No Battle Fought

Book 2 of the
No Glory Sought Series

by

Phil Geusz

Published by
Melange Books, LLC
White Bear Lake, MN 55110
www.melange-books.com

Credits

Copy Editor: Nancy Schumacher
Line Editor: Mae Powers
Format Editor: Nancy Schumacher
Cover Artist: A.Bratt

No Battle Fought
by
Phil Geusz

"Today's mission, Commander, is revenge. And may God have mercy on your soul."

Even the ordinary sort of war is awful enough— people die, resources are wasted, and the survivors are scarred forever. But when unstoppable force comes up against an indomitable will to resist and the nukes begin to fly, well…

Does war have a purpose? Or is it all just a meaningless blood-drenched spasm? When you're outfitted with thermonuclear weapons and you and your squadronmates are giving all you have just to stay alive in the same sky with the enemy, well… Perhaps that's not the best time and place to ask such deep questions.

Yet when you're a seventeen-year-old naval officer who doesn't expect to survive another hour, how can you *not* ask?

* * * *

Dedicated to CDR Lawrence A. Wise, USN (Ret)

Other books available by Phil Geusz from Melange

No Oath Sworn, Book 1 of the No Glory Sought Series
'December Moth' in the Hearts of Tomorrow Anthology

Author Contact:

www.resistingarrest.net

Chapter One

"War isn't easy," I heard my amplified voice say over and over again as it reverberated off of the auditorium walls. "In fact, becoming involved with war is the worst, most profound tragedy that can ever befall a human being. Fighting a real battle isn't like what you see in the holos. It reminds me more than anything else of stumbling around in the bottom of a dark sewer, up to your waist in filth and trying to murder someone before he can kill you. It's not glorious, it's not fulfilling, it's not something to be proud of. In fact, when it's over and done with what you yearn for, more than anything else you've ever wanted, is to be clean again. But, no matter how hard you try, you never can quite scrub the stink of death away." I looked out over the crowd I was supposedly selling war bonds to. They were very quiet now, where when I'd first been introduced they were cheering and waving flags.

"Yet war has been thrust upon us," I continued, voice grim and face hard. "It's up to us to bear the stink, to accept the moral responsibility for the truly terrible things that we now *must* do. To make the sacrifices that must be made, that we may live on as a free people. To embrace darkness for a time—that our children and our children's children might know only light." I sighed and looked down at the notes that the United Systems Board of War Finance had prepared for me; they had nothing whatsoever to do with the speech I was actually giving, and were therefore of only limited help. I'd been ad-libbing for ages now, saying what was in my heart instead of what the professionals judged best. No one else would've been able to get away with it. But I was Thomas Longo, Killer of Battleships. It wasn't like they had a replacement hero waiting in the wings. Besides, when I spoke my heart, bond sales went up so much that even the professionals had been forced to recognize the fact. *Well, Thomas,* I whispered to myself. *You talked yourself into this corner; now you'll just have to find a way to talk yourself out of it.* "We must sacrifice, that they may be free," I concluded lamely. "We must bloody our hands that they may live. We must stand and fight, that they might not be burdened with the mark of Cain. We must support this war, because history tells us that strength is the surest foundation of peace. And, above all, we must not shrink away from our duty before history. We must not allow evil to triumph! We *must do what it takes to win this war, no matter how hard it is or how much we must suffer along the way. We must win!*"

"Arrrrgh!" the crowd replied, a wordless, primeval utterance. Then they made fists and waved them threateningly in the air. Every single one of them was a California millionaire; in order to get in, they'd been required to buy a hundred-thousand credit war bond. Some had bought several. If recent history was any guide, they'd buy even more after hearing what I had to say.

"We *must* win!" I repeated. "For the sake of everything's that's good and decent! We *must* win!"

"We must win!" the crowd agreed, taking up the chant. "We must win! We must win!"

They were still chanting and fist-waving minutes later; I could tell because the floor of my little anteroom was still bouncing up and down to the tempo of stamping feet. I was sitting in a folding chair, mercifully alone with Father Murton. "I hate speeches," I observed as my tutor massaged the place where my neck and shoulders came together. It shouldn't have mattered that he rubbed me; my plastic skin wasn't nearly as sensitive or flexible as human flesh, and I didn't even *have* muscles to get all knotted up. But Father Murton had done it when I'd been frightened or upset as a small boy, and lately he'd taken up the practice again. It seemed to work, at least a little. "Speeches make me feel almost as dirty as fighting does."

"I know," the priest replied, shaking his head. "But, if it's any consolation, you seem to have a real gift for it."

I closed my eyes and false-sighed, since my mannequin-body wasn't equipped for the real thing. "So, I have a gift for making war-speeches, and a gift for aerospace combat. But not for much of anything else. Why can't I be good at something I *want* to do? Something that doesn't get people killed?"

Father Murton stopped rubbing for a moment then started again. "You're hardly the first teenager ever to flunk calculus, Thomas," he began. "As your tutor, I'm officially supposed to be disappointed in you. However, under the circumstances—"

Suddenly my dressing-room door swung open; it was Heiko, my chief bodyguard. I didn't like having a bodyguard, but was hardly in a position to argue. Mostly, though, I didn't like Heiko. He always treated me like a little kid. "VIP to see Commander Longo," he reported, speaking to Father Murton as if I weren't present. "A Commander Knight."

My jaw dropped, so that my tutor spoke first. "Is he in a wheelchair?" he demanded.

"No, sir!" Heiko replied. "He's got facial scars, though. Want me to tell him to get lost?"

"Then he's the younger Knight." Murton looked at me and I nodded. "We know the Knights rather well," Murton explained to the plain-clothed Marine officer. "From Churilla. Both of them are welcome *any* time under *any* circumstances, and are to be treated with the utmost respect. Am I clear?"

"Yes, sir!" Heiko replied, saluting smartly and coming "about face" with parade-ground precision. Father Murton didn't like him very much either, I knew. But he tried to be nice, so I did too.

It was a little while before Commander Knight showed up. That always happened whenever someone came to see me unexpectedly; even Father had trouble sometimes. Slowly the distant foot-stamping died away. As it did so, I changed out of my uniform and into gym shorts and a t-shirt. By the time Ted arrived, I was half-immersed in a game of Rocket Sledder. One moment I was schussing back and forth across the ceiling, and then...

...not only was Ted standing in front of me, but his younger brother Jimmy was with him! "Hi, Tommy!" he said, smiling and looking up at my game-in-progress. "You're only on Level Six? And just one life left?"

My grin widened. "Only because you haven't been here to help!" I answered tossing him a controller. Then I turned to face Ted. "How are you, Commander?" I asked, making a point of using his new rank. He'd been promoted to lieutenant-commander just like me, and had a bunch of new medals, too. He was in the navy for real, however. So in his case, it actually mattered. "And, how's your father?"

"Dad's great," Ted replied, shaking first my hand and then Father Murton's. "In a year or two, he'll be fit for limited duty again. Though there'll be almost as much metal in him as there is in you. He asked me to send his regards."

I nodded and smiled. "I'm glad to hear that. He didn't seem the type that'd take well to life in a wheelchair."

Ted grinned. "Not hardly." Then his eyes narrowed slightly. "We were in the audience for your speech."

"It was *great!*" Jimmy exploded, waving his arms for emphasis. "We must win! We must win!"

I looked down at the ground. "Not really," I said slowly. "But... They want me to stand up there and talk about heroes."

"Heroes?" Ted asked.

I would've blushed, if I could have. I'd known *far* too many heroes. Most of them were dead. "Yeah," I agreed after a time, digging into the carpet a little with a fake toe. "Heroes. And... I just *can't*. So I make stuff up to say instead."

"Hmm," Ted replied, meeting Father Murton's eyes for a moment. Then he turned back to me. "Well, to be honest, I don't think that I could give a speech on that particular subject either. Not anymore at least." He frowned.

"Yeah," I answered. "If it wasn't for who I am and who my father is, they'd never let me get away with straying so far. But then, they haven't had a problem yet with what I've said either. So I guess it's all right." Then I changed the subject. "Have you heard yet?" I asked Jmmy.

He grinned, and that was all I needed to see. "All *right!*" I declared, reaching out to slap my friend on the shoulder, but not quite pulling it off. Electric motors turn only so fast, which can sort of spoil a good slap.

Still, Jimmy took the ruined gesture as it was intended. "Yeah," he replied, blushing and looking away. "I'm going to be a Skybolt pilot" He looked me in the eyes. "Just like you! There's going to be a dozen of us to start with, the nucleus of a whole squadron!"

I nodded slowly, not really sure of what to say. It wasn't a nice thing, being a Skybolt pilot in time of war. Not nice at all. "It won't bring you any joy," I offered. "I can promise you that."

"I know," Jimmy replied, reaching out and wrapping an arm around his Polecat-flying brother. "In my family, Thomas, we *all* know. But still. We *have* to."

I shook my head. Jimmy hadn't quite yet turned fifteen; he'd be undergoing the brain-core procedure even younger than I had. What was the world coming to, anyway?

"We *must* win, Thomas," Father Murton reminded me. "We *must*."

I sighed and looked away. "I know."

There was a long, awkward moment, then Ted spoke. "Look," he said slowly. "Things have to move through channels; it's the navy way. But, they're going to tell you tomorrow anyway, so I might as well spill the beans tonight." He tousled his younger brother's hair. "I'm going to be part of the new squadron as well. A special technical liaison. Which is just fancy navy talk for general helper-outer." He looked at me. "I'm supposed to have special insight into the headaches we're going to have bringing what amounts to a bunch of kids into the navy, as well as knowing a thing or two about the realities of aerospace combat."

"That can't be right," my tutor objected. "It makes far too much sense. Are you sure this is the same navy that I know and love?"

"I can't believe you're not in command," I observed. "You're one of only a handful of combat-experienced veterans, you're both an Academy graduate and a Top Banana, and as you said you really *do* have some unique qualifications and insights to offer."

"I probably *would* be in command," he admitted. "Except that the people upstairs have someone else in mind." He shrugged. "And, I happen to know the guy. Respect the hell out of him, too. His qualifications are even better than mine. If it were anyone else, or if this particular individual weren't available, I might feel like I'd been slighted. But no, not with *this* guy around." He looked me in the eyes. "Besides, it's one of the most sacred principles of military leadership that a combat officer has to *lead his men into combat* in order to be effective. He can't ask anything of his men that he's not willing to do himself." He paused. "I'm too old to be brain-cored, Thomas. So is every other experienced officer in the navy; every brand-spanking-new Academy graduate too, for that matter. So, as much as I'd like to, I *can't* be in command. I can help out. I can advise. I can smooth out rough spots, and kick the asses of the idiots who'd take advantage of the poor kid who's trying to do one of the toughest jobs there's ever been while far, far too young. I can even offer him my shoulder for him to cry on." He swallowed. "But, Thomas, I can never, ever command a squadron of Skybolts. I can't lead them in combat. No one in the galaxy can. Except you."

Chapter Two

It so happened that Father was in California too, on business. There were three extra seats in the navy 'hopper I'd been allotted for my speaking tour, and no one much cared how they were used. So, the next day, Father hitched a ride back home to New Orleans with us.

"...can't believe you're even *considering* doing this, Thomas!" he was complaining, striding up and down the aisle and waving his arms. "You've done your part and more; no one can deny that. And, I *need* you! To test-pilot for me! It's not like your talents would be wasted!"

I sighed and looked down at Arizona as it rolled past. It was brown as far as the eye could see, except for the golf courses.

"He's right, you know," Father Murton pointed out. "There's plenty of important work that still needs to be done on the Skybolt. If you're going to be an engineer someday, Thomas, you could do a lot worse than on-the-job training. In the long run, it might even be better for the United Systems."

I shook my head, but said nothing.

"Gott in himmel!" Father continued. "It's only a miracle that brought you home to me this last time! I love you too much to let you... let you..."

"Volunteer for combat?" I asked at last. "To go out and kill or be killed, just like all the other kids my age?"

"*Not* your age," Father countered, his hands balled into fists. "Older than you, except for the Skybolt pilots. Much older- two or three years! And not already veterans, like you are." He frowned. "Son, I'm so very proud of what you've done, prouder than I think you can ever understand or know. But you've *done* your part, at a dark and dangerous time. And done it well! Test-piloting is an honorable profession in time of war." He looked away. "*Why*, Thomas? *Why* won't you stay home with me?"

Something clicked inside of me; we'd just crossed the state line into New Mexico, according to the new inertial guidance system one of

Father's top assistants had mounted in me. But, somehow, everything looked the same. Barren. Void. Empty. "Open up the envelope again," I suggested to Father. "Go ahead. Read my orders aloud."

Father frowned, then did so. "Lt. Commander Thomas Anthony Longo, USN," he began. "Holder of the Parliamentary Order of Merit, Founder of Churilla, Most Noble Chevalier of the Esteppan Order of Blood—"

"Not that part!" I protested, interrupting Father in mid-honorific. "Please!"

He smiled slightly. "But that's my *favorite* part, Thomas!" I opened my mouth to protest, but he cut me off at the pass. "Anyway… You are requested and required, upon receipt of these orders, to prepare yourself in all respects for command of the First Special Aerospace Combat Squadron."

"I suppose the 'special' part is because all of the pilots will be underaged," my tutor suggested.

"You will report immediately to the New Orleans facility of Longo Enterprises in order to familiarize yourself with the latest production variant of the Skybolt and to take the remaining two weeks of shipwreck leave due you, at your discretion. During this period you will also confer extensively with Lt. Commander Ted Knight regarding the structure and composition of the Special Aerospace Combat Squadron. Your mission, it should be emphasized, is not to take command of an extant organization but rather to find a way to integrate the Skybolt weapon system into the navy's existing combat structure. Consideration must be given not only to developing the Skybolt itself as a weapon system, but also to the unique needs, sacrifices, and nature of its pilots, as well.

"The Board of the Admiralty hereby congratulates Lt. Commander Longo on his new command, and expresses its unlimited confidence in his ability to overcome the numerous obstacles that lie before him. In closing we offer both Lt. Commander Longo and Lt. Commander Knight our full support, as well as our gratitude for past services. Either of them should feel free to call upon us personally in the event that substance should need to be lent to our promises of support. Signed, Admiral Raymond Kretzchmeyer." Father smiled. "Then he added his personal phone number in ballpoint. Even *I* don't have that."

I sighed and shook my head. "Father… I've read that thing twenty or thirty times, and now I know that you've read it as well. Where exactly in that document do get the idea that any of it is *optional*?"

He closed his eyes. "Thomas," he said slowly. "I'm well-connected in places that matter. And, I *do* need a test-pilot. The navy is moving very fast on this—faster than Parliament, even. Technically, forming this squadron is still illegal. The Skybolt funding bill hasn't been passed yet; I of all people ought to know. All it would take would be for me to make a few discreet calls…"

"No!" I screamed, suddenly angry for no reason that I could really understand. "I *won't* have you pulling strings!" I leapt to my feet, hands formed into angry metal balls. I was taller than Father now; my mannequin-body had been updated to reflect the growth of the real one. "I *won't*! Not while everyone else is fighting!"

Father Murton reached out to steady me, afraid I'd tumble my gyros. "A few months ago, Thomas," he said slowly," I'd have agreed with you. I *did* agree with you, even. But now…" He shook his head. "The navy is being led by fools these days, and Parliament is even worse. Obeying these orders wouldn't be courageous. It'd be stupid. You're worth ten squadron commanders as a fundraiser alone. Anyone can see that. In fact, that's another good option for you; raising money is also an honorable way for a hero to spend the rest of the war." He frowned. "I mean, imagine if you were captured, after what you've done!"

I frowned, not having thought of that one. Being captured *would* be pretty bad, wouldn't it? But… "Well, it's a chance that I'm just going to have to take, I guess. I mean, if Ted Knight thinks I need to do this, then it's what I need to do."

Father grimaced. "Ted Knight! He's just a fighter jock, Thomas! The man's brave enough, I suppose. And a gentleman. But—

He might have said more, but I didn't hear a word of it. "Ted Knight," I roared at the top of my volume-scale, "is a hero! And my squadron-mate, to boot! We flew *combat* together and I won't have you—"

Just then, my vocal speaker squealed and died, overdriven beyond all reason by my outburst. Father grabbed his ears at the hideous screech, while my tutor merely winced. Mute, I formed a snarl with my lips and pounded the table in frustration. It was bad enough being seventeen, without having a body that failed at all the worst moments!

"Thomas," Father finally said, half-opening his arms for a hug. "I'm sorry for what I've done to you, and the position I've put you in. But—"

I wasn't having any though, not just then. I snatched up a pen and pad and scribbled out the rest of what I'd meant to say. "I love you both," my note said when it was finished. "And I know you both want what's best for me. But neither of you has ever flown combat, and neither of you has ever watched a squadron-mate die. I'm doing this, regardless of what you say and regardless of however you try to stop me. I'm doing it because it's my sacred duty.

"And, even more, I'm doing it because we simply *must* win."

Chapter Three

My two weeks of leave didn't amount to much. But that was okay, since I hadn't really been shipwrecked. Originally, the rule creating a special allocation of thirty days leave was enacted in order to give distressed navy men a little time to get their lives back in order after not only going through a traumatic and life-wrenching experience, but also as likely as not losing a fair share of their material possessions. Over time, however, the interpretation had been stretched to include those assigned to dirtside duties who'd in effect become refugees as the result of real-estate changing hands. While I technically qualified for the extended leave under this interpretation, it hardly made sense in my specific case. I'd lost nothing except good friends; all the time off in the world wouldn't bring *them* back. And, while I couldn't deny that I'd undergone a traumatic experience, I didn't think a piddly little two weeks was going to make much of a difference on that score, either.

Besides, as a brain-core there was very little to choose between work and play for me. So, I spent my leave-time soaring over Lake Pontchartrain in Father's new prototype. A Skybolt was a delightful thing to be, far better than a clanking monstrosity of a mannequin body, and it'd been *much* too long since I'd worn an airframe. I did loops, made low and fast firing passes, and even landed a dozen times on the *Glorious First of June* in high Earth orbit to officially carrier-qualify the new type. Father was relieved that I chose to spend my leave test-piloting for him; Parliament hadn't authorized any more brain-core operations since mine, and his shiny new 'hopper had been gathering dust for months. The navy had instructed Father to begin tooling up for a run of two hundred and fifty and Parliament be damned, but then a judge showed up at the plant with a restraining order. It was all a terrible mess! Besides, my flights were good for morale at Longo Industries, especially since the new machine performed so well. Father was less pleased about the fact that I was bound and determined to go back to combat flying, but was respecting my wishes. We hugged long and hard after he told me, and I loved him more than ever.

"They won't even let me make *parts*!" Father complained at dinner one night, stabbing his fork in the air for emphasis. "Not even spares for the verdammt prototype!" He rolled his eyes. "If anything important breaks, the whole program will stop dead. Absolutely dead! We made more progress *before* there was a war on!"

"Yes," my elder brother agreed. Sven was much older than me, and looked so much like Father that it was frightening. I, on the other hand, favored our mother. "At least the Autarchy knew how to cut red tape."

Father's fork froze in midair, then he frowned and put it down. Clearly, he'd rather suddenly lost his appetite. "I'm forced to admit," he said finally, "that on bad days I agree with you."

My eyes widened slightly as I looked down at my full, untouched plate. The shrinks had agreed that I should always sit in on family meals, even though I had no stomach. There'd been bitter disagreement, however, as to whether or not I should have food on my plate. Finally, after endless battles, it had been decided that I should. When I ate at home Anna, the cook, used the wasted food to feed her beagles. As it happened, *I* preferred an empty plate; none of the psychologists had bothered to ask. On my bond-peddling tour, Father Murton had winked and let me have my way. But now I was back home, sitting at a heavily-timbered Esteppan dining-table in an Esteppan-decorated home that was at the same time both comforting and oppressive. Father Murton was gone and wouldn't be back for days; he'd received orders to form a group of special one-on-one counselors for the proposed squadron of brain-core pilots.

"You know," I said slowly, looking at Father, "I think that's the first time I've ever heard you say anything nice about the Autarchy."

He snorted. "You're probably right, Thomas."

I frowned, and picked at the steaming sauerbraten. I liked sauerbraten, a lot. But now I could hardly remember what it tasted like. Or, even, what *tasting* was like. There was a limit to how much one could do with a mannequin-body, and neither taste nor smell had made the cut. "They say that the Esteppans fought like demons," I said. "Or, at least my navy friends do. That the average Esteppan was so well-trained and so well-indoctrinated that he was worth three United Systems sailors or soldiers." I met Father's eyes. "Or maybe even more."

Father's frown intensified. "It's natural that you're curious, Thomas," he said at last. "Especially with what you've done personally.

But…" His voice trailed off.

Then Sven wiped his mouth with a napkin and spoke up. "Thomas," he said slowly. "I was in the Esteppan Aerospace Force. You know that."

I nodded. "For a few months. Right at the end."

"No," he said. "That's not quite true. I went to Hammerfjord, the Academy. For three long years. That counts as military service. It would've been four, except they graduated us early for the war." He shook his head. "Thank god for that! Combat was *nothing* after Hammerfjord."

I tilted my head to one side; my brother had seen combat, too? We never, *ever* spoke of such things.

He read my gesture and smiled. "My experiences don't compare with yours, Thomas. I was in command of an aerospace-defense platoon. Mostly, I supervised a bunch of radars. We did shoot down over a dozen Polecats one day, however. When they tried to knock out the airbase we were guarding."

Father shook his head again then sighed and resigned himself to the conversation. "Sven holds the Order of Merit," he added. "It's the award just under your own Order of Blood. The Autarch himself pinned it on him for that day's action. It was a trap. One that Sven dreamed up. He found a way to modify his missile software, you see. The United Systems people were caught totally unawares when his weapons didn't behave as expected."

My brother's face colored. "They were so afraid of the Stormcrows that sometimes they forgot we had missiles, too. They hardly paid any attention to us." I nodded; it was easy enough to understand. The Stormcrows were the older Esteppan fighters that the Skybolt was derived from; Father's first great design. Trying to win aerospace superiority over Stormcrows with Polecats must've been a suicidal nightmare; it was a miracle that it'd been managed at all.

"What I did was nothing in the greater scheme of things, Sven continued. "In fact, today I regret the whole incident. Good men died, and an evil war was prolonged. It's difficult to be proud of something like that. The medal never leaves my dresser drawer."

I nodded. We all three knew that it was hard enough just being an Esteppan, living on the United System's capitol world. I could understand in full why my brother didn't want his victory remembered. "But why?" I asked. "How was it that the Esteppans fought so well? For such an evil cause?"

There was another long, awkward silence. Then Father finally spoke. "Military excellence," he explained at last, his face screwed up as if the words themselves had a foul taste, "can often best be derived from a total unity of opinion. The reverse is also true. Divided opinion is almost always a recipe for defeat."

I leaned forward; the navy had given me a whole pile of edu-tapes to read, so many that I was officially excused from all other studies indefinitely. But they were all about geometric tactics and fleet formations and stuff like that, not what was *really* important.

Sven smiled. "They taught us at Hammerfjiord that an army must strike with one purpose, supported by many minds. In the videos I see here on Earth about the war, we Esteppers are portrayed as blind followers—robots who obeyed our orders at all costs. But it wasn't that way at all! Every single man, most especially small-unit leaders like me, were encouraged to use our heads at every possible opportunity. In training, for example, we were often issued impossible orders just to see if we were foolish enough to try and follow them to the letter. Those who made the attempt were flunked. The highest marks were given to those who found a way to honor the *intention* of these impossible orders, even if what the student officer actually did was something completely different than what was instructed." His smile widened. "If anything, the United Systems officers were the blind followers. We found them to be very predictable."

"But," Father said, cutting off Sven, "the freedom to think only went so far." He looked at his eldest son. "As you said, the watchword was 'Many minds, one purpose'. God help the man who dared questioned that purpose; no one else would." He sighed. "Not that there were many who *wanted* to dissent; that was the truly sad part." He shook his head and looked me directly in the eyes. "Thomas, I know that you'll find this hard to believe. But the fact is, the Autarch was, in the beginning, the most popular leader Esteppe ever knew. Our planet is cold and wintry, you know that. So cold that it's hardly survivable. We have huge deposits of rare elements, however, so rich and pure that they hardly need refining. Plus, we found ourselves gifted with a flair for technical achievement. Our planet became rich beyond our wildest dreams. Soon we began to think that we were smarter than everyone else."

"And that's where things went wrong," Sven continued. "When some idiots began to think that economic and technological superiority was the same thing as moral superiority. They began to assume that we had a special destiny."

Father sighed. "Here on Earth, some nations *have* had special destinies," he admitted. "They dominated the planet during crucial periods for one reason or another, and spread key technologies or ideas until their time in the sun was over. Rome was one such nation, and the United States another. Even more nations, however, have *thought* they had special destinies, but did not."

I looked down at my plate again; the food was congealing, as always. What a terrible waste of perfectly good sauerbraten!

"We haven't been colonizing planets for all that long yet, in the historical sense," Sven continued, taking over from Father. "And, it's proven far more difficult to establish ourselves on an alien world than colonizing, say, Australia, ever was. There's usually no soil and no fisheries. Very often there's also an alien climate to try and cope with. Earth's offspring-worlds are developing slowly as a result, so slowly that up until recently she's dominated them with ease whenever and wherever she's chosen to exert herself."

"Up until the Esteppan war," I guessed.

"Right!" Father agreed. "We were rich, like I said. Rich and arrogant and overweening." He sighed. "And, perhaps in some regards not very bright. It was fertile ground for new ideas, yes. Some of them, like the Stormcrow fighter, succeeded like nothing ever seen before. But, the ground was also fertile for very old ideas. Bad ones, most of them."

"The Autarch promised that science could lead us to a whole new level of humanity," Sven explained, his words a near-whisper. "He claimed that, with him in charge, we could re-engineer and re-wire ourselves into godhood. That was our unifying purpose, the goal we were not permitted to question."

"And perhaps we could've done so, if the United Systems hadn't stopped us by force," Father admitted."Doctor Schumann was a brilliant man before he became Autarch. I studied under him at Tellersberg, you know. In fact, I was one of his grad students."

"Really?" I gasped. No, I hadn't known that at *all*!

"Heh!" Father snorted. "Perhaps we should've had this talk long ago. Yes, son, in the beginning, before the military became so influential, I was one of the Autarch's favorites." He waved his arm around us. "That's why we continue to prosper to this very day, ultimately. Why we have so many good things." He looked down at the carpet. "And, it's also why I stood trial for war crimes. I was guilty, even though they acquitted me. I confessed."

I nodded, having seen the films on my teaching machine. Father had confessed over and over again after turning himself in, blubbering and apologizing and so distraught at what'd befallen his dreams of man-become-god that for a time he'd been ruled mentally incompetent and his trial suspended. Guilty as he'd indeed been of converting human beings into cyborgs, there was never any danger of a conviction. Father began meeting secretly with United Systems intelligence assets the moment he realized the Autarch was mad, and gave them information on the Stormcrow that was so sensitive it was *still* classified. Most historians believed that he was tried merely in order to make his exoneration as public and as complete as possible.

"Anyway," Sven continued. "We're drifting off topic here. 'Many minds, one purpose'. That was the mantra of the Esteppan Armed Forces, and both halves of the equation were seen as vital to success." He sighed. "One way to ensure unanimity of purpose is to kill anyone who asks too many inconvenient questions."

Father nodded. "And, in a dictatorship, there are always mechanisms for doing exactly that. In the old Fascist regimes, there was the secret police. Enemies were 'disappeared' without a trace. But the Autarch considered that inefficient. Instead, he took a page from the old Soviet Union and worked his enemies to death."

"Not just enemies," Sven pointed out. "The 'useless', as well. Babes in arms, in other words. The sick and infirm. Anyone who couldn't do 'useful' work." Sven colored. "I attended classes explaining why this was just and honorable, Thomas. Classes that I did well in. Useless mouths were an impediment, an anchor holding the Autarch back from making us all into gods. I was taught that all of us were nothing in our current states, that only our future godhood mattered. And, since useless mouths endangered the transition…" He shrugged.

I looked at my brother with new eyes. "Did you…" I asked hesitantly. "I mean…"

He sighed. "No, thank god. But, I would've, if ordered. One purpose, you see. No individual's scruples could be bigger than the One True Purpose."

"It was hideously efficient," Father explained. "And, here's where we finally get around to answering your original question, Thomas. Every form of social organization has its plusses and minuses. A dictatorship brooks no dissent, tolerates no arguments, and acts with a unanimity of purpose and decisiveness that no democracy or republic can ever hope to match. All shoulders are put to the same wheel, or else. No energy is wasted on infighting."

"But," Sven continued. "There are prices to pay for this. In a society where certain opinions are forbidden, for example, then the facts that support the banned opinions must be done away with as well. Then, the secondary facts that, upon study, lead to the banned facts must also be hidden away. And so it goes, on and on and on until the most absurd lengths are reached and the average citizen is trying his best on a daily basis not to notice that the sun isn't actually rising in the west like the government say it's supposed to."

"Heh!" Father chortled. Then he turned back to me. "The final result is a citizenry that isn't sure about anything anymore, except that they're being lied to. But it usually takes decades or sometimes even centuries for things to progress that far." He scowled. "In the short run, a dictatorship is a very dangerous thing indeed."

"Dissent spreads doubt, and *nothing* is more corrosive to a military organization than doubt," Sven continued. "That's why even in free societies the military operates as a legally-sanctioned dictatorship within the larger political body. There's no room for doubt or debate when it comes time to plan an invasion, or for that matter to charge a weapon emplacement. A soldier goes where he's told when he's told to do it, period. It *must* be that way, or else organization totally breaks down. And, when *that* happens..." He shuddered.

I shuddered too, having seen exactly that on Churilla. It hadn't been a pretty sight. "So," I said at last, "You're saying that a dictatorship is just like a big navy, sort of. It's efficient, but not progressive or open to new ideas."

Sven nodded. "Or respectful of individual needs. It *can't* be, and do its job." He sighed. "Free nations, on the other hand, are very good at inventing things and maintaining human dignity. But in all honesty they fight poorly. Especially when the war is unpopular and politicians are constantly trying to intervene. Things are better when there's wide public support, but only a little because the habit of endless debate dies hard. Decisiveness, in and of itself, is a potent weapon in time of war. Try to imagine a navy where objectives and strategy are publicly debated and voted on and you'll see what I mean."

I frowned, remembering how the politicians on Churilla had tried to order the precious handful of remaining Polecats to protect dozens of completely indefensible objectives. "I see," I said slowly.

"Now," Father said, "For the other side of the picture try to imagine an entire nation run like the fleet, complete with court martials and firing squads for disobeying orders or falling asleep at the wrong times. In the long run, it'll choke on itself. But in the short run..." He shrugged.

"That's why Drakkus is doing so well in this war. Why the Dracans might well win, even. They're all unified behind their Emperor—that it's at bayonet-point doesn't matter much in the short run. It's only in the long term that free nations out-invent and out-produce dictatorships."

"Many minds, one purpose," Sven said, smiling. "A good slogan for a purely military organization, but a bad one for a society. In the long run, at least."

* * * *

Father and I had planned another test-flight for the next morning, but it wasn't to be. Something had broken in the 'hopper's interface module, the "critical failure," that Father had so feared. "Can you feel *anything*, son?" his anguished voice asked me though my crew-chief's circuit.

"No," I answered. "Nothing. I'm totally dead."

He cursed then, both violently and fluently, employing crude Esteppan oaths I'd never heard before. For that matter, I'd almost never heard Father curse *at all* before. It was a little overpowering, given that just then his voice was the only sensation in my universe. "I'm sorry, Thomas," he said eventually, realizing what he was putting me through. "We'll get you out of there right away. I just… just…."

"It's all right," I answered. Father was having the hardest time imaginable, trying to balance the navy's demand for progress against the ever-growing stack of stop-work orders that were flowing so impressively from the local courtrooms. It wasn't just the anti-war people; a lot of local churches were upset about the Skybolt program as well. "Take your time."

"Right," Father agreed, though already his tone was distant and I knew that I was half-forgotten. That was all right; it was just how Father was. "I'll get Steve on the diagnostics; he's a good tech. Maybe we can fly tomorrow."

"Maybe," I agreed, though I rather doubted it. I'd never before failed so completely to hook up to a new body of *any* kind, much less a Skybolt. The interface was fried, I knew deep in my heart. Totally and completely fried. Worst of all, it was one of the most specialized and exotic components in the entire airframe. There was no spare, and at least a dozen judges were determined to ensure that there never would be a spare. "If not, then can we schedule the design conference that Ted wants so badly? He says it's the most important thing on tap, save for the test flights."

Father snorted, and blind as I was I could still see the curl of his lip.

He thought that designing fighters was *his* job, not the navy's. "Maybe," he said. "I'll make the calls. In the meantime, let's get you unplugged."

As it happened, Father learned everything he needed to know about what was wrong with the Skybolt as my braincase was being wheeled away. "You should have seen the thing!" he complained to my brother as we stood up from the breakfast table the next morning. "The whole module was burned to a crisp. Burned! You could tell just by looking that the superconductors were garbage."

Sven frowned. Technically he was the engine and airframe guy while Father was in charge of the control systems, especially the euphemistically-named "biological interface". In reality, however, they worked so closely together that they were almost interchangeable. "Earther workmanship is garbage!" he countered. "To this day, despite all of our tuning we get four percent more power out of the port antigrav than the starboard. There's no imaginable reason for this, save for poor craftsmanship!" He sighed. "We imported the first machine's motors from Esteppe. They were a perfect match. *Perfect!*"

I frowned. The twin antigravs of a Skybolt had to operate in synchronization for best results; their overlapping hyperfields worked together to create an effective output equal to the cube of an unsynchronized powerplant. It was the latest tech available, and was also why the loss of even a single motor in combat was so crippling. I frowned. "No wonder this 'bolt felt a little mushier than my other one," I commented. "I thought maybe it was my imagination."

"No, Thomas," Sven observed, crossing his arms. "I read your log. Your observations were dead-on accurate. They matched my predictions perfectly." He looked at Father. "This is ridiculous. We have no flying prototype, we have no suppliers worthy of the name, we don't even have any *production tooling*, for god's sake! So, tell me again. How exactly is it that we have a fighter program going? And, while I'm at it, can you remind me again where the return-on-investment part comes in?"

Father looked away. "Now, Sven," he said, employing exactly the same tone of voice that he'd so often used on me when I was small and fractious. I blinked; most of the time, Sven felt more like my uncle than my elder brother. But every once in a while something came up that reminded me of the true relationship. "Keep in mind what's at stake here, son. We've got one hell of a battle to fight, yes. And it seems like everyone in the universe except the navy is working against us. But... But..." Father looked at me.

Sven scowled mightily, then turned to look out the window. Our dining room faced the factory; what should've been a bustling war-priority manufacturing center stood empty and waiting for the big orders that'd been promised and promised, but which had somehow never shown up. "Yes," Sven acknowledged. "We owe it to Thomas not to give up. To Thomas, and all the others like him."

Father nodded, then smiled grimly. "The Dracans are at the Henderson Nexus!" he marveled, shaking his head. "At the Henderson Nexus! Only two jumps away. Practically next door."

"It's a wonder, our government is. The best government that money can buy, I think sometimes." The new voice came from behind us; it was Ted Knight, arrived early for the design conference. He'd been made an honorary family member for the duration; Father had assigned him the best room at the gasthaus out back, where he usually put only the highest-ranking VIP's. Given how closely we were all going to have to work together given his and my new jobs, and how time-consuming it could be to get through all the security surrounding the Longo facility, it made sense for us to give him a room. That he'd received the *best* room, however, and been accepted into the family itself, was Father's way of honoring me and supporting my decision to command the new squadron. I'd tried to thank him for his thoughtfulness; the words hadn't come out right, but somehow he seemed to understand.

"Hah!" Sven countered, raising his orange juice as if in a toast. He and Ted had taken an instant liking to each other. Perhaps it was because both had graduated from military academies, although I thought there was maybe a little more to it than that. "The question is, who are the biggest fools? Those who lead or we who follow?" He shrugged. "Care for a waffle, Ted?"

Knight frowned. He was so thin as to be nearly skeletal, like all Polecat pilots, and lived on the strictest diet imaginable. "Thanks, Sven," he replied. "But no thanks. I'm still drawing flight pay."

"Indeed?" my brother replied. He gestured towards the conference room just off of the kitchen, and all of us began walking in that direction. "Admiral Vlasilov is coming through security now," Ted explained. "But he's asked us to go ahead and get started without him."

"I'll take notes," Father agreed. He hated conferences with a passion, and would do almost anything to shorten them. We all took our seats. "What's on the navy's mind today?" he asked.

"The usual," Ted replied. Sven inhaled, but Ted warded off the upcoming explosion with his hand. "I know," he answered. "Believe me, I know. It's not your fault, any of it. Everyone knows, back in London."

He sighed. "You may not realize it, Sven, but you and your Father are dreams to work with compared to most other navy contractors. Especially, contractors for something so important and high-profile." He frowned. "We have one outfit who wants us to name a destroyer after the owner's grandfather; every time we tell them it can't be done a shipment is mysteriously delayed. Another is lobbying Parliament to require us to lower our acceptance standards, so that they won't have such a terrible reject rate." He shook his head. "And all of this in wartime! You gentlemen have no idea how refreshing it is for us to deal with people who actually seem to want the same things we want, at no more than a fair profit." Ted smiled; his scars and obviously-artificial eye would have made the result seem sinister to anyone who didn't know him. "Of course, there *is* Thomas to consider. But, somehow, I think you guys would've been just as easy to work with even if he wasn't your son."

Father nodded. "Our interests are indeed in alignment," he agreed. "We want to produce the finest combat skyhoppers in the world."

"And," Sven added. "We also have no interest in becoming slaves of the Emperor."

"Nor do I," Ted agreed. Then he sighed. "But we can't fix the politics, gentlemen. Not at our level. All we can do is make and fly fighters." He inserted a cube into the conference table's dataport. "Now," he began, "Let's skip over all of the production-readiness stuff today; there's no point in rehashing all of that. Instead, let's take a look at the navy's wish-list for the production version of the Skybolt. If, by some miracle, any should ever accidentally happen to be produced…"

Chapter Four

We were talking about hardpoints when Admiral Vlasilov arrived. He wasn't much on formality, so no one had to stand up and salute when he entered the room. Not that I had to anyway; one of the few good things about having been awarded the Parliamentary Medal of Merit was that I was permanently excused from that sort of thing—in fact, everyone else was supposed to salute *me*, regardless of rank. The whole "Attention on deck!" thing was baffling, really. It was supposed to be essential for discipline. But… Couldn't people just do as they were told without all of the nonsense? There hadn't been any saluting at the underground headquarters back on Churilla; people had often risen to their feet out of respect for Spencer and Alicia, but no one *made* them do it. Yet, everyone had followed orders, even when they led to the deaths of those involved. Wasn't Spencer's way better?

"…too many hardpoints," Father was explaining to Ted as the admiral smiled at me in greeting, then sat down across the table. "Hardpoints cost weight, Commander. More than you'd think, at the kind of gee-load generated by a Skybolt. And weight saps performance. It takes a lot of structural support to hold a bomb or missile in place during fifty-gee-plus maneuvers."

"Ja," Sven agreed, slipping into Esteppan dialect. He often did when absorbed with technical issues. "The Stormcrow only had two hardpoints. We've already added significant mass, going for four."

Knight frowned. "The navy wants to be able to use the Skybolt as both an aerospace-superiority fighter *and* as an attack-craft," he countered. "We're never going to have enough Skybolts; we can see that already. So each airframe is going to have to be able to deliver as many weapons as possible. It's *worth* it to sacrifice a little performance, in exchange for versatility."

I was still looking at Vlasilov, who was peering intently at the notes Father had taken for him. He must also have been listening, however.

"Indeed, Theodore Loftonovitch," the admiral agreed, slipping into his own native dialect. He set the notepad down and leaned back in his chair. "Young Thomas here scored four hits with four missiles, the one time a Skybolt has flown combat. A remarkable score, to be certain! But, imagine what he might have done if he'd had *eight* missiles to fire! This is what we call a force-multiplier."

I gulped and looked down at the tabletop. I didn't like planning conferences any more than Father did. I'd had to sit through dozens back on Churilla, however, and had learned how very important they were. So, I spoke up where otherwise I might not've. "I'd have scored the same four hits, Admiral. Exactly the same four. Or more likely, less than four."

Vlasilov's bushy eyebrows narrowed. "How could this be so?" he demanded.

"You've seen the films," I explained. "The whole time I was making the attack, every light gun in the Dracan fleet was firing on me. Some of the heavies, too."

Vlasilov nodded. "You were very lucky. As well as brave."

* * * *

I tried to wave my luck and bravery aside, but the electric motors in my arm spun so slowly that the gesture was ruined. So, before the moment could grow even more awkward, I plunged on. "No, sir. I *wasn't* lucky. I flew around the incoming fire."

The admiral blinked. "That is not possible," he declared.

"It is with a Skybolt, sir. There's almost zero reaction time; the nerve impulses hardly have to travel any distance at all. Plus, no split-seconds are lost manipulating a stick or pedals. And the power-to-weight ratio is so lopsided that the Skybolt responds instantly to my thoughts." I looked down at the table. "Sometimes, when the fire was at its heaviest, I had to just hope it missed. I admit that. But mostly, I flew around it."

The admiral's jaw dropped, then he snatched up a pad and began taking notes. "Why have you never mentioned this before?" he demanded."

"Because I thought it was obvious. How *else* did you think I survived?" I sighed, then nodded towards Father. "If I'd had eight missiles to lug around, and even more, if I'd had the built-in structural supports for eight hardpoints slowing me down, I think some of those near-misses would have struck home. I probably wouldn't be here today, many more troops would have landed on Churilla, and the *Imperial Throne* would still be the Dracan flagship." I shook my head. "Father's right on this one, Admiral. Or at least I think so. If anything, I'd like to see the production model equipped with *two* hardpoints, like the Stormcrow. Sometimes, less is more."

Vlasilov was still scribbling furiously. "Da," he answered. "We will table this issue for now and see what they have to say in London." He scowled. "The navy has no further modification requests, gentlemen." He turned to me. "How about you, Thomas?"

I gulped. The navy was going to spend billions of credits on Skybolts, and that was the least of it. What I had to say clearly mattered; it might even be an important factor in whether the war was won or lost. But who was I to make design suggestions? Just a pimply-faced engineer's kid, was all. "I… Uh… Not with the 'hopper itself, sir. It's almost perfect. A world-beater, even. But, there are some things I'd like to see changed in the associated systems."

"You once told me that you thought a video game ought to be part of the interface package," Ted suggested. "Because it gave you something to do on the liferaft."

I nodded. "Plus, it's a useful diversion at other times. Father already knows about that one. He says it's no problem. But…" I looked at Father again. "I've also suggested that our survival pods need to be more flexible. They should be equipped with some kind of hands."

Sven sighed. "We've been over this, Thomas…"

"I agree," the admiral said, scribbling again. "Thomas was practically non-functional for weeks, due to his lack of hands. A cripple, really, even though it must be acknowledged that he proved able to travel. We don't like it that a shot-down pilot becomes so helpless." He sighed. "Thomas, we acknowledge that you did all that you could. No one blames you in any way. But a fellow shot-down pilot died, where perhaps if you'd been equipped with hands he might still be alive today." The older man looked at Father. "That, sir, is well worth a few additional ounces of mass. From the navy's point of view, at least."

I thought about how Lt. Eaglish's little light had slowly faded to nothing. "And to me," I declared firmly. "We need a suicide option, too."

"Thomas!" Father declared, obviously startled. "How can you…"

"Agreed again," Vlasilov replied, his eyes now boring deep into mine."There are many situations a fighter pilot might well face in which a painless suicide switch is the greatest blessing we can offer." He nodded slightly in acknowledgement, though of what I wasn't sure.

Father sighed and looked down at the table. "Forgive me," he explained softly. "You have to understand, with my personal connection…"

"Of course," the admiral replied, smiling. "It must be very hard for you, Doctor Longo." He reached out and patted my father on the shoulder. "If it's any consolation, my own favorite nephew applied for the Skybolt program. He finished sixtieth. Someday, as likely as not, he will be flying under your son's command." Vlasilov turned back to me. "All of this is highly irregular, Doctor. All of it. We're placing our finest weapons, our very fates, in the hands of children who by rights should still be at home with their mothers. We do this not because we find it somehow desirous or noble, but rather because we have no choice." Then the admiral smiled. "It's insane, really, to ask so much of those still so young." He turned to face me again. "I thought at first that my superiors had lost their minds. And yet, now that I have met you, Thomas, I must acknowledge that I feel confident that our fates are in good hands after all."

Chapter Five

The next item on our plate was creating what Ted called the "United Systems Navy Lite". This discussion didn't involve Sven or Father, so they went back to the shop. Meanwhile, we three navy types sat down and began to work out just exactly how the new Skybolt squadrons and their underage pilots were going to fit into the organizational structure of the fleet. It wasn't nearly as easy as I thought it would be; in fact, it took us many hours of hard work.

The first problem was reconciling navy discipline with our new pilot's known immaturity. The fundamental difficulty was that kids are not and cannot be grownups. All of us recognized this, just as we recognized that there were excellent reasons why the laws of all civilized nations made special provisions for those below a certain age. Nor did successful militaries make a habit of arming children and expecting them to survive on a battlefield. Yet we had no choice, just as we had no choice about so many other things. "Look, Admiral," I said finally, about a week into the process. "Let's get real here. We're trying to make sense out of nonsense."

"Yeah," Ted agreed, sighing and pouring both himself and the admiral another cup of tea. "I agree." He gestured at the pile of proposed organizational charts that lay scattered all over the table. "The more complicated things become, the less sense they make." He frowned. "Admiral, headquarters is asking us to develop a system to force a bunch of teenagers to behave as soberly and as responsibly as adults." He shook his head. "In all honesty, about a million generations of parents have torn their hair out over exactly the same problem and gotten nowhere. We've only got a few more weeks before the surgeries begin, with any luck. Somehow, I doubt we'll find the answer before then, where so many others have failed."

Vlasilov looked as if he'd bitten into a rotten apple. "Bah! What would you propose instead?" he demanded.

"Employing common sense," Ted shot back. "The same as successful parents always have." He smiled. "Admiral, if you go back far enough there's a history of young men serving in the world's Navies. In fact, in the Royal Navy, a midshipman frequently went to sea for the first time at twelve. Sometimes he saw combat."

I nodded. "There were other kids aboard those ships, too. Powder monkeys, for example."

"Right," Ted agreed. "So, maybe we should use their system as our model. After all, it worked." He cleared the big conference-room screen and began drawing a new chart. "Historically," he began, "Young officer-lads were referred to as 'midshipmen'. Today, we reserve that term for Academy students." He frowned and looked at me. "How about we call them 'cadets' instead?"

I smiled. "That works. And, we can give them cadet-rank. So that we have our own internal chain-of-command." Chain-of-Command was very important, I knew. Or at least Admiral Vlasilov certainly seemed to think so, which made it important to me as well."

"Good!" Ted replied, scribbling furiously. "And... We can give the cadets their own part of the ship, preferably near the hanger. We'll call it the 'gunroom', after the old midshipman's quarters." He turned to the admiral. "Sir, even in the old days, boys were boys. They'll need space to run around, roughhouse, play games..."

"Da," Vlasilov agreed, ceding the point with a small motion of his hand. "There was never any doubt of this. They must have an area where discipline is relaxed. Some of the captains may be unhappy with this arrangement. If they become *too* unhappy, there will always be other more flexible captains to be found."

Ted grinned. "Good! The gunroom will be free of all naval discipline then, except when at action stations." He scribbled some more. "And, all cadets will be under the direct personal supervision of the ship's captain."

Suddenly, Vlasilov wasn't smiling any more. "Why is this?" he demanded.

My friend didn't back down. "Many reasons, sir. First and foremost, because we owe our cadets nothing less. They're giving up *so* much, sir, at an age where under ordinary circumstances they'd not be asked to serve at all. But there are also issues of practicality. We're not going to have time to train all of the engineering officers, for example, in how to handle cadets. There are a lot of single, childless men in the navy, sir, and it's not reasonable to expect them all to be able to deal with all of these new issues without extensive training. But we *can* hand-pick a half-dozen or so captains with families, and trust their common sense. It worked in the old wooden navies, sir. And, don't forget that this time around each cadet will be accompanied by their own personal counselor. Having an adult assigned one-on-one to each cadet ought to help a lot."

Once we got that much settled, the rest was simple. After all, depending on common sense usually made things work out better. It was decided that enlisted men were to salute cadets but not be obliged to obey a cadet's orders. Counselors were to fill a role analogous to the one that Father Murton filled for me, serving as individual tutors, and confidantes as well as physical therapists. Brain-cored people had special needs, many of which were remarkably time-consuming to fill; the consumption of so much manpower was therefore not an extravagance. Counselors were to effectively be in *loco parentis*, answerable only to the ship's captain.

"There are still many loose ends to deal with," the admiral observed as we finished up what all of us profoundly hoped would be the last meeting on the subject. "Detailed insignia design, for example. But we can delegate that."

"Yes, sir!" Ted replied, looking almost as tired as his superior. He was all in favor of delegating details, I knew. It was one of his basic principles of life, in fact.

Vlasilov shook his head and sipped at his tea. "I can't believe we're making so much progress so quickly," he observed "You'd think there was a war on, or something."

"I can't wait to see the new rank badges," I added. "Maybe we ought to just take the standard ones and put a big red 'c' over the top of them."

"Could be," Ted answered, adding a line to his notes. Then he frowned. "Admiral? There *is* one more question we need to deal with here."

The older man closed his eyes and sighed. "Yes?"

"Thomas himself," Ted said, nodding my way. "Is he a cadet?"

I started to say that of *course* I was a cadet, but then Vlasilov cut me off. "Nyet! How could he be? He's been wearing normal navy insignia for months now. Plus, he saw combat before the cadet program was even begun. This is not to say that he isn't terribly young to be an officer, mind you. Or that, being young, he isn't entitled to, shall we say, special considerations which I'll make certain his CO's are painfully aware of. Like, perhaps, freedom from military discipline in the gunroom. The navy is a large organization; we can afford to make one or two special exceptions." He smiled and tousled my fake hair, then pointed to my sleeves. The stripes there were straight, not wavy. "You're even a Regular, by special provision of the Board of Admiralty. Not Naval Reserve. If you stay in, you'll surely fly your own flag someday. And, be advised, all of us who've met you are very much hoping you'll stay in. You're a natural. Already, even at your age, you're a better man than half the Regular Navy people I know. Especially, you're more flexible." He smiled. "Tell me, Thomas. Do you think we'd let just *any* seventeen-year-old sit in on the biggest restructuring of the officer corps in a century, dead Imperial battleship or no?" His smile widened, and he extended his hand. "You've done well, son. Damned well. Thank you."

My mouth opened, but no words would come. Me, an admiral someday? I'd never even thought about it. Then I shrugged and shook hands with Vlasilov. "I don't know what I'm going to do after the war, sir." My face hardened. "I was going to be an engineer, but… Well, it doesn't matter. What *does* matter is that, after what I've seen, I'm going to do all I can to beat the Dracans in the meantime. Promise!"

Vlasilov smiled. "It's been a pleasure, Thomas. A great pleasure indeed." He turned to Ted. "You've done magnificently as well, Commander. You're as sharp as your father, and even your grandfather. I think you're going to do a fine job working with Thomas." He gathered up the scattered folders and tucked them into his briefcase. "I'll write up our findings and submit them to the Board; they'll be adopted, of course, in their entirety. They don't have time *not* to adopt them. This is why I was sent to expedite things to begin with."

"Unless Parliament keeps dragging its feet," Ted replied.

"Da," Vlasilov replied, his smile fading. "There's always that." He frowned, then turned back to me. "Thomas," he said slowly. "I can't be absolutely certain of this; my assignment is getting the Skybolt integrated into the fleet and working out its impact on the organizational structure. But you might want to spend a day or two polishing up your medals. The Assistant Minister of the Navy, in charge of working with Parliament, happens to be my old Academy roommate. And, a little bird tells me that, now that I'm done with you, he's next in line to put you to work."

Chapter Six

Admiral Vlaslov was right; I didn't even have time to take my uniform off before I got an e-mail from Assistant Minister Li informing me that a navy 'hopper would pick me up at Father's private airport at 0600 sharp to take me to Europe. Below this bald statement appeared an itinerary much too full to be comfortable. I was scheduled for breakfasts, luncheons, dinners and teatimes with politicians, media types, labor union leaders, war-bond buyers, and even movie stars. Furthermore, I was specifically ordered to wear all of my decorations at all times. I'd been around the block a few times by then, and understood what PR was all about. It was going to be my job to sit quietly, pretend to eat, and try to smile as my time was wasted posing for pictures when in any rational world I would have been immersed up to my ears in getting the first-ever Skybolt squadron set up and running and ready to fight Dracans.

How many full-time jobs was I expected to hold down, anyway?

At least the navy let me keep the 'hopper full-time; there was no way I would've been able to pull off such a schedule without it. We flew direct to Italy, where I formally accepted the little estate in the Alps that I'd been awarded in gratitude for my having destroyed the *Imperial Throne* during the fight for Churilla. I felt pretty bad about getting something so nice when so many had died without receiving any recognition at all. I didn't have any choice in the matter, though; the navy wanted me to appear grateful and stay there whenever I had business in Europe. And it *was* a nice little chalet, though perhaps more to Father's taste than mine. From the balcony you could see far into Austria; when I got my body back I'd be able to go skiing any time I wanted to without ever leaving my own land. There was even a tow-lift left over from the previous owner.

As beautiful as the view was, seeing Father Murton waiting for me in the den was better still. I walked up to him as quickly as I could and threw my arms around him. "It's wonderful to see you!"

"Heh!" he chuckled, pushing me away slightly and admiring all the glittery hardware dangling here and there from my person. "Well, don't you look like the result of an explosion in a jewelry store?"

I smiled and looked away; Father Murton knew how shy I was about my medals, and teased me all of the time. "I *have* to wear them," I explained. "Orders."

He placed a hand on my right shoulder, one of the few remaining unadorned locales. "I know, Thomas," he reassured me. "Though I must say that you look good that way." He paused, then reached out and gently turned my face towards his. "You *earned* those, Thomas. Every last one of them. You were both brave and successful, on a huge scale. Traditionally, that's how medals are won."

Father Murton had told me that a dozen times before, but I still didn't believe it. So, as always, I changed the subject. "Look!" I said, pointing at the fireplace. "Someone's left us plenty of wood. Let's get a fire going! I have to testify before Parliament tomorrow, and from then on every single minute of my life is pre-scheduled. And, therefore, yours too. But tonight, we have an hour or two for ourselves. You can tell me all about the new Counselor Corps you're setting up!"

Chapter Seven

London in winter was not a pretty place; a nasty mixture of sleet and snow was falling as our 'hopper landed on the "Official Business" pad just inside the United Systems Capitol Complex. Low, brooding clouds blocked much of what little sunlight was available this far north, so that everything appeared drab and gray. It was probably even darker for me than it was for everyone else, what with me having camera-eyes. Combined with the wet chill in the air, I could think of quite few other places I'd have rather been.

Others, apparently, didn't feel the same way. The 'hopper pad was located within a few yards of the complex's main gate, clearly for the purpose of offering the public an opportunity to watch their elected leaders come and go. A sizable crowd had gathered there to greet me, waving Union Jacks and other national flags. They cheered their lungs out when I climbed down the 'hopper's little boarding-ladder, and in acknowledgement I smiled and waved my hat, like I always did. My reaction was almost automatic I'd done it so often. Though of course, I really was always grateful.

This time, however, something unexpected happened. One section of the crowd erupted in angry shouts and frenzied sign-waving at my gesture; presumably, they'd used it as a preplanned signal. "Crim-in-al!" they chanted. "Crim-in-al! Crim-in-al!"

I looked at Father Murton, whose lips had formed a thin, taut line. "What's all that about?" I asked him. "I've never seen anything like it before!"

"War protestors," Murton explained, grasping my arm. "Come on, Thomas. Let's—"

I shook off my tutor's arm, suddenly quite angry. "No," I protested. "Let's find out what's going on here. I'm *not* a criminal!" And with that I was off and marching towards the chanters, trailing perhaps half a platoon of confused bodyguards.

"Here he comes!" one of them, a sandy-haired teen of perhaps my own age declared. His eyes seemed almost to be bugging out of his skull. "Bloody 'ell!"

The chanting slowly died away as I pressed up against the fence. "I'm *not* a criminal!" I declared as soon the noise level dropped low enough. "I'm many things, yes, and not all of them good. But I've broken no laws."

"You're the worst kind of criminal!" a voice from the crowd answered me. It belonged to a large man with a dark mustache. He was wearing a Che Guevera t-shirt and jeans despite the cold. "First you had yourself altered into an inhuman monster, at a cost of millions. Then, you went out to sell war toys to whore-politicians so that your war-criminal Esteppan plutocrat daddy could get even richer."

I opened my mouth to protest, but then a red-haired woman spoke before I could find the right words. "And that wasn't enough, was it? Oh, no! Not by half! Then, Thomas Longo, you had to go fly a combat mission in your war-criminal daddy's cruel, inhuman Esteppe-tech death-machine and kill thousands, maybe even tens of thousands, of poor working-class soldiers. It must run in the family, huh?" She smiled in triumph. 'So, how does it feel to be a mass-murderer, *Commander* Longo?"

My jaw worked, then my fists balled in rage. It hadn't been like that at all! But, before I could speak, the chanting started back up. "Crim-in-al! Crim-in-al! Crim-in-al…"

The protestors made up only a small part of the crowd that had come to greet me; most of the rest were now looking on in disgust.

"Do it, Jeanine!" the Che Guevera guy directed, turning towards someone standing a few feet behind him. "Do it now!"

Suddenly a rather small woman rose above the rest; she was wearing a pair of illegal anti-grav boots, and carried a United Systems flag in her hand. She waved it to the crowd, smiling, then soaked it with something.

And lit it on fire.

Suddenly the crowd changed chants. "Burn it down!" they declared in unison. "Burn it down!"

"Power to the workers!" the leader cried out in counterpoint. "Power to the people!" Everywhere, cameras were recording the scene; it was clear what the lead story on tonight's news programs would be.

Suddenly, I realized that somewhere along the line I'd grabbed the heavy wrought-iron fence that separated me from the protestors with both hands, and had actually succeeded in bending one of the rails. I tried to let go, but couldn't. In my anger, I'd stripped out the gears in my right hand. Even worse, some of the shredded metal must have landed in exactly the wrong place. The hand was locked up tight.

"Burn it down!" the group continued to chant, bouncing and leaping about in something not unlike religious ecstasy. A single rock came winging in; it probably hit someone, though I couldn't be sure. Then there was a second, and a third. This one, finally, was well-aimed. It struck the woman with the anti-grav boots square in the temple; still carrying her burning flag and container of liquid, she fell among her cohorts. More flames sprang up, then there was screaming. Out of nowhere, squads of police appeared in full riot gear. Whistles blew, more rocks filled the air, the flames grew ever taller...

And all the while I stood in place, locked to the fence by my own padlock of a right hand!

"Come *on!*" my tutor hissed, tugging me towards the Parliament building and safety. "Thomas! Listen to me!"

Suddenly I realized that he'd been tugging at me for some time; I'd just been too bull-headed and angry to notice. "I... can't!' I explained, looking down at the sidewalk. "My hand's locked up. Someone's going to have to release it manually."

"Damn it, Thomas!" the priest exploded; Father Murton almost never cursed, but when he did it meant that he was angry to the core. "Look what you've gone and done, not listening to me! Are you still a child after all?"

All I could do was stand and stare down at my feet; he was right, of course. There I was, a highly-decorated Naval officer, and I'd acted like... Well, a seventeen-year-old boy, I supposed. So I guessed I deserved a seventeen-year-old style dressing-down. Still, though... "Does this mean I'm grounded?" I asked my tutor, meeting his eye at last. "And, if so, is that before or after I testify for Parliament? Do I have to skip combat missions, too?"

"Gah!" Murton replied, not appreciating my sense of humor in the least. "Let me see your arm..." Surrounded by a solid phalanx of Marines whose bodies would with any luck serve to block the lenses of paparazzi and tourists alike, my tutor slit my dress-jacket sleeve with his penknife and opened up the access hatch in my forearm. "What a mess!" He dug at my inner workings with the tiny blade; Father would never have approved of his choice of tool, I was quite certain. Then something snapped inside of me, and I was free. "All right!" Murton ordered the chief of my detail. "Let's get him inside. Send someone back to Italy to get his spare jacket. Right *now*; there's not a moment to spare! Naturally, he doesn't wear a standard size. That'd be much, *much* too simple. And, someone call Longo Industries; we need to get the arm fixed, too. He can't use it until we do."

We were halfway to the main entrance by then, where a gaggle of distressed-looking VIP's stood waiting to greet me. One of them was my own Member of Parliament; I dry gulped.

"And," Father Murton whispered into my right ear as we ascended the stairs with what little remaining dignity was possible under the circumstances. "The answer is 'yes'. You are *so* grounded, Thomas Longo! More grounded than you've ever been in your whole life! But, like so many other things, it'll have to wait until the war's over. There's no way to work it into your schedule until then."

Chapter Eight

I spent the next hour or so sitting in my shirtsleeves and feeling guilty. The Head of Protocol was nothing if not unflappable; he not only found a little room at zero notice to hide us away in, but calmed us with hilarious stories about other social disasters he'd had to deal with. My favorite was the time a previous Prime Minister had stepped on the hem of her own skirt while climbing the staircase outside. She'd not only disrobed herself, but had been wearing the sexiest of underthings…

"…and Prime Minister Gardner ended up sitting in that very chair, Thomas," he finished up his story. By then, I was laughing as hard as I could. Even Father Murton was grinning. "She managed to hush the whole thing up, of course; even the paparazzi wouldn't dare cross *her*." He smiled, then turned to my tutor. "Don't sweat it, Father. You'd be amazed at how often this sort of thing happens around here. Everyone will understand."

Just then the door opened and a familiar figure burst through, followed by a huffing-and-puffing security guard. "Deputy Prime Minister Alicia Wiston," he announced belatedly, from over her shoulder. Alicia was still walking with a limp from the two broken legs she'd suffered while escaping with us from Churilla, but even so she still moved briskly. Apparently, gengineered beings healed both quickly and completely. "Thomas!" the rabbit-woman declared, pressing me back down into my chair when I tried to rise to my feet in her honor. "What on earth's happened to you?" She dropped down to one knee, produced a handkerchief seemingly from nowhere, and wiped a nonexistent spot of dirt from my plastic cheek. "Are you hurt badly?"

I looked away. "No, not really. It's something that we could fix in ten minutes if we had parts."

"Which we should have anytime now." Father Murton smiled and nodded at Alicia in greeting; she nodded back by way of reply. "Though Thomas could testify as he is, if necessary. There's no pain."

"Is that true, Thomas?" she asked, turning back to me. "No pain at all?"

"None," I agreed, studying the carpet intently. I'd joked with my tutor about being in trouble. But somehow I couldn't do so with the Deputy Prime Minister, who'd clearly come running to see that I was all right the second she'd heard that I'd been injured, abandoning heaven-only-knew what important government business along the way. "I messed up," I admitted. "It was all my fault. I shouldn't have incited them."

Alicia frowned, then turned to the Head of Protocol. "Have the police arrested that rabble yet, Henry?" she demanded.

"I'm not certain, Ma'am," he replied. "I've been busy making our guests comfortable. If you'd like…"

"Yes," Alicia replied, nodding decisively. "I would. Please, report back to me personally when you have all the details." Then she turned back to me and sighed. "Being a public figure isn't always easy, Thomas. Don't blame yourself. We should've spent more time preparing you for this sort of thing. It's much too easy for the rest of us to forget how young you really are."

There wasn't much I could say to that, though Father Murton was glowering at me over Alicia's shoulder. He *had* prepared me as best he knew how, and it *had* been my fault. But somehow in Alicia's eyes I could do no wrong. That was really nice; in fact, it made me feel good in a place that I hadn't even known existed, but which seemed terribly important nonetheless. "Well," I said slowly, trying to change the subject. "I'll ignore them next time. I promise!" Then I smiled as best as my plastic face allowed. "Congratulations on your new job, Madam Deputy!"

Now it was Alicia's turn to study the carpet. "No one was more surprised than me," she admitted. The linings of her ears were darkening; her husband Spencer had once explained to me that this meant she was blushing. "It's all symbolic. For the sake of the war effort; embattled Churilla, and all of that." She smiled a little. "There's nothing to the job, really, except that I have to attend a few extra briefings and go to Cabinet meetings. I'm still on all the same committees, which is where all the real work is done."

Father Murton's eyebrows rose in the way they always had when he'd caught me telling tall tales as a child, but he didn't say anything. So I changed the subject yet again. "Still," I continued. "Spence must be very proud."

Suddenly Alicia seemed almost to melt; her ears lowered, and it was if she'd lost half a foot in height. "Oh, Thomas!" she whispered. "I'm so frightened for Spence! They found the cave, you know."

My heart froze. "No!"

She licked her nose. "Someone talked. Probably under torture or something; I don't blame them or anything like that. But still… The Dracans came in the middle of the night. Our snipers held them off for a few minutes. That was long enough for Spence to get away, along with a few others. The rest, though… "She closed her eyes. "They died destroying important records."

I didn't know what to say, so instead I spread my one working arm out invitingly. In an instant I was comforting the Deputy Prime Minister, who was now wailing away like a distressed bunny. "Oh, Thomas! I'm so terribly scared! I mean, we knew the cave would fall someday; it almost *had* to. And, he has other safe places. But, they came so close! Much closer than we ever imagined! All of our friends are…"

There wasn't much I could do besides hold Alicia nice and tight, so that's exactly what I did until she was all cried out. "He sends his regards to you, Thomas. Spence does, that is." She let go of my shoulders and stood up. "He always liked you very much, you know. He thinks you make good war-bond speeches."

I couldn't help but smile. "Coming from him, that's the highest of praise."

Alicia dabbed at her face with the little handkerchief she'd first used on me. "Thank you, Thomas," she said eventually. "I've needed to cry ever since I heard, but I haven't had anyone to cry with. It's so hard for me, being alone." Then she smiled the expression still pretty despite her red, irritated eyes. "I'll be seeing you again soon, once we get everything rescheduled. But you know what? I'm *glad* you stood up to those demonstrators, at least just this once. Spence will be so tickled when he hears!"

Chapter Nine

It didn't take long to get everything rearranged; apparently, my Parliamentary appearance was the navy's number-one overall priority that day. While it proved impossible to repair my arm on the spot, someone procured a black satin sling from somewhere; it looked very distinguished when worn with the borrowed jacket that some other poor lieutenant-commander had been forced to part with, probably without any compensation whatsoever. Then the Parliamentary Tailor, whose shop was located right across the corridor from the equally-improbable Parliamentary Beautician's place of business, showed up and altered the jacket to fit me. Or, rather, she altered it to *almost* fit me. Which, under the circumstances, was as much as could be hoped for. Besides, with all the medals and other gewgaws acting as distractions who could tell the difference?

The Army was all about 'hurry up and wait', I'd been informed by a notably incompetent sergeant while walking across the rocky barrens of Churilla. Parliament, it seemed, operated on the same principle. Henry, the smiling Head of Protocol, moved us to another little anteroom just as soon as all the sewing work was done. This one was located just outside the regular meeting room of the Defense Committee, and was better furnished. There was a nice pot of hot coffee waiting in the middle of the long table, and Father Murton wasn't at all shy about sitting down right next to it. "Thank heavens," he muttered, pouring himself an extra-large cup and sweetening it, as usual, to a syrup. "I've been dying for some of this stuff ever since we left Italy."

I couldn't drink coffee, or much of anything else for that matter. Still, it was nice that they'd also left a half-dozen cherry-colas in an ice-bucket for me. I lifted one halfway out, then idly let it fall back into place.

"Need help with that?" my tutor asked, half-rising.

"No," I answered. "There's no sense wasting it." There was a long silence as we stared at the monitor on the wall; it showed what was happening in the Committee meeting. The volume was down real low, but I could still tell that they were debating an ethics issue, of all things. Why the Defense committee would debate an ethics issue, I couldn't imagine. Supposedly, those were the concern of the Rules Committee. Yet there they were, calling each other fancy names. Even more, there was Alicia sitting right in the middle of the group, slamming her fist on the table to emphasize every point she was making. I sighed and shook my head, then turned back to Father Murton.

"You know I'm sorry for what happened outside," I said at last.

"I do," he agreed, nodding. "I also understand why you did it. It must've been very hard for you."

"It was hard," I agreed. "But not the name-calling part."

My tutor's eyebrow's rose. "Really?"

"Really." Then I frowned. "I don't know why, but when they said those things and then set the flag on fire it was like being back at the bridge that time, when the Major ordered his private to kill him so that the Dracans wouldn't kill the private instead. Or, when the neutron bomb went off, and everyone except me knew that they were going to die." I shook my head. "It felt exactly like those times."

Father Murton frowned, then set down his coffee cup. "It felt like that to me, too," he agreed. "I thought about different places, yes. And different people doing the dying. But it was pretty much the same, I'd imagine."

I shook my head. "Father," I said. "I understand that some people are against all wars; I can understand and even respect that, a little. But, judging by his t-shirt, the leader wasn't a pacifist; not by half! Che Guevera certainly wasn't, at least. And..." I shook my head again. "Pacifists don't burn flags."

Father Murton sighed and sipped at his coffee again. "No," he said. "As a rule, they don't."

I turned back to the monitor again, where someone was pointing at Alicia and shouting. "So, who were those people?" I finally asked. "And, why were they there?"

My tutor looked towards heaven before answering, as if for inspiration. "I really don't quite understand them myself," he began after a time. "We had the same kind of thing back when we were fighting the Esteppan war." He frowned. "Now *that* war, there was honest room for disagreement about. There were very much two sides to the issue of whether or not we should've been fighting, and so when people protested I gave them the benefit of the doubt. Even when they were rude and stepped way, way over the line. Like that mob did today."

I nodded.

"But now...Thomas, I have to admit to you that I don't entirely understand it myself. At first we were totally unified. But these last few weeks... The Dracans are only two Jumps away; conceivably, they could get here in a single battle. The navy isn't at all certain they can stop the Dracan fleet if it concentrates." He sighed. "Even now, there are food shortages occurring here and there, from all the upset in interstellar trade. Metal shortages, too. Earth is practically in the front lines! And those morons..." He made a visible effort to control himself. "Thomas, some people think that the Dracans are funding the radical peace movements, though no one's been able to prove it yet. That's probably why Alicia wants them arrested; so that their finances can be examined. But we can't hold them, as much as most of us would like to." He looked me in the eyes. "Truth be told, I respect the average patriotic Dracan more than *that* bunch."

I looked down at my broken right hand, then up at the bickering Members of Parliament. "Is this why democracies don't fight wars very well?"

The priest smiled. "Pre-cisely," he answered. "For example... You noticed how Alicia played down becoming Deputy Prime Minister, didn't you? How she said it was 'just symbolic'?"

"I thought that was kind of weird," I agreed.

"It *is* weird," my tutor answered, frowning again. "I mean... She's *legal* as an MP, sure enough. Just as legal as Spence's Churillian Government in Exile. And, she's undoubtedly competent. But... I mean, *look* at her. She's an *anthro* for heaven's sake, the most obvious of all sorts of gengineered beings." He looked at me. "It's all a complicated dance, Thomas, more complicated than I can follow. She's a symbol, all right. But..."

Just then the room's warning buzzer went off, and text appeared over the screen's main display. "Five minutes," it said. And, sure enough, the Parliamentarians were rising to their feet for a break. "Wow!" my companion exclaimed, paling a little. He tended to suffer from stage fright, right at the last moment. "That was sudden."

I shrugged. So far, Parliament was the most unimpressive thing I'd ever seen. "Maybe they ran out of nasty things to say about each other."

"Heh!" Father Murton snorted. "I doubt that." He took one last sip of coffee, then rose to his feet. "Stand up, please?" he asked. "So that I can straighten up your uniform?"

I nodded and complied. "Okay. But, I need to know one more thing."

"I'm your tutor, Thomas," Father Murton answered, smiling. "Answering questions is my most important job."

"Before the buzzer interrupted us, you said that Alicia really *is* a symbol, in her present job. But I can't figure it out. What is she a symbol of? Total resistance to the enemy?"

"Oh, no!" Father Murton replied, adjusting the replica of Admiral Togo's rank insignia that adorned my left shoulder. "It goes far deeper than that. She's a symbol of the future. A bright, shining example of what we can be, perhaps even what we *should* be. What we could've been long ago, if we hadn't run away screaming from our destiny and tried to stuff the mushroom cloud back into the little metal box." He looked at me, and smiled gently. "As are you, Thomas."

Chapter Ten

I didn't really understand what Father Murton meant about Alicia and I being symbols of the future. But I didn't have time to ask any more questions either, because it was time for us to go testify.

The Members of Parliament were already seated when we came in through the little door. The Defense Committee consisted of a dozen members, two of whom were the Ministers of the Army and Navy; the Constitution required that. That Alicia was also Deputy Prime Minister was just a coincidence. Or perhaps not; I wasn't sure of *anything* anymore, with Father Murton's words still spinning through my mind. Everyone stared at us with cold, hard eyes except for Alicia. She winked, which made me smile. That in turn made Navy Minister Tonga smile, and suddenly everything felt a lot better.

Once Father Murton and I were seated the Committee Chairman, John Nichols, greeted us. "Commander Longo, Father Murton, I'd like to thank you both for coming here today." He smiled. "It is rare that we're privileged to play host to such distinguished warriors. And, I dare say, heroes." He smiled as the rest of the Committee applauded quietly. "Your adventures are well known here, gentlemen, and know that each and every one of us is grateful for the sacrifices you've made."

I smiled even wider then, not because I liked to be told that I was a hero but because it was so rare for anyone to acknowledge the brave things that Father Murton had done to help me. Without him I couldn't have achieved anything at all, and it was good to see that at least someone understood that.

"Now," the Chairman continued, "Let me make it clear that this room is among the most secure places on planet Earth. There's nothing, absolutely nothing, about the Skybolt program that the men and women now present are not cleared to know. The cameras are shut off; there will be no public record of what follows." He smiled again. "Thomas, we just want you to tell the truth. You don't need to worry about what's

46

classified and what's not."

I nodded; there wasn't all that much I knew that was classified, anyway. Or at least I didn't think there was.

"Good," he continued, still smiling. "Now, can you please tell us why you think we ought to build more Skybolts."

I blinked; this was the *last* question I expected. *Anyone* could see why we needed Skybolts, couldn't they? "Well…" I said slowly, gathering my thoughts. "Mostly because they're easily the most effective weapons we have."

I was going to say more—maybe even a *lot* more—but was interrupted by an MP. Parliamentarian Nagano, according to his nameplate. "The Dracans don't seem to think much of them," he countered. "They're not producing anything like the Skybolt. Instead, they're building more battleships." He raised his voice. "The same battleships that've beaten our fleet in five separate engagements now, I might add. Big-gunned, heavily-armored vessels that're leading our enemies to victory, while we talk of mass-producing helpless little fireflies crewed by mutilated children!"

The Navy Minister scowled, but before he could speak another MP chimed in. Her name was Clark. "Does that statement have anything to do with the fact that the only armory within many parsecs capable of producing big naval guns lies within your district and provides thousands of jobs?" she demanded.

Nagano grinned coldly. "No more than the fact that Longo Industries plans to buy parts of their airframes from a plant in *your* district!" he countered. Then he turned towards the Committee Chair. "Sir!" he demanded. "I request that Mrs. Clark's remarks be stricken from the record. I'm interested solely in the good of the people of the United Systems! Any other implication is despicable."

"Of course," the Chair replied, his tone sarcastic. "Your desire to build battleships the navy doesn't want has nothing to do with the narrowness of your last re-election. Anyone can see that!"

"No more than *your* desire to put my constituents out of their jobs has anything to do with your party wanting to take over my seat!" Nagano's eyes were flashing now and his right hand was balled up into a fist.

"We *do* want to build gun-armed ships!" the Navy Minister declared. "Lots of them! But with small, rapid-fire guns to defend them against Skybolt-type aerospace craft! Everyone knows the Dracans *have* to adopt them sooner or later, if they can. It's the next logical progression. We want to be one step ahead."

"But for now we have the technological lead!" Chairman Nichols declared, scowling mightily. The expression didn't suit him. "We *must* move ahead! Just as quickly and as forcefully as we possibly can!"

"Not without me, you won't!" Nagano countered. This time he actually pounded the table, like he'd been doing while Father Murton and I were watching from the anteroom. "You by god do *not* have a solid majority! And if I have my way you won't ever have one! My ass will fit the Prime Minister's chair just as well as his does, sir!"

I closed my eyes and sighed. This was ugly, even worse than I'd ever imagined. I *knew* that Parliament was very narrowly divided, of course. Everyone did! But, still…

"…there are many facilities that can make smaller guns," the Navy Minister was explaining, as patiently as he could. "Plants that usually make Army weapons, even. Your district would still get a share of the work"

"A pittance!" Nagano roared. He turned to Army Minister Kowalski. "How about you? What do you think about the navy using your plants and taking your guns? I bet you don't care for that at all!"

Kowalski sighed and closed his eyes. "The army's position is clear," he said eventually. "We can't fight until the navy takes us where we need to go. In essence, we're a bullet fired by the navy. Therefore, their needs *should* come first."

"Traitor!" Nagano cried, slamming the desk again. "I *put* you in that job, you bastard! And I can take you out!"

Everyone shouted at once after that, all except for Alicia. She just stared angrily down at the tabletop. It went on and on…

…until suddenly the meeting-room's door opened. Angrily, the bickering Defense Committee turned to see who dared interrupt them. It was the Prime Minister. "Go on," he declared, turning a front-row visitor's seat around backwards and seating himself in it. "Don't let me interrupt. The sooner we have all of this out, the sooner we can get something done."

There was a long silence, then Alicia finally spoke up. "It's all about featherbedding, Matthew," she said finally. "This whole damned argument comes down to featherbedding and party-line politics. I never imagined I'd see the day. Some of us want to featherbed while Churilla burns! You don't see me trying to have guns made in *my* district! Some of us have *real* problems at home! Like Dracan armies of occupation, for example!"

The Prime Minister scowled, then looked at Nagano. "There's a war on," he said slowly. "We're spending a gazillion credits an hour. Your district is industrialized." He sighed. "Look, I'm a politician too. We all are, here." He waved his arm to include the whole group. "Backroom deals are hardly an unknown phenomenon among our kind. What would it take to bring you along?"

Nagano frowned and folded his arms, but before he could speak, a new voice interrupted. "Nothing," the bird-like Parliamentarian from Sweden declared. Her name was Dagan. "Nothing under the sun could ever even *begin* to persuade me that it's all right for us to make monsters out of our children and send them to war." Nagano's mouth opened, but once again he was forestalled. "You *need* us, Isoroku," she warned him. "Or you don't have even a chance at a coalition." She looked the Prime Minister dead in the eye. "He's for sale," she acknowledged. "You're absolutely correct about that. I, however, am not. And if he ever wants to be PM, which we all know he wants like a drowning man wants air, he won't sell me out. At least not on this issue. He can't afford to."

I'm not a monster! I tried to say. But before I could speak Nagano cut me off. "You're losing this war," he declared, looking at the PM. "You and your whole coalition. Eventually, when things get bad enough there'll be a vote of no-confidence. You'll lose it. When that happens, I'll get my battleships despite you. They'll have to expand the big-gun arsenal a dozen-fold."

The Navy Minister scowled. "Not necessarily. If the Dracans invade and take Earth, no one will be expanding *anything* in Seattle."

Nagano half-grinned and dismissed the idea with an airy gesture. "Very funny, Frederick. Next you're going to tell me that the Emperor really *is* going to sign the peace treaty here in this very building."

"He might well," Minister Tonga answered, his face darkening. Then he turned to the Prime Minister. "Sir, the navy *needs* the Skybolt. And we need it *now*. This is what is required to defend the people of the United Systems and the population of Earth itself. If it's not provided, I can no longer make any promises whatsoever."

"We'll darken the sky with our battlefleet!" Nagano protested. "Damnit! I'm not talking about leaving Earth defenseless; anyone with sense knows that. We can outproduce the Dracans three battleships to one!"

"Eventually, perhaps." The navy man shook his head. "But it takes two full years to produce the main battery for a major warship. There's no known method of doing it any faster. For half a decade, we chose not to build any new capital ships so as not to 'provoke' a naval race. Now, we simply don't have that kind of time anymore." He turned to the Prime Minister. "Sir, we should've moved on the Skybolt before the war even started. The delays became inexcusable when young Thomas over there showed us what this weapon can do. Battleships are obsolescent, except in those rare cases where a system's Nikita Points lie far away from sizeable masses. There heavy ships will still be useful, and therefore they'll have to remain a part of the fleet. But…" He shook his head. "We're depending on Skybolts to give us our edge. Nothing else we know of will do the job. Nothing!"

"You will never build Skybolts!" Parliamentarian Dagan declared, scowling. "*Never!* They're an ethical abomination!"

"You're damn right you won't!" Nagano echoed. "What kind of naïve fool do you think I am? Take this issue to the Parliament floor, and you'll come back with a no-confidence vote quicker than you can say John Robinson." He leaned back, folded his arms, and smiled. "And then *I'll* be picking and choosing which committee meetings I want to walk in on unannounced."

No one formally adjourned the meeting, or at least not that I could see. There was just silence for what felt like a very long time. Finally the Navy Minister slammed his computer shut, stood up, and strode towards the door. He wasn't halfway there before the Army Minister slammed shut his own computer and followed him. "I see what you're doing!" Nagano threatened Kowalski. "There will come a day of reckoning!" But the Minister didn't slow down at all.

I rather liked Army Minister Kowalski, I decided. Then Nagano and the Swedish woman stood up and walked out together, smiling and chatting. Almost everyone else followed them, leaving just the Prime Minister, Alicia, Father Murton, and me.

"I'm sorry, Thomas," Alicia said eventually. "I know how valuable your time is. And…" She shrugged. "I'm even sorrier you had to see *that*. In some ways, no battle fought is uglier or fouler than a political one."

"It's all right," I answered. Then I shook my head. "How can they worry so much about who's Prime Minister or where the expensive weapons are built when everything that's good and decent is at stake? Don't they understand that we really *can* lose, or how awful that'd be?"

"I don't know, Thomas," the PM replied, shaking his head. He walked over and put his hand on my shoulder. "Just like I don't understand how people can call you a criminal, and burn flags in front of you. It's absolutely beyond me, all of it." He shrugged. "Maybe I *should* step down and let that rotten bastard run things, if it means we'll have *something* to fight with instead of nothing." He stared off into the distance a moment, then shook his head. "Anyway… Thomas, I'm also sorry about what you've had to see and hear today. All of it, from the very moment you arrived." His face hardened. "I've closed my eyes for too long, perhaps. Maybe I need to take a page out of your book, and face down a few hard-core bastards myself."

Chapter Eleven

I usually didn't follow the news very closely, especially not the political news. But this time I expected to find my own name in the headlines. Sure enough, when I woke up the next morning and checked my computer there I was. In extra-large type, even. "Thomas Longo Testifies Before Defense Committee", the headline read. "Majority Party Hopes to Clear Legislative Logjam by Invoking Hero of the Orion Nexus; Longo's Entrance Marred by Protestors"

I read the story over and over again—at least three times all the way through before Father Murton came and knocked on my door to see if anything was wrong. It was still kind of strange, reading about where I'd been and what I'd done in the headlines. Especially since this time the reporters didn't seem to have gotten much right beyond the fact that I'd indeed gone to London to testify. There were four or five paragraphs on the protestors, for example, including an interview with the group's leader. But, there'd been a lot more non-protestors than protestors; at least ten times as many. They'd been as offended as I was when the flag was burned. Yet the reporter hardly mentioned them at all, much less asked them any questions. Plus, they seemed to have some awfully good "anonymous sources" in the Parliament Building. The things said at the meeting were supposed to have been secret, but Parliamentarian Nagano's words were quoted almost verbatim, time and again. "We can build enough battleships to darken the sky!" he was reported to have said. "We can outbuild the Dracans three to one!" Yet there was nothing about how the big naval ordnance factory was in his district, or about how the navy didn't actually want more battleships.

Or, for that matter, about how the Dracans were only one battle away from Earth.

It was just as well that I didn't actually eat breakfast anymore; I wasn't sure that I'd have had the stomach for it. "So," Father Murton eventually asked me between bites of cereal. He still ate the same sugary stuff that I'd liked as a little kid; it was kind of strange to see him sitting there with his long gray hair, staring fixedly at the back of the goofy cartoon-character box. "How's your hand, Thomas? Is it giving you any more trouble?"

"No," I answered, my frown deepening. Father had called last night, all in a stir. The minute he'd heard about my injury, it seemed, he'd dropped everything and assigned his lead machinist to make me a whole new arm. He'd never trust the old one again, he'd explained. But the work hadn't been underway for more than an hour when a sheriff's 'hopper landed and delivered yet another court order. This one prohibited Longo Industries from working on my social body in any manner whatsoever unless my life was in danger, on the grounds that it constituted part of an illegal weapons system. Technically the courts were entirely within their rights to issue such an order; the original Skybolt work was done under a temporary Act of Parliament that'd since expired. But knowing this didn't help much. I wouldn't have a working right hand again until either Parliament passed new laws or Father gave up, put me back in my own body, wrote off much of his once-substantial fortune, and sold out.

Maybe that'd be for the best. Then when the Dracans came I'd have two arms with which to fight them. Perhaps I could use part of an incomplete battleship as a club?

There was a long lull in the conversation, until Father Murton finally spoke up again. "I saw the write-up on our little adventure yesterday," he commented. "It seems that Parliamentarian Nagano is a hero."

"A gifted, noble leader," I agreed, rolling my eyes. "Clearly our best hope for victory."

He sighed, then got up and walked towards his bedroom. "Whatever," he said his voice flat and dead. "I don't make the big decisions, thank heavens. All I can do is follow instructions. Today we're instructed to go sell war-bonds. Let's just hope that the proceeds don't go towards battleships we don't need."

Chapter Twelve

Father Murton and I weren't the only ones on the war-bond circuit. We'd crossed paths several times with an Army type, for example, who'd found and defused a live thermonuke during the smuggled-bomb attacks on the first day of the war. There was also a lady who'd written a rather catchy little song about the Emperor's personal sanitary arrangements. Alicia Wiston was also selling bonds in her capacity as a representative of an occupied planet. Parliament kept her so busy, however, that she had little time to tour. Raising money was important work, yes. But making good decisions was even more vital. So it was a very pleasant surprise indeed when I caught sight of Alicia silently reading and drinking a cup of coffee backstage at the Geneva rally.

"Hi, Alicia!" I called out, walking up to her as fast as I could. "Good to see you! And two days in a row at that!"

She raised her eyes from the book, and for just an instant I could read in them the accumulated pain of her almost two centuries of eventful life. Then she sort of lit up from the inside and was on her feet, limping towards me at her usual quick pace. "Thomas!" she greeted me, spreading her arms for a hug. We embraced for a moment, then she took Father Murton's hand and shook it eagerly. "I didn't know until today that we were going to be here together," she explained, smiling. "It never occurred to me to cross-check my schedule against yours. Or else I'd have scheduled lunch or something with you."

Father Murton smiled back. "We didn't know either," he admitted. "Once you've done one of these things…"

"…you've done a million," the Deputy Prime Minister agreed. "And all you want after that is to have them done and over with forever."

"Amen," my tutor agreed. "Then his face brightened. "We *could* do dinner, however," he offered. "Thomas was supposed to visit a Swiss shopping mall tonight, but they've cancelled due to heavy snowfall. That doesn't happen very often in Switzerland, I'd imagine."

"Probably not," Alicia agreed. Then she pursed her lips and consulted her computer. "I *can* do dinner," she agreed finally. "Assuming nothing comes up, that is. And, assuming we can find a place here in Geneva at such short notice."

"It's a date," Father Murton agreed. "I'll get Security right on it." Then the band was playing one of Alicia's most famous compositions, *Winds of a New Planet.* I recognized it because Spence used to hum it all the time.

"Oops!" she exclaimed. "That's my cue! Please, meet me here afterwards. Right at this very spot!"

* * * *

I stood in the curtains to watch Alicia make her speech. It was professional curiosity as much as anything; I wanted to see what I could learn from her. But, sadly, from the very beginning I could see that her methods would never work for me. She began by curtseying to the crowd, then sat down at a grand piano. Everyone clapped for her, even harder than they did for the woman who sang about the Imperial Bedpan. Then she seamlessly joined in with the house orchestra. They gradually faded away until only Alicia's instrument was left, thundering and roaring and majestic as *Winds of a New Planet,* her own composition, climaxed in an ending that was both perfectly logical and yet totally unforeseen. Then the house was on its feet and roaring for more. I'd never heard Alicia play a *real* piano before. Or for that matter, I supposed, *real* music. By the time she was finished I knew that I would've been weeping if I'd been wearing a real body, and Father Murton actually was wiping tears away. It was the most gorgeous thing I'd ever heard! No *wonder* Spence had hummed it so much!

Alicia didn't stop there, however. Next she played some Churillian patriotic songs, then a medley of the ancient marching songs of Earth. I knew a lot of these songs, like *The Battle Hymn of the Republic*; after all, who didn't? But somehow Alicia made her rendition of them something special and different. Was she subtly improvising somehow, at a level inaccessible to us non-geniuses? Had she grown more skilled than any normal woman via so many extra years of practice? I couldn't even begin to guess, but for whatever reason her mini-recital was the most unforgettable display of sheer talent I'd ever been privileged to witness.

"All right," she finally called out over the closing strains of *It's a Long Way to Tipperary.* "You all know why we're here and what we're trying to accomplish." She reached the end, and the wonderful music stopped dead cold. "You're already aware that my homeworld is under siege and that my husband is fighting there in a war so savage that most of you probably can't even imagine it. The odds are against his survival, much less victory."

She stood up and limped across the stage, pursued by a single spotlight. "You also know that even as we sit here in this nice warm room, sipping at good drinks and enjoying fine music, young men and women are fighting and dying by the thousand, often in the most barbarous possible ways." She nodded towards me, though the crowd couldn't have known it. "One of these brave young men is here with us tonight, scheduled to appear next. He's willingly risked his life in your name, won great victories in your defense, and is eager to go back and risk everything for us yet again. It's my privilege and honor to share the evening with him."

By then she'd wandered back to her piano. She struck a hard, discordant note; the instrument seemed to howl in pain. "Good men everywhere are fighting and *dying*, ladies and gentlemen! Not fighting and dying in the cold, distant intellectual sense, like numbers on a scorecard. Rather, they're fighting and dying in the vicious, screaming-your-life-out-as-the-bayonet-strikes-home sense. I've seen it and Thomas Longo has seen it, up close and at first hand. We're here to testify that the war is real, that the war is terrible, and, worst of all, that we're losing." She let her eyes run back and forth across the audience, as if trying to meet every single eye. "So, ladies and gentlemen," she said slowly. "Distinguished guests. Enjoy your drinks, and your afternoon getaway from your offices and classrooms. Enjoy them in full measure, and enjoy my music as well, if you will. But..." Her fists clenched. "Please remember now and always that we're in a fight for our very *lives*. That the Emperor's values are not our values, and that he *can* win. *Will* win, even, if we don't work together. If we don't stand together in time of need." She looked down at the stage floor. "Some of us have talents to contribute. Others have blood and courage." Then she looked up again. "But *you* have money. Each and every one of you bought a war bond to gain entry this afternoon, a bond worth more than two years of an average workingman's wages. That's a good beginning. But you can afford *more* bonds, can't you? *Many* more, if you're honest with yourselves, for those who face cold steel and death in your name! We need every dime. That's not exaggeration. It's cold, hard fact."

A murmur passed through the crowd, then ushers appeared everywhere, handing out promissory notes. "Yes," Alicia continued, nodding. "I see that you can indeed afford more." For the first time, she smiled. "Thank you all," she said, "From the bottom of my heart. Thank you in the name of my husband. Thank you in the name of the people of Churilla. And, most of all, thank you in the name of children yet unborn, who will know freedom instead of slavery due to your generosity."

Chapter Thirteen

"...tried my hardest," I explained, looking down at my elegantly-folded napkin. Napkin-folding had been raised to a high art at the *Edelweiss*, where Alicia and Father Murton and I were having dinner together. Mine was an origami-Skybolt in snowy linen.

Edelweiss was an expensive place, but they were able to provide us with a private room on short notice. Even better, the manager explained as he showed us in that my money wasn't any good; dinner was on the house. We weren't even to leave a tip!" Sven tried taking over as my tutor towards the end. He's *great* at math! Better than Father, even! He tried so hard to help. But..." I shook my head and sighed. "I'm sorry, Alicia. I just didn't get it. I've let everyone down."

Alicia smiled. "Don't sweat it too much, Thomas. After all that you've done, I just can't find it in my heart to worry too much about your failing calculus." Her smile faded. "Seriously—you have *so* much else on your plate just now. And..." She looked at Father Murton, who nodded slightly. "Thomas, you don't like math, do you?"

"Not really," I admitted. "In fact, I sort of hate it."

"Well," Alicia continued softly. "Engineers deal with math all day long. You know that. So, why would you want to do something you hate all day every day for the rest of your life?"

I frowned. "I don't know. But... I'm a *Longo*. My grandfather was an engineer, my great-grandfather was an engineer... It's sort of just how things are."

Alicia nodded. "Family traditions are important," she agreed, dabbing at her face with her own origami-napkin. Hers, predictably enough, had been done up as a bunny. "But individual needs are important as well. Sven's a good man, by all accounts. I imagine that he'll be perfectly able to take over when your father is ready to step aside. And, I'm also quite sure that all of your relatives are proud of you just as you are." She met my eyes. "Traditions are important. But they aren't meant to be straitjackets." She tilted her head to one side. "Tell me. What did your mother do?"

"She was a housewife," I explained. "On Esteppe, that was considered highly honorable. But…"

Alicia's eyebrows rose. "Yes?"

"*Her* mother was Governor of Zeeland Province, before the takeover." I looked again at my napkin; they'd even added perfect little antennas in just the right places! Perhaps they'd let me take it home with me? "I never knew her."

"Hmm," Alicia answered, through a mouthful of something green and crunchy. "Well," she continued after chewing and swallowing. "That explains that."

"Explains what?" I asked.

"Why you're so good at making speeches," she explained. "Thomas, you have a gift. Give Spence and I a couple-three years, study up a little on the art of genteel backstabbing, and we'll make you Prime Minister."

I gulped; just a few days before an admiral had promised me my own flag someday, if I just stayed in the navy long enough. Everyone seemed to think I was chock-full of potential. Or at least everyone except my math-tutors did. "I don't know," I answered in a whisper. "I mean, I'm honored, but…"

"Heh!" Alicia grinned, then turned to Father Murton. "I envy you," she told him. "Neither of us, you by reason of faith and me by reason of law, are allowed children. But you," she continued, pointing at me with her fork. "You have *him*, all day every day. How wonderful it must be!"

"Usually," Father Murton replied. "Except on those rare occasions when he acts his age." His smile faded. "Alicia," he said slowly. "I've wanted to say this for some time now, but I haven't been able to. It was never the right time or place." He frowned, clearly searching for words. "I'm a man of strong faith. But I also think for myself. It's against official doctrine, but I think that you and Spence would've made wonderful parents. Would still, if it isn't too late. And it's a tragedy that you haven't been allowed. You're wonders, both of you. The sheer human potential being thrown away is… staggering. If we'd produced even a few thousand more individuals of your caliber, I believe this war would never have happened. Your kind would've found another way."

The Deputy Prime Minister smiled, then took another bite of salad before replying. "Spence and I have obeyed the law. But, don't imagine for a moment that we've liked it. Or, that either of us agree with the premises that underlie it."

Father Murton nodded. "I can't change things any more than you can. Still, I wanted to tell you. I *had* to, somehow."

Alicia nodded, smiling once more. "Thank you, Father. You'd be amazed at how few have ever taken our side."

As usual, it was at dessert-time that I most regretted being unable to eat. Father Murton consumed a delicious-looking sliver of German chocolate cake, Alicia was served a sparking crystal dish of sherbet, and I had to watch while their eyes rolled in sheer delight. Then dinner was over and my companions were drinking what was very clearly a special kind of coffee. "Superb," my tutor declared. "Absolutely superb." He grinned. "Yes, Madam Deputy, being Thomas's tutor does indeed have its fringe benefits."

"Heh!" Alicia agreed. "As does being a Founder of Churilla, Ephraim." She raised her cup, the priest matched the gesture, and then the two delicate bits of crystalware clinked in the middle of the table. The gentle collision created a sweet ringing tone.

Just then the concierge entered our little room, looking worried. He looked back and forth between the three of us, then decided to address himself to Alicia. "Madame," he began, bowing apologetically. "You are, I presume, aware that there are other Parliamentarians present here tonight?"

Alicia scowled. "Word got out," she agreed.

"Not on our end, I assure you!" the tuxedoed man explained. "We're nothing if not discreet. But still…" He frowned again. "Word did indeed get out. Several Parliamentarians and other dignitaries were hoping to dine with you and Thomas. While they've respected your privacy up until now, two of them are demanding to see you." His frown intensified. "They're Army Minister Kowalski and Navy Minister Tonga."

Alicia's eyes closed halfway. "Indeed?" Then she looked at my tutor and I; we nodded in agreement. There were more important things going on in the universe, after all, than private dinners. She turned back to the concierge. "Send them in, please. And thank you for your discretion."

"Good evening," Minister Tonga greeted us as he and Minister Kowalski strode in. We all stood to greet them and exchanged hearty handshakes. "We're sorry to disturb you during your private time," he explained as the *Edelwieiss* staff brought in chairs and poured drinks for them. "We both regret it very much."

"Of course," Alicia agreed, her professional smile locked firmly in place. "What can we do for you gentlemen this evening?"

Tonga looked at Kowalski, who shrugged. "Well," Tonga said,

clearly a little unsure of where to begin. "There's two important matters. One involves our friend Nagano."

Kowalski nodded. "You know I'm technically opposition," he began. "Even though, Madame Deputy, I've never been so tempted to switch parties in my life." He sighed. "I might still do so, before all's said and done. But, that's beside the point." He met Alicia's eyes. "There's to be a vote tomorrow on funding the Skybolt. Nagano intends to make it a confidence-issue."

Alicia's ears rose. Then she crossed her legs and took a large sip of coffee. "Really?"

"Really," Kowalski replied. "He's pulling out all the stops. And he thinks he'll win." He reached into his breast pocket and pulled out a sheaf of papers. "Based on this. It's maybe an hour old."

It was a Defense-Committee report of some kind, I could see, marked "Eyes Only". It was at best a couple of pages long; Alicia required only a few seconds to read it. "Oh, my," she said, when finished.

Tonga nodded. Then he looked up at Father Murton and I. "You're cleared," he said. "So I won't leave you out of the loop. Our intelligence services estimate that an all-out attack at New Nippon is imminent. We expect it within days. Maybe even within hours."

I nodded. New Nippon was only one Jump away. Even worse, since the solar system had only one Nikita Point, if New Nippon was lost Earth would be cut off from the rest of the United Systems.

"We've been expecting it," Father Murton answered. "Though not so soon."

Kowalski frowned. "We'd have had Skybolts ready and waiting for them, if it hadn't been for all this political horseshit. We'd have achieved total surprise." He looked down at the floor. "Madame Deputy, I am *so* sorry for what my party has done." He balled up his fists. "If only, if only…"

"There, there, Hubert," Alicia answered, reaching out and placing her hand on his knee. "It wasn't *your* fault. None of it was. You did your best in an impossible situation. I have complete faith in both your competency and your honor." She turned to Tonga. "What are our chances?" she demanded.

"Slim," he answered. "Though not nonexistent. We've got a few surprises in store for them, and some of our new smaller ships, like the *Chief*-class destroyers, are world-beaters. But then, you already know about *them*."

I nodded, remembering the heroic struggle of *Roman Nose* and *Tecumseh*. Without them, none of us would've escaped Churilla.

"Of course," Alicia agreed. Then she frowned. "But the new ships are very few, overall. We hardly have a main battle-line left."

"They'll never land on Earth," Kowalski added. "Or not anytime soon at least. That'll be the biggest fight the Dracans have ever seen. There's still plenty of Polecats, and we've got a lot more missile batteries than either Churilla or Meade's World had."

"But," I interrupted. "If they take New Nippon they can raid Earth anytime they want to. At high speed, just like they did Churilla. And, like our navy did to Chruilla again to get us out." I frowned. "They can raid us with nukes. I don't think the air defenses can stop hit-and-run raids. For sure, they can't stop all of them."

"Plus there's all the imports," Tonga agreed. "Food, especially." He frowned. "Once word gets around, the en-route merchantmen will all turn back. Our trade's ruined."

Alicia sighed, then stood up. "We have to get back to London," she declared. "Now. This will be an all-nighter." She looked at Minister Kowalski. "Thank you, Hubert," she said softly. "If there's any justice in the universe, this won't be forgotten."

"Heh!" he snorted. "I gave up on justice a decade or more ago," he explained. "How can I believe in justice, when Isoroku Nagano is the head of my party?"

Chapter Fourteen

While the *Edelweiss* had indeed been able to provide the three of us a private room for our dinner, there was no other way to leave except via the main dining room. Not that there was any terrible hurry; security, it turned out, wouldn't be ready to escort us to our 'hoppers for a few more minutes anyway. So after meeting and thanking the chef and his staff, the least we could after receiving a free meal, Alicia decided to step out into the lobby and greet anyone who cared to see her. Shaking hands wasn't exactly my favorite thing to do with my spare time. Nor did I think Alicia particularly cared for it. But she was a politician, so it was expected of her. And, with her about to need so much support, I volunteered to tag along and help out in any way I could.

But things didn't work out as planned. Truly exclusive restaurants are generally quiet and genteel places. The patrons are by definition rich, and many are also famous. Therefore, as a rule, the patrons tend to fail to be impressed by celebrity; if anything, in such places, the atmosphere is even quieter and less-intrusive than in that of a mere five-star establishment. Yet when we emerged from our private room there was a virtual cacophony of conversation. Even more unusually, the diners were all clustered around a half-dozen or so tables, their own meals left half-eaten. "Mrs. Wiston!" an elderly gentleman cried out from near the heart of the largest cluster of diners. "Madame Deputy! Have you heard?"

Alicia's eyebrows rose. "About what?" she asked innocently, as if she hadn't seen the intelligence report.

"The big attack!" the man replied. He pointed at his computer, which everyone was staring at. "My god! They're attacking! The Dracans are attacking! We were just about to come and get you."

Alicia limped over to where she could see the screen. The others made room for her in deference to her rank, and then for Father Murton and me as well.

"…three friendly destroyers have come through already, Paul," a

63

female voice was saying. The holoscreen showed nothing but a patch of ordinary-looking space, save that it was flanked by the three flashing blue navigational beacons that marked a Nikita point. The shot had been taken at extreme magnification; you could tell by the way the beacons trembled with every little vibration. "Two of them heavily damaged. And... wait a moment, Paul!"

Sure enough, even as we watched, a United Systems battle cruiser flashed into being, its after-turrets still blasting away towards the Dracan vessel that presumable was at the other end of the wormhole. And it was shooting back, too! A huge Dracan-orange laser-bolt struck home abreast the battle-cruiser's rearmost turret; it must've penetrated deep because the battle-cruiser slewed heavily to port, revealing the name painted across her bow. She was the *De Ruyter*, once-proud flagship of the battle-cruiser squadron. Now, she was little more than a wreck.

Still, she was a fighting wreck. Instead of trying to stabilize his ship, her captain let the sickening skid continue until she hung broadside across the approach to the Nikita, now able to fire with her forward guns as well as those aft-mounted weapons still functioning. She poured out salvo after salvo, then inexplicably stopped.

"What's happening, Darlene?" the man at the news desk, presumably Paul, demanded to know. "Can you see anything at all?"

"No," Darlene answered, her voice thick with fear. "I... Wait a minute!"

Then suddenly ship after ship was pouring through the Nikita; battered cruisers, shot-up destroyers, even a charnel-house of a battlewagon with torpedo scars up and down its sides and all of its guns pointed this way and that, whichever way they'd been firing when the Dracans had knocked them out. It was a miracle that anyone was still alive aboard her, and an even bigger miracle that she was still responding to her helm. Flying junk, that's all she was. Radioactive flying junk. Eventually, every single man aboard her would surely die. There was no hope for them, after having taken so many torps. "My god," Darlene whispered. "Oh my god."

"May He have mercy on their souls," Father Murton prayed.

"Amen," Alicia echoed. Her hand found mine, then squeezed.

I hadn't thought to count the vessels coming through, but it was clear that only a tiny portion of the fleet had made it out. The last vessel through, the battleship *Yamamoto*, was almost clear when another one of the titanic orange laser-bolts struck home, penetrating even deeper into her vitals than the similar bolt which had crippled *De Ruyter*. There was a huge explosion, and then another battleship and her crew were dead.

"Dear god!" a wealthy female customer whispered. She was weeping openly. "All of those men…"

Alicia squeezed my hand again, but said nothing.

For a long time, no one else said anything either. "It was an *Imperial Throne-* class battleship," I finally explained, breaking the silence.

"What?" Father Murton asked.

"That laser bolt—the one that killed the *Yamamoto*. I've seen them that big before. It was fired by an *Imperial Throne*-class battleship." I pressed my lips together as the camera zoomed in to show individual spacemen kicking out their lives in hard vacuum. "Someday, I'll kill *that* one, too."

Things happened pretty quickly after that. Within seconds of *Yamamoto's* death there were security people running around doing who knew what. A navy lieutenant appeared out of nowhere, saluted me, then handed Alicia a message form. "It's urgent, Ma'am," he explained. "You're to return to London immediately."

Alicia frowned, her eyes passing disapprovingly over the chaos that'd so suddenly descended around her. Then she read the message and frowned again. "Destroy this," she ordered the lieutenant when she finished. "Immediately." Then her eyes turned to me. "Thomas," she said slowly. "Do I recall you mentioning that you have extra seats on your 'hopper?"

I nodded. "Three."

She frowned again. "I need more than three, I fear. But I'm going to borrow your 'hopper anyway." She turned to Father Murton. "I need to get as many Parliamentarians back to the capitol as possible. Hubert was telling the truth, as I believed all along. There's a constitutional crisis developing." She frowned. "If you two were anybody else, I'd commandeer the thing altogether. But as things are we'll just have you leave some of your security detail here. It should be all right; we'll be getting a fighter escort just as soon as I can arrange it."

Then a Parliamentarian came scurrying up. "Madame Deputy!" she wailed. "Madame Deputy! I… I mean, did you see…."

"Of course, Marie," Alicia said smoothly, accepting the distraught fellow MP into her arms. "And we're going to make everything all right."

"Battleships!" the weeping woman declared. "We need more battleships! We'll darken the sky!"

For just a moment Alicia's features went cold and hard. Then, so quickly that it was as almost if it'd never happened, the storm cleared and Mrs. Wiston was all sympathy again. "We'll fight them," she not-quite-agreed. "And win. You have my word on that."

Chapter Fifteen

London wasn't very far away, by skyhopper standards. So Father Murton and I didn't have to spend too long answering foolish questions about space battles and Nikita Points. "How long would it take to *manufacture* a second Nikita Point?" one Parliamentarian demanded of me; I suggested that he consult an astrophysicist. "They'd never dare nuke us," another assured his colleagues. "Never." I was less certain, having personally been neutron-bombed myself by precisely the same Dracans that he was referring to. But I didn't say anything. There wasn't any point. Or at least not any that I could see. In fact, I didn't want to talk to anyone just then, except maybe Father Murton. And his lips were sealed as tightly as mine. Probably this was because he knew as well as I did what was about to happen in London, even if these silly peacock-politicians whose endless hair-splitting arguments and power-dances had just gotten thousands of good navy men killed for no good reason hadn't tumbled to it yet.

There wasn't any crowd waiting to greet us this time as we took our turn landing in front of the Parliament building, though it was still sleeting. "The traffic's insane," our pilot explained over the intercom. "I've been asked to encourage Your Honors to disembark as quickly as you possibly can.": But his words made little difference; it took forever to unload as the Parliamentarians lollygagged and jibber-jabbered in the hatchway as if they had all of the time in the world. Father Murton and I were the last ones off; my foot had barely cleared the companionway when the 'hopper pilot upped-ship.

The Prime Minister himself was greeting the Parliamentarians on their way in, smiling and shaking their hands as if he hadn't a care in the world. You had to look closely indeed to see that the lines in his already-craggy face were indeed a little deeper than they'd been just a few hours ago. "Thomas!" he greeted me with genuine surprise. "Father Murton. What... I mean..."

"They're with me, Matthew," Alicia explained. "I had to commandeer their 'hopper."

"Ah," the PM answered, understanding instantly. "But... I mean...."

"Where's Henry?" she demanded. "Henry?"

Out of nowhere, the Parliamentary Head of Protocol appeared. Though surrounded by frazzled politicians dressed in everything from formal dinner wear to athletic gear, his tuxedo somehow was freshly pressed. "Yes, Madame Deputy?"

Alicia pointed at us. "Those two are my personal guests," she answered. "It's my fault they're stranded here. Please, give them the full VIP treatment that you're so famous for. Keep them handy, as well. It's unlikely, but I just might need them."

"But of course!" Henry replied bowing and smiling in obvious pleasure. Apparently he *lived* for chaotic nights like this one. "Please, gentlemen. Follow me!"

Apparently, personal guests of the Deputy Prime Minister rated quite well in the capitol building's scheme of things; in mere seconds Father Murton and I and both of the guards we'd managed to hang onto were festooned with special passes and tokens that, we were assured, gave us the freedom to do pretty much anything we pleased on the Government Floor short of demanding the microphone or voting. Then we were escorted to first-row seats in the VIP section, offered refreshments, and instructed about how to call for personal service at any time.

We had an excellent view of the Parliamentary floor, which was rapidly filling up with agitated, harried-looking MP's. It was fascinating to watch, really, the kind of thing that you never saw on newsclips. A tiny handful of fringe-types excepted, the Parliamentarians all belonged to five major parties, three of which were relatively small. And there they were, standing in the middle of their debating arena in precisely five groups, three of them much smaller than the other two. Even in this hour of disaster, they were socializing and arguing along party lines.

The place looked pretty full by the time that the PM appeared behind his podium and gaveled the special session to order. "Our first order of business," he began, "will be to—"

"I object!" a harsh voice rang out. It belonged, predictably enough, to Parliamentarian Nagano. "I have a confidence-vote on the agenda, sir! When a confidence-vote is scheduled, the PM is *not* to chair the meeting!"

The Prime Minster scowled, then began again. "The first item on the agenda is—"

"I object!" Nagano cried out again, this time leaping out of his chair and charging the rostrum. "You have no right—"

The PM pointed at his number-one opponent. "Arrest that man!" he declared. Suddenly a dozen Marines appeared from backstage. "Arrest him!" the Prime Minister repeated, pointing again. His voice sounded a little surer this time.

Nagano's jaw dropped in shock, and there was a sudden roar of outrage. "You can't arrest me!" Nagano declared as the Marines marched steadily towards him. "I'm a sworn Parliamentarian! And therefore immune from arrest within this building. Besides, I've done nothing wrong. I *do* have a confidence-vote scheduled! You are *not* supposed to be holding that gavel, sir! And, I'll win for *sure* now!"

At this, the Marines hesitated. Suddenly the Navy Minister was on his feet as well, in the full admiral's uniform that the political masters of the navy almost never wore. "Arrest that man!" he repeated, pointing at Nagano. "That's an order!" And just that easily the Marines were advancing again.

Nagano's eyes went wide, and his ally Parliamentarian Dagan rose to her feet. "You wouldn't *dare*!" she screamed, her fists balled and pumping up and down. "You wouldn't *dare*!"

The Prime Minister didn't even blink. "Arrest her, too!" he ordered, pointing again. "We *shall* have order here tonight!" Yet another squad of Marines appeared. This time they didn't hesitate at all. It was over in thirty seconds; Nagano resisted, Dagan didn't. In neither case was the outcome ever in doubt.

"Good lord!" another voice cried out. "This is a goddamn coup!"

"The exits!" another cried out. "Look! They've blocked them!"

I turned around, and sure enough there was a half-platoon of Marines stationed at each doorway. A coup it might well be, I decided. But at least it was a well-planned one, executed with daring and singleness of purpose. Attributes, I couldn't help but note, that'd been conspicuously absent from the United System's decision-making process since long before the shooting had started.

"Our first order of business," the PM continued as the marines dragged Dagan and Nagano away, "will be for me to announce that a state of martial law has been declared for the entire Solar System and its associated jurisdictions. Habeus Corpus is hereby suspended. Freedom of the press is hereby suspended. Elections are hereby suspended." As he spoke, Army Minister Kowalski appeared at the PM's left shoulder, and a few seconds later Navy Minister Tonga appeared at his right. Clearly, the military had chosen sides. Then, behind him, Alicia stepped out onto the little stage in support as well. "The right of free assembly is suspended," the prepared speech went on. "The populace is hereby informed that strict rationing of food and other strategic materials will be instituted within a fortnight…"

Father Murton was shaking his head, a tear crawling down his cheek. "I had so hoped that it wouldn't come to this," he whispered.

"We're going to be under siege," I answered. "And under repeated nuclear attack as well." I frowned. "Didn't we talk one night about the weaknesses of a democracy in wartime?"

He nodded. "Yes. Even back then I knew deep down in my gut that this was coming. This, or something very like it. It had to, really." He sighed. "Abraham Lincoln did pretty much the same thing, and so did Winston Churchill. Not to the same extreme, granted. But, to be fair, they weren't facing the threat of repeated nuclear strikes."

"And I bet their Parliamentarians weren't quite so stupid," I growled. The legislators had done it to themselves, so far as I could see. Years back they'd decided to stop building battleships, believing that the Dracans would do so as well. Then, once it was crystal clear that the Dracans hadn't even slowed their construction programs, they could've voted to start laying down hulls again. Instead they'd kept their heads firmly buried in the sand. Even two years ago, they could've voted to build Skybolts en masse instead of merely allowing for the completion of a single demonstrator. But Parliament had done none of those things. So far as I could see, everything which followed was the logical, totally-predictable outcome of such poor decision-making. When democracy failed, I decided, it tended to do spectacularly. Or, at least it had this time.

"…no intention of imposing a dictatorship," the PM continued. "Once the immediate danger is past, civil liberties *will* be reinstated. Free debate will be encouraged once more. I also swear that I won't make use of these emergency powers to any greater degree than is absolutely necessary; there'll be censorship, for example, but legitimate political debate and commentary will be permitted insofar as it doesn't interfere with the war effort." His face hardened. "*Nothing,* from this point forward, must be allowed to interfere with the war effort…"

"That explains Nagano's arrest," my tutor pointed out. "He was obstructing the war effort, sure enough."

Apparently, there wasn't anything else on the agenda except the imposition of martial law. "I will inform you when it is necessary for this body to meet again," he said in closing. Then the Prime Minister gaveled the meeting to an end without seeking a motion of closure, and that was that. For a long time the Parliamentarians simply sat and stared at one another in shock. Then there was another angry roar. It didn't last long, however, once the Marines filed in from their posts at the exits and lined the hall. Unlike the ones who'd made the arrests earlier, these wore full battle gear.

"My god!" one of the legislator's voices cried out. "What are we going to do?"

"Win the war," another answered. "Unless you expect a better deal from the Dracans." He shrugged. "Me, I say that it's about goddamned time."

Chapter Sixteen

Neither Father Murton nor I had anywhere to go, nor any pressing business which needed attending to. Besides, we were effectively stranded. "…could try and call up Newton again," my tutor said, looking thoughtful. Newton was our pilot. "Though with the world having gone totally nuts—"

"Excuse me, sir," a young man interrupted. He was a naval officer, an ensign probably fresh out of the Academy. Which meant that he was both much older and infinitely more qualified to serve as an officer than I was, even though he had to call me "sir". It was awkward, but since neither of us had any choice in the matter we carried on exactly as if our disparity in rank actually reflected something meaningful.

"Yes?" I replied, raising my eyebrows.

He reached out and tried to hand me a canvas envelope. Then he realized that my arm was in a sling and gave it, along with another, to Father Murton. "My name is Roberts, and I'm carrying orders for you gentlemen," he explained. "I'm instructed to wait here while you open them, then put myself at your disposal to aid you in carrying them out."

I nodded again, then looked over my tutor's shoulder as he used his penknife to slit the heavy material open. Naval orders were always sent in canvas envelopes, made of genuine sailcloth. There was also always a musket ball inside, so that the package would sink quickly if thrown over the side of an ocean-going-type ship of war. This was all nonsense today, of course. But in the navy, tradition died hard. Many officers kept the musket balls and displayed them proudly on shelves in their private offices. "We're to report immediately aboard *The Glorious First of June*," Father Murton explained. He was a much faster reader than I was. "To take up your squadron command."

The Ensign nodded; clearly he already knew. "Yes, sir," he agreed. "I'm here to assist you with your dunnage; Admiral Vlasilov is well aware that you've had no chance to pack, and he also recognizes that no

72

one but you two can possibly have any idea of what you'll be wanting or needing aboard ship."

"That's sensible," Father Murton agreed.

The ensign produced a blank tablet and a pen. "If you'd each be so kind as make lists for me," he continued, "and perhaps indicate where I might find things, I'll go pick them up for you. I can't be too specific, but I'm authorized to inform you that this won't be an extended cruise. You'll be hitting dirt again in fairly short order, in a place where you can buy things." He turned to me. "And, sir, it might also be helpful if you were to contact your father and let him know to expect me. I'll also be bringing along a few ratings to help."

Since I wrote legibly only with my right hand, Father Murton had to make both lists. He didn't seem to mind, though I stammered a little while figuring out what I wanted to bring. It was a little embarrassing, asking a stranger to go through my dresser drawers for me. There was still plenty of kid-stuff there, like the stuffed zebra that Father bought me when I was six and my all-time favorite coloring-book. Even worse, the most important thing I wanted to take with me was my best video-game joystick. But there wasn't much I could do about it, short of up-shipping without any of the stuff I really cared about. Maybe Ensign Roberts still had a few suspiciously kid-like articles lying around in his own chest of drawers? If so, perhaps he'd understand.

We were just finishing up when Navy Minister Tonga stepped up. "Hello, Thomas," he greeted me, reaching out to shake my left hand.

"Hi," I answered, smiling. Ensign Roberts was standing at rigid attention, I noted, and seemed terrified out of his mind at the sight of so much brass on one uniform. Perhaps I was better off never having been an ensign after all?

The Minister noticed the torn canvas envelopes sitting on our chairs. "Well," he said. "I see that you've received your sailing orders." His smile faded. "Thomas, maybe we *are* asking too much…"

"No, sir!" I countered, shaking my head. "Not at all! I wouldn't be anywhere else for the world."

Tonga pressed his lips together, then nodded. "I'm essentially a civilian," he said slowly. "Though I was an enlisted man for a few months, so long ago that it feels as though it was part of another life. As the Navy Minister, it's my job to ensure that the fleet gets what it needs to perform its function, yet doesn't become so powerful that it becomes dangerous." He sighed. "I'm supposed to be a manager of resources, not a leader of men. A bureaucrat, not a strategist. The less interfering I have to do, the more successful my term of office is deemed to have been. Yet it was on my watch and on my orders that the navy backed a coup. And, it is again on my watch and at my orders that we're for the first time ever deliberately and in cold blood sending children to war."

"History will vindicate you," Father Murton predicted. "You and the PM both will go down as great men. Kowalski, too. Maybe even *especially* Kowalski."

"Maybe," Tonga answered, looking down at the floor. "Or maybe not. I've done my best, is all I know. And all that I'm sure of." Then he turned back to me. "Anyway, Thomas. It seems that I'm doing a great many things lately that a Navy Minister shouldn't ever do. Another thing that my predecessor warned me about was playing favorites, getting to know individual sailors and taking an interest in their lives and careers." He smiled and extended his hand again. "Once again, I'm guilty, as charged." His face softened. "Thomas, if there is ever *anything* you need, or that I can do for you…"

I could've accepted the extended hand and shaken it. I also could've merely stood and saluted with my still-working left hand. Instead I stepped forward and wrapped my good arm around the Minister's back in the nearest thing I could manage to a hug. "Thank you," I whispered. "For everything."

"No," he answered, squeezing back. "Thank *you*." Then he pulled away, stood at attention, and saluted *me*. "Go," he ordered. "Right now! Time is much shorter than you imagine."

Chapter Seventeen

The *First of June* was wallowing in a heavy North Sea swell as we approached in the fleet 'hopper, just like all the rest of the navy vessels present. Not that there were all that many of them; practically everything space-worthy had been committed at New Nippon. *June* had missed the defeat there only because she'd first been held back so that I could run carrier-acceptance trials with the prototype Skybolt, and then to have her armament upgraded. My old friends, *Roman Nose* and *Tecumseh* were also tied up to the big central dock; both were clearly still under repair from their ordeal during the Orion Nexus Raid. A pair of larger vessels were also floating nearby; they were cruiser-sized but had very destroyer-like lines. "Those are something new," Father Murton explained as our pilot hovered, waiting for traffic to clear. I'd never seen the sky so full of 'hoppers! "They're called 'heavy escort cruisers', and are named after aviation pioneers. Because, you see, they're designed to support carriers." He smiled. "The near one is the *Jimmy Doolittle*, and the other is *Wilbur Wright...Louis Bleriot* is still in the yards." He frowned. "Now, she'll probably never see space."

"They look funny," I observed. "I mean, they're practically covered with little guns, but don't have any big ones."

"They're proof that the navy is capable of growth and change," my tutor answered. "Think of them as improved and enlarged *Chief*-class ships, designed to back up hit-and-run raids like the one that got us off Churilla. They're all about speed and close-range rapid fire, plus they carry an enhanced torpedo armament." He smiled. "Behold the future of the cruiser."

I nodded slowly. "I'd hate to fly even a Skybolt anywhere near all of those guns."

"Exactly," the priest agreed. "The Dracans will have a Skybolt-equivalent soon enough. It's always best to have a counter already up and running ahead of time."

"Only *Doolittle* is operational," a new voice added. It was our pod's co-pilot; like the pilot he was a civilian contractor. "*Wright* is still short most of her internal fittings. The only reason she's out here instead of back at the dockyard is because of all the repairs. They needed the slip."

I nodded; London, Philadelphia, Tokyo... Every navy yard on Earth was overwhelmed with urgent battle-damage repair work. And that was *before* the slaughter that'd just taken place a few hours ago. What things would be like when the remains of the fleet hit dirt, I couldn't imagine.

"It would've been a whole new fleet, eventually," the co-pilot mused. "All high-speed and dependant on the Skybolt as the primary offensive weapon." He sighed, then shook his head. "Too late now, though."

I frowned. "Maybe it's too late," I answered. "And maybe it's not. When are we going to be able to land? Our flight-orders are stamped 'urgent.'"

"So are everyone else's," he countered. "In fact, I came back to let you know that we're going to be holding position here for at least another half-hour. " He pointed down at the landing platform. "Look for yourself. There's not an empty square-inch to be found down there."

I nodded and looked out the porthole. I didn't like the co-pilot very much, but that didn't mean he wasn't right. There were three medium-sized cargo-'hoppers and a jumbo-oversized job all unloading at once, in a space that would have been cramped just for the jumbo. Freight-spiders were crawling everywhere, disappearing with pallet after pallet of all sorts of stuff into the hull of the *Jimmy Doolittle* and, even more frequently, that of the much-larger *June*. Some of the pallets were unidentifiable, but... wasn't that the prototype Skybolt lying on one of the skids, minus her wings? And... My heavens! One spider was loaded down with gold bars! Hundreds of them!

Finally, after an interminable wait a tiny corner of the landing area was cleared for us. Our pilot touched us down just as smoothly as you please, and then Ted Knight greeted us as we stepped out into the bone-chilling North Sea wind. "Hi! Follow me, and let's you get you guys settled into your cabins. It's cold out here!"

Neither of us argued. But joining our ship proved a much more difficult task than we'd bargained for. Due to the unceasing cargo-spider traffic and the fact that the landscape was continually changing, Ted kept getting us lost. It was pretty hard on Father Murton, as we hadn't caught up with our dunnage yet and that included our pea jackets. But I didn't mind so much, except of course that I didn't want him to suffer. There was all *kinds* of interesting stuff plied up everywhere I looked; circuit boards, machine tools, and in one corner a big pile of crates marked "Rhodium .99999" that was surrounded by armed Shore Patrol types. There was even a bunch of factory stuff painted in Longo Industries colors that looked as if it'd been sawed off of its base and strapped to whatever size pallets had been near to hand. Father would never have approved of *that*, I thought.

Or perhaps he would've after all. "Thomas!" a familiar voice cried out. It was Sven, dressed in a parka. He came striding up, smiling around the stem of his pipe. "I knew that you were coming, of course. But I didn't think we'd get to see each other. Father's billeted in *Roman Nose*, and I'm going to be aboard *Doolittle*. With Dean; they let us bring him, too. It didn't take too much arm-twisting." He winked.

Dean? Even Dean was coming? "Why… I mean…"

My brother's smile widened. "Haven't they told you yet, Thomas? We're going home! To Esteppe! Where we can produce Skybolts without worrying so much about our facilities being nuked on alternate Tuesdays. That's very bad for component standardization, you **see."**

I blinked again; Sven had just attempted a joke. This was unheard-of; he must be excited indeed! "Home?" I repeated dumbly. "To Esteppe?"

"T-that's right," Ted agreed, his teeth chattering. Apparently his pea jacket hadn't caught up with him yet, either.

"But…" Father Murton asked. "What about the Dracans? How are we going to get past their fleet at New Nippon?"

"We're going to fight our way right through the middle of them, if we have to," Ted replied. "We figure our odds will be best if we move immediately, before they have time to make contingency plans. Hopefully they won't be expecting us to try anything this crazy, especially not so soon after getting our asses whipped." He crossed his arms over his chest and shivered theatrically. "Come on, guys. The quicker we move, the better our odds of catching the Dracans still licking their wounds."

Chapter Eighteen

Things were just as insane inside the hull of *The Glorious First of June* as out on the cargo platform. People were running everywhere, very often carrying datapads or complicated-looking fittings and tools, and the hanger deck was practically alive with cargo spiders. You couldn't look anywhere without having at least one or two sweating ratings in view, busily strapping cargo to the tiedown-points normally used to secure Polecats and Gladiuses.

It was clear that this was going to be a pure freight-run; all of the 'hoppers were gone, probably retained to help defend Earth from dirtside airbases. Instead, we were as full of cargo as space was of black. Even if we'd held onto a Polecat or two, we couldn't have operated it with the deck so cluttered. Nor, for that matter, would we have been able to operate the prototype Skybolt even if it'd been operational. But it clearly still was not. My 'hopper sat on its side all the way up against one of the hanger deck's outer walls, forlorn and lonely with its detached stub-wings neatly chained atop the fuselage. Clearly it was still not flyable, and wouldn't be any time soon.

The pilot's ready-room was located right next to the hanger-deck; though I'd visited *June* during carrier trials, I of course had been wearing the Skybolt as a body and therefore hadn't been able visit the host squadron, as tradition dictated. So even though I'd been aboard *June* a dozen separate times, all I'd ever seen of her was the hanger. Ted saved the day by pointing towards the most distant hatchway, and, slowed considerably by the ship's rolling in the heavy North Atlantic swells, I headed that direction.

Everyone was staring at me, of course. Even though the crew was so busy, they still tapped each other on the shoulder and pointed as I passed. Sometimes, they met my eyes; when that happened, I smiled. Most of the time, they smiled back. That made things a little easier. Still, I felt like I was on stage every second of the trip, right up until the ready-room door closed behind me. "Whew!" I said to my tutor. "That was—"

"*Attention on deck*!" a voice bawled out. There was a crash of heels, and suddenly the room was full of people standing at attention. My mouth opened slightly; then I turned to Ted.

"At ease!" he ordered after meeting my eye. Technically speaking Ted was junior to me by virtue of time-in-grade, but that was so totally ridiculous that we'd cut a private deal between us to ignore the fact. It was one of those common-sense decisions that we'd spent so long discussing during our planning sessions. He met my eye a second time, and I nodded again. "Formalities," he continued, "are suspended in this room for the duration."

"Thank you, sir!" a shaven-headed petty officer at the back of the room replied; he was at least fifty years old, and sounded as if he ate crushed rocks for breakfast. He turned to me. "And thank you too, sir!"

I nodded awkwardly, then looked around. It wasn't at all like the last ready-room I'd been in, back on Churilla. Sure, there was a display-board at the front of the room, and a big pipper was mounted on the wall there so that we pilots could keep up to date on the action. But, the place was practically sterile. There were no pin-ups on the wall, nor any squadron keepsakes to be seen. Presumably the Adam-and-Eves, our predecessors, had taken all of their stuff with them. Even the coffee-pot was gone! I couldn't have drunk coffee even if I'd actually liked the stuff; my mannequin body didn't deal well with hot beverages. But there was something fundamentally *wrong* about a ready-room that didn't have a coffee pot. Even worse, it wasn't full of pilots. Instead, for the most part it was full of kids. All of them were still standing at whatever they thought passed for attention and staring at me with big, scared eyes. Even Jimmy Knight, the only one I'd ever met, looked scared. That, I decided immediately, needed to change. "Hello," I said, meeting their eyes one by one and smiling. "I'm Thomas Longo. And, I'm a kid just like you."

Jimmy smiled back, though no one else did. "I've wanted to meet you guys for ages," I explained. "But I've been pretty busy, and there've been a lot of people trying to block this project. Between the two, it just never happened." I looked down at the ground. "I'm sorry about that."

"Less than half of us are here," Jimmy pointed out.

"The navy's trying to locate the rest of the pilots," Ted explained. "But everything happened so quickly! Some, for example, are on vacation with their parents." He frowned. "We're probably going to have to space without some of them."

I nodded back, and counted heads. There was Jimmy, and twelve others. Fourteen of us, total. About a third of a traditional squadron. More like a single flight.

"Well," I replied, "We'll just have to make do with what we have." I smiled again, then held up my one good hand and spread its fingers. "The docs told me that when I met you, I should above all else make certain to show you as well as I can what it's like to live in a mannequin body, sort of to help prepare you. But because things are so crazy, I'll have to offer you the short version instead. It sucks. Period."

"Heh!" one of my future pilots chuckled. "It don' look like no fun 'tall." She was from the Caribbean, judging by her lilting speech and sunny smile. Jamaica, perhaps. "But we're signed up solid, Tom Longo! We're ready, fun or no."

I smiled back. The navy hadn't been able to allow women to fly combat for many years, due simply to their too-high body-fat ratio. But, what difference did that make to a disembodied brain? I'd already heard of Delana. She'd finished number one overall in the competition, and probably would be flying rings around me in no time flat. Delana was pick-of-the-litter, while I'd never had to compete at all.

Then I nodded at the adults, who were all gathered together in the back. "Is that your new outfit?" I asked Father Murphy.

He nodded. "Yes, Thomas. The counselor team."

I nodded and smiled at them as well. "I was supposed to meet with you, as well," I explained. "Individually, one-on-one, so that you could gain some insight into what it's like to be around someone like me." I let my smile widen. "Well, here's insight number one. Nothing involving me ever seems to go as planned. Probably that'll be true for your own individual pilots, as well."

The elderly petty officer smiled. "We're adaptable, sir," he promised. "And, we're honored to be here."

I blinked; somehow, I'd been under the impression that all of the counselors were going to chaplains and therefore officers; apparently, this wasn't the case. Not that it particularly mattered; the counselors were Father Murton's bailiwick. I had enough problems on my own personal plate. "All right, then," I continued. "I guess—"

Then, the ship's klaxon rang. "Attention all hands!" the annunciator declared. "Prepare for acceleration! Up-ship in ten minutes! Repeating, up-ship in ten minutes!"

Chapter Nineteen

One of the advantages of being aboard a fighting ship was that the navy tended to think things out pretty well in advance. All forty of the briefing room's chairs could double as acceleration couches. Since we had only one flight of pilots aboard, there was plenty of room for their counselors, as well.

"This is going to be our battle-station later," Ted explained. "Once we're actually flying combat. So, I suggest that we settle in here. Anyone who wants to is free to go to their cabin." He nodded at the pipper. "But in here you'll be able to see what's going on."

No one took Ted up on his offer, which was completely unsurprising. It only took a few minutes to get everyone strapped in; Father Murton had to help me due to my bad arm, and I was pleased to see that the rest of the counselor corps took care of their principals, as well. The gravel-voice petty officer, I noted, was assigned to Jimmy Knight. That seemed to fit, somehow. But more answers would have to wait for another day.

When the high-gee hit it didn't bother my mannequin-body; it'd been so long since I'd experienced the effect of gee-forces on flesh-and-bones that it was hard to remember what it was like. The *June* accelerated first at about three gravitires, then smoothly worked up to nine for a time before shutting down her motors and drifting. According to the pipper, we were in orbit.

"I've never been in space before!" I heard a cadet exclaim. His voice was cracking something awful. "This is so cool! I'm floating!"

"Don't unstrap, David," his Counselor warned him. "We'll be maneuvering again any second now."

But we didn't maneuver for minute after long minute, even though the acceleration-warning lights remained steadily on. "Maybe part of the cargo broke loose," I speculated to Father Murton, "and they had to re-secure it."

Ted blinked. "Maybe," he allowed. "Or…" He pointed at the pipper. "There you go."

Sure enough, suddenly there were more blue pips moving in to join our little formation. Along with *June*, we'd brought *Tecumseh*, *Roman Nose* with both forward guns still dismounted, *Jimmy Doolittle*, the unfinished *Wilbur Wright*, and two more brand-spanking new Chief-class destroyers that probably hadn't even been shaken down yet, *Ten Bears* and *Osceola*. Now we were joining up with an armada even more powerful than our own. It consisted of my old friend the battlecruiser *Andrea Doria*, along with a motley collection of various cruisers and destroyers.

"My god!" Ted hissed, so quietly that I'd never have heard him if I hadn't been in the next seat over.

"What's wrong?" I asked.

"That's the training fleet," he explained. "Obsolete, every last one of them. And manned by the greenest crews there ever were. Most of the men will have only been in the service a few weeks." He closed his eyes. "They're going to be *slaughtered*."

My mouth dropped open. Now that Ted mentioned it, I *did* recall that the elderly *Andrea Doria* had been relegated to training duty after escaping from the Nexus. And yet there she was, swinging smoothly into formation next to us just as if she still belonged anywhere near a line of battle.

I thought that we'd be getting underway, once the *Doria* and her consorts showed up. But there was still another delay, until yet another group of ships rose out of the Atlantic towards us. These, I noted, didn't even try and maintain anything like a formation.

"Merchantmen," Ted explained. "Every last mother's son of a merchantman that'd rather run the gauntlet than sit around and wait to be nuked." He shook his head. "My god! There's *dozens* of them!"

I nodded again; it was almost like a regatta. "Some'll get through just by sheer numbers," I replied, beginning to feel a little hope. Perhaps this wasn't quite as insane as it felt after all. "The Dracans can't possibly shoot us all up."

"Not at New Nippon," Ted agreed. "The Nikitas are especially close together there."

I nodded; by a happy coincidence, a system's Nikita's points tended to occur about the same distance from the sun as the liquid-water zone. If there also happened to be a sizeable planet near that orbit, its mass tended to concentrate them fairly nearby. New Nippon, however, wasn't a planet. It was the moon of a gas giant, whose titanic gravity field clustered the Nikitas even tighter than usual. "This could work," I agreed. "Especially if the Dracans aren't expecting us yet, and don't have patrols set up."

"They won't be ready," Ted promised. "It's still only been a few hours. I've seen the preliminary intel reports on the big battle. Yes, we got our asses waxed. But by no means was it totally one-sided. We killed three battlewagons, and a disproportionate number of smaller craft." He smiled his one-sided smile. "Precisely the same smaller craft they'll need to catch us. I don't know it for fact, but I'd bet money that was no accident. The Dracan heavies are obsolete, just like ours. We'll kill them someday with Skybolts." His smile faded. "Not that I'd feel particularly comfortable about selling us life insurance just now," he added. "We're obviously the most valuable target. And, the *Imperial Scepter* was just on the other side of the Nikita, the last we heard. If she's still there..."

"Right," I agreed, remembering what the huge orange laser-bolts had done to the heavily-armored *Yamamoto*. Our hull had practically no armor at all...

The thrust-warning bonged again; we took a few stomach-churning lurches this way and that until we were square in the center of the formation. With us were five fast passenger liners. *Jimmy Doolittle* and *Wilbur Wright* hovered nearby in close attendance, along with the Chiefs. "All of the modern stuff is staying together," I observed.

Ted nodded, then pointed at the training fleet, which had formed a thin sphere around the rest of the merchantmen. "And they're staying together, too, the poor bastards. I wonder what their captains are telling them, just now."

Then the warning bonged again, our own captain ordered full emergency thrust, and we were racing balls-to-the-wall for the solar systems sole Nikita Point and the Dracan fleet just beyond.

Chapter Twenty

High-gee acceleration pinned most people into their couches. I, however, was not most people. The electric motors in my neck barely felt the strain as I raised my head and looked around at the others.

At my first command, I suddenly realized. The people I was ultimately responsible for. The ones already looking to me for strength and leadership.

I frowned, then let my head fall back. Everything seemed to be as all right as it possibly could be, considering that I was strapped to an unarmored light carrier just setting out on what promised to be one of the epic death-rides of all time, in a room full of children I mostly didn't even know. I was just a kid myself, but I still knew what needed to be done. "It's going to be all right," I lied. "We're in the best-protected ship in the formation, the one that's *got* to get through. It'll be rough going, but we're going to make it."

"Yeah," Delana agreed in her heavy Jamaican accent. "We'll be making it for sure." I raised my head again and looked over at her. Eyes closed, she looked so calm that she might well have been asleep.

"The easier it is for us, the harder it'll be for everyone else," Jimmy Knight observed. He'd been a navy kid all his life, and probably knew more than half the adults in the room about battle-tactics.

"Surprise counts for a lot," I countered. "Surprise and audacity matter more than mere numbers."

"The secret to victory is usually sheer bloody-minded aggressiveness," Ted chimed in. He made a terrible effort and shifted his head slightly so that he could half-smile at his younger brother. "That's what Dad taught me, what Thomas has already learned, and what we need to teach the rest of you."

I nodded to myself, turning to watch the pipper. Our formation was stretching out now, for passage through the narrow confines of the Nikita

Point. The squadron looked a lot more impressive than it really was; the obsolete, trainee-manned cruisers and destroyers created exactly the same image on our combat display that a modern, properly-manned ship would've. Presumably the same would prove true on Dracan equipment. Pippers couldn't tell you if a ship's guns were well-manned or not.

We hit the Nikita hard, and the sick-making feeling that I always got when passing through one was far more intense than usual. *June* could've done it a lot faster; she'd been equipped with the latest gear for high-delta-vee hit-and-run raids, after all. But most of the other ships in the formation were not so-equipped. Besides, there'd been no time to build up much velocity. The tunnel-effect pressed on our minds for an instant…

…and then we were through, in enemy space!

It always took the pipper a little time to catch up after a Nikita jump; lightspeed was lightspeed, after all. Luckily the ready-room was gifted with a porthole, and as squadron commander my chair was located near it. I turned my head…

…and felt my jaw dropping. There, right *there*, was a Dracan destroyer so close abeam that she was *between* us and our nearest escort, the *Doolittle*. Even our vectors must've been nearly identical; she was holding position on us as neatly as if everything had all been planned out in advance instead of being a near-collision. Suddenly she seemed to awaken; before I could even exclaim in surprise her guns began to slew round towards us.

But they never made it. *Jimmy Doolittle* seemed to explode in flame, and for an instant I thought she'd blown up. Then her light, fast-firing guns struck seven, twelve, three dozen blows, and the Dracan blew up before she could get off a single shot. It was the most impressive thing I'd ever seen, even more than salvoes from the main battery of the *Imperial Throne*. *Doolittle*'s guns might be small and short-ranged, but there were a *lot* of them. Within their reach it seemed to me that nothing could live except by her captain's permission.

The porthole's view was limited, and the Dracan's destruction had been so sudden and complete that already there was nothing left to see. It was almost as if the vessel had never existed at all, had been merely a trick of my imagination. But then I heard distant cheering from the rest of the crew.

"We got a destroyer already," I explained aloud. "Or *Doolittle* did, rather."

"We came out right on top of the poor bastard," Ted amplified. He'd had a good view, too.

Then the pipper flashed for attention, and painted its first, necessarily incomplete, picture of the battlefield. My jaw dropped again, the second time in under a minute. The sky was full, absolutely full, of Dracan ships!

"My god!" Ted whispered. "There's a hundred of them!"

"More," Father Murton countered. "And, look at all the wrecks!"

I nodded, gulping. My tutor was right; there were even more wrecks in the sky than live ships, most of them in faint United Systems blue. Near one side of the screen a whole line of dead dreadnoughts still drifted in ragged formation, killed at so nearly the same instant that they'd never had the chance to maneuver independently. Near them floated a few faint pink wrecks, the Dracan dreadnoughts they'd taken with them. But, there were many more blue corpses than red. "Jesus god almighty," Ted whispered. I wasn't sure if it was a curse or a prayer. "That's the heart of the main battle line. The pride of the fleet."

"Right," Jimmy agreed. "And look! The Dracans are between us and Nikita Three!"

We'd hit Earth's Nikita on a vector calculated to carry us towards New Nippon's number-three jump-point, which was the most direct route to Esteppe. But, probably by pure chance, the Dracans had chosen to re-form their squadrons directly between us and it. If we'd wanted to force an engagement, it would've been perfect. However, as things were, the tactical setup couldn't have been worse.

Suddenly *June* slewed hard to starboard; clearly the fleet admiral was reading the pipper too. "This'll be a long burn," Ted predicted. "We're going to aim for Nikita One, I bet. It's a round-robin trip to Esteppe, but doable."

I looked out the porthole; *Doolittle* was thrusting along with us, as was *Roman Nose*, easily distinguished by her two missing guns. But… There was the *Doria*, just beyond *Nose*. And she didn't seem to be altering course at all. Instead, she and the rest of the Training Squadron were standing directly towards the main Dracan line of battle. Seven apparently still-healthy dreadnoughts, three battlecruisers, and more light vessels than I could easily count. Ten times the effective strength of our ships, even if they'd been manned by skilled veterans instead of trainees! And that wasn't even counting the *Imperial Scepter*, which at first had stood a little off from the rest but was now accelerating with regal dignity to her proper place at the head of the Dracan line.

I closed my eyes and sighed. "Sheer bloody-minded

aggressiveness," I said quietly. "That wins battles, all right. But sometimes you have to also be willing to sacrifice yourself that others on a more important mission might live."

Chapter Twenty-One

Ted was right; our burn *was* a long one. Slowly our force divided into two parts, the Training Fleet steadily closing in on the Dracan's main body, and a smaller force made up of the merchantmen plus *The Glorious First of June* and our little group of fast, modern escorts. The Training Fleet maintained very nearly its original course, thrusting only slightly to starboard, while our group was turning in earnest. Meanwhile, the Dracans had formed up and were closing for all they were worth.

"I bet that's one surprised admiral on the bridge of the *Imperial Scepter*," Jimmy Knight offered. "He *never* figured we'd try something like this."

I nodded. "It's gutsy and bold. The *last* thing they've come to expect from the likes of us."

"Our admiral's no dummy, either," Ted added. "Look at how we're deploying. The Dracans have to know that there's all kind of valuable stuff aboard the merchantmen, and probably aboard *June*, too. But he's only got so much time to get at us before we hit the Nikita, which from his vector he can't follow us through. He only has time to run straight in."

"So," Delana added, suddenly understanding, "To get at us he has to turn those pretty, pretty ships of his all broadside-ways to torpedoes from the Training Fleet!"

"Exactly," Ted agreed. "He's riding the horns of a dilemma. He can shoot our transport group up plenty good if he wants to badly enough. He'd get a lot of us, though probably not all. Once the survivors have Jumped, he could finish off the Training Fleet at leisure. There's ultimately nothing in the sky that can challenge him. But if he does things that way, he'll take disproportionate losses. Probably even lose a couple dreadnoughts. That never looks good on an officer's resume."

"Right," I agreed. "If he stands in to fight the Training Fleet first, he'll kill large numbers of warships without losing much of anything at all. Our group will get away clean, of course, if he does that. But what does that matter from his point of view? The blockade of Earth will be assured, so far as he knows, and that's his primary mission. Besides, you get bigger medals for killing warships than merchantmen."

"Heh!" Jimmy chuckled. "You oughta know."

I wanted to answer that, but somehow couldn't come up with a proper reply. So we watched in silence as our forces deployed, *June* leading our group and *Andrea Doria* heading up the Training Fleet. Suddenly the pipper flashed as *Doria* opened fire on the *Imperial Scepter* at maximum range.

"Why is she doing *that*?" Jimmy asked, his brow wrinkling. "You can't get hits from that range. All it's gonna do is drain her batteries."

We watched as the shots went wide; *Doria* corrected, then fired again. This time against all odds one of her bolts struck home, though it didn't seem to do any damage. "She's trying ta' make a big fuss," Delana opined.

A heavy cruiser, the *Perth*, joined in. By a further stroke of luck, her first salvo found and blew the stern off of a Dracan destroyer; its engines died and instantly it was left behind, out of the battle. Our gunnery was too good to be true; perhaps the forward weapon-mounts were being operated by the instructors?

"Well," another young voice commented; I didn't know his name yet. "If that didn't get their attention, I don't know what will."

"Go on!" Ted hissed. "Take the bait, Admiral Dracan! Go for the big medal!" *Doria* fired again, missing but not by much. Then the pipper flickered as it was momentarily overwhelmed by a flood of new data. When it cleared, *Imperial Scepter*'s guns were slewing around to face the *Doria*. Even better, the entire Dracan fleet was thrusting as hard as it could towards them.

"We've made it," Ted opined, sighing and letting his head fall back onto his headrest. "They'll never catch us now."

I nodded as *Scepter*'s guns spat a wall of fire. *Perth*, one of the oldest and feeblest ships in the fleet, disappeared almost without a trace, And so did the three hundred or so men who manned her. Just like that, they were gone. Then the rest of the Dracan line opened fire, and ship after United Systems ship flared and died with hardly an effective shot fired in return.

"Can we turn that thing off?" one of the counselors asked as *Doria* took her sixth or seventh fatal hit. The battle was less than ten minutes old and already it had degenerated into a massacre. "Please?"

"Not while we're at battle stations," Ted answered. "Regulations."

"Regulations be damned!" the counselor countered. "Children don't need to see this sort of thing!"

Ted's remaining eyebrow rose, but I cut him off. "These 'children' will be *doing* this sort of thing to the Dracans soon enough, if I have my way." I explained. "Slaughtering them without mercy." I turned back to the pipper, where *Doria* and her thousand-man crew now glowed the pale blue of death. "I feel sorry for the victims too; don't get me wrong. I even feel sorry for the Dracans I've killed; they'll haunt me for the rest of my life and perhaps beyond. But we're at *war*, Counselor. And a cruel, pitiless war it's been so far, without any prospect whatsoever of getting any better. If you can't deal with wholesale slaughter, then resign your commission. You're in the wrong business. And you're looking for sympathy from the wrong man."

Chapter Twenty-Two

We held a task-force wide memorial service the next morning for those killed in the Battle of New Nippon, both those who'd died in the original major fleet action and then the brave men and women of the Training Squadron who'd made such a suicidal attack that we might get away. "…they gave all that we might escape to forge the tools of victory," I explained to the men aboard not only the *First of June* but also our escorts and the merchantmen, via closed-circuit. "We must stand ready to repay their sacrifice in kind. We must produce and wield these weapons that we may live up to their courage and example. Victory must be ours!"

A memorial service wasn't the right time or place for wild applause; instead, the room erupted in a sort of angry mutter of approval. *June's* crew was in an ugly mood, experiencing the kind of anger and pain that only Dracan blood could assuage. Most of *The Glorious First of June's* crew had previously served aboard vessels that were now dead, and had close friends and relatives who now drifted cold and silent between the stars. Some people might've been cowed by such an impressive display of Imperial might. But these were *navy* men. They wanted vengeance more than anything else in the universe. More even than life itself.

"Victory *must* be ours!" Sir Robert Morgan agreed, meeting me at the little podium that had been rigged up in a corner of the cluttered hanger deck. He was *June's* captain. "Thank you for speaking, Commander Longo," he continued, pumping my hand enthusiastically. "You do our departed a great honor."

I nodded looking down at the deck, then went and sat down between Father Murton and Admiral Vlasilov, who was in command of the whole task force. The Russian smiled approvingly, and my tutor patted me gently on the shoulder. Apparently they thought I'd done well, though I knew that mere words were nothing when measured against the terrible self-sacrifice we'd all witnessed just the day before. The battle was still raging when we hit the Nikita, but there'd been no hope whatsoever of victory for our friends. Nor even of mere survival.

Alicia was the next to speak; she'd been sent along with us to act as Head of State for the colony worlds while Earth was cut off. "War," she began, "is the scourge of history…" She was a good enough speaker, and what she had to say was probably very important. But my adrenaline was still flowing from my own time at the podium, so that I couldn't concentrate on her words. "…in support of values that are eternal, unlike our mortal bodies," the Madame Deputy was saying.

I liked Alicia a lot, and I didn't want to be disrespectful towards the dead. Still, however, my eyes kept wandering towards where my would-be pilots all sat together in a cherub-faced row, with their respective counselors gathered behind them. It wasn't my fault, perhaps, but I hadn't spent any time at all with them. The only one I knew at all was Jimmy, and I wasn't really close even with him. I sighed to myself. These kids were two whole years younger than me; how could we possibly get to know each other across such a huge age gulf? Especially, I admitted to myself, when I'd never been very good at making friends to start with? When I'd been a kid, I'd been a total loner. Weeks, sometimes even months had gone by without my ever seeing, or wanting to see, another child. Some pick *I* was to command a squadron of kids!

Soon Alicia finished talking, and everyone stood up to leave. Several officers came by to congratulate me on my speech. Then Admiral Vlasilov pulled me aside. "We need to hold another conference," he explained. "Your father and brother, Commander Knight, and us two. To make final plans."

I nodded. We'd not been able to meet since everything relating to the Skybolt program had been turned topsy-turvy. "Whenever you'd like."

"This evening, then," the admiral replied. "Right after dinner. We'll meet in Briefing Room A." Then he smiled slightly. "I heard what you told one of the counselors yesterday, when he wanted to turn off the pipper. I couldn't have handled it better myself."

I looked down at my shoes, then shrugged. "I was just being truthful, sir."

"Keep it up," the admiral advised. "And you'll go far."

* * * *

Father and Sven didn't physically board *June* for the meeting; instead, they joined us by video-link. My brother brought Dean along with him so that he could wave and smile at Father and I for a moment;

under the circumstances no one complained of the waste of valuable time. Then Vlasilov spoke. "Dr. Longo," he began, addressing Father. "It should be clear to you by now that the navy is totally committed to the Skybolt weapons-system, and that we consider it the key to victory."

Father nodded, but did not speak.

The admiral looked down at his computer. "I'll add that the navy fully appreciates the difficulties you must now find yourself in. In fact, I'm informed that you still don't have an accurate inventory of your equipment. Is this correct."

"That's right," Sven answered. "We know what was shipped from New Orleans, but the loading process itself was total chaos." He shrugged. "You were there."

"Da," Vlasilov agreed. "So I was. And yet, even though I appreciate that your information is incomplete, I fear there are decisions which must be made very soon regardless. Preferably tonight." He scowled. "Once we get to Esteppe, how long will it take to get Skybolt production rolling?"

"That depends on many things," Father replied, his eyes suddenly hooded and cautious. "One of them is the work force. Skybolts are not ordinary consumer goods, as you well know. They require assembly by skilled craftsmen of the highest order." He shook his head. "The Stormcrow plant has been shut down for over a decade; who knows where my former employees have gone?"

"And then there's the condition of the plant itself," Sven pointed out. "It's radioactive, you know."

The admiral pressed his lips together. "No," he answered. "I did not."

"It was near-missed during the last days of the assault," Father explained."And ended up right in the heart of a fallout pattern. Fortunately, production was shut down at the time due to lack of parts so almost no one was there. And, because of the radiation all of the tooling is probably still intact. Certainly, no one's sought to buy it from me."

"How bad was it?" Vlasilov asked. "I mean, was it at a lethal level?"

"Back then it certainly was," Father answered. "Now…" He shook his head and sighed. "If we make an intensive cleanup effort, who knows? But, my honest guess is that it'd still be an unhealthy place to work."

"Right," Vlasilov agreed, his frown deepening. "So not only do we have a potentially hostile work-force, one that has no reason to love the United Systems, but even with anti-rad drugs we'd be asking them to risk their lives for us just by reporting to work." He sighed and shook his head. "How long to start in a new location?"

This time it was Sven's turn to scowl. "When we pulled out of New Orleans, the navy told us to assume that we were going to move into old Stormcrow plant and decontaminate it. We picked and chose what we brought with us accordingly. So we'd have to dismount some of the Stormcrow machinery, decontaminate it, remount it, reprogram it... All of this, of course, on top of all the remounting and calibrating we're already going to have to do with what we brought with us." He shook his head. "Proper calibration work can only be done by the very highest tier of skilled workers. It takes time; there's no known way to rush things along. Call it a year."

Vlasilov's eyes narrowed. "Before the first fighter rolls off?"

"Oh, no!" Sven replied. "Before production can even *begin*."

"But..."the admiral spluttered. "I mean..." Then he made a visible effort to calm himself.

"We can save maybe half a year by not decontaminating the old plant," Father pointed out. "Everyone can work in safety suits."

"That'll also slow things down quite a bit, however. Just in a different way," Sven warned. "Production can begin sooner, yes. If everything is still intact the way that we hope it is, I mean. But each worker's productivity will be halved, at best. And we believe that skilled workers are going to be our major bottleneck. So you can have your Skybolts a little sooner that way, but in the end you'll have far less of them."

"I see," Vlasilov replied, drumming his fingers on the tabletop. "Your arguments are both reasonable and persuasive; this I grant you. But..." He sighed and shook his head. "We must find another way. There has to be a counterattack to relieve Earth. They cannot hold out for so long."

Sven had been filling the bowl of his pipe; now he lit it, taking his time to make sure that it was drawing well. "You can't simply wish Skybolts into existence," he pointed out eventually. "You're not hearing anything here that you haven't heard before."

"And," Ted added, speaking for the first time, "You can't just pull skilled Skybolt pilots out of any available orifice either, much less a working squadron. We need time to train. Hell, we haven't even developed Skybolt tactics yet; we need time to stage maneuvers to see what works and what doesn't. Plus, the surgeries haven't even begun. We estimate that most of our pilots won't even be able to *begin* training for six months after being cored."

"Da," Vlasilov agreed, conceding this point as well. "This is a hard limit, Commander, one that cannot be altered under any circumstances. People can only recover just so quickly; flesh and bone is no more amenable to being rushed than uncalibrated equipment. And yet…" He looked around the table, meeting all of our eyes. "Earth cannot hold out a year, gentlemen. Not under any circumstances. And when she capitulates, the war is lost. We will all become slaves of the Emperor."

There was a long silence. "We should begin the surgeries immediately then," I suggested. "Assuming the sick bay here is capable of them."

"It is," Vlasilov answered. "I have verified this personally. But only at high risk of failure. Therefore we will attempt only the bare minimum number, plus one as a backup." He looked at my father again. "Your estimates for starting production; those are all based on using production-series tooling. This is correct?"

Father nodded. "Ja. The sooner we start using the production tooling, the more Skybolts we can produce overall."

Vlasilov nodded. "But you've built two prototypes by hand, no? The original, and the one down on the hanger deck? And you built them without using the tooling that needs so much calibration?"

"Yes," Sven answered, nodding and beginning to understand. "At an extreme cost in skilled labor, however. Skilled labor that will also be needed to get full production started. Keep in mind, this is our projected bottleneck."

Vlasilov waved the objection away. "We're fifteen weeks out from Esteppe. If you build entirely by hand and if we can find you all of the labor that you need, how many Skybolts do you think that you can have flying in, say, another fifteen weeks?"

Father looked at Sven, who gulped visibly. "We'd still need to use the old facility. Specialized tools are still required, even for building by hand. Plus, we'd have to hyperwave ahead and get the motor-subcontractor started. Perhaps we could get a head start on the plant cleanup, as well?"

"I didn't ask about difficulties," Vlasilov replied, his eyes hard and cold. "I asked, how many in fifteen weeks?"

Sven shook his head and shrugged, then Father turned to Vlasilov. "You *do* understand the sheer impossibility of what you're asking us to do, don't you?" he asked. "There are so many unknowns… We can only make our best guess."

The admiral nodded once, stiffly. "I accept this."

Father nodded back, equally stiffly. "Then, in that case I'd estimate that we can have perhaps six machines ready for you, including the prototype we're bringing with us. That's under the best foreseeable conditions, mind you."

"A half-flight. If that's all there can be, then that's all there can be. Thomas, and five others." Vlasilov shook his head, then turned to Ted and I. "You gentlemen will select six candidates from the young men and women available to undergo brain-core surgery. Written orders will follow." He scowled and looked away. "You have one week to accomplish this; sick bay's still not quite ready. It's not nearly enough time, I know. But it's what must be done."

Chapter Twenty-Three

I didn't sleep very well that night; Admiral Vlasilov's last words kept running through my head over and over again like a mantra as I tossed and turned and slipped in and out of consciousness so frequently that I often couldn't tell if I was asleep or awake. "Six candidates… It's not nearly enough time… Written orders will follow…."

After Admiral Vlasilov was through with me, Father Murton and I spent most of the rest of the evening debating how to make the big decision. We had tons of test scores to go by, since the candidates had all been chosen through competitive testing in the first place. But the testers had spent a lot of effort on stuff like hand-to-eye coordination; how could that matter, when Skybolt pilots had no hands? I'd been on the clumsy side myself before being cored; in fact, there wasn't the slightest doubt in my mind that I'd never have made the grade if I'd had to compete to become a pilot. Yet, even I had to admit that so far I was doing all right. Clearly there was something more involved, something that no test could possibly measure. "Lofton Knight understood," I explained to Father Murton. "He looked in my eyes and somehow just *knew*. So did some of the other pilots."

"What about asking Ted for help, then?" my tutor suggested. "He's a good judge of character."

"We will, before it's all over," I promised. "But, in the end, this is *my* squadron. I'm going to be giving orders, and they're going to be following them." I frowned. "Some of us will die. So I have to do this myself; I owe the other pilots that much. Or, at least I have to try."

The priest's eyes narrowed. "My, Thomas, but you're growing up fast." He sighed and shook his head. "Well, then. Perhaps I can make a suggestion…"

And so I found myself venturing out into gunroom mess for the very first time, barefooted and pajama-ed, with my hair still uncombed.

"Attention on deck!" someone called out, and suddenly I was

standing amidst a bunch of wide-eyed, ramrod-erect fifteen-year-olds, some of whom were still chewing mouthfuls of breakfast cereal.

"Belay that!" I commanded. "For the duration." Then I turned to the mess attendant who'd spoken up, "Jeez! This is the *gunroom*, for heaven's sake! Can't a bunch of kids eat their cereal in peace?"

"Jose is new here," a counselor pointed out; there was one assigned to the common areas at all times, something I intended to change. The navy would soon be trusting us with thermonuclear weapons; the least they could do was let us babysit ourselves when off-duty. So long as we behaved, at least.

I nodded. "All right. Jose is new." I nodded and smiled at the young rating, not all that much older than me. "But please, make sure that word gets out." I ran my hand through my uncombed hair, then sat down between Delana and a young man named Peter; I knew him only from the picture in his file.

"Would you like a bowl, sir?" Jose asked.

"No, thank you," I answered. "I've found that I don't like pretending to eat. Though every once in a great while I drink a cherry-cola for old time's sake. Don't offer me one unless I ask, though. It's not something I want very often."

"I worry about that," Peter said. He must've been shy, because his voice was very quiet, and he didn't look me in the eye. "I like eating."

"You'll miss it," I agreed. "A lot." Then it was my own turn to look away. "I'm so sorry I haven't been around to meet anyone," I explained. "But I've been so busy. And, well… We had a schedule. You saw what happened to it."

"Yeah," Peter agreed. "Father Murton explained a hundred times about that. We understand." He smiled. "But at least we're getting to meet you now."

"Yeah," I agreed, smiling back. I'd been fifteen myself when brain-cored; the shrinks had done their best to convince me that I still had a growing and developing body, despite the fact that I really didn't. They'd even built adjustments into my mannequin-body's legs, making me a bit taller every week or so. The fact was, however, that I hadn't led anything like a normal social life for almost two years, not that it'd been any great shakes before then. Practically the only people I'd interacted with had been adults. So maybe I still had more in common with the average, garden-variety fifteen-year-old than I thought?

It was a fine line I had to walk between familiarity and respect, between leadership and friendship. But it was the *only* way to decide who could fight and who couldn't, so far as I could see. And in the end, it'd be the only way to build a solid, reliable military unit; adult forms of discipline simply wouldn't work.

So I held my smile and turned to the rest. "It's Saturday, my day off," I lied. In point of fact, I hadn't had a day off since I couldn't remember when. This certainly wouldn't be one, either. "So, what's there to do around here?"

"Not much," a boy named Steve said. He looked sad and morose; how very different from the bright, happy face in the file! "There's never anything to do except study."

"You can't study all of the time," I declared, standing up and smoothing my pj's. "Don't we get to have any fun at all?"

"There's the video games," Jimmy Knight suggested, just as I'd hoped he would. He turned to the rest of the cadets. "Tommy is a *killer* Rocket-Sled player."

"Wow!" Piet Skolhammer answered, his eyes narrowing slightly. "That's my best game!"

I let my smile transform itself into a cold, challenging grin. He answered in kind, and deep down I suspected that I'd just selected my first pilot. "Excellent!" I replied. "Let me go get dressed, and get my controller. " I turned to Piet. "Find a partner," I said. "Pick a good one. Jimmy and I are going to kick your ass."

Chapter Twenty-Four

"…it *is* a lot like a videogame," I explained as Delana twisted and spun her aerospace fighter through a vortex of flame. She was very, *very* good. I nodded at the screen. "In fact, it feels just like that. Though, of course, you aren't piloting a Polecat. And your enemies aren't Stormcrows."

I smiled to myself, remembering the first time that Father had walked in on me while I was playing *Invasion: Esteppe!* I'd been right in the middle of shaking a stubborn red-nosed Stormcrow off of my tail, and he'd gone white as a sheet before walking out without saying a word. Would I have the same reaction, I wondered, the first time I saw someone simulating Skybolt missions over Churilla and trying to shoot down an *Imperial Throne* class dreadnought? Quite probably, I decided. It could never be a game, for me.

"Except that when you get killed, it's all over." The comment came from Steve, who I'd already decided not to have cored despite his truly outstanding test scores. He was a little *too* smart, it seemed. Watching the death of the Training Fleet had affected him deeply, and not in a good way. "You never, ever get a replay."

"True enough," I agreed noncommittally, making a mental note to talk to his counselor. Though if he wasn't already aware of the problem the man was utterly incompetent. Perhaps Steve would get better with a little support, and be stronger by the time I was ready to select again.

"An' no one be gettin' no replays when the Dracans be runnin' things," Delana muttered as her fighter twirled and weaved amidst the simulated laser-bolts. A surface-to-air missile roared up; she dipped her port wing just as pretty as you please, before most of the rest of us even knew it was there. The projectile flashed past harmlessly; would it still have missed, I wondered, if it'd been reprogrammed with my brother's altered software package? "Not a one."

"All right," I said finally. My score was second-best; either I was better at video-games than I'd ever realized, or else maybe I might have done pretty well on the tests after all if I'd ever taken them. "I give up, Delana. You can play this thing all day long and never get shot down. You're the champion. But… How do you do it?"

She smiled as she put the game on "freeze". The expression was very pretty; her eyes seemed almost to glow. "You don't be thinkin'," she explained. "You be movin' all the time. If you stop and think, well, by then everything's gone bad and you've lost it all."

I nodded slowly. "It's a lot like that for me, too. Though you're better at it."

Delana's eyes twinkled. "It's a trick you learn." She put the controller down beside Jimmy, who was sitting crosslegged on the floor and gazing up at our only female cadet with something like awe in his eyes. Jimmy was hell on wheels when playing cooperative games like *Rocket Sledder*, and was also the only cadet who knew more than I did about strategy and tactics. But he was miserable at *Invasion: Esteppe!*, so miserable that even though everything else about him screamed "fighter pilot" I didn't know if he was going to make the grade or not. Yes, he was an excellent strategist. But we didn't *need* a strategist; we had his brother Ted for that. Perhaps it'd be better for him to grow up and enter the Academy the normal way, like so many of his ancestors? And, maybe, it might even be better for the United Systems?

Delana smiled and tousled Jimmy's hair. He was a runt of a boy, and she treated him like a kid brother. "You're not *quite* beyond hope," she suggested. "Come dance with me, and maybe you can pick up a little magic too, eh?"

I blinked. "Dance?"

"Oh, yes!" Delana replied, her eyes flashing again. "Delana dances *beautiful*, every single morning-time!"

"That's true," Piet confirmed. "And, it *is* beautiful." He poked Jimmy with his finger. "Maybe we can get you all dressed up in a tutu, too?"

"Bite me!" Jimmy answered, blushing and giggling. He giggled easily, which would've made him seem a bit immature to anyone who didn't know that his highly-decorated combat-veteran father and brother giggled too.

"I'm no lyin'," Delana said. "The dancing, it helps. It puts you in the here and now of things." She stuck out her chin playfully. "Maybe our squadron commander man come and try some fancy steppin' bright-and-early, eh?"

Now it would've been my turn to blush, if I still did such things. A mannequin-body was well-suited for preserving one's dignity, however, if little else. "Well," I said, getting up slowly from the couch. We pilots had been gaming for nine hours now, our only respite being a peanut butter-and-jelly break at lunchtime. It'd been a very successful session indeed; I'd identified two potential pilots for sure, I decided, and maybe a third. Perhaps more importantly, I'd weeded out five others, some of them probably permanently. The fact that I'd also made more friends than I ever had before in my life didn't matter. "It's been fun, guys. But I have homework to do."

"Aww!" Jimmy protested. "We almost set a new record! Just one more game?"

The offer was more tempting than it should've been; in point of fact, I'd been excused from classwork indefinitely. What I faced instead was yet another endless technical meeting on the Skybolt followed by a long, skull-splitting session with Father Murton regarding who I was leaning towards picking and why. Mostly, I suspected, Father Murton was insisting on getting involved so that I wouldn't feel so guilty later when some of my new friends got killed; he'd then be able to claim that it was at least partly his fault, to help take the sting out of it. It was pretty noble of him, especially since he really *would* experience a share of the guilt. "We only have a week," he'd pointed out. "Your method is no crazier than anything else we might conceivably throw together by then, or at least not that I can see." As always, he meant nothing but the best for me. Since I wasn't supposed to be old enough to be able to figure out his motives, it was wisest to let him "help" even though I was maybe being less than totally honest.

Besides, when one of my friends *did* eventually die, well... Maybe I'd need him after all.

Chapter Twenty-Five

The rest of the week went by in much the same fashion. I went to class sometimes with the cadets when my schedule allowed; it was probably good for me, as they were learning important stuff that I'd never formally studied. Father, for example, had taught me to recognize most navy rank-badges before sending me out on my sales mission. But, I'd never learned how to read specialist enlisted-man's insignia, and I was downright startled to realize that I was completely unable to describe an army lieutenant-colonel's symbol of authority when the question was posed to the class. Thank heavens I wasn't called on! Not only were the cadets better-chosen than I'd been, I decided, but they were being better trained for what they had to do. All in all, I figured they'd eclipse me as "the hottest pilot in the sky" in no time flat. And someday become real officers as well, instead of a make-do phony like me.

We played video games too, of course, and one morning before school I made it a point to arrive early enough to catch Delana doing her morning dance routine. Sure enough she was wearing a simple tutu; somewhere along the line, she'd learned classical ballet. I'd believed that her smile alone was something special, and had even been charmed in some inexplicable way by the way she handled a video-game. All of this was as nothing, however, to watching her twirl and dip to her favorite piano recording. She was as totally in control of her own body as she'd been of her mock-Polecat; every muscle, every breath, every little flounce of her costume part of a greater, more perfect harmony. I wasn't spying on Delana; she'd invited me to come and watch. I'd even made a small noise, so that I wouldn't intrude. But she didn't hear me, and once I'd caught even a glimpse of such perfect beauty I couldn't find it in my heart to distract her even the tiniest bit. The music built, then crescendoed and stopped. Delana raised a perfectly-sculpted arm in acknowledgement of the applause of her imaginary audience, curtsied with studied elegance, then faced me and stuck out her tongue. "Sneak!" she accused, her voice playful.

"I… Uh…" The moment was broken, yet there still were not words. "That was…" I tried. "It was… beautiful."

"I be loving to dance," she acknowledged, curtseying again just for me. Then she grinned. "Come dance with me?"

My jaw dropped. "I… Uh… The electric motors, you see…"

She rolled her eyes. "Come now, Thomas Longo! I'm an idiot, you think? I know all about the motors; soon enough I'll be a lumbering junkpile just like you! So today, it's all the more important that we make do with what we have. You're being the one who always says that, at least." She got up onto her toes, took my good arm, and twirled beneath it. "Just stand and smile, Thomas Longo, and Delana does the rest."

Then the music started again and Delana was dancing. It was even more bewitching, so close up. Even though every last step had to have been improvised, it all flowed as naturally as if she'd been rehearsing for a thousand years. She spun under my hand, tiptoed around me in a delicate, fragrant circle, and at the very end fell backwards so unreservedly that I had to catch her to prevent a fall. Then, as the last note died, she closed in and threw her arms around me. I wanted desperately to kiss her, but… but… Instead, I pushed her gently away. "No," I whispered. "Delana, we can't…

"I know," she whispered back. "In a few weeks, 'twill be ridiculous to even be t'inking such thoughts."

"It'll *never* be ridiculous," I countered. "Not after seeing you here like this today." Her cheeks darkened, and I smiled. "You're beautiful. But I'm your squadron commander."

"Yeah," she replied, looking down at the floor. "You are that. And someday, I'll have me a squadron of my own to look after. It can't, might never be."Then she met my eyes again and smiled. "But Thomas Longo, remember you always that once upon a time Delana Jones thought that you were quite the catch indeed."

Chapter Twenty-Six

By Friday Father Murton and I had it all worked out. It'd be Delana, Piet, Jimmy Knight, Lai Ming, Li Han, and Viktor Oudh. "So," my tutor said, weighing the files in his hand and looking across the table at me. Try though he might, even he couldn't meet my eyes at this final juncture. "This is final, then? Even on Jimmy?"

I nodded with far more conviction than I felt. I'd thought hard, and really *did* believe these were the best choices. But how could I ever be really, truly *certain*? "Jimmy did a lot better when we quit playing the Esteppe game," I explained. "I think it was just a psychological-block thing. I mean, his father talked about the big battles against the Stormcrows all of the time, and he grew up playing with his cousins, whose fathers got killed there."

"That makes sense," Father Murton agreed, his eyes narrowing. "In fact, it makes a *lot* of sense. You're becoming quite good at this sort of thing, Thomas."

I shrugged. "Too good. It makes me cynical." Then I sighed and looked out my porthole. There was nothing to be seen there but an endless well of hard vacuum; the room's lights were bright enough to wash out the stars. "Delana's the standout, in every conceivable way. She should have my job."

"Don't sell yourself short," Murton replied.

I shrugged. "Whatever. I figure she'll be an element leader and my second-in-command for now, until there's enough fighters for her to get her own unit. Piet's aggressive as well; he'll command the third element."

"Right," Father Murton agreed. "For what it's worth, so far the Counselors agree with your choices. We agree about Lai, Li and Viktor as well." He frowned. "But… Are you *sure* about Jimmy? He can still be your friend, you know, even if he doesn't ever become a pilot at all."

I felt my lips press themselves together. So *that* was what was worrying the priest! I'd known Jimmy longer than any of the others. He'd been my only real friend for ages, now. "He *did* do better once we got away from the Esteppe game," I countered. "Everyone loves him—all the cadets, not just me. You can see it, if you watch close enough." I shook my head. "A squadron has to be a *team*, you see. We're just kids, so the only way we can manage that is to really, actually *like* each other. Jimmy's the glue that's going to keep everything stuck together. Besides," I pointed out. "He and I work better together than any other pairing at team-games. That one *Rocket-Sled* game we played, when we stayed up until eleven? That might be an all-time record for *anyone, anywhere*." I smiled. "In fact, I can't wait to get Esteppe just so we can register it." I let my face grow serious again. "He's gonna be my wingman, Father. My personal wingman, the guy I'm counting on to get me home alive. Jimmy's the one I want for that job; no one else."

"He's immature," the priest countered gently. "Childish. He's got a very bright future ahead of him, I acknowledge. No one's putting him down. But, Thomas, some kids grow up later than others. It might be best to wait."

"He's immature?" I asked. "So's his brother, if by the word you mean playful and full of fun. And his father too, for that matter. Haven't you been paying attention? The other Counselors might not see it; they haven't been around the Knights. But you have. A certain kind of immaturity is *required* in a fighter pilot. Otherwise, we'd be too terrified to take off, like that poor Steve kid. Look at how grown-up *he* acts. You'd rather I picked him instead?"

This time it was Father Murton's turn to press his lips together. "So be it," he said at last, nodding. "After all, you're right about your own life being one of the ones at stake here. And, maybe even about the maturity level of successful fighter pilots in general. So I'll back your decisions all the way, even though the other counselors think you're wrong about Jimmy." He sighed. "I missed that bit about the Esteppe game. Maybe I'm getting too old for this line of work after all."

Chapter Twenty-Seven

Things were a little easier for me after that; I'd made my big decisions and now faced something of an interlude. The same couldn't be said for the rest of my family; Father and Sven were going quietly insane chasing seven projects at once. Not only were they making plans for retooling the old Stormcrow factory, but there were about a million other details for them to chase down as well. Sven, for example, was trying to train the navy fitters as much as possible about how to troubleshoot and repair a Skybolt, using the dead prototype as his example. Meanwhile, on top of everything else, Father was spending hour after hour down in the ship's workshop trying to get a few key components made. If he could pull it off, it'd save manufacturing time later. But, neither of them met with much success. The only good news, from my point of view, was that they'd both transferred their quarters to *The Glorious First of June* so that they could work more closely together; they were even sharing a cabin, so that not a minute of their valuable time would be wasted. So I got to see them sometimes, though not nearly often enough.

The counselors were busy, too. Sick Bay was capable of performing only one brain-coring operation a day; there was only one surgeon qualified to oversee the process, and he had to rest sometime. Father Murton had planned out an extensive training agenda for his counselors, who would have to serve as physical therapists and even body-servants as much as mental-health professionals. Like everything else, however, his plans had been cast to the winds by the deteriorating military situation. And, like everyone else, he was improvising as best he could. With my blessing, he set things up so that for the better part of every day I was attended to not by Father Murton, but by one of the other counselors. This not only gave them hands-on experience, but freed up my tutor to work with the others behind the scenes. It was a little embarrassing to have someone other than the priest or one of my own relatives doing things like tying my shoes for me. But it was good experience for them, so I did what had to be done. Besides, I found that I rather liked most of the other counselors.

This proved especially true for Petty Officer Brooks, Jimmy's counselor. He was the very first cadet to undergo surgery; sick bay had scheduled things to suit themselves, and I had no idea why they'd chosen one before another. He'd be unconscious for a week or so while his nerve endings resituated themselves; after that, Chief Brooks would have what amounted to a fifteen-year-old quadriplegic on his hands until Jimmy learned how to handle a mannequin body.

"...don't need you to help me comb my hair," I explained as Chief Brooks tried to assist me through my morning routine. It was taking twice as long as usual, because he didn't know what I could and couldn't do for myself. It was a little aggravating, but that was the whole point of the exercise-- so that he could learn such things. "But, I *do* need you to put on my shoes and socks. Plus, you'll have to check to see that all my ribbons are right, and button me up. I can't manipulate small objects very well.

Brooks nodded, meeting my eyes in the mirror over my sink. "Yes, sir," he replied.

I sighed, then shook my head. "Chief Brooks?"

"Yes, sir?"

"What's your first name?"

"Gregory, sir." He smiled.

"May I use it?" I asked. "Please? And you can call me 'Thomas'."

"Yes, sir." He frowned. "Yes, Thomas. Of course."

I nodded at my uniform jacket, spread neatly on the back of a chair and waiting for me. Even my informal daily clothing was bedecked with enough decorations to choke an elephant. "I understand that you want to call me 'sir'," I continued. "It's a reflex. You've been in the navy longer than I've been alive. Twice as long, probably."

He colored slightly. "More than twice as long. Though not by much."

I smiled for the first time. "And you have kids older than me? Grandkids nearly as old?"

Brooks nodded again.

"Just think of me as one of them," I said. "Please. And treat me accordingly. There's no naval discipline in the gunroom, and that goes for everyone. Including the counselors." I smiled. "Sometimes I *need* to be treated like a kid. Want to be, even. It's for the best."

He sighed. "I know, Thomas. But you're a regular officer, you see. That makes it harder for me to break my old habits. With Jimmy it's easier to relax; I've known him since he was little. And—"

"Really?" I asked, though I shouldn't have interrupted. Father Murton was always reminding me that it wasn't polite. "I've wondered how you came to be his counselor, with all of the others being chaplains."

Brooks smiled, and this time the expression was natural and unforced. "Captain Knight arranged it," he explained. "Lofton Knight, I mean. He pulled strings from his sickbed. Said he didn't want anyone else for his son." The smile faded. "He called me in to see him, and when I saw how shot-up he was… I mean, how could anyone say 'no' to such a badly wounded vet? I was already retired, though he didn't know it. And he never will, if I have my way. It was a pleasure to come back to the colors, for the likes of him."

I nodded. "Then he knew you well?"

"Heh!" Brooks chuckled. "I was Captain Knight's drill instructor his first year at the Academy. He was the best damned boot I ever knew. I tried to make him sweat, but all he ever did was smile and turn it all into some kind of a joke. Our paths crossed after that, too; we were shipmates several times. In fact, I was with him when he watched one of his brothers die. I got him drunk afterwards." His face fell. "What a proud family that one is."

I took a moment to wash my face; the process was a lot like that of washing a human face, except that when I was done I needed Brooks to help me clear my camera-lenses. "I hear the counselors think I shouldn't have picked Jimmy," I commented as the petty officer dabbed at my simulated eyeballs.

The big man sighed and shrugged, his massive shoulders mere blurs to my smeared eyes. "I'm no professional shrink," he said slowly. "But, it's been my job to evaluate people from time to time. It so happens that I think you were right. That particular apple didn't fall very far from the tree, Thomas." He paused, then looked deep into my eyes. It might've been part of the lens-cleaning process, but it wasn't. "You're an okay officer yourself," he said eventually. "Guys like me, we appreciate the way you don't strut around and put on airs. God knows I wouldn't want to be in your shoes. No sane man would. We understand that you didn't come up the normal way, and we know that it's not your fault when you get something wrong. We're willing to make allowances because of that. But, to be completely honest, we don't have to make all that many.

You're doing really well, considering."

I nodded and blinked; my vision was now perfectly clear. "Thank you," I said finally.

"I got all the smears?" the petty officer asked, suddenly anxious. "I've never cleaned anyone's eyes before."

"I can see fine," I assured him. "But, that's not what I was thanking you for. And you know it."

Chapter Twenty-Eight

Even though things were going a little easier, there were still plenty of demands on my time. I was still dropping in on the cadet's classes whenever I could; in fact, I never missed Military History and Tactics once. I'd already learned a bunch of stuff about fleet-handling and the like back on Earth. But my knowledge was shallow, so shallow in fact that I'd had no idea of how little I really understood. I knew that battleships fought in linear-formations so that the maximum number of guns would bear on the enemy, for example, and that the best angle to deliver a torpedo from was the ship's side. But, I'd never learned the really basic stuff, concepts so fundamental they were easy to overlook.

"…formed the very first disciplined military units," Commander Bard explained. "The Greeks were the earliest to understand that a disciplined body of men, standing together in close order and actively cooperating, could accomplish far more on a battlefield than a scattered mass of individual warriors seeking single combat."

I nodded, fascinated, as the commander sketched out a little drawing that showed how in a Greek phalanx, every soldier's shield helped to cover the man on his left. "That leaves the whole formation more vulnerable to attack from the right. In time, this led to the first attempts to maneuver on the battlefield, to try and shuffle units around in such a way as to exploit this weakness. And thus was invented a new kind of soldier; the general…"

I mostly did pretty well in school, but I'd never been so fascinated by a subject in my life. "…is commonly accepted to have achieved its height under Alexander of Macedon, also known to history as Alexander the Great. His greatest achievements may well have been political and logistical in nature, even though his campaigns of conquest have occupied the lifetimes of a thousand scholars. On the battlefield, however, his true genius was to be found in his keen understanding of human nature."

I blinked, but before I could ask a question the instructor explained herself further. "Alexander was practically always heavily outnumbered in his battles. Ten to one, or sometimes even more. Yet, he was never defeated."

"How can that be?" Steven asked.

Michele dimpled. "That's why he's called 'Alexander the Great' instead of 'Alexander the Pretty Darned Good'." Everyone giggled, including me. "Alexander's great advantage was that, man for man, he had far and away the best army in the world. At even odds, they could win *any* battle. And, weapons were relatively short-ranged back then. So Alexander's enemies could never make use of their whole army at once, when fighting a smaller force. There simply wasn't physical room." Her eyes swept the room. "So, what do you think Alexander's secret of success was?"

There was a long silence, then brainy Steven raised his hand. "He was good at seeing weak points?" he guessed.

"No," Michele replied. "Not usually. He fought many battles, and sometimes he did indeed exploit unseen weaknesses. But that wasn't his usual method."

I gulped and raised my own hand. "Thomas?"

"He chose his own battlefield," I guessed. "Like the Dracans usually do. When you're on the attack, you can choose when and where to fight, and only do so when you're sure to win."

Michele smiled. "That's partly right. He did indeed choose his battles, and his battlefields, wisely. But..." Her smile widened. "His most decisive tactic was that he *always attacked the enemy where he was strongest.*"

I blinked. That sounded *stupid*, not smart!

"Keep in mind", Michele continued smoothly, "That back in those days, fighting-units varied greatly in strength and capabilities. Some units could put up a much better fight than others. And, the battlefield was small. You could see the whole thing, no matter where you were."

"Sort of like watching a space battle on a pipper," Tommy Hager pointed out.

"Exactly!" Michele answered. "Certainly, there'd be dust clouds and such. Plus, if you were fighting for your life what was going on a little distance away might not be your number one priority. But still, if something important happened, pretty soon everyone knew it."

Suddenly, I understood. "So, when Alexander's men beat the best enemy unit..."

Michele smiled. "He didn't just *beat* them, Thomas. He'd *destroy* them. Very often, the enemy general stationed them in the very best and most important defensive position, so that Alexander's men had to climb a hill or cross a ditch to get to them. After all, the opposing general knew that they were the best, too. He'd design the rest of his position around the strongpoint."

"So," Petty Officer Brooks blurted out. Clearly, he was fascinated as well. "When Alexander's men wiped them out despite all their advantages…"

Commander Bard smiled. "When they were wiped out, not only had the enemy lost his best troops and his key position, but the rest of his soldiers had *watched it happen*. They *knew that they were next*. If Alexander had made such short work of the elite units, with all the advantages against him, then what chance did *they* have?" She turned off the chalkboard and placed her hands on her hips. "Before you knew it the enemy was running away, disorganized and useless as a fighting force. Very often the enemy king ran as well; he was human too and panic is a very contagious thing. If they'd stood their ground regardless, then who knows? With such a numerical advantage they might well have won in the end. After all, there were only just so many Macedonians. Eventually even warriors of the caliber of Alexander's men would have grown tired and been overwhelmed."

"So," I said slowly. "Alexander's enemies basically advertised their own weak points, by putting the best troops there."

"In a way," Commander Bard agreed. "Others might just look at it as another example of why offensive warfare is inherently more powerful than being on the defensive. But that's another lesson for another day."

Chapter Twenty-Nine

I was still thinking about Alexander and his Macedonians later that afternoon, while helping Sven with his training program. The broken prototype Skybolt was the only bird we had available for the fitters to practice on; that was bad enough. Even worse, mine was the only brain module available as well. Though Jimmy and Li's operations were complete, they'd have to remain in sickbay for some time to come. So, there was no choice but to let the ratings practice hooking me up and then disconnecting me just like any other Skybolt component, over and over again.

"Are you all right in there, Thomas?" Sven asked, his voice tight and annoyed. Several of the fitters had already made errors while handling me; once, I'd even been slightly damaged. Normally my brother was icy-calm, but he'd dressed down the responsible rating with such harsh Esteppan oaths that the poor man had fled weeping. Now the rest of the work-gang treated both Sven and my capsule with a whole new level of respect. Which suited me just fine; where would the Skybolt program be if I somehow got broken?

Where would the entire *United Systems* be, for that matter?

"It's *boring*, being a spare part," I complained to Petty Officer Brooks, whose turn it still was to attend me. "That's why I keep wanting to talk to you, I guess."

Gregory nodded; his image was dim and fuzzy. My video input was currently coming from a little monitor-camera that my brother had found lying around somewhere; it'd been very kind of him to improvise me an eye. Ordinarily we didn't bother with sensory inputs while I was being mounted in a Skybolt, because being blind and deaf didn't matter for such a short period of time. But now the operation was being performed over and over again by markedly inexpert personnel, with breaks for Sven to curse. I *could* have gone without input for that long, but it wouldn't have been a lot of fun.

"It's quite all right," Gerald answered, reaching out and wrapping his arm protectively around my brain-case; it looked kind of funny to see him do that when my own viewpoint was a good five feet away, since that made it seem like he was comforting someone else. He meant well, though. "I've got nothing else to do and nowhere else to go."

I would have nodded if I could've, but as things were I wasn't even capable of blinking my camera's monitor light. "Whoops!" my helper said suddenly, looking past my camera. "Here they come again."

"Yippee," I answered without enthusiasm, beginning the boot-up process for my internal video game. I was growing heartily sick of this particular drill, and wanted something new. But how could I ask for something so selfish and trivial when Father and Sven obviously had all the work they could handle and more?

I watched as Sven picked up my braincase and explained for the thousandth time which leads were especially delicate and which weren't. Then suddenly someone called out "Attention on Deck!" Everyone except my brother stood straight and still; in the process one of them bumped my camera, so that all I could see was the hanger ceiling.

"At ease!" Admiral Vlasilov's voice ordered. "Dr. Longo, where is your brother Thomas? I was informed that he was working with you."

"Right here!" I called out.

There was a long pause while Vlasilov figured it out. "Oh... Da! Forgive me, Thomas."

"Yes, sir," I replied. "Can someone please fix my camera? I can't see anything."

"Of course," Brooks answered. He stepped over and for just an instant I was looking up into his face. Then the camera slewed around until it was pointed at the admiral. Or almost pointed at him, rather. I could see his face only from the nose down. This didn't seem like a good time to be fussy, however.

Vlasilov scowled, then turned away. "Dr. Longo, I fear that I must interrupt your training session. I assure you that I do not do so lightly. It's necessary that Thomas and I speak immediately in private. If I could take him with me to a conference room and leave you in peace, I'd do so. However..." He gestured at the tangled wires.

"Ja," Sven answered, making a short bow and clicking his heels in the Esteppan fashion. Then he turned to the camera. "I'll be right back, Thomas. Will you be okay while I'm gone?"

I tried to nod, then remembered. "Uh-huh."

He smiled. "Good." Then he nodded to the admiral and left,

followed by the fitters he'd been working with.

Suddenly the admiral raised his arm and addressed someone behind my camera. "Not you, Counselor," he said, presumably to Petty Officer Brooks. "You may stay."

That didn't sound good at all, I decided. "Did I do something wrong?" I heard myself blurt out. "Am I in trouble?"

Vlasilov frowned again. "No, Thomas. In fact, I think more highly of you every day. We were lucky, so very lucky…" He sighed and looked away for a moment, then turned and faced me again with an almost military motion. "Son, I have bad news."

I tried to raise my eyebrows, but of course didn't have any. Of all the miserable, awkward timing…

"We all knew that there was some risk involved in performing the brain-corings aboard ship," he continued. "The only facilities equipped properly for such procedures are your father's facilities in New Orleans and on Esteppe." He closed his eyes. "Thomas, we've lost a cadet. One of your pilots."

I was just a brain. I couldn't feel my throat tighten, and since my camera had no tear ducts, my vision didn't blur. "Yes, sir?" was all I could think of to say.

Vlasilov shook his head, then looked down. He was weeping, even though I could not. "The doctors did everything they could. It shouldn't have happened at all, they say. No one quite understands what went wrong."

"Who was it?" Chief Brooks asked, his voice a near whisper. "Please, sir? Who?"

"Young Piet Skolhammer," Vlasilov answered, reaching out, I presumed, to clasp Brooks on the shoulder in the Russian fashion. "The very last to go under the knife. He was fifteen years and seven weeks old."

Chapter Thirty

Piet's death didn't stop the program, of course. *Nothing* could be allowed to stop the program. But even so, things slowed down a little. Sick bay doubled and redoubled their checks on the rest, and classes were cancelled so that the counselors could spend some time in private with their charges. That included Father Murton and I; it took a little while for Sven to get me repaired and reassembled. But still, my tutor and I had several hours to talk.

Not that we spent most of them doing what we were supposed to. Once we got past speculating on what might have gone wrong and sharing what little we knew about Piet's death, we mostly sat in our shared stateroom and stared gloomily at the walls. "I should never have touched this," Father Murton said at last. "The minute your father broached the subject of brain-coring you, I should have talked him out of it. Failing that, I should have resigned and walked out." He shook his head. "I should resign now, even."

I shrugged. "What if you had?" I asked, my voice flat and dead. "Then either the United Systems would've had to surrender to the Emperor by now, or more likely Father would've gone ahead with someone who couldn't do the job half as well as you have." I shuddered. "I'd never have survived Churilla without you! Isn't fighting against the greater evil worth tolerating lesser ones?"

The priest looked away, still angry. Then he sighed. "I used to think I had a pretty good grasp on right and wrong," he said eventually. "Sure, there were slippery areas. But ever since the fighting started…"

I nodded. "Spence and I used to talk about war a lot, while he was fishing. Combat, he believes, by its very nature perverts all standards of ethics. It turns all of our value-systems upside down, and makes mockeries of the concepts of good and evil. There's nothing democratic about a bullet, nor anything intrinsically moral or immoral about a bayonet. Everything is gray; there's no black and white. War is the use of force to coerce one's enemy into doing something they don't want to do, and the degree of coercion required is directly proportional how obnoxious the enemy society finds one's demands to be. Spence thinks that very few people today understand what defeat really means; it's not just a bad thing that happens to generals and a few political leaders. Defeat means that *everyone* has to alter their culture and their way of life to suit the victors' desires rather than their own. It means abandoning sacred ethical principles, religious beliefs… It means that your kids will be taught to believe different things than you do, things you consider wrong and evil, while you can do nothing about it but stand and helplessly watch everything you thought important become part of the past. Your enemy's culture is perpetuated, not your own." I sighed. "Culture, according to Spence, is pretty much everything that really matters to most people. The penalties for defeat are so overwhelming that virtually *anything* can be justified in the name of preventing such a catastrophe. The people of Esteppe fought on for months beyond any hope of victory because they didn't want United Systems ethical standards rammed down their throats. Spence told me he predicted that they'd fight like demons before the war ever began, and that he knew the same thing would happen on Churilla if he could just offer his people a little hope and someone to rally around. The Esteppans fought on and on and on, even when things got so bad that everyone was starving and the navy was nuking them at will." I half-smiled. "They never did formally surrender and accept defeat Instead, the United Systems occupied the whole planet and captured the government."

Father Murton nodded and closed his eyes. "Millions died," he agreed. "For nothing. Or at least it seemed like the last stand was purposeless to us, up in orbit. Obviously the Esteppans didn't agree." He sighed and looked at me. "Have you ever read any of Spence's books?"

"I've wanted to," I explained. "But with all the stuff I have to do…"

My tutor smiled. "If academic-type classes are ever re-started, I'll let you do reports on a couple-three of them; that way, it'll be an official part of your schedule. Wiston's books are well worth reading, and now that you've met him I think they'd be more educational than ever. His specialty is the period of history between the development of industrialization and the beginning of space colonization."

I nodded. "No wonder he's so depressing when he talks about war. Those were the bloodiest, most brutal years in human history."

"Until now," Father Murton corrected me gently.

We talked on and on into the night, mostly about the nature of war and that of right and wrong. "You claim that right and wrong are absolutes," I said at one point. "Spence says that morality is at least partly an illusion at the nation-state level, that countries or planets will do whatever it takes to survive." I cocked my head to one side. "So, imagine that the Dracans finally get to where they can produce a fighter like the Skybolt, something that can turn the whole war around in their favor. And, let's imagine that we know where the plant is, right smack in the middle of a heavily-populated city. So, we *could* put together a big raid, come popping out of their Nikita Point at a huge delta-vee with just enough time to make a single pass, nuking the plant and the city along with it before the carrier's out of range." I looked up at my tutor. "Or, we could do nothing, let the plant produce its fighter-planes, and allow the war to drag on and on and on, killing *lots* more people than if we'd fried the place once and for all while we had the chance. So, what's right and wrong in this case."

"The Church says to leave the city alone," he answered.

"What if we really, truly believe we're going to lose the war if we don't? That everyone forever after will have to bow to the Emperor every morning, and drink to his good health at every meal? That no one will ever be free again?"

"It's still wrong, Thomas."

"All right," I said. "Back in the Cold War, the United States and the Soviet Union faced each other off with hydrogen bombs. Neither country was as pure as the driven snow, but the Soviet Union held thousands of political prisoners and didn't allow even the most basic of human freedoms. If the Soviet Union had fired off all its missiles, everyone in the United States would've died. Right?"

"Right," the priest agreed, looking uncomfortable.

"So," I asked. "What moral right did the US have to shoot back, if that happened? If they were all going to die for sure, anyway? But, if they ever decided that they wouldn't shoot back, or even appeared as if they might not be nasty enough people to shoot back, the Russians could've made the United States do whatever they wanted just by making threats."

Father Murton colored. "Thomas, I—"

"Spence says that there no right or wrong to any of this," I continued. "That war has a terrible morality all of its own, a morality that makes no sense whatsoever in any other context. He says that the surprising part isn't that people are such savages when fighting wars.

Rather, the surprise is that we recognize any limits to our barbarity at all. 'War is hell', he says a great general once wrote. But, any attempt to reduce the suffering or make the fighting less awful is counterproductive, in that it makes the suffering and dying last longer and drags the conflict on for years and sometimes even decades without any kind of true resolution."

Father Murton turned away. "Perhaps," he said eventually, "I shouldn't encourage you to read Wiston's books after all."

"I've watched Spencer deliberately mutilate enemy dead," I answered. "You were there too. He didn't do it because he's a bloodthirsty savage. He did it because he thinks it'll help his side to win, and that nothing could possibly be worse for the future of Churrila, or even for the future of mankind, than losing to the Dracans." I pressed my lips together into a hard, thin line. "I never really had much of a chance to think about who I was killing and how up until now; somehow, everything was just moving too fast." I shook my head, then turned to Father Murton. "I've murdered a helpless woman myself, in the name of war. I strangled her to death, while she begged for mercy. It was Sara Fowler. Back on Churilla. She was hiding in that closet in the penthouse with me. I never told you until now. It didn't seem right."

The priest's mouth fell open, then closed with an almost audible snap. "Thomas... I mean...." His eyes darted back and forth. "Would you like to make a confession?"

"I can't," I replied, for the first time understanding who I was, and maybe even catching a glimpse as to what I was really meant to do. What my real purpose in life was. "In order to make a proper confession, I should feel remorse. Which I don't, any more than I do for the battleship." I pressed my lips together again. "Killing her was the right thing to do, by the contorted, perverted logic of war. No battle fought is ever without its casualties. The first among them is justice, and the second is usually innocence. I was just beginning to understand that, back then. Spence would be proud of me for doing what I did, though he'd regret that the task fell on me while I was still too young. Alicia certainly feels that way. She's said so more than once."

My tutor paled, but said nothing.

"I should've told you before," I continued. "I owed it to you. But I just couldn't, somehow. Until today, when Piet, poor Piet..." Suddenly I could say no more; of its own accord my face screwed up, and in an instant I was hugging the priest and blubbering like a little child. No tears came, of course, nor a wet flow of mucous. Still, I was weeping nonetheless. "He was just a kid," I whispered in Father Murton's ear. "Just a brave little kid, caught up in the scheming of the Emperor and Spence and the Prime Minister and…"

"It's all right," Father Murton crooned. He was weeping too, I suddenly realized.

"And all the thousands of other little kids! Millions, maybe, before it's all over!"

"I know," my tutor whispered.

"And I… I *picked* him! *Murdered* him, just like I did Sara Fowler!"

"It's all right," the priest whispered in my ear. "The God I know and love would never blame you, Thomas. Not for either of them, in the midst of all this madness." I must've cried for almost an hour; it was bedtime when I was done, and Father Murton was wise enough not to try and restart our conversation. Even so, I didn't go to sleep right away. Instead, I got up and booted up my computer. There was one obligation that I absolutely, positively, had to at least get started on before I could allow myself to rest.

"Dear Mr. and Mrs. Skolhammer," my letter began. It was damned awkward, typing with electric fingers. But finding the right words was by far the more difficult task. "It's my sad duty to write to you regarding the circumstances of the death of your son Pieter. He was a wonderful boy; I enjoyed playing with him very much…"

Chapter Thirty-One

We held a little service for Piet, just as we had for the sailors who'd died at New Nippon. Alicia spoke, as did Admiral Vlaslov. Both wept unashamedly. I wasn't asked to say anything, even though I was Piet's commanding officer. Father Murton probably had something to do with that; in any event it suited me just fine. I didn't really feel much like making a speech anyway, right then. Nor would I have known what to say if I'd tried.

I'd never travelled on a navy ship before, but in some ways it was a lot like a voyage aboard a liner. There was a lot more to do, what with all the meetings and drills and such. However, there was the same sense of daily rhythm, of being our own little world isolated from the universe. Day after day after day, we greeted the same individuals in the same passageways with the same little nods, our schedules eternally invariant. Time passed quickly, so quickly that that it was a bit of a shock when *The Glorious First of June* burst through the last Nikita Point into the Esteppe system and splashed down in the navy harbor at New Narvik.

I'd been born on Esteppe, of course. But I couldn't remember a thing about it, except maybe for the fleeting memory of an icy wind on my face as Father and the rest of us boarded ship for Earth. I never could decide if the memory was real or just something I'd imagined, but the wind was certainly icy enough as Father, Sven, Admiral Vlasilov, Father Murton, and four specially-trained Marine bodyguards dressed diplomatically as navy junior officers crammed into a small old-fashioned Esteppan skyhopper with me for the short trip to Father's old plant. Not a minute would be wasted on diplomatic niceties, we'd decided; Alicia could take care of that sort of thing. The navy needed to know the state of the Stormcrow plant, and it needed to know *right now*.

The crowding was made even worse by the fact that everyone except me was wearing a full rad-suit; while it was hoped that the radiation wouldn't be too bad, there was no way to know for sure. The little 'hopper seemed almost to groan under its burden, and Father Murton finally asked the question that had been on the tip of my own tongue. "How much of an overload can this thing handle?" he demanded, waiting for Vlasilov to seat himself; he couldn't get into his own seat until this happened, things were so tight.

"Plenty," Sven replied, more gruffly than usual. He was wearing the Esteppan Order of Merit he'd once earned at his throat, and wasn't at all happy about it. Vlasilov had all but ordered him to do so, in the name of helping us all to make a good first impression on any Esteppeans we might run across. For the same reason I was wearing my own red Order of Blood. On Esteppe, it was traditional for those who'd earned high honors to display them at all times. People even wore their war-ribbons to the corner grocery store. "See?" he said, pointing at the maker's plaque. "It's one of ours."

I leaned forward in my seat to look; sure enough, the maker was listed as Longo Gravitonics; we were riding in one of my father's earliest products! "Well," Father Murton grumped as he sat down. "In that case, I'll shut up and quit worrying about it."

Sure enough, the old 'hopper's heart was sound and true. Our flight was completely uneventful, right up until we touched down on the plant's main landing site. "We used to fly our test Stormcrow from this very pad," Father explained to me as we settled in. He pointed. "And that house over there is where you were born."

I craned my neck, trying to see out the little porthole. There wasn't any house, only a pile of broken-down rubble. Atomic weapons tended to have that effect on residential structures, I knew. Most of the Stormcrow factory was underground, but the surface facilities had been exposed to the edge of the blast zone.

Once everyone's suits were sealed, we unzipped the 'hopper and stepped outside. The ground was covered with a nasty mixture of ice and black goop that was probably the remains of a thousand fires. It would've been very ugly indeed had we been able to look at much of it. But the overly-distant sun was already slipping below the frigid blue horizon, so that we had to use flashlights to see where we were walking. Remaining upright required intense concentration, especially for me. Vlasilov had been around mannequin-bodies enough by now to anticipate my needs at least sometimes, so he ordered two of the bodyguard-types to hold my arms. They saved me from nasty falls at least twice.

While the Stormcrow plant itself was underground, the HVAC

systems had necessarily required contact with the outside world. The filters had faced directly towards the blast, and the fractured, twisted remnants of them testified with mute eloquence as to what happened to an unreinforced structure when it was struck by the blast wave from even a relatively distant nuke. "It was stupid engineering," Father explained, shaking his head from side to side the way he did when seriously vexed. "Stupid, stupid, stupid! I tried to protest, but the Autarchy claimed there were no military-grade filtering installations to spare."

"Forgive me, Dr. Longo," Vlasilov countered, his face cold and hard. "But you have no idea how many good men we lost trying to kill this place. The only reason the bomb was dropped so far away was that we couldn't successfully penetrate any closer. So, I'm just as glad that there *weren't* any correct filters."

"Ja," Father agreed, his head now bowed and subservient. "Forgive me, Admiral. I was—"

"Right," Vlasilov agreed, waving his arm in dismissal. "And if the bomb *had* landed any closer, you'd be a corpse and I'd be a Dracan POW. Let the dead bury the dead, I say. It was another war and another time." He smiled. "Besides, you've proven your true loyalty many times over, Doctor. You've lived most of your life in a very difficult situation. This is understood."

"Look!" Sven pointed out, smiling at Father. "My cyclescoot!"

"Heh!" Father chuckled. "It's still there, right where you dropped it." He turned to me. "Sven was on leave the day we were nuked. I had no idea he was within hundreds of miles of home. Then he came running into my office. 'Air raid'! he screamed, right before the plant-sirens went off." Father waved his arms as if in panic, and made his eyes bulge out. "'Air raid'!"

Sven smiled and nodded. "I was still carrying my air-defense network communicator. It must've been quite a sight."

"Then the bomb exploded," Father continued. "It wasn't so bad at first. We had no idea of how dirty it was. Up until then, the United Systems had limited itself to blast-bombs."

"The Autarchy evacuated and treated the few workers who were present, or else we'd be dead," Sven finished up, looking glum. "Not everyone in the area was so lucky. But we were essential, you see. No one else could build Stormcrows."

There was a long silence after that, as we walked past the rest of the shattered ventilators and around the corner to the main plant entrance. Surprisingly, a single light bulb glowed above the door. "Well," the admiral grunted. "I left messages here and there, hoping someone would relay them. Perhaps one got through."

"Ja," Sven agreed, pointing to the commuter-train rails. They shone clean and bright, a sign of recent use. "Someone's gotten the tramway running again, at least." He smiled. "That's a positive step."

"Indeed," Vlasilov agreed, nodding. "Come, what are we waiting for? Let's go inside."

It was a good bit warmer once the main doors were behind us, though still not warm enough for us to remove the coats we were wearing on top of our radiation suits. And there were more lights. We entered a worker's locker room; Sven pointed his radiation-detector at the ground. He frowned. "Not good," he complained. "Not good at all." We started walking again towards the room's exit and what I figured must be the shop floor beyond. "We can't ask anyone to work here without full gear; there's too much risk of long-term effects." He sighed, as we turned the last corner…

…and came face to face with two or three dozen Esteppen workers, all of whom were busily engaged in hanging up long strings of work lights and none of whom were wearing rad-suits. Everyone froze, staring at each other. Then, one of the Esteppans, his hair iron-gray and his stomach bulging, stepped forward. "Herr Doktor-Professor?" he asked, hat suddenly in hand. "Mein Gott! Is that you?"

"Schmidt?" my father replied, taking a small, cautious step forward. "Schmidt?"

"Mein Gott!" the worker repeated, his voice this time filled with joy. He spread his arms, then Father fell into them and the two danced a little jig of glee. I'd never, ever seen my father dance before!

Meanwhile, a few of the others removed their own hats and cautiously approached the rest of us. "Your Excellency?" one of them asked Sven, addressing him in the manner proper to one who wore the Order of Merit. He might almost have been Schmidt's twin, for age and paunch. "Are you…" My brother smiled and nodded. He turned to me. "And you… You must be…." I smiled and nodded as well.

"Well!" the older man declared, his eyes widening. Then he bowed to each of us, again appropriately, given the decorations we wore. "I'm *so* glad you're finally here," he gushed. "So very, very glad! We were wondering if perhaps the United Systems had forgotten us and our broken-down old plant."

"We can *never* forget this plant," Vlasilov answered diplomatically, extending his hand and doing his best to appear friendly. "We're most grateful that you and your friends have come to help us."

The old man smiled. "How could we not? The honor, after all, is ours. I'm a skilled machinist, one of the finest on this world. Yet what have I been producing these past few years?" He sneered. "Instruments! Medical instruments! But now! Now I shall be making weapons of war once again!" His eyes met mine proudly. "Weapons fit for the hands of heroes such as yourself. My life is complete again!" He smiled so wide that I thought his face would break, then extended his hand. "I'm Hans, your father's chief machinist in charge of prototypes. We've worked hand in hand many times, I'm very proud to say." He gestured widely. "And, welcome to the Nordwerks, home of the finest aerospace fighters ever manufactured by human hands! First the Stormcrow, and now the Skybolt!" He shook his head theatrically, then placed his hand over his heart. "My life is complete!"

Chapter Thirty-Two

We all shook the chief machinist's hand as he blushed and sputtered in joy. Then Father, Sven, the admiral and I formed a sort of impromptu reception line, shaking the hands and receiving the bows of each and every one of the Stormcrow workers. It was moving, even as much as I hated to be bowed to. The workers didn't hesitate for a second to shake Vlasilov's hand, though we'd been terribly afraid that he'd be spurned. Instead they all called him "admiral" with what certainly appeared to be genuine respect in their voices. As Vlasilov himself had observed just a few moments earlier, perhaps the less that was said about previous unpleasantries the better. In any event, it was clear, these old men wanted nothing more than to help beat the Dracans; when Vlasilov asked one of them why they weren't wearing rad suits, he was told that the workers had found them too confining.

"We held a meeting, then took them off the first day," he explained with a fierce glitter in his eye. "Yes, we know the numbers as well as you do. Better, perhaps, and they aren't pretty. But we're old, mostly. And don't have so much to lose, ja? The Dracans are messing with Esteppans now, you see. And I swear to you they'll break their teeth on the likes of *us*! No battle they've ever fought has even *half* prepared them for what they're going to find waiting for them here. We may lose, but if we do we'll take millions of them along with us! Maybe even billions, with luck!" His eyes narrowed. "There *are* still people in this universe who know how to fight a proper war."

Vlasilov's smile froze at the implied rebuke, but the expression vanished in an instant as he remembered who he was speaking to, what the man standing before him had once been a key part of accomplishing in the not-so-distant past, and that he was even now standing unprotected in a 'hot' environment in the service of their common goal. "Da," Vlasilov finally acknowledged, extending his hand a second time for shaking. "I acknowledge this. You people *do* know how to fight a war—more effectively than anyone else I've ever seen. That is exactly why we've come here. Working together, this time."

"Working together," the Esteppan agreed, accepting the extended hand and shaking it a second time. His smile was noticeably warmer now. "And, glad of it. I'm Duncan Mac Ewen, by the way, head of the Worker's Council. That would equate to chairman of the labor union, in other places." He pointed at the pile of discarded rad suits. "This is what these men are willing to do for you, Admiral, and for all free peoples everywhere. Even more, this is what they're willing to do for the Longos, who never forgot them even during the worst of times. Others starved. Herr Doktor-Professor shared his personal fortune. Treat them equally well, and I can promise you no problems."

"You'll receive the very best," Vlasilov answered, taking his left hand and clasping it over Mac Cloud's. "The best wages, the best materials, the best equipment. My word of honor, and the navy's word of honor." He shook his head. "On Earth, the workers would never have volunteered to do such a thing! Never! I'm deeply moved." He smiled again; this time the expression was icy-cold. "The Emperor should fear men such as you and your fellows. If he's asleep, then he should be suffering a terrible nightmare."

The rearmost areas of the plant weren't so badly damaged as the front, though the fallout was just as bad. The light fixtures either had already been repaired or else had never been seriously damaged in the first place, so that we could see a lot better. All of us were walking the plant together now, we visitors and the proud workers traveling in an undifferentiated mass, taking a sort of tour.

"We've focused on getting the precision-machining operations cleaned up," Mac Ewen explained, pointing at a large machine whose clean Longo-blue paint seemed almost to glow against the general drabness. "Like that polymill, for example. We weren't certain, but suspected you'd want it first."

"You were right," Sven answered. "Good work! We have a broken prototype that requires its attentions immediately."

Mac Ewen grinned, and suddenly I knew that this had been *his* decision though he'd never try to take credit for it. "It's still not calibrated," he explained. "And sometimes it's glitching for no apparent reason. Maybe it's the ionization from the fallout. But the problem's over our head, and we haven't been able to get a factory rep out here. They claim they're busy with other war-work."

"That will change in the next thirty seconds or so," Vlasilov declared. He gestured at a staff officer, who nodded and raced off to find a telephone.

Mac Ewen bowed gratefully. "We'll be waiting for him with open arms." Then he turned to Father. "Sir, there's something else. The plant's still full of Stormcrow subassemblies. I even found my old lunchbox sitting on one, right where I left it."

Father's eyebrows rose. "Really? That's too bad, in a way. The Skybolt shares no common parts, or at least not of any parts of importance. A lot of the specs are relatively close, but since I was starting all over again from nothing anyway, I re-engineered everything to accommodate Earth's standard manufacturing practices." He sighed. "Apparently, that was a very poor decision."

"Apparently, Herr Doktor-Professor," a new voice replied. It was cold and imperious. "You seem to have rather a talent for making bad decisions. Fine fighters, yes. But very poor decisions indeed."

Father's eyes narrowed as if he was in pain. Clearly he recognized the voice. "Many of we Esteppans have made bad decisions, Jurgen," he replied without turning around. "Yourself included."

"Perhaps," the stranger replied as I turned around to face him. The newcomer was dressed in the old pre-war Esteppan fashion that I thought had died with the Autarchy. He wore a heavy black robe trimmed in sable, with matching riding boots. Even worse, he still shaved his high-domed head in the Autarch's favored fashion, so as to show off the golden socket just above the base of his skull that marked him as a special favorite of the Autarch, a socket that could never be removed without killing him. My father had one too, I knew; it was the means by which an Eliteman could mentally link to the planetwide computer network. Once upon a time, Father had shaved his head too. Nowadays, however, he wore his hair unfashionably long so as to hide his socket as thoroughly as possible. "Perhaps I've made an error or two in my time," Jurgen admitted. "But then, I've also never been quite so skillful in reversing my loyalties at just the right moments as you have, Willy. When I swear an oath, for example, it tends to remain sworn."

When Father finally turned to face his old acquaintance, his eyes were cold and his face hard. "I saved you too Jurgen, like it or not. You'd be dead without me."

"You *did* save me," the bald-headed man acknowledged, nodding once. "After all, they could hardly hang your chief assistant after letting you off scot-free. I even got to keep my estate, just like you did." Jurgen looked up, noticing Sven and I for the first time. "Excellencies," he acknowledged us with a slight bow. "I'm honored to greet men of your respective Orders of Heroism. You've fought well, both of you."

Neither Sven nor I acknowledged the compliment; instead, my brother spoke in a near-snarl. "Why are you here, Jurgen?" he demanded. "And, for god's sake, why aren't you wearing a radiation suit?"

The former Autarchy official shrugged, then addressed me. "You don't know me, Thomas, though I remember you. Even as a baby you were a noble-looking little thing. I once was to your father what Sven is now," he explained. "His right arm. I knew that it was a family business, and that someday you and your brother would supplant me. That was the natural order of things, something I could accept in exchange for the privilege of working for a man like the great, Autarch-beloved Herr Doktor-Professor. Back then, I was your father's plant manager." He sneered, so powerfully and effectively that, once upon a time, he must've practiced in a mirror. "The new government, lickspittles that they are, decided that I could be of help here. They're correct, of course. I've spent the last few years building heavy cargo floaters in my own plant. So I know where to obtain precisely the types of materials and expertise you'll so badly need. My contacts are fresh, where yours are all more than a decade old." He turned to Sven. "And I wear no rad-suit out of tribute to the workers. What they suffer, I shall suffer. It's the Esteppan way."

Vlasilov frowned. 'We could get by without you," he pointed out.

Jurgen smiled. "Oh!" he countered. "I wouldn't have missed this little reunion for the world." Then his face went cold again. "I was required to swear an oath of loyalty in exchange for my release from captivity, Admiral. As I've already said, *my* oaths are good, and *my* honor is intact. I served the Autarch willingly until he died, and now I shall serve you." He bowed slightly.

Vlasilov turned to Father and raised his eyebrows. "Ja," Father eventually agreed. "Jurgen was always a man of his word, even in the darkest of times. And he's a brilliant engineer in his own right." The black-robed man smirked, then bowed slightly in acknowledgement of the compliment. "We can put him to work in sourcing, as he suggested. We need someone local for the job, and Jurgen is probably the best-suited man on the planet." He looked up at his former assistant. "I'll accept your word and your assistance, Jurgen, and I don't doubt your honor. However, I have a question for you before you begin, one that I must insist that you answer."

"Ask it, then," he replied, folding his hands at his waist.

"I have *three* sons, Jurgen, as you well know. Not just the two healthy ones who are here. The third is still aboard ship, probably playing with his favorite stuffed doll. He's there instead of here helping us because my friend and mentor the Autarch, whom I did indeed betray, ordered that his brain be turned into mush before my eyes as punishment for a crime that he then could only suspect me of." Father's eyes glittered. "You knew Dean before they ruined him, Jurgen. He often visited you in your office and played with the model Stormcrows on your desk. Sometimes he called you 'Uncle Jurgie' while you sat and smiled. He was *so* bright, once upon a time! I also once had a wife, who as often as not made your lunches with her own hands. And we both know what happened to her. So, Jurgen Grunwald. Will you come with me up to *The Glorious First of June*, and explain to Dean why his mistreatment was necessary for the advancement of mankind, so that we might evolve to a higher level? Will you do that for me? Or perhaps you'd like to begin by explaining to Thomas how his growing up without a mother was necessary so that Elitemen like you and I might fulfill our higher destiny? Would you do these things for me, Jurgen? And when you're done explaining these things, will you still shave your head and walk around with a swagger-stick up your ass, demanding to be treated like a minor god because once upon a time you were able to commune with a cold, soulless machine? Will you still boast of your loyalty to the men who committee such crimes?"

Jurgen looked away, but said nothing.

"The past is the past," Sven interceded, stepping between the two men. "Best forgotten, or else we'll all soon be worshipping the Emperor. None of us want *that*." He looked back and forth between his elders. "Jurgen, you'd be dead if Father hadn't done as he did. You've admitted it. I'll also add that I've never once heard him speak a single ill word of you. That's the truth, on my honor as a Brother of the Order of Merit."

Jurgen nodded once, coldly.

"We need you," he continued. "Everyone everywhere needs you. You know how important the Stormcrow was to Esteppe's defense, and therefore you also know how important the Skybolt will become." He raised his arms as if in supplication. "You say that you're willing to help, and I believe you. You say that your oath is good, and I accept that as well. But, we need something more." He frowned. "We need your active cooperation, Jurgen. We need for you to bury the past and commit yourself to this project without reservation. Or else we need for you to go back to building your cargo floaters in peace. Take your choice. We'll respect you either way. But no middle course is acceptable."

Jurgen looked my brother in the eyes. "You've grown up, Sven. Tall and proud. I salute you." Then he turned to Admiral Vlasilov. "I believe in the enhanced superman, Admiral, with all of my heart and my soul. It's the future of mankind. I've had my mind expanded; you can never, ever ask me to deny what I know to be true." He sighed, then turned to Father. "And you've grown larger too, old man. You're right. I can't look Dean in the eyes. Sometimes I still have nightmares about him, even all these years later." He sighed again. "Your wife, as well. She was a wonderful woman. I try not to think about either of them and have perhaps been too successful for my own good." He frowned, then extended his hand. "I came here prepared to demand an apology, Willy. I was angry to the core at how you'd betrayed the future of Man. But, I find that instead I'm the one compelled to apologize. Perhaps you're the brave one after all." He extended his hand; Father accepted it into both of his and shook it firmly. "I'm sorry," Jurgen continued. "For what you've been through, and for what your family's been through."

"I'm sorry too, Jurgen," Father replied, his voice thick with emotion. "More so than you can ever know."

The robed man nodded. "We'll work together again. You and Sven and Thomas and I, and the whole Longo crew. Like old times. And between us we'll shake the universe."

Chapter Thirty-Three

From that moment on, the old Stormcrow plant didn't know a moment's peace. Father and Jurgen sat down with the skilled workers and divided them up into three crews so that things could keep right on happening twenty-four hours a day, seven days a week. Eventually, they'd provide the nucleus for a staff of hundreds, maybe even thousands. Vlasilov promised to fill the vacancies as soon as humanly possible; even as he was making this promise the machine-repairman for the polymill arrived in a military 'hopper, rad-suited and escorted by an armed Marine. She looked more than a little frightened, but nothing else could've done more to boost the admiral's credibility with the Longo workers. By the next morning specialists from the fleet were arriving to help with the decontamination work. Though the plant could never be made safe for unsuited men within the time available, the admiral did all that could be expected and more.

The Esteppans paid him back in spades, smiling and joking with one another as they scrubbed down and then restarted one machine after another. "It's time to change rags, James! That one's glowing brighter than the arc-welder!"

Father and Sven took off their own suits as well; when the admiral protested, Father suggested that it was perhaps time for him to take me back up to *June* and work on developing tactics. Other men might have lost their tempers, but Vlasilov merely glared for a second and then nodded and accepted that he was now merely in the way. I shook everyone's hand again, told Jurgen that I was pleased to have met him, then left with the admiral.

Actually it wasn't Vlasilov's job to develop a tactical manual for the Skybolt; it was mine and Ted Knight's, though of course the admiral took an active interest. Ted and I had already spent hours discussing how best to operate a group of 'bolts. Now, working with a computer specialist, we ran detailed simulations and tried out the different approaches we'd come up with.

"I don't like it," Commander Knight complained after what must have been our tenth simulated attack on a Dracan fleet one afternoon. "It goes completely against doctrine. But you're right; no matter how we slice it, maneuvering independently gives the best chance of survival."

I nodded. "That's because we can actively dodge incoming rounds," I explained. "And, doing that means we have to be free to move in any direction we like instead of tied to each other."

Ted's frown intensified. "But... It's still all wrong. We're only going to have six Skybolts, armed with a total of twenty-four torps, against an entire Dracan fleet." He sighed, then shook his head. "If every pilot maneuvers independently, how can we get any concentration of fire? It'll take more than one torpedo to kill a dreadnought. And those *Imperial Throne*'s! You were damn lucky to kill one with only two hits."

I nodded; that was true enough. If both torps hadn't hit in exactly the same spot, the ship would never have blown up. "But," I countered, "how are we going to hit *anything* if we don't survive long enough to deliver a weapon? I was lucky that first time, Ted. Partly it was because the Dracans hadn't ever seen a Skybolt before. But mostly I was just lucky."

Ted nodded grimly. "I know, kid. The fleet ran simulations; based on the volume of fire, your 'bolt should have been shot down a lot sooner than it was." He sighed, then tossed his pen on the table. "All right. Let's get down to the nitty-gritty. Traditional fighters operate in pairs in order to cooperate against other fighters. Check?"

"Check," I agreed. "That's what the Thach Weave is all about. And why it's been around for so long."

"But," Ted continued, "Bombers work in larger groups in order to achieve decisive concentrations, both in terms of saturating the defenses and putting enough warheads on the target to kill it." He sighed. "I think we were right the first time, Thomas. Three two-plane elements. It's a tradeoff, yes. Pilots will lose some of their independence in dodging individual rounds. But, not nearly so badly as they would with three 'hoppers in an element."

I nodded, though only reluctantly. "We'll have to game it out more, but I think you're right. It's the best compromise between individual freedom of action and strike-coordination." Then I frowned. "But Ted, we still don't have anything like enough Skybolts. Not to break the blockade of Earth. You know that as well as I do."

He frowned. Our gaming might've sent a few mixed messages, but on this issue it was loud and clear. "I know, Thomas. No matter how we organize them, it's not enough. But what else can we do but try?"

I looked away a moment. "You haven't been down to the plant," I observed.

"There's been no reason." He shrugged. "It's pretty hot, after all. Off limits to anyone who doesn't have vital business there. Except you, of course." He grinned. "You're immune."

I nodded. "Yes. But, I *did* visit, you see. And…"

Ted's eyebrows rose. "Yes?"

"And… Well, there were a lot of incomplete Stormcrows there. One of them looked ready to fly, even. It was sitting in the final test area."

My friend's eyes narrowed. "You're not configured for a Stormcrow, Thomas. Neither is anyone else. The format is totally different. We're not producing new pilots for them."

"Yes. And the hospital where the conversions were done was leveled after the war," I answered, having already done my homework. "The equipment was destroyed and most of the doctors were hung because they were the same ones who made Elitemen. But…"

"But?" Ted asked.

I shook my head. This was going to make things harder than ever for me, I knew. It'd multiply my woes a thousandfold. Still, it needed to be done regardless. "Well… I just got an invitation in the mail. Father Murton and Admiral Vlasilov want me to accept it, for the sake of interplanetary relations. I didn't want to. Still don't want to, really. But…"

Ted's jaw dropped, and his face went white. "You got an invitation to meet Colonel Rotte?" he whispered.

"I did," I agreed. "He's the head of the Order of Blood, and takes the position very seriously, it seems. I'm the newest member, even though I don't like it very much."

"He also shot down over a hundred Polecats," Knight added. "And personally took out I don't know how many navy ships."

"Right," I agreed. "Like I said, I don't want to go. He's completely unrepentant, they say, a dedicated Autarchist. A little mad, even. And…." I hesitated again.

"And?"

I shook my head. "He's still Stormcrow-configured," I explained. "He and I'm still not sure how many others. A brain in a bottle. Back then, you see, a pilot's body wasn't preserved for re-uniting, like mine has been for me. It was just another useless mouth."

Chapter Thirty-Four

I hadn't expected to have time to play tourist on Esteppe, any more than I'd been able to do so during my Skybolt sales tour. I'd visited a dozen worlds, and seen practically nothing of any of them except for during simulated attack runs. Yet now that I was doing what was surely the most important work of my life, at the same time that I was at my absolute busiest and every second mattered, I was sitting in a veritable snail of a tour bus, crawling my way through the New Alps towards Stormcrow Pass.

"…were Estppe's most famous native species, Your Excellency," my private guide was explaining. His name was Uri, and he seemed a little overwhelmed by my presence. I was being 'Excellencied' at every opportunity. "As you certainly already knew. They were rare even before Esteppe was colonized. Though an effort was made to preserve them, the war finally drove them over the edge." Uri smiled sadly. "Today, the only Stormcrows left are preserved specimens in museums. Someday, it's hoped, we'll be able to clone them back into existence. However, as of now native Esteppan DNA still isn't understood well enough to make this possible."

I nodded, admiring the majestic scenery. So far it was even better than the Italian and Austrian Alps. It wasn't hard to imagine the lean, dark lines of a huge stormcrow wheeling to and fro in the updrafts, seeking prey. Stormcrows were still the biggest winged creatures ever discovered anywhere, so huge that several humans had been taken as prey in the early days of the colony. It was no wonder that they'd been adopted as the symbol of Esteppan valor.

"And up there," Uri pointed out to the bus's left, "is the Aerie. At the top of Mount Blood."

I nodded again. "How long until we get there?"

"Just a few more minutes, Your Excellency," Uri gushed. He'd be telling the tale of his journey with the famous hero Thomas Longo for the rest of his life. I'd been wildly popular on Earth; here, where military valor was the highest and most esteemed of all virtues, I was practically worshipped. It made me terribly uncomfortable.

"This place is just as beautiful as I remembered it," Faher Murton pointed out, smiling through his thick beard. "Beautiful, and deadly. See over there, on that far ridge? There's been an avalanche recently. You can tell by the color of the snow."

"I just wish we could've traveled by 'hopper," I replied, though I knew Uri's feelings would be hurt. "This is a nice-enough trip, sure. But, I don't have time for pretty scenery just now. There's a war on." The motors of a skyhopper interfered terribly with the function of all but the simplest and most heavily-shielded electronic devices. On Earth, traffic was restricted to very high altitudes, except for narrowly-restricted landing zones. Here, where the population density was so much lower, the rules were for the most part considerably less stringent. It was just plain bad luck that the Stormcrow pilot's retirement home happened to be located in one of the few proscribed areas. Over half of Esteppe's largest computer manufacturers and software developers were headquartered within a few miles of the rest home.

Father Murton smiled, then turned back to his window. "Enjoy the R&R while you can, Thomas. I certainly am."

I sighed, then turned my attention back to the scenery. Now the imaginary Stormcrows circling the peaks were the sooty-black kind that I'd seen back at my father's old plant. My mentor was right; I *should* try to get my mind off of my problems while I had the chance. But how could I, when I had such an important meeting with Colonel Rotte ahead of me?

* * * *

The Aerie was all that it was rumored to be. My tutor and I were greeted by an impeccably dressed butler. He bowed so deeply that I feared he'd snap his elderly back. "Welcome home, Your Excellency," he greeted me. Then, he turned to Father Murton. "And to you as well, esteemed sir. Colonel Rotte awaits you in the reception room. However, I've been instructed to take you to your rooms first, so that you can make yourselves at home."

I nodded as Uri carried in our luggage. As a Knight of the Order of Blood, I'd been awarded the irrevocable right to a suite of rooms in the Aerie for however long I might live. Though, the company being what it was I didn't think I'd be visiting too often.

Despite my misgivings, I found the Aerie's architecture to be rather fetching. It featured the same heavy wooden beams and somber colors common to all the buildings of Esteppe, and the furnishings were simple and ruggedly built as well. Only the windows could be said to be opulent. Given the natural beauty of the surroundings, however, to be any less extravagant with the glasswork would've been a crime. I'd grown up surrounded by such architecture and furnishings, and as much as I hated the thought in many ways I felt very much at home as the butler withdrew and left me alone with my thoughts. A long time ago, just before I'd taken off on my one and so far only combat mission, Father Murton had claimed that I'd been raised in the Esteppan tradition, at least mostly. At the time I'd thought he was wrong. Indeed, I'd even been a little offended. Now, however, I had to wonder where my roots truly lay. Indeed, when I thought of the Longo workers laboring away without their rad suits I even felt a small stab of guilty pride. After all, how could I possibly be ashamed of any sort of kinship with such men?

I was just tucking my most-prized video game controller into a dresser drawer when there was a light knock at my door. "Thomas?" Father Murton's voice asked. "Are you ready? The colonel is waiting."

"Just a minute," I answered, adjusting the Order of Blood that I wore up close to my throat one last time in the mirror. Father Murton would have to adjust it for me again, I knew; I was too clumsy to get it right. Of all my decorations, the Order was the most visually prominent and therefore the most difficult to center properly. It was the most uncomfortable as well; I'd only worn it a handful of times before coming to Esteppe. I could hardly turn my head; in fact, the thing was wearing a nice little groove in the flexible plastic of my neck. It was just as well that all living Brothers of the Order were cyborgs. Normal flesh probably couldn't survive the abuse of wearing the decoration continuously, as demanded by local custom.

Sure enough, Father Murton adjusted the Order again for me out in the hallway, then we were on our way to the reception room. The butler was surprisingly accommodating; for once, we didn't have to ask our host to slow down on the stairs. There were *many* cyborgs here it was slowly dawned on me. And, therefore, life was arranged to suit *my* needs. "Remember," my tutor hissed in my ear as we slowly descended a grand, sweeping staircase far too elegant to replace with an elevator. "Rotte's a nutcase, but he's an honorable man by his own reckoning."

"Duh!" I whispered back, irritated for a moment that, with all my responsibilities, I was being treated like a child. "I'm not stupid, you know!" Then I shook my head and sighed; I *was* a kid, still, and the priest was merely trying to help. What an ass I was being! Was seventeen like this for *everyone*, or just for cyborgs? Given how important my duties had become, maybe I should talk to the docs and try and talk them into readjusting my puberty a little? "Sorry, Father."

My tutor grinned. "It's all right, Thomas. Thank god you're still normal, after all you've been through. I keep saying that to myself, and it helps."

I looked down at the ground. "Colonel Rotte's an Eliteman," I recited, repeating back the briefing I'd received over and over again the night before. "Like Jurgen and Father. And an unrepentant one at that. He wasn't hung because during the war he was just a soldier like my brother, not involved in anything illegal. As the leading Esteppan ace he runs the Order of Blood, which is still quite influential behind the scenes here on Esteppe. People listen respectfully when Knights of the Blood speak. He thinks the Autarch was right about most things, though he acknowledges that the mass killings were wrong." I sighed. "See? I remember."

"You do indeed, Thomas," Father Murton answered, smiling. "But you've forgotten the most important part of all."

I sighed again, then shook my head. Probably my own Order of Blood was hanging awry again as a result, but I didn't care. "No, Father. I haven't forgotten the important part. We need him. In fact, the whole human race needs him. And I'm our best shot at bringing him on board."

Chapter Thirty-Five

"Good afternoon, Commander Longo," Rotte's mellifluous voice greeted me as I entered the Aerie's reception room. "I'm deeply honored that you were able to find time at what must be such a busy juncture to come and visit your Brothers."

I blinked, and looked around the empty-seeming room again. Suddenly what I'd taken to be a footstool spun around to face me, then sprouted legs and rose to man-height. "G-Good afternoon," I spluttered in reply.

"Forgive my appearance," the thing I assumed to be Rotte responded. It was back-lit by the oversized windows and snow-reflected sunshine, so that I couldn't make out a face. If it had one, that was. "I've been experimenting in recent years. This body, I believe, is far more practical for my needs than the mannequin I used to inhabit. Though yours is far more attractive than mine ever was, I fear. Esteppe generally treats its veterans well, but our plastics industry simply isn't up to Earth standards. No one culture does everything well, I suppose. And few do everything badly."

"I suppose not," I replied, wincing inwardly at my inane and perhaps even nonsensical choice of words. But I recovered smoothly, extending my hand for the colonel to shake. "Pleased to meet you."

Somewhere within the footrest's inner workings an electric motor spun. Then a small trap-door opened and a metal five-digit manipulator not unlike my own simulated hands popped into view. I nodded and smiled as we completed the greeting ritual, electric motors spinning away inside both of us. It was damned awkward, far more so than I'd have guessed. On the second stroke, we actually broke physical contact. With normal humans, I just sort of maintained a loose grip on their hand and let them do the pumping. But with another being like myself, this approach didn't work. "We need a new greeting, we cyborgs," Rotte observed. "As in so many other things, flesh and blood institutions are impractical." He withdrew his arm and turned his headless trunk slightly from side to side.

I smiled wordlessly; Rotte was still backlit so strongly that I couldn't make out whatever it was that he used for a face these days. He had one, I was sure; a face was too useful in communicating emotions to do without, and too important psychologically as well.

"I was just working on my models when you came in," he observed. "They're rather a passion of mine. Would you care to see?"

I blinked; Rotte had been sitting in the middle of the floor when I arrived, a good ten feet away from anything. "Of course," I replied. "Models of what?"

Rotte's body spun around, though his legs remained still. For the first time I was able to make out a rudimentary visage, two naked camera lenses, suspended above a very obviously artificial plastiflesh mouth. It was mounted at about the height of my navel. The mouth smiled slightly. "Spacecraft," he answered. "Warships of all kinds. My father used to laugh at me when I was a boy, for spending so much time and effort on trifles. Nowadays, however, they're my only source of joy." The smile widened. "I think you'll recognize the ones I'm about to show you."

We walked halfway across the large room before we arrived at what looked like a cross between a remote-handling facility, the sort suitable for dealing with highly toxic materials, and a machine shop. There were manipulators and cameras everywhere, of all sizes from that of a child's hand down to microminiature. The whole thing was enclosed in a large glass cube, making it look even more like something out of a xenobiology lab. But instead of containing samples of possibly-dangerous alien life-forms, Rotte's cube held several highly-detailed model spaceships in various stages of completion. And he was right; I recognized them all at a glance. I'd had intimate encounters with each of them.

"That's the *Imperial Throne*," I said, pointing at the still-incomplete model. It was spinning on a spindle in front of a fixed paint sprayer, half-finished; clearly, this was the task I'd interrupted. "And there's *Tecumseh* and *Roman Nose*." I frowned. "You're not supposed to have blueprints for them. They're still secret ships."

Rotte's artificial mouth smiled again; it was quite expressive, I decided, despite also being so obviously unreal. "They weren't easy to come by," he acknowledged. "However, my model-making is harmless and the shipyard engineer who supplied me with the line-drawings knows that I'd never share them." The manipulators suddenly came to life; instantly the *Chief*-class models were placed aboard a little train and whisked away. "They're not for public display. Rather, I brought them out of storage to honor the heroism of my newest Brother." The headless torso bowed slightly. "Forgive me if I've offended you."

"Not at all," I answered. After all, the media had been shooting video of the *Chief*-class vessels for months now. You could almost model one from the public data alone. And… And…" Suddenly my jaw dropped. "You're directly linked to that case!" I suddenly realized. "Those manipulators; they're directly controlled by your mind!"

The diaphragms behind the lenses of Rotte's camera-eyes opened in a quite-passable display of surprise. "Of course!" he replied, extending his clumsy hand-analogs and waggling the slow, awkward fingers. "How else could I possibly get any fine work done?" Even as he spoke the spindle holding the model *Imperial Throne* began to spin, and the spray gun issued forth a fine gray mist of wet paint. "Modeling spaceships would be impossible with mannequin-hands. Surely you of all people understand that."

My mouth was still hanging open. "I… Uh…"

Rotte's eye-diaphragms narrowed to pinpoints. "You think that my little breadboard setup is illegal, don't you? A violation of the Interplanetary Conventions against cyborging?"

"Uh…"

The artificial smile widened, but the camera-eyes remained cold and narrow. "My whole existence is a violation of the Conventions, Thomas. As is yours."

"That's not true," I countered. "They passed a special bill for me."

"A bill that's been expired for months, I might point out." Rotte sighed and shook his whole torso from side to side. "In fact, as near as I can tell the entire United Systems government has been illegal since the Prime Minister declared martial law. Every single action they've taken under that proclamation is utterly without a legal foundation. If everything had been done according to proper procedures, assuming the media has the story correct, our current emergency war-leader would've failed a vote of no-confidence and Isoroku Nagano would today be losing the war for us all in a most decisive manner indeed." The camera-eyes looked up to meet mine. "That's where paying too much attention to legality gets one, Thomas."

I pressed my lips together. "That's different."

"Really?" Rotte asked. "I might ask you to explain just exactly how. In fact, I probably *would* ask if I were half as sadistic as I'm rumored to be." The *Throne* stopped spinning and Rotte's camera eyes widened, making his expression seem warmer. "Instead, I'll point out that, by failing to execute me and the other five Stormcrow survivors, the United Systems government implicitly accepted the existence of mind-controlled machinery." He thumped his chest, creating a hard, metallic sound. "Our mannequin-bodies, to be specific."

I closed my eyes impatiently. "Your biological bodies were dead," I replied. "You have nowhere else to go. Of *course* they allowed you to keep your mannequin-bodies; the United Systems could hardly take them away, now could they?"

"They *could* have hung us," Rotte replied. "Probably should have, if they truly wished to make an end of our kind. But, they *did* allow us our bodies, as you've acknowledged, even though their existence is an ongoing violation of the law." He smiled again, then pointed a manipulator finger at the cabinet. "And I say that's part of my body."

My jaw dropped open again. "Come now!" Rotte continued, leaning forward slightly. "You're reputed to be quite bright, Thomas. Just because I control my modeling-box via radio signal instead of physical wire is irrelevant. I lack proper hands, and this is my prosthesis." His smile went cold again. "You wouldn't take away a man's prosthesis, would you?"

I closed my eyes again. "No," I answered. "I suppose not."

"And you wouldn't even consider doing so, would you?" the colonel continued. "If I wasn't an Esteppan Eliteman, that is."

I shook my head and looked away. My head was beginning to hurt; this meeting had gotten off on the wrong foot entirely and now was spinning entirely out of control. "Excuse me," I said. "I'm just a kid, really. Just like you were when they first brain-cored you."

Rotte's camera lenses glittered. "Yes."

"Because I'm a kid, I'm not supposed to know all the answers. Maybe you're right. Maybe that cabinet *is* your hands. Maybe it's legal, maybe it isn't. I'm not really sure of anything anymore." I looked down at the ground. "Forgive me if I've offended you."

"How could you offend me, Thomas?" Rotte asked, extending a manipulator and letting it come to rest on my shoulder. "You're a brave young man under terrible stress, as I myself once was." He smiled again. "I've formed a fighter squadron too, you know. One much like your own, and not so many years ago at that." His eyes narrowed again. "Tell me, did you adopt the two-ship formation? Or go for singles?"

Eventually, I knew, I was going to have to trust this man with my life and more than my life. We *needed* his Stormcrows. "Pairs," I replied evenly. "Even though I'm aware you chose singles for most actions."

Rotte's body bent at the waist in a recognizable nod. "But of course. We operated almost entirely on the defensive, and thus optimized everything to cover as much ground as possible." He pointed at the now-painted *Imperial Throne*. "To kill one of those monsters you need concentrated firepower, which dictates larger elements. Different tactical imperatives dictate different techniques." He turned to face me. "If we'd attacked capital ships more often, we'd have done the same thing."

I false-gulped; it'd taken Ted and I who knew how many hours of computer time to figure out the answer to a problem that this man had clearly solved over a decade ago. "You and your squadron fought well, "I answered, my voice carefully neutral. "So well that you're a legend in the navy. They speak of you with hushed voices. "

"I did what I had to do," Rotte answered, though he was clearly pleased by my words. "Just as your brother Sven did. I worked with him personally on the big missile interception that he was decorated for, you know. He planned the whole thing, and it was my report on the engagement that got him his Order of Merit. Which he earned in full, I might add." He turned to face me again. "And, as head of this Order I also personally approved your own entry into the Brotherhood of Blood. Which you also have well and truly earned."

There were a thousand things I wanted to say, most of them about how deep down I wished that he hadn't bothered. And yet, when I finally said the words I'd so dreaded speaking, somehow they weren't quite a lie anymore. "Thank you," I said softly.

"You're a hero," Rotte answered, turning away and walking two or three steps to the nearest window, where he stared off into the distance. "In our line of work, one tends to end up either dead or highly-decorated. It's simply the nature of things." He sighed, then extended his arms and gripped his manipulators together behind his back. Given the nature of his physique, the result could've been a grotesque parody of human posture. But, somehow, it was something more than that. "When, Thomas? When are you going to ask me to fly combat with you? I've known about the Stormcrows in the plant for years. Given who I once was, how could I *not* know? One of my best men died in the blast during the attack that shut down production. He was on his way to pick up a new bird. It's probably still sitting there, almost ready to fly."

"Not until tomorrow," I answered, telling the absolute, complete truth. "The plan was for me to spend today buttering you up, and let you

145

get to feeling all fatherly-like towards me. Then, we hoped that you wouldn't be able to turn us down. And yes, as of three days back, it *was* still sitting there. I saw it with my own eyes."

"Hmph," Rotte answered, still staring off into the distance. "I have no reason to love the Dracans, Thomas. But I also don't care so much for your United Systems, either." He turned to face me. "Until the war began and things became desperate, the Autarch was *good* for Esteppe. He was elected to office with the full understanding of the populace that it was to be for life. And, you can't name one single act of aggression committed by Esteppe prior to the opening of hostilities. Not one! Because there weren't any!"

I gulped. "The history books say that creating cyborgs was threat enough."

Rotte shook his torso again. "It was self-determination. We had a dream, and no one else had the balls to follow us. But they couldn't let us succeed, either. For if we had, we'd have left everyone else in the dust. As things were, we came far closer than was comfortable." He turned to face me. "We nearly won, Thomas. You know that. Thirty Stormcrows and thirty Elitemen, against the universe."

"Yes," I acknowledged. "You almost did. But…" I turned to face him. "Along the way, your leadership sold out their humanity. They slaughtered the weak and the innocent. Millions died, so that your precious Elitemen could live." I shook my head. "You know of my brother Dean, I'm sure. How can anyone possibly rationalize what was done to him?"

"I can't, of course," Rotte answered. "No one can. I'll admit something now that I never have before, Thomas. During the last few months, I was tempted to defect on every mission. In my heart, I knew that it was the right thing to do. Had I done so I might've arranged to take the whole squadron with me. I was never, however, quite brave enough to try." He sighed. "I've killed hundreds of men in honorable combat, Thomas. Thousands, probably. But I shamefully slaughtered millions by failing to surrender, once the Autarch went mad. Without the Stormcrows, immediate capitulation would've been unavoidable." He looked down at the carpet. "Millions. And that is why, Thomas, even in the heat of anger and the shame of defeat I've never called your father a traitor. He's a great man, a far greater man than me. And braver, as well." Rotte reached out again and clasped my shoulder. "You've achieved much, Thomas. But, I fear, you've far more yet to live up to."

I pressed my lips together. "Yet they say that you still believe in the

Autarch. And, in the destiny of the Elitemen."

"I do," Rotte acknowledged softly. "Thomas, you've never jacked into a master computer. You've never known the speed, the rapidity, the clarity of thought…" He shook his head. "Thomas, why do you think that the United Systems trusts your father to build fighters? Not why they pardoned him and let him keep his wealth and estates—that's not what I'm asking. He earned that by stepping forward and sharing the information that ended a bloody, pointless war. Still, he's got a socket in his skull, and was once the nearest thing the Autarch ever had to a son and heir. He even did key work developing the cyborg interface. So, why did they let *him* develop the Skybolt, instead of just handing some equally bright and totally politically-reliable Earther engineer the blueprints and telling him to hop to it?"

I blinked, suddenly confused. "I… I don't know."

"There's a thousand reasons why the United Systems would want to do just that. How much easier would it have been to get the Skybolt past Parliament, for example, if no Esteppan Elitemen were involved?" He sighed and turned away. "Thomas… It's because no one else *can* do it. No one else alive has ever live-wired his mind to a computer and thought so much or so well about gravitic motors. For example… Both the Stormcrow and I presume the Skybolt have engines capable of generating a synchronized feedback loop. They're nine times as powerful with two engines functioning as one. Isn't that right?"

"Right," I agreed, even though it was classified.

"Have you ever heard of any other application for synchronized antigravity feedback? Any other application anywhere?"

"No," I acknowledged.

"That's because your father came up with it while wired to a computer," Rotte explained. "The math that underlies the phenomenon is beyond the range of unenhanced human understanding. A normal human brain can't deal with the complexities. But your father still retains enough of what he learned while plugged in to be able to work with the concepts."

I tried to speak, but no words would come.

"Now," Rotte continued. "How many *other* important discoveries are waiting for us out there? Waiting for geniuses like your father to enhance themselves electronically and master? How far might we grow, and how fast?" The colonel shook his torso again. "The possibilities are limitless! Absolutely limitless! And yet we cower in fear, hiding ourselves away from the light and hoping that it will simply go away."

"Technology *never* goes away, Father Murton always says," I answered slowly. "It just waits for its time to come."

"General Schumacher was an Eliteman," Rotte continued. "He was in charge of all of our strategic planning. Sometimes his orders appeared to be nonsense, but they never, ever were. The computer connected to his brain wouldn't *let* them be. The tribunal hung him, but if he were commanding the United Systems Navy I doubt if the Dracans would ever have gotten past the Orion Nexus." He shook his head in disgust. "I've killed millions through cowardice and inaction. Yet how many more have the Parliamentarians killed through superstition and idiocy?" He turned to face me. "All we wanted was to develop the human mind as far as we could stretch it. Instead, we found ourselves at war. And, they say that *we* were to blame!"

I closed my eyes and made my hands into fists. "Look, colonel. I can't change the past. Nobody can. All we can do is face the future. Together, preferably."

"Ja," Rotte agreed, his artificial lips now twisted up into a smirk. "We can kill the Dracans together, you and I. They'll give us more big medals in gratitude, and let us lead a few parades. Then they'll shuffle us back here. Or at least they will us Stormcrow-configured types, if any survive the fighting, because we don't have the kind of bodies we're supposed to anymore and that reminds them of possibilities too unpleasant to consider." He sighed, then shook his torso. "Thomas, I'll gladly fly with you. I don't love the Dracans—Indeed, I'll will swear by the Order to do everything I know how to do in order to defeat them. And I'll bring my Brothers along with me—we've already discussed this many times. But…" The diaphragms behind his lens-eyes narrowed again. "Thomas, there's a price."

"Name it," I replied, my own eyes narrowing as well.

"I want to jack in again, Thomas. All of us want to be free to jack in again. In the same way that my model-making box is my hands, computers are my true mind. We want you and the Skybolt pilots to be configured to jack in as well, if you choose. It should be easy enough, in the state you're in. We'd *like* for everyone everywhere to be free to reconfigure their minds, though we know that's too much to ask. So instead, we'll settle for just us pilots, and those Elitemen still alive and able." He smiled. "The rest of mankind will just have to take care of itself, I suppose."

Chapter Thirty-Six

Alicia *always* had time to see me, no matter how full her schedule grew. It was very full indeed these days, judging from the crowd waiting in her outer office. What with her being effectively the head of state and wartime dictator for all of the United Systems outside of Terra, I couldn't even *begin* to imagine what her schedule must be like; mine was bad enough, after all, and I hadn't a fraction of her responsibilities.

It was just as well that Father Murton and I weren't kept waiting for long. The other petitioners for Alicia's time recognized us instantly, but the unexpectedly short delay meant that they weren't granted enough time to figure out how to open a conversation with us. Alicia had promised back in the cave that she'd see me instantly if something was truly important, and the fact that she was now leading the war effort of many worlds had no effect on her promise. Neither Alicia's mind nor her heart worked that way; indeed, it seemed that she *liked* being interrupted by me, so long as I didn't do it too often. It reassured her that she still had at least a poor sort of adopted family that genuinely cared about and needed her as a person rather than as a political leader, and who would still love and respect her even if she never saw Spence again. Besides, both my tutor and Admiral Vlasilov had reassured me that the Stormcrow issue was indeed important enough to bring to Alicia's immediate attention. "I have similar privileges, Thomas," the admiral explained. "Due to my position as acting wartime fleet commander. But this time, it'd be better if the request came from you. I fear that in recent weeks I've been at her door more often than I would've liked."

Alicia had grown sufficiently in importance that she maintained both an inner and outer waiting room; there was a small crowd in the inner room as well, though fortunately they didn't gawk like the people outside did. I even recognized several whose hands I'd shaken at bond drives; they smiled when I nodded at them, and sort of glowed.

We hadn't been waiting three minutes when Alicia's secretary

Benjamin threw open her private door and, smiling and bowing, ushered a very well-dressed Esteppan from his mistress's office. The supplicant didn't look happy, and when he saw Father Murton and I in the anteroom it didn't take him long to put two and two together regarding why his long-sought interview was being cut so short. Still, he managed to remain civil, bowing and calling me "Your Excellency" on the way out.

"Thank god you've come by," Alicia greeted us as she half-leapt up from behind her desk and, old-fashioned skirt rustling, walked around to hug Father Murton and give me a quick peck on the cheek. I was glad there wasn't anyone else around to see; it would've been more embarrassing than I could stand. "That man who was just in here? He runs the local shipyards. I can't imagine how he ever found his way into a position of such responsibility. All he can do is find reasons why things can't be done on the necessary time-schedule." She shook her head. "Normally, high-achievers aren't so negative."

"I didn't know Esteppe even *had* shipyards," I answered.

"They do," Alicia confirmed, her ears twitching in apparent pain at the remembered conversation. "Quite small by Earth standards, but absolutely vital to us here and now. And growing very, very quickly." She sighed and looked down at her desktop. "I fear that I may have to remove him from his job entirely. That's generally a bad business, and here even more so because feelings are still so sensitive. But he just can't improvise. For him, everything has to be just-so, like in peacetime. All i's dotted and every last t crossed." She shook her head, then turned to me. "Anyway, what's up, Thomas? Girl trouble?"

"Not yet," I answered, though I'd have blushed a beet red were I capable. "It's navy trouble, ma'am. Admiral Vlasilov asked me to see you instead of coming himself." I shrugged. "Though I'll admit I don't understand quite why."

Alicia pursed her lips, then returned to her seat behind the desk. "That's fair enough," she admitted eventually. "Though I have to admit my curiosity is piqued. Are you sure you wouldn't rather talk about girl trouble?"

I smiled. "If I could," I promised her, "I would." Then I let my smile widen. "Perhaps Admiral Vlasilov has girl trouble he might wish to discuss with you?"

"Ha!" Alicia replied, grinning from ear to ear and looking a lot happier than she'd been before my tutor and I had walked in. "That'll be the day." Vlasilov was reputed to be the most confirmed bachelor in the fleet. Then Alicia's face hardened a bit. "Seriously, Thomas. I have only so much spare time in a day, even for you and the fleet."

I nodded, then explained about the Stormcrow pilots. "…and," I finished. "I have a personal message from Admiral Vlasilov. He told me to tell Madame Deputy that he can make plans to engage a fleet with a mere half-squadron. He can order new vessels from inadequate yards that have never built warships before, and even turn a blind eye while heroic civilians work in a radioactive environment to try and further the war effort. He says that he can and will do *anything* to win this war for the Unites Systems. 'But', he said, and I'm quoting him now. 'But, I cannot turn the United System's value system upon its head. It's beyond my authority. As badly as I need those Stormcrows, I cannot make this sort of promise to these men.'"

By the time I'd finished, Alicia's mouth was a hard, cold line broken only by her harelip. "Tell me, Thomas," she asked. "How badly do we need these so-called Elitemen? Honestly, now."

I frowned and looked down at the carpet. "Even with them fighting on our side," I answered, "our chances of winning a major engagement with the Dracan fleet are pitiful. Ted and I have been gaming it out over and over again, all day every day except when we've been visiting the new pilots. Without the stormcrows, there isn't any chance at all." Then I looked up again. "Admiral Vlasilov says that we won't have to fight the whole Imperial Navy at once, though I don't see how he can make that promise. Concentration of force is a basic principle of naval strategy." I shrugged. "If it was me, I'd have the whole Imperial fleet enforcing the blockade of Earth. That way they're invincible, and they win automatically. Why their guy would do any different is beyond me. The admiral won't talk about it."

"Don't underestimate Vlasilov," Alicia countered. "He's brilliant in his own field of expertise." Then she looked down and sighed. "How soon must we make a decision?"

"Yesterday," Father Murton interjected. "Literally yesterday. I called up Sven last night; his third-shift men were just getting ready to cut up a Stormcrow fuselage to convert it into a jig for the Skybolt line. They've stopped work for now, but something has to be done soon. The plant's jammed with 'crows, and they have to be either finished or moved out of the way. As incomplete as most of them are, moving them is pretty much the same thing as ruining them. A decision is called for immediately."

"All right, then," Alicia answered, turning to me. "Go tell your Ace of Ace's that he's got a deal. He and his buddies will be able to jack in just as soon as the emergency's past and the shooting's over. You can swear on your Order's honor that you heard me make this promise with your own ears, Thomas. I'll write up a secret memo for you later." Then she turned to Father Murton and sighed. "It's all a lie, of course. *No one* can promise the Elitemen anything remotely like this without a long, public debate in Parliament. One that they'll almost certainly lose, I'll add, even with the public grateful to them for their services." Her face hardened. "Vlaslov isn't the only one, you know. I'll do *anything* to win. *Anything!* Because nothing could possibly be worse for humanity than a Dracan victory. I don't like lying, least of all to honorable fighting men who are putting their lives on the line. I don't like it at all. But, there's no choice that I can see."

My tutor turned to look at me, and I shrugged. "What?" Alicia asked, not understanding the interplay. "What now?"

I shrugged again, and Father Murton kindly took the lead. "I'm afraid that's impossible, Alicia," he explained gently. "You see, all the Stormcrow build-data is encrypted in a format that only an Eliteman's brain-jack can decipher. If we're to finish the Stormcrows anytime before we're all old and gray, *someone* has to start jacking in on a regular basis. In fact, most likely several *someones* will have to." He looked at me.

"Father suggested that his assistant Jurgen would be a good choice," I said, very quietly. "He's still fully configured. So is Father himself; he says he can save several weeks, maybe even several months, if he can jack in to work on Skybolt series production as well. And, he says to tell you, things would go even faster if Sven received an implant as well, to cover the needs of the third shift…"

Part Two

Chapter Thirty-Seven

That night, it so happened, both Father and Sven had pressing business aboard *The Glorious First of June* in the late afternoon. Despite our high-powered schedules we (along with Dean) were still a family, and therefore both wanted and needed to spend time together. When I found out that they'd be aboard, I asked Father Murton if he could help me borrow part of the wardroom, so that even if we didn't have very long to visit at least we could sit down and have dinner. What we got was far better than anything I'd expected; instead of the cold sandwiches which were all that was usually available to crewmen who chose not to eat at the standard times and places, someone rolled out the whole nine yards for us Longos. This included the ship's finest silver service and snowy-uniformed mess attendants. Apparently, Father Murton had a lot more pull than I'd ever realized.

I didn't eat, of course. Instead, I just sat quietly and felt good as Father and Sven mostly talked about production issues and the difficulties of getting the sensitive factory equipment properly calibrated in a radioactive environment. Father was looking better than I could ever remember; on Earth, he'd been a very quiet, unassuming sort of engineering and scientific genius. Yet here, on his homeworld, he seemed almost a different person, confident and bold. Even his accent was more profound.

"I tell you what!" he declared, waving his fork airily in a way I'd never seen before. "If we get that polymill back on-line, we have that prototype up and flying in a week." He grinned and turned to me. "A week! Then we have you make more test flights, ja?"

"Yeah," I agreed, smiling even though something was really beginning to bother me. "I'm looking forward to flying again."

"It must be wonderful," Sven agreed, stuffing his pipe for an after-dinner smoke. Their 'hopper wasn't due to launch for another forty-five minutes. He shook his head. "To wear a Skybolt for a body. I can't even imagine it."

I sighed and looked down at the table. "It's not easy to explain. In fact, I can't put it into words at all." Then I raised my eyes and met Father's. "Any more than you explain what it's like to jack into a computer network and have your mindpower multiplied."

My father's gaze didn't waver. "You're right, Thomas," he agreed. "There aren't any words to explain such a thing, or even any commonality of experience that can be built upon. That's why it's so hard."

Sven frowned and studied me closely. "Is something wrong, Thomas?"

I sighed and shook my head. "I don't know," I answered, being as honest as I knew how to be. "I really and truly don't know."

Father smiled slightly. "You're seventeen, Thomas. It's a confusing age to be, even when the universe around you is halfway making sense. But, living in the middle of a vortex the way you do… Well, I can't even imagine it." He put down his fork and tapped the tabletop. "Come. Spread it all out right here, and we'll do what we can to help you work things through."

"Well…" I said slowly. Then I looked up at Father again. "I just don't get it. I mean… The United Systems fought a big war to stop cyborging, right? Lots and lots of people died."

"Yes," Father answered. "They did."

I frowned. "Maybe that's part of the problem," I said slowly. "I'm getting more and more confused every day. Who is 'they', anyway? And who exactly are 'we'?"

"Ha!" Sven barked, slapping his thigh as if I'd just made a joke.

Father smiled. "You're growing up fast," he observed.

I closed my eyes and sighed. "I grew up knowing you were the Autarch's favorite, but I also watched the films of you weeping as you confessed your crimes. Yet, now, in some ways you're talking like an Eliteman again. Like you think the Autarch was right all along." I shook my head. "And even the admiral is taking your side! Doing all he can to help you jack in! After he fought and killed to stop you from doing exactly the same thing when I was a baby!"

Father sighed, then wiped his mouth with the expensive navy napkin. "The Autarch was mad," he explained eventually. "Or he went mad, rather. Bernard, I fear, was never particularly good at dealing with setbacks. When he ran out of options that seemed acceptable, his sanity broke. He should never have taken up politics, should have stayed in his lab and done what he was good at. What he had a special gift for." Father met my eyes again. "He went mad, Thomas. But that doesn't mean he was wrong. And, if you paid strict attention, I never apologized once for creating brain-cores. I wept for my guilt in supporting a man I knew to be deeply flawed and helping him achieve a level of power that he was grossly unsuited for. I wept for the war-dead, Thomas. I'm in part responsible for them. We pushed too far too fast; the reaction against us was, I can now see, inevitable. I remain deeply sorry."

I shook my head. "You set this all up," I accused. "Didn't you? From the very beginning. To make your Eliteman dreams come true. And now, the United Systems *has* to let you have your way." I balled up my fists, suddenly angrier than I'd ever been before. "You even used me. Your own son."

He winced as if I'd struck him. Then his eyes softened and he looked away. "I didn't make the Dracans attack," he replied eventually. "Be reasonable, Thomas. I couldn't have made that happen if I'd wanted to. Nor did I weaken the fleet so much that it couldn't win a conventional war, or divide Parliament so closely that it couldn't function. I'm not responsible for *any* of those things; the universe was what it was." He sighed and shook his head. "All I did was design truly excellent aerospace fighters. I had nothing to do with starting *this* war, thank god! Nor, Thomas, did I 'use' you. I *had* to brain-core my own son, to prove that the procedure was good enough for the sons and daughters of others."

"And, Thomas," Sven pointed out, "you *could* have said no."

"But…" I replied. "Esteppe *lost* the war! And yet, now, everything is starting to go just as if they'd won. Or, as if *we'd* won. I mean…"

"Who's carrying the war effort here and now?" Sven asked, his tone irritatingly reasonable. "Whose defenses have failed, and to whom is Earth looking to for salvation?" He shrugged. "This is the nature of things, Thomas. When power-balances alter, the rules shift to favor those on top." He shrugged. "Don't you see that today Esteppe is the most important planet in the entire Union? That Earth has come to us on bended knee, begging for deliverance? Facts are facts, and new realities have new implications. If they want our help, they must accept our morality." He shrugged. "Esteppe never acknowledged that cyborging was wrong, Thomas. Instead we were simply forced at bayonet point to cease doing it for a time. This is a different thing entirely. Is it any wonder that underlying differences between our cultures would remain?

Or that now, when we're strong again, we seek to have our own standards of right and wrong re-adopted?" His eyes narrowed. "And, once Earth has been saved and returns to its status as richest and most powerful of all worlds by such a huge margin, perhaps things just might reverse themselves again. Unless, of course, they decide that 'borging is too useful to ban, even in times of peace. As I expect they might, once they've had their noses thoroughly rubbed in the fact."

I put my elbows on the table and cradled my head in my hands. Suddenly, it ached. "It's all wheels within wheels within wheels!" I complained. "No one cares about just doing the right thing!"

"Oh, but we *all* do!" Father corrected me. "Doing the right thing is one of the most powerful of human urges. It's just that we don't agree on what 'right' is. So, we fight, fight, fight, and the most powerful get their way, so that *their* standard of right and wrong is the one that gains legal sanction and is imposed on everyone else. It's as simple as that. I mean, don't you think that the average Dracan soldier believes that he's fighting for the holiest and most noble of goals? He does, you know. Even if we don't agree."

"As I believed in the Autarchy of Esteppe," Sven added. "I killed and would willingly have died in order to help free the minds of mankind." He sighed. "I still might get to do the dying part, you know. The fallout in the plant is no joke. One of the workers started getting nosebleeds yesterday; the doctors say it might be from the radiation."

"Ja," Father agreed, looking grim. Then he turned to me. "Thomas... Forgive me for saying something very hard. But times are hard, and growing up is hard. I love you very, very much."

I nodded. "Go ahead. I've seen a lot of hard things."

"You have," he acknowledged with a little bow. "More and harder things than I'd ever have wanted for you." He sighed, then spoke. "Thomas, you just accused me of using you in order to further my dreams for the future of mankind. That hurt, and it hurt a lot."

I nodded again, without speaking.

"So..." he said eventually. "Am I 'using' your brother Sven by allowing him to work in the factory without anti-radiation gear? And did I 'use' your brother Dean when I sat and watched them lobotomize him instead of admitting that I was leaking secrets in order to end the war as soon as possible, to put a stop to the useless bloodshed?" He stood up and spread his shoulders; I'd never really appreciated before how wide and powerful they were. "We live in hard times, Thomas, and those of us who end up in positions of responsibility often live the hardest lives of all. We must do difficult things, and bear hard consequences. You've already experienced some of this, certainly more than your share. Yet your life is only now truly beginning. I fear there is more hardness, perhaps much more, yet to come." He bowed his head. "I'm sorry for the pain that being my son has caused you, just as I'm sorry for what happened to Dean. Neither of you deserved to suffer. And yet, what were my alternatives? Should I have chosen not to employ my talents, for fear of the suffering that success might bring me? If so, what if *everyone* took such an approach? How would anything ever get done? How would we ever learn new things? How would our species ever grow? It's just the way things are for mankind. We're grossly imperfect beings living in a grossly imperfect universe, struggling along as best we know how." He shook his head. "I'm sorry, Thomas, for what my life has done to yours. And yet, at the same time I'm also not sorry at all. Things *had* to be as they are. It was as inevitable as the next sunrise. But know that I love you more than life itself, and that I'm prouder of you than you can possibly imagine."

Chapter Thirty-Eight

Father loved me, I knew that well enough. In fact, it was one of the few unshakeable truths of my universe. Just as I loved him. And yet, right then I didn't want to talk to him anymore. It was just as well that he and my brother had a 'hopper to catch, and that I had other duties.

My five remaining future Skybolt pilots had been a lot more interesting to be around as playful kids than they now were as featureless and immobile metal vessels. During the initial phases of recovery, it was normal procedure for brain-core patients to be kept in an induced coma to promote healing. Once the drugs were stopped, it usually took several more days for normal consciousness to return. That was the worst time, I remembered, when I'd been awake but hadn't yet learned to interpret my new sensory inputs. It had been like floating in an endless, timeless void filled with meaningless snatches of sound and flashes of impossibly-colored lights, all flavored by the taste and smell of chocolate-chip cookies I couldn't quite eat. Eventually the sounds had switched over into voices, and the random lights into a nice, steady camera image. But, in the meantime it was a pretty rough ride. I'd been by to visit my pilots every single morning since their surgery, but now that two of them had woken up I was stopping by in the evenings as well. Their being awake made no difference to the outside world; the only way to tell was by the brain-wave monitors. But it'd been important to me, back when I'd been so lost and alone, to know that my family was by my bedside, so I'd promised my future subordinates that I'd be around, too.

"Come on!" Petty Officer Brooks was whispering to Jimmy Knight's cylinder when I entered the room. "Come on, kiddo! Light that light!"

I smiled; illuminating the signal light was the very first thing a newly-bottled brain-core learned to do directly with his mind. Once he could blink it off and on, limited communication became possible and that made all the difference in the world. "How's he doing?" I asked, startling the counselor badly.

"Oh!" he exclaimed, leaping to his feet. "I didn't hear you come in, Thomas!"

I smiled, gesturing him back to his chair. "I didn't mean to scare you. How's he doing?"

"All the needles are in the green," Brooks answered, gesturing at the display. "He's conscious, but not hooked up yet." He turned and looked at me. "They say that's the worst part."

"It is," I agreed, nodding. "The absolute worst."

Brooks nodded, then scowled and turned back to the metal cylinder that contained his charge. "And there's not a thing I can do to help."

I felt myself smile at the sight of the muscular, crew-cutted former drill instructor behaving in such a tenderly maternal fashion. Perhaps Commander Knight had known what was best for his boy after all. "It'll happen eventually," I reassured him. "They do that thing with the induced voltages before we're bottled, you know. So that we kind of know what to do."

"Right," Brooks answered, still staring at the cylinder. He frowned. "They're asking so much of you youngsters," he said eventually. "Maybe too damned much."

I frowned, then an idea struck me. "You're a veteran of the Esteppan War, you told me once."

He nodded."Yes, sir."

I gestured at Jimmy's cylinder, then down at my mannequin body. "What do you think of all this?" I asked him. "I mean, this rain-bottling is the very thing that you fought against. What you might have been killed trying to stop. And yet here you are, helping the process along. Doesn't that bother you?"

The petty officer shook his head. "Not really, sir."

I tilted my head to one side. "Why… I mean, how can it *not*?"

Brooks smiled. "I'm in the navy, sir. I go where I'm told, and do what I'm told to do when I get there. Back then, I was a gunner. So, I blew the crap out of whatever I was told to blow the crap out of." He gestured at the gold rings on my sleeves. "Thinking about that kind of thing is for officers, sir."

I grinned; how wonderful it must be to be an enlisted man! "So, you only fight because you're told to fight?"

Brooks's eyes narrowed. "No sir," he said slowly. "I fight because I believe in men like you. Why should I worry myself to death about things like right and wrong, when you do it so much better than I do?" Then he looked back at Jimmy's cylinder. "I also fight for my shipmates, of course. And for freedom."

"Of course," I echoed. Then I looked away. "I've got news for you, Gerald. You're no better at figuring out right and wrong than the rest of us. And certainly, no worse."

"Heh!" he chuckled. "Let me tell you a secret, Thomas. I've always known that, deep down. But I try not to let it worry me. If you try to figure all of the political garbage out, you'll never get anywhere in this universe. No battle fought is ever half as complicated as the peace settlement usually is. Or as scary."

I shook my head. "Maybe I'm just having a bad day, Gerald. But I don't know what's right and wrong anymore." I pointed at Jimmy's tank. "I mean, there's a child inside that thing. A little boy. He's scared and upset and helpless and if he's anything like me, probably trying to cry his eyes out. And we helped do it to him, you and I. Plus, we've already killed another kid. He's *dead*! How can that be right?"

Brooks shrugged. "It's not, of course." Then his eyes met mine. "Would you like me to call Father Murton? I'm sure that he'd be glad to talk this through with you."

"No," I answered instantly, though I didn't know why. "I mean… This time, I'd rather talk to you, if you don't mind."

Brooks smiled and nodded. "Of course."

"Except that I don't quite know what to say," I said after an awkward pause. "I mean, why do we fight wars in the first place, if we *still* haven't settled things after all the killing is done?"

"I haven't a clue," Brooks replied. "But… Look at it this way. Somewhere out there across space, a young Dracan officer is probably asking someone pretty much the exact same question. I mean, they're human too, right? So, they wonder about things just like we do."

"Right," I agreed.

"And when he's done wondering about the right and wrong of his cause," Brooks continued, "he's gonna go to sleep. Tomorrow when he wakes up he'll spend all day learning how best to kill you and me." Brooks smiled. "When the time comes, he'll *do* it if you give him half a chance. And you'll be just as dead as if your executioner had never asked himself questions about the rightness or wrongness of things. At a certain point you just have to accept that the universe is the way that it is, and sink everything you have into trying to figure out how to waste that other poor son of a bitch before he does the same to you, and maybe everything and everyone you love and care about along with you." He shrugged. "Warriors can't afford to ask themselves the big questions, Thomas. Too many doubts aren't healthy. Sometimes you just have to shoot first and not ask any questions at all, ever. We're all cogs in a much larger machine. It's as simple as that. Even our so-called leaders spin in place with the rest of us, slaves to forces we barely even comprehend. We can't help it if the machines are essentially blind and brainless."

I nodded, then looked down at the floor. Maybe Brooks was right, maybe he was wrong. How could I ever be sure? For that matter, how could I ever be sure of anything at all?

Brooks placed his hand on my right shoulder. "It's all terribly complicated, Thomas. So complicated that no man can ever grasp the truth of it Me, I do what feels right, and what feels right is serving in the navy. What feels right for you, only you can say."

I sighed again, then raised my head and smiled. "Thank you."

"You're quite welcome, sir," Brooks replied, grinning. "Your concerns reflect well upon you." Then he looked away. "It looks to me like I'm going to have an all-nighter here, Thomas. Why don't you go and turn in early? A man needs a little rest, after a talk like we've just had."

Chapter Thirty-Nine

I did manage to sleep an extra couple of hours that night, and it felt good indeed. It was also probably the best investment I could possibly have made, for the next week and a half was my most hectic yet. There were classes to go to, meetings to attend, and war bonds to sell. Any one of these three would have been a full-time job for anyone else; as things were, Admiral Vlaslov finally gave in and appointed a petty officer to serve as my full-time personal secretary, aide, and scheduler. "It's the only way that I know I'll be able to reach you when I need you, Thomas," he explained as he introduced me to Peter Bosche, a naval reservist. Peter had been the private secretary of a major Earthside movie star, until she'd committed suicide. I rather hoped she hadn't been driven to it by poor scheduling.

Though Peter did his best, there were still only twenty-seven hours in any given Esteppan day. I had so many obligations it wasn't even funny; selling bonds, planning tactics, selling bonds, visiting my future squadronmates and monitoring their recoveries, selling bonds, establishing a working relationship with Colonel Rotte, who it now appeared certain would command the Stormcrow squadron, selling bonds, attending classes I just *had* to take, selling bonds...

Did I mention that I was still selling a lot of bonds?

One morning I was walking across the weather deck of *The Glorious First of June* on my way to the "bond 'hopper'", as everyone was beginning to call it, when suddenly a large ship became visible in the sky. I paused and looked up. "What's that?" I asked Commander Knight, who was accompanying me in his capacity as a fellow-hero so that we could continue our discussions en-route.

"I don't know," my friend replied nervously. Then he realized that whatever it was, it must be friendly or else the navy would be doing something about it. "We're ahead of schedule," he suggested. "Let's watch her come in."

And come in she did. The vessel was a light carrier, we realized in a moment or two, with lines very similar to those of *June* herself. She splashed down not a thousand yards away from us, the ripples bobbing us up and down like a cork in the normally placid waters of Lokiskur Fjord. "She's the *Skagerrak*," Ted finally said after shading his eyes so that he could read the name on her hull. "Brand new, produced locally. Not quite a sister-ship, but damn close."

My fake eyebrows rose. "I didn't know we were building any warships here."

"Oh, yes!" Ted answered. "Not nearly as many as we could on Earth, but some. We need all the help we can get."

I nodded. So far the only reinforcements we'd received were two *Chief*-class destroyers that'd been built and crewed on New Zion, and a smattering of elderly light cruisers and destroyers that'd been on patrol away from Earth when the final attack had taken place. Certainly, the *Skaggerak* was welcome. "And look!" I answered, pointing upwards. "Here comes another!"

We stood and watched the second ship come in as well, though we could in all honesty no longer claim to be ahead of schedule. It was smaller than *Skaggerak*, leaner and tougher-looking. "Another *Doolittle*!" I cried out, beating Ted to the punch. "Now we have three. *That's* good news!"

"It certainly is," Ted agreed, smiling as best he could. "Those are the meanest little ships I've ever seen."

Sure enough, the new *Doolittle*-class vessel landed just ahead of the *Skaggerak*, once again bouncing us up and down like a toy in a bathtub. "Heh!" Ted chuckled, reading the vessel's name with shaded eyes again. "Not quite a *Doolittle*-class vessel after all. She's a modified and improved version, also built locally. Care to guess what she's called?"

I titled my head to one side. "Well… The *Doolittle*s are named after aviation pioneers. And this is Esteppe; it's traditional to try and give ships names relevant to the culture of the planet they're built on, when you can follow the class-theme as well.…" I frowned. "But, I guess I don't know that much about the early days of flight. So, I give up. What's she called?"

Ted's half-grin widened. "The *Graf Zeppelin*," he answered. "Don't be ashamed, Thomas. As obvious as it is once you've heard it, I wouldn't have gotten it either."

"Ha!" I laughed aloud as the fleet blew their sirens to welcome the newcomers, and curious sailors lined our rails.

"Look at those guns!" one petty officer declared, pointing at the *Zeppelin*'s turrets. They carried triple mounts instead of the usual twins. "Jesus Christ! I'd hate to be downrange of *those* things!"

"They're Esteppan-made," an ensign explained. "A design the navy's been considering for years but only just adopted. They're each a little lighter than *Doolittle*'s guns, but the rate of fire is something to behold."

Ted gave a low whistle, and I nodded in sympathy. We'd both seen *Doolittle* fire her guns in anger; it was difficult to imagine anything beyond that experience.

"Well," Ted said eventually, clapping me on the shoulder. "Someone's got to pay for those bad boys, I suppose. So, it's back to the salt mines for you and me."

Chapter Forty

Either selling bonds was getting easier with practice, or else I was developing psychological calluses in all the right places. Instead of dragging on forever and ever, like it used to, the three-hour hard-sell session seemed almost to end before it had really begun. Indeed, I was a little upset to realize, as Ted and I trudged across the snow towards the bond 'hopper, that I could barely recall giving my speech. I'd repeated the spiel so many times that the Rotary Club sort of blended in with the Chamber of Commerce, which also reminded me very much of the Citizens Club of New Hamburg. I was still trying to decide if I should feel guilty or not when Sergeant M'Bengi, the Marine bodyguard left behind to watch the 'hopper, stuck his head of the hatch. "Commander Knight!" he cried out. "Commander Longo!"

"What?" Ted replied for us both.

"A message has come in for you both," M'Bengi yelled. "We're not going directly back to *June*. Instead, Commander Longo finally has a working Skybolt to fly! And I can't wait to watch him take off!"

Sure enough, the prototype Skybolt that I'd flown back on Earth was sitting out on the tarmac when we arrived at the Stormcrow plant, and most of the staff was standing around it bundled up in overcoats, waiting for me to arrive. It was easy to see who the regulars were and who was just there to gawk. The kibitzers wore rad-suits; the real workers were protected only by proud smiles and a defiant attitude.

Father himself was waiting to greet us when Commander Knight swung our hatch open and trotted down the ramp. "We weren't expecting this to be such a big deal," he said as Father smiled and pumped his hand.

"Our polymill's faulted out again," Father explained. "So for the next hour or so there's not much for the staff to do inside." He smiled. "Besides, they deserve to see." He smiled up at me as I negotiated my slow, painful way down the ramp, then gave me quick hug. "It's been too long, Thomas," he observed. "Sven also sends his love."

I smiled back. "I miss you both."

Then Father was all business again. "The prototype is ready for you, Thomas. It checks out a hundred percent. We don't have a specific test regimen for you today. Mostly we just want you to take her up for a little joyride, to help you sharpen yourself back up again." His features grew serious. "It's been a long while, Thomas."

I nodded. "Yes, it has. Though I've been hitting the simulator almost every day."

"Of course," Father agreed. "But that's hardly the same thing, as we're both well aware." He grinned. "The men have worked hard, Thomas. Very hard indeed. If you could spare them a few words…"

"Right," I agreed. I'd liked the Stormcrow workers from the minute I'd met them; it'd be a pleasure to shake a few hands.

"Excellent!" my father replied. "And… I have more news!" He turned towards the east and shaded his eyes. "Any second now…"

Ted stiffened. "No!" he said. "Don't tell me that you've already—"

But, sure enough, Ted's words were cut off by the roar of a soot-black fighter soaring by overhead, unmuffled military antigravs screaming as it waggled its wings at us. Before we could grasp quite what it was we'd seen, the ghost from the not-so-distant past was gone. "A Stormcrow!" I whispered. "You've got a Stormcrow flying already, too!"

"No," he answered, gesturing at his staff. "*They* have a Stormcrow flying already. They're miracle-workers, all of them." He turned to Ted. "By the way, we're going to be sticking with our original estimate. We feel that a half-dozen Stormcrows will be the optimal solution. Any more, and we'd be trading first-generation Stormcrows for state-of-the-art Skybolts." He shrugged. "We only completed thirty Stormcrows during the entire war, you know. Producing *either* of these aircraft is a major industrial effort. It's a miracle that we still have enough parts to complete six 'crows, but we do. Counting the birds we're robbing out of the museums, of course."

Ted nodded. "And, conveniently, we have six Stormcrow-configured pilots. It works for me." He looked sidelong at Father. "How's it feel to be jacking-in again?"

"Absolutely divine," he replied, face suddenly dead-serious. "It is like living again, after being dead for more than a decade. As Thomas observed the other night, there's no words to explain it."

"Right," Ted agreed. Then he shook his head and changed the

subject. "Was that the great Colonel Rotte who just flew over? Back when I was in flight training, my instructor used to use him as a bogeyman. 'If you'd made that mistake in the presence of Colonel Rotte, young man,' he used to say, 'he'd have splashed one more Polecat'." Ted shook his head. "I'm a little in awe of him, I'm afraid."

"Ja," Father agreed. "That's him. He'd hardly allow himself to be second to fly. If you knew him, you'd understand."

"He's a fighter-jock," Ted answered with a shrug. "We're all alike. Hell, I'd be doing exactly the same, in his shoes." His eyes narrowed again. "Is he still sharp?"

"Emil was a little awkward on takeoff," Father allowed. "But, after all, it'd been a decade since he'd flown. He didn't even have access to a simulator for all those years. Plus, the 'hopper he's flying is of a later mark than his old fighter. All of these things considered, he's doing quite well." Then Father turned back to me. "Come, Thomas! The men are waiting. Let's get you hooked up, and then you can judge Rotte's skills for yourself."

Chapter Forty-One

Takeoff wasn't something that happened quickly with a Skybolt; indeed, quick-reaction time was the one important performance parameter where the Polecat outshone its replacement. This takeoff was even more delayed than usual because I had to do my walkaround surrounded by a gaggle of Longo technicians, many of whom were still working on the Stormcrow line and thus had never seen a Skybolt before.

It was also extra-hard because the Longo workers had thoughtfully painted the nose of my machine bright red, the mark of a Brother of the Order of Blood. I'd agreed to wear my medal, yes, out of respect for the people of Esteppe who'd bestowed it upon me. There were even good, sound tactical reasons for an ace to have his fighter painted up in an easily-recognizable fashion; historically, a handful of high-scoring aces tended to shoot down far more enemy aircraft and do far more damage in other ways than all the far more numerous low-scorers combined. Ever since the Red Baron had painted his Fokker scarlet-red, high-scoring aces had been quite deliberately striking terror into the souls of the merely mediocre. During the Esteppan war, entire Polecat squadrons had been known to turn and flee from a pair of red-nosed Stormcrows.

But… It was *wrong* for my aircraft to carry a special paint-job, just because I'd shot down five Dracan aerospacecraft and a few other ships! Even worse, it wasn't the navy way. But there were the Longo workers, smiling and beaming in pride at their handiwork as they stood and slowly died of radiation poisoning so that we could win our future battles. What could I do, except grit my teeth and fly? Damnit, red didn't even *look good* on the nose of a sky-blue Skybolt, the way it did against the soot-black of a Stormcrow! And, when I looked closer, sure enough some overzealous artist had hand-painted little representations of each craft I'd downed in a neat row just above where my brain-capsule mated up to the fuselage. *Gaah!*

If selling bonds had taught me anything, it was how to keep right on smiling and shaking hands even when I was miserable. I made it a point to greet each Longo worker personally, and to especially thank the man who still had red paint on his hands from the hurry-up job he'd just completed in my honor. Then, I let the clumsy and unpracticed navy ground crew mount me into my alternate body.

It was always good to be a Skybolt, and never better than when I'd not had the opportunity to fly for a very long time. Once the checklist was complete I taxied a little way out onto the snow-covered tarmac, then goosed my throttles just a wee bit. And just that easily, I was aloft and underway.

Flying a Skybolt was so easy that most of my training-time had been spent learning the rules of the airways and correct radio-procedure. A Skybolt could sustain twenty-five gees of thrust when anywhere near a planet-sized mass, and twice that for brief periods. With such power on hand it was virtually impossible to make an unrecoverable mistake at the controls. Short of either plowing into the ground or building up such a vector that one ended up too far from a mass to maneuver, what could go wrong? There were no stalls to worry about as in early aircraft, any turbulence short of a once-in-a-century tornado was virtually unnoticeable, and the airframe was so stout that one had to work at breaking it "Go there!" I thought, and the Skybolt did it. No weapon of war in all of history had ever been so simple to operate.

So I felt pretty good as I went zipping across the featureless tundra, flying so low that when I looked through my rear-facing camera I could see the swirls of snow kicked up by my turbulence. I'd take it easy for a while, I decided, and get used to my fighting body again. Then—

"Horrido!" a harsh voice suddenly cried out directly into my inner ears. Then a soot-black 'hopper went hurtling by in a blur, rocking its wings in triumph. "Horrido!"

A sudden chill passed through me; "Horrido!" was the Esteppan aerial victory cry, the equivalent of the navy's less demonstrative "Splash one!" Even worse, Colonel Rotte sounded in real life exactly like the sound-track of his avatar in the "Invasion: Esteppe!" video game; I hadn't realized that they'd used an actual recording. I activated my intercom circuit, then counted to ten before speaking. "You're not going to count *that* one, are you?" I asked. "I mean, we weren't even dogfighting that I knew of."

"Ha!" Rotte countered, spinning his fighter in glee. "Perhaps you're right, Thomas; that was indeed a foul blow. But…" He stopped his spin, then reversed it. "I'm *free*! For the first time in over a decade, I'm free!"

I'd have smiled, if I hadn't been a skyhopper. I knew just how he felt. "It's good to be flying again," I agreed. "I can't imagine what it would be like to be grounded so long."

"It was a living hell," Rotte replied, stopping his spinning and forming up on my left wingtip. He seemed very close, so I eased away a little. Then the colonel spoke again. "I just realized something," he said. "You've never flown formation before, have you?"

"Nope," I answered, putting a little more distance between our 'hoppers. "Except with a camera 'hopper for publicity photos. After all, so fr there's never been more than one Skybolt in the universe at any given time."

"Hmm," Rotte answered. "Well, it's hardly your fault then." He paused. "I've long wondered what you do and don't know, Thomas. You're plenty brave, I acknowledge that. But there's so much more!"

I sighed to myself, then keyed my microphone. "I've studied as hard as I know how. I've been listening to and learning from all the pilots I've had the chance to."

"But not from me," Rotte pointed out. "So, let us begin your first *real* lesson. Which is that what appear safest is often the most dangerous thing of all." He waggled his wings once, somehow, I understood that this represented a smile. "Formation flying is an essential skill, Thomas, one that you should've mastered long since had there been any other aerospacecraft of comparable performance for you to work with. It's essential because, when attacking a target like a missile base or enemy ship, it's necessary to concentrate one's forces against a single point. An uncoordinated attacking group stands a good chance of colliding with itself once the shooting starts. And in fighter-versus-fighter combat we pilots have to systematically cover each other. The formation is the key to mutual defense."

I keyed my mike twice in silent acknowledgement; this was kindergarten stuff and Rotte had to know that I'd at least read about it. Even if I had no hands-on experience.

"So, Thomas," he continued, edging in closer. "Which do you think is safer? An open formation, or an extremely tight one."

"Open," I replied. "So everyone doesn't have to concentrate so much on not running into each other."

"Wrong!" the colonel replied, bouncing his Sotrmcrow up and down in emphatic little bursts. "The closer together you are, the safer you are. If your wings are almost touching, a little bump won't do any real damage; there won't be any momentum behind the impact. But, if there's a little distance between the wings, then there's space for the energies to build up." There was a little pause. "If you look closely at the archive photos, you'll see that the older Stormcrows had little dents all over their wings. They came from flying close formation."

I gulped. This *was* something new. And it made perfect sense as well. "All right," I responded eventually. "You want me to try and get closer?"

"No," Rotte answered. "Let me close on you. Flying lead is always easiest." He began easing in slowly, talking all the while. "The lead pilot is responsible for safety and navigation," he explained. "That's you, and I'm trusting you utterly. You can always tell a good wingman by what happens when the leader the leader flies into a mountain. If the wingman crashes right beside him, not having broken concentration for an instant, then he was a good one."

I worked harder at flying straight and level than I ever had before, trying not to notice the Stormcrow looming ever-closer alongside me. It was a lot more difficult than I'd imagined. "You can't possibly fly combat like this," I said eventually. "Neither of us are even looking for the enemy. We couldn't if we tried."

"Of course not," Rotte replied easily, his wingtip now overlapping mine by about six inches, and separated vertically by perhaps the same distance. "In combat, our formations will be much looser. But as I said, closest is safest. This is particularly true for learning. So, we'll master ultra-close formation first, then gradually open things up." He paused. "Now, if we *were* in combat and a Dracan suddenly appeared, what would happen?"

"We'd collide," I answered, not really having though about it. Rotte was down to maybe four inches, now.

"Correct!" the colonel replied, his voice registering approval. "Because we have no pre-existing plan as to what to do, nor have we practiced it over and over again until it becomes second nature." Rotte was within two inches now; involuntarily I flinched a little, and our wingtips bumped. But... The veteran was right! Nothing happened except for a little tap; we were too close to damage each other significantly. "Careful now," Rotte said, his voice as soothing as he could manage. He backed away a little. "You're really doing quite well, you know."

"Maybe," I acknowledged. "But I obviously still have a lot to learn."

"Ha!" Rotte answered. "Don't we all?" There was a short pause. "Let me show you something, Thomas. Don't do anything sudden, all right? Just fly straight and level."

I clicked my mike twice again, then Rotte's Stromcrow blurred as he applied a huge vector. Quite suddenly, he was four inches from my *right* wingtip. "Don't try that one anytime soon, Thomas," he urged me. "It's an advanced lesson. But not as hard as it looks."

It *couldn't* be as hard as it looked, I decided. Because it looked *impossible*, and yet I'd just seen it done. 'Wow," I said at last. "That was impressive."

"Thank you," Rotte replied smugly."It was an illegal maneuver, back when we were the Butcher-Bird squadron. Too risky."

My jaw would've dropped, if I'd had one just then. "Colonel," I said. "If it's too risky…"

"Ha!" Rotte replied, the single syllable somehow communicating both disdain and arrogance. "And 'Ha!' again! What do those idiot groundlings know?"

I didn't really know what to say to that, so I concentrated on flying straight and level instead. I didn't want Rotte to dent my wing again.

"Thomas," the colonel continued after a little while. "You *do* have a lot to learn. For example, you probably already know that turning away from an enemy, particularly a determined and skilled enemy, is the worst mistake you can possible make."

"Right," I agreed. That was tactics one-oh-one. "Everyone knows that."

"Of course everyone *knows* it," Rotte replied. "But how many can *do* it?" Suddenly his fighter blurred and vanished. "There are certain eternal truths about wars and warriors, Thomas. So long as Man is Man, they'll hold without exception. Let's give you a chance to learn a little something about yourself." There was a long silence, then Rotte spoke again. "So far, Thomas, according to the tapes I've seen you haven't had to deal with any kind of aggressive, coordinated fighter opposition; the Bananas took care of that for you, while in turn you took care of the Dracan heavies for them. And you did well. Don't get me wrong; you earned your Order of Blood, and there's no higher award. But still, you've never faced down a determined enemy in another fighter. Man to man."

"That's true," I acknowledged.

"Good," Rotte replied. "*Very* good." There was another long pause, during which I checked every camera I carried, and found nothing. Where had Rotte *gone*, anyway? I suddenly missed my pipper, which hadn't been installed on what was supposed to be a mere joyride. Then the colonel spoke again. "Now, Thomas. I'm a Dracan. What do you do now?"

If Rotte was a Dracan, I thought to myself, he was an invisible one. I looked everywhere; up, down, sideways…

…until I finally picked up his scarlet nose, pointed directly at me and closing like an express train.

"*Shit!*" I exclaimed, unfortunately over a live circuit.

"Ha!" Rotte replied. "Scared, are you?"

There wasn't time to think, not really. My mind *screamed* for me to turn away, *demanded* that I break right, left, up, down; *any* which way! The red nose grew and grew and grew, and the heart I didn't have any more grew icier and icier…

…until I realized that if I *did* flinch, as likely as not I'd break the same way as the colonel and all that'd remain of either of us would be a little cloud of smoke. There wasn't anything I could do; I was helpless!

Suddenly alarms were ringing and red lights were flashing in my non-eyes. "Collision imminent!" my automated assistant Otto sang out. "Collision imminent! Collision imminent!"

Lack of body be damned; an iron band was tightening around my lungs, and my heart was racing away at triphammer speed; thudthudthudthud! My non-palm itched and sweated all at once as it gripped the joystick that didn't actually exist and *demanded* that I do something, *anything* to escape the impending catastrophe.

But, if I did, that'd be even *more* likely to kill me!

Then Rotte passed in a blur of black; he missed me by inches, pulling up at the last possible nanosecond. "Oh ho! So you *do* have the soul of an ace, young Thomas! I salute you! Welcome you to the club!"

"You *bastard*!" I screamed into my intercom; my whole being was charged with adrenaline, and it showed. "You lunatic *bastard*! Are you out of your godamned mind? You could've killed us both!"

"So?" Rotte replied. "Everyone dies. Today is as good as a day as any." He waggled his wings. "I'm running low on charge, Thomas. Time for me to head back to base. I'm afraid a Stormcrow doesn't have quite the legs of your Skybolt, and I was in the air for quite some time before you took off." Then his aircraft blurred again and was gone.

"You asshole!" I screamed, this time with the intercom carefully turned off. "You incredible piece of…"

Then, with the adrenaline and other fear-juices finally burned off, I was laughing my ass off. Rotte was right to test me, of course. Our lives were going to depend on each other; fighter pilots had to know up front if there were any weaklings among the squadron. If there was a better way to find out who had enough guts and self-control to cut the mustard, I couldn't think of it.

Then, my laughter ceased. For it was abundantly clear already that there was nothing funny about what was going to happen to those Dracans unlucky enough to find themselves flying against Rotte and his pitiless Butcher Birds.

Nothing funny at all.

Chapter Forty-Two

I made only one more flight from the little factory runway, then my base was moved to the Courland Heights airfield just outside Esteppe City. During the recent war, Courland Heights was the primary operational center for the Stormcrow unit; conveniently, all of the hardstands and such fit the Skybolt like a glove. At first the navy types didn't seem to want to associate with the natives, but I put a stop to that by, in full uniform, spending most of an afternoon showing the locals my Skybolt and explaining to them what all the upcoming noise was going to be about. They were very understanding and supportive; many brought fruit baskets and such that went a long way to smoothing things over. I also joined in with the locals singing an old Esteppan hiking song, reminding both them and the navy types of exactly where I'd been born. I was rather proud of myself for thinking of that one. It seemed to help a lot in bringing everyone together.

Rotte's Stormcrow arrived the day after my Skybolt did; from that point onward we flew together every moment we possibly could. This wasn't a matter of friendship or even of camaraderie; frankly, I could barely stand the egotistical bastard. He was, however, almost certainly the universe's leading combat pilot. Despite his repulsive personality he was also an outstanding instructor, if a bit crude in his methods and mannerisms.

Within two days we had the formation-thing all worked out, and before another week passed we were flying perfect scissors-like Thach-weaves, the best known defense against the super-high-performance fighters the Dracans didn't even have yet. We broke right and broke left in perfect unthinking symmetry, and screamed full-throttle down narrow alpine passes, vectoring our thrust like madmen and triggering large-scale avalanches with the fury of our passage. We shot up target panels together, too. I thought I was a pretty fair shot until Rotte's tiny spreads made mine look like shotgun patterns. We flew and flew and flew, and I learned and learned and learned. Both Ted and Father Murton worried about me spending so much time with Rotte, even though I assured them that I didn't like him at all. But I *did* admire him as a pilot, I admitted when pressed. And perhaps as a warrior as well. Which worried them all the more, though there wasn't a thing they could do about it.

Then another Stormcrow arrived. It was piloted by Gustav Schwartz, of a mere fifty-eight kills. He'd have had many more, Rotte assured me, except that he'd sacrificed his own score in order to serve as the colonel's perfect combat partner in the sky. Then a third 'crow arrived, with Stanislaw Davinsky at the controls. He was the only other living pilot besides me to ever have killed a dreadnought with torpedoes; during the final invasion of Esteppe he'd blown up the *Mikawa*. He was a lot nicer than the other two Butcher Birds, and sometimes when no else was around we talked about skimmer racing and video games.

Then the score began to even up. Jimmy Knight arrived in his brand-new Skybolt; he and I stayed up well past midnight playing video games and catching up with each other. Because we were in such a hurry my pilots had to virtually live in their simulators. As a result, they were far more comfortable and capable as Skybolts than they were in their mannequin bodies. It broke my heart to see Jimmy stagger down the barracks hallway gripping the rail like a quavery old man, barely able to wobble into his room. But we had a deadline to meet, and what had to be done had to be done. At least his hands still worked well; we set another new record at *Rocket Sledder*.

And, speaking of hands, Jimmy's Skybolt carried a gift for me. The Stormcrow workers had pitched in together during their spare time and made me a new right arm. It was downright heavenly to be fully-functional again; after talking it over for a long time with Father Murton I send them an autographed poster-sized blowup of my final attack on the *Imperial Throne*. I didn't do that kind of thing very often; in fact, I'd turned down every autograph request I'd ever received, and so far as I knew the poster was one-of-a-kind as well. But, there wasn't anything else I could think of that the people there would like half as well. And, how could I deny them? The worker who'd been first to start having nosebleeds had developed full-scale radiation sickness, and despite the fact that the navy provided the best available drugs and doctors his prognosis wasn't good. Apparently he was unusually rad-sensitive, but if the others had quit no one would've blamed them for an instant.

They didn't, however, which was just as well for Vlasilov and his plans. It was easy to forget while soaring high and free above beautiful

Esteppe that Earth was in mortal danger. There was almost nothing about the siege in the news, but that was now censored. Instead I judged the Dracan's progress by the depth of the lines in the admiral's face. As near as I could tell, things weren't looking good at all. "You have six weeks, Thomas," he told me in an elevator on the day that Jimmy arrived. "At that time we shall raise the fleet and go into battle, with however many pilots may or may not be ready. If we put it off any longer, we might as well not space at all."

Chapter Forty-Three

Six weeks wasn't long enough, not by half. Even though everyone flew every day that their bird was airworthy, there was far too much for rank beginners to learn and master in such a short space of time. Even some of the Butcher Birds needed longer; not all of them were as quick to find their legs as Rotte. Of course, the situation with my new pilots was a thousand times worse. The colonel was in overall charge of training, though he hissed and spat whenever the subject came up. "It took me a *year* to learn to fly combat!" he'd complain. "How can anyone expect me to do anything with these apple-cheeked children in such a tiny fraction of that time? What kind of miracle-worker do you lunatics think I am?"

A pretty good one, apparently. We were three days from the admiral's deadline, and Rotte had done an amazingly good job with the time available. He felt that Jimmy had nearly unlimited potential, and thought very highly of Delana as well. "Esteppe failed to make use of female pilots," his fitness report on her read. "In this, I can see now that we were severely mistaken." He also was pleased with Viktor Oudh. "Given a few months," Rotte claimed, "I could make a combat pilot of him." But the colonel didn't seem to think much of Li Han and Liu Ming. "They're rank beginners, both of them," the Esteppan ace declared. "They were the last to receive their Skybolts, and it shows. Both of these pilots are gravely deficient in all areas of training, and are progressing relatively slowly. I won't be held responsible for either their lives or those of their squadronmates if they're exposed to combat at their current states of development."

Ted whistled a single low note when I handed him Rotte's report on Li and Liu. "Well," he said slowly. "Our Esteppan friend certainly doesn't mince words. That's about as emphatically-negative a downcheck as I've ever seen from an instructor-pilot in my life."

I shook my head. "It's not their fault. Even the colonel understands and accepts that. They just need more time, is all."

Ted frowned. "But there just plain *isn't* any more time, Thomas." He looked up from his datapad. "Have you flown with either of them?"

"No," I answered, not having to explain why. I hardly had ten minutes in a day to call my own any more. Father Murton was complaining, but for once wasn't getting much sympathy. I had a job to do, and that was that.

Ted shook his head again. "We *need* them," he said eventually. "If we didn't, I'd be all on Rotte's side. We can give them the easiest combat assignments, perform training underway…"

I shook my head. "We're going to be attacking the main Dracan fleet. Tell me where you're going to find an easy assignment in *that*." Then I looked away. "You're right, of course."

"Yeah," Ted answered, leaning back in his swivel chair. "But Rotte's righter than either of us, I'd bet my pension." Then he sat back up erect again. "Tell you what," he suggested eventually. "You're a few training-hours short yourself this week, and Li and Liu are scheduled for advanced formation-flying with Rotte this afternoon after the squadron meeting. How about you go out yourself and look in on them? Maybe you'll come up with a good idea or two on what to do with the time we have left." He shrugged. "Rotte's done well for us so far; I've got no complaints. But, maybe these two you ought to train yourself? He thinks you're up to it."

I looked down at my shoes. Rotte's report on me said that I was an outstanding natural dogfighter, and the only true killer of men among the "new kids", as the Butcher Birds referred to us youngsters. "He needs more practice with his weapon," Rotte had claimed. "But then, so do I. One can *never* be proficient enough. What's far more important is that Thomas is gifted with aggressiveness, clear-headedness, tenacity, and the moral courage so necessary to kill other gifted, well-trained men day after day in battle. He's the only one among my new students whom I would today allow to fly with the Butcher Birds, and I believe he'd give a better account of himself than some of my old comrades, toughened veterans and close friends though they may be. His skills will continue to develop until he's killed or otherwise removed from flying duties; this is the natural course of things for one with so much potential. What's far more important is that he understands the true face of war, a rare gift indeed in someone with so little battle experience."

Of course, to be fair he'd written these words the day after he and I spent an entire afternoon in a series of wild one-on-one simulated dogfights, during which he'd shot me down twice and I'd returned the favor once, making use of a convenient railroad tunnel and one of Lofton Knight's better tactical concepts to help me out along the way. More importantly, however, the colonel hadn't once been able to bomb the target I was defending; it'd taken everything he had just to stay alive in the same airspace with me. In the larger sense I'd won the battle and we both knew it. My fighter out-performed his, which was a partial explanation for my success. But it was only a partial one, given that defense was always so much more difficult than offense. I allowed myself a small smile. My beating him had served the bastard right after the way he'd played chicken with me. Who did Rotte think I was, anyway? Just some dumb kid, to be intimidated so easily? "All right," I agreed. After all, it didn't take much persuading these days to get me in the air, or at least not when the alternative was office drudgery and more meetings. "I'll give them a little time to get started, then head out after them."

Chapter Forty-Four

Our noon squadron meeting was rapidly becoming a daily affair. Training flights tended to be about four hours in length; anything longer resulted in fatigue and too many mistakes. So we tended to have a morning sortie, meet at noon for an informal discussion of what we had and hadn't learned, then go out for more lessons in the afternoon. Generally speaking we "new kids" were left to ourselves during these meetings; that way, if a spitball barrage seemed to be in order there was nothing to keep us from firing away. It helped us relax, and we *needed* to relax, or so our counselors kept telling us. Sometimes Ted sat in, but that was okay since he was almost as hardcore a spitballer as the rest of us; we liked him a lot.

Therefore, we were surprised to see Admiral Vlasilov waiting for us in the ready room, hands clasped behind his back as he admired the *Rocket Sledder* poster that the Action Game Company had sent Jimmy and I in recognition of our recent high scores; we hadn't gotten the best ever, sadly. But we'd rated within the top one-hundred, which was good enough for an award. The whole ready room was decorated with video-game posters nowadays; instead of being dull beige, our walls were now riots of unusual shapes and colors. The counselors delighted in finding us new game posters, once they discovered that we prized them; all of our favorites were represented. But the *Rocket Sledder* one was still the best. Or, at least, Jimmy and I sure thought so!

"Good afternoon, Admiral," I greeted my superior officer as I entered the room. Vlaslov had already barred saluting there for the duration. "What brings you hereabouts?"

He turned around and smiled, the deep lines in his face almost disappearing. "A matter of immense military importance, Thomas," he explained. "Something so critical that the navy would never forgive me if I didn't attend to it personally."

The rest began arriving then; Viktor and Jimmy leaned on each other as they unsteadily tottered in; our pilots were still spending so much time flying that they hadn't mastered their mannequin-bodies. Liu and Li leaned on each other as well, placing their feet with exaggerated care as they staggered their way across to their usual seats near the back of the room. Only Delana could move halfway normally, though even she didn't look as if she'd be dancing again anytime soon. I felt a little stab of pain at that; the universe was a sadder place without Delana dancing in it. I could only hope that she'd be back on her toes again soon, and that I'd live long enough to watch her greet the dawn again.

"Thomas," she greeted me with a coy little grin, her camera-eyes somehow as bright and full of life as her natural ones had once been. "How are you this fine day?"

I felt myself smile back. It was impossible not to smile when Delana was speaking to me. "Pretty well," I acknowledged as Ted closed the door behind her. Then the moment was past and it was time for business. I nodded to Vlasilov. "Admiral? You wanted to talk to us?"

"Da," he agreed, smiling at Delana as well. She affected lots of people that way, I suddenly realized. Then the admiral strode to the front of the room. "As I just explained, I must deal with a matter of vital military importance today. With Commander Knight's able assistance, of course. And, I hope, Thomas's." With that, he gestured for us to come up in front and stand beside him.

"What?" I asked. "I mean…"

"Come on," Knight urged, pointing to a spot next to him. "You're keeping an admiral waiting."

I shook my head, wondering what key briefing I'd missed, then stood in the spot he indicated.

"A navy is composed of more than people and ships," Vlasilov began. "It's also built of ideas and traditions. 'England expects every man to do his duty,' a famous admiral once signaled his outnumbered squadron as they ran downwind towards the muzzles of thousands of grimly waiting cannon. Nelson would've become a legend regardless, but his most famous signal and the attitude behind it has shaped the soul of every admiral since. 'We have not yet *begun* to fight!' another naval hero once declared when asked to surrender his crippled vessel; he then proceeded to turn the battle around and defeat his more powerful enemy despite the heaviest imaginable odds." Vlasilov looked each of my pilots solemnly in the eyes. "Ships have souls, units have histories, and navies have traditions. It's the way of things when men go to battle in dangerous places, trusting their lives to their vessels and to each other."

Then Commander Knight spoke up. "Squadrons have traditions, too." He indicated the garish artwork on the ready room walls. "You've started well; I don't doubt that a hundred years from now, some of these same posters will still be hanging on whatever passes for a pilot's lounge in that time and place. They'll be considered treasures beyond price."

Vlasilov took over again. "You have the right to begin new traditions like these posters," he continued. "Indeed, you almost have a duty. However…" Vlasilov frowned. "The larger traditions of the fleet must also be considered. In your case, one of these traditions is being imposed upon you, for the good of the service as a whole."

"Therefore," Knight said, suddenly grinning, "it is both my duty and my honor as a member in good standing of the Top Banana squadron to induct all of you into the Sacred Order of the Banana!" Suddenly both he and Vlasilov pulled chunks of banana of their pockets and began slinging them at the other pilots.

"I'm throwing for Captain Knight," Vlasilov explained, grinning like a boy as he pelted the flinching mannequin-bodies. "Not being a Banana myself, I'd otherwise not be entitled. He delegated me this vital task before we left Earth."

Finally all the banana-munitions were expended, and Delana was unsuccessfully attempting to comb mashed fruit out of her hair. Everyone else was giggling and smiling, including me. "Your drinks are free from here on in," Jimmy explained, practically glowing with pride. "Once you're old enough to order them, that is."

"You're all Bananas," Ted repeated, handing out insignia to everyone but making sure that his younger brother was served first. No one seemed to mind. Then Vlasilov was pressing something into my hand, as well. "Congratulations, Thomas," he said. "I 'm pleased to see these go to you. And to Ted as well. Under the circumstances, it's both proper and necessary."

I opened my fingers, and realized I was holding a full commander's insignia. "Sir!" I protested. "Please! It was enough of a joke that I was a lieutenant-commander! This is… ridiculous!" I tried to hand the rank-badges back.

"No, Thomas," the admiral replied, shaking his head. "It's not ridiculous at all. The leader of the Top Bananas has *always* been a full commander, alone among all squadrons." His eyes narrowed. "It's partly in compensation for the reduced life-expectancy." Then he handed me something else, a pair of Banana-emblems embroidered in metallic-gold instead of yellow. "This is your personal badge. Only the active commander of the Top Bananas is authorized to wear it. May it see you through the perils to come."

Chapter Forty-Five

It took half an hour to mate me up to my Skybolt even now that my ground crew was fully trained, and then another twenty minutes to fly out to the practice range where the rest of my squadron (and, for that matter, most of the Butcher Birds) were training just as hard as they could. With only three days left and one of them scheduled to be taken up carrier-qualifying everyone except me, every minute counted.

The minutes counted for me, too, and I should've been deciding what I most needed practice at as I winged north across the endless steppe that, in combination with a corrupted data transmission, had given my homeworld its name. Should I ask to have a gunnery set up and waiting? Or perhaps I ought to have a dogfight with any of the Butchers who might be willing, once I was done observing Li and Liu? Instead, however, I wasted the time second-guessing the navy. All of we Skybolt pilots were being force-fed books on air combat just as quickly as we could assimilate them. As the unit's commander, however, I was also devouring the standard works on military leadership and discipline. Though hardly any of them seemed to have much relevance to leading a bunch of teenagers into battle, some of the general principles made a lot of sense. I should never expect my men to follow where I wasn't willing to lead, for example. And, when making choices on a battlefield, it was as important to be firm and decisive as it was to be correct. Or perhaps even more so. I'd learned a lot from the leadership books, I admitted to myself.

So why, then, had Admiral Vlasilov and Ted Knight broken one of the cardinal rules this afternoon by rewarding the new Skybolt pilots with an honor they'd done nothing to earn, and which deep down they *knew* they'd done nothing to earn?

I sighed to myself mentally; being a 'hopper at the moment, I could hardly do so for real. Perhaps I was a little over-sensitive, having myself been the victim of far too many rewards for my single combat sortie to date. While I just might barely, by dint of shared risk and reasonable success, be able to claim a sort of honorary membership in the Sacred Order of the Banana, by no means had I earned any of the rest of the honors or rank that had been deluged upon my person. In the same way, my other pilots weren't even *close* to ready to become Top Bananas. Most navy pilots worked like fiends their entire careers in the hope of one day having fruit thrown at them, and the vast majority never succeeded. My pilots weren't even really out of kindergarten-level combat training yet; indeed, the lack of progress on the part of two of them was why I was out flying today instead of selling bonds or filling out the endless forms that my job made me responsible for. There could be no question at all that my pilots weren't ready to be Bananas; the very idea was laughable.

And yet... Ted and Vlasilov had made them exactly that, after planning that stretched at least as far back as our time on Earth. Indeed, Lofton Knight himself was part of the conspiracy. Ted and the admiral were hardly fools, and Lofton was one of those rare and special sorts of leader who transcended description. If *they* thought that it was proper to make me the top banana of the Top Bananas, then they *had* to be right.

But *why*?

Maybe it was for the benefit of the rest of the navy, I reasoned to myself. Maybe the men left sitting and waiting aboard *The Glorious First of June* and the *Skagerrak* would feel better and more secure, knowing that the Top Bananas-- in name at least-- were out fighting for them. Or perhaps the brass though that the 'hopper-wranglers and ground crew would do a better job for the Top Bananas than, say, for the New Kids In Town. Or perhaps it was like painting the nose of my fighter red, to put fear in the bellies of our enemies. It could've been any of these things. But they just didn't feel right; in my heart, I knew that I'd not yet found the true answer.

Li and Liu were practicing formation flying as I approached the exercise area, with Colonel Rotte following them at a discreet interval. I keyed in Rotte's frequency. "...must move as one," he was saying. "As *one*! Not as a pair of goddamned cats running away from a hot bath!"

"Yes, sir," Li replied meekly. He and Liu were both very good indeed at video games, and it went without saying that they'd tested out superbly at everything else or they wouldn't have been chosen for brain-coring. Yet Liu was boyishly shy, and Li even more so. Was this perhaps part of the problem?

"I've fought against the Top Bananas!" Rotte railed. "They waged war like *men*, not ignorant little boys!" He paused a moment, presumably to calm himself. "Now, let's try it again. Li, form up on Liu. When you're ready, break right."

I eased myself in alongside Rotte; by now forming up on him was as easy and as natural as sitting down to dinner with Father and Sven. Sadly the same couldn't be said of my two least-accomplished pilots. Instead they closed up in little fits and starts, clearly still afraid of running into each other.

"You see?" Rotte cried out on our private commander-to-commander channel. "It's goddamned well hopeless, at least in the time we have left. Utterly futile! Surely *you* can see it, Thomas, even if that arrogant fool Vlasilov cannot."

I bounced up and down once in silent acknowledgement, though inwardly I was smiling at the improbability of Rotte calling someone else arrogant.

"Watch!" Rotte continued. "They've left the interval too large. When Li calls for the break, Liu will be totally lost."

Sure enough, when Li called out "Break right!" Liu found himself seemingly alone in an empty sky as Li rocketed off unsupported. "Hopeless!" Rotte repeated on our private line, even as he patiently explained for what must have been the thousandth time what'd gone wrong to the participants. "Form up again," he ordered when finished. "This time, we'll break left."

I nodded to myself; Rotte had reversed the turn so that I could see both students performing; if everything went correctly the hoppers would emerge from the maneuver with Liu flying lead, whereas in a right-break Li should've ended up as the leader. I sighed with impatience as they too-carefully edged into position, Then Liu gave the order. "Break right!"

"Abort!" Rotte and I screamed at once, instantly aware of what was about to happen. But it was already too late; before the counter-order could even form in our minds, Li had begun the *left*-break that he'd been led to expect. It was over in an instant—the Skybolts turned inwards towards each other, there was a flash of light, and then all that was left was a puff of smoke to mark the sight of the first-ever mid-air collision between Skybolts.

"No!" Rotte screamed; he would've been pounding his instrument panel in anguish, had he been capable. "I tried to tell them, Thomas! I *tried*! We pushed them too hard!"

"We did," I agreed, swinging out of formation and racing across the sky in the hope of seeing two parachutes blossom forth. But instead there was none, until after what felt like much too long a time a single blaze-orange canopy popped open. "Oh, god! We've killed one of them!"

It didn't take long for Rotte to get a grip on himself. "Mayday, Mayday, Mayday," he declared on all frequencies, his voice now cold and emotionless. "We have two birds down, due to mid-air collision. I repeat there are two birds down. I confirm this visually."

"Roger that," our air traffic control center responded instantly. "We caught it on the pipper, sir. We've already dispatched a 'hopper and crash-response team to pick up the survivor."

I couldn't close my eyes while I was a Skybolt, but I could shut down all visual feeds for a moment. I did so before speaking again. "*The* survivor?" I asked. "As in one? We've only got a visual on one 'chute, but…"

"Only one survivor, sir," the tower confirmed. "The life-support telemetry is still functional on both victims. I'm very sorry, sir."

"Who?" Rotte demanded, his voice unusually thick. "Who, damnit?"

"Li Han, sir. Li Han is alive. But Liu Ming… Well, sir, according to the data we have here he probably never knew what hit him."

We followed Li's bright orange parachute all theway down; Rotte and I circling it protectively as if a thousand enemies were poised to strike at it given the slightest chance. He landed within a mile of one of the crashed 'bolts, so that the pyre of smoke rising from it would serve as a useful landmark when the pickup 'hopper eventually arrived. Predictably Li went staggering off towards the downed bird once he was free of his 'chute, and I was forced to become very severe indeed in order to prevent him from marching cross-country towards Liu Ming's 'hopper to see if he could help his buddy and wingman. "Shut up and obey orders, Ensign!" I snapped at one point, feeling like a real heel. "Exactly what part of 'Stay put until you're rescued' don't you understand?" Once I even had to hover in front of Li's little tripod and physically hold him back, he was so determined to go on. But there was no way, no way at all, that I was going to allow him to see his best friend's blood-spattered Skybolt laying smashed and broken atop the remains of Liu's shattered braincase. Indeed, I only wished that I could edit the sight from my own memory as well.

Fortunately the crash crew arrived promptly and spirited Li away before undertaking their more gruesome duties. All further training was cancelled for the day; we all flew home slowly and somberly in one big mixed gaggle, Skybolts and Stormcrows alike, with none of the usual radio banter.

I'd already landed and was taxiing towards my hardstand when I finally understood why Vlasilov and the Knights had been so eager to make us Bananas before we'd really earned the honor. Yes, it was for the morale of the fleet and all that other stuff. But the *real* reason was now crystal clear. "I'm so proud, Commander!" poor Liu had told me as our squadron meeting broke up. "I'm one of the very best! I can't *wait* to tell my parents!" Vlasilov and the Knights were wise indeed, and I was deeply grateful for their insight, and even for their mercy.

Due to their consideration and willingness offer recognition before it was truly earned, Liu Ming had been made a Banana while he was still alive to appreciate the fact.

Chapter Forty-Six

The next couple days were pretty rough for us pilots, Bananas and Butcher Birds alike. The navy had a rule that called for an automatic grounding in the event of a training accident, and at first it was rigorously enforced. So instead of getting right back onto the horse that'd thrown us, we spent our last really useful training day sitting around listening to recorded safety lectures given by officers who'd never seen a Skybolt and never even dreamed that they might be addressing the pilot of a Stormcrow. Most of the advice we were force-fed was useless or worse, so much so that I stood up and gave a quick counter-lecture after each required showing. Rotte, I knew, was doing the same with his Butcher Birds. Meanwhile, it was beginning to look like we might lose Li as well.

Despite everything the counselors could do; indeed, despite everything we fellow pilots could do, Li was withdrawing further and further from reality by the hour. A disembodied brain isn't half as wired to its environment as one carried in a human body; the senses are less vivid, and there's a general sense of remoteness. In some rare cases, brain cores had been known to reject reality-at-a-distance in exchange for something else that wasn't very well understood. This was apparently especially true after serious emotional shocks, and among brain-cores who'd not proven particularly successful in their new roles. Whatever the cause, halfway through his debriefing Li's answers became vague and sometimes even nonsensical; by the time they got him down to sick bay he was so far gone that he only intermittently replied to blinking-light signals.

As I sat and fumed at the irrelevant-but-still-absolutely-required safety lectures, part of my mind was worrying away at the prospect of having to write yet another letter. Last night's had been rough indeed, far worse than the one for Piet. I'd sat for most of an hour and stared at the first line, totally unable to figure out what came next. It was still burned into my brain, and probably would be for life. "Dear Mr. and Mrs. Ming," it read. "I know that I can't possibly imagine how distraught you must be at this moment." The rest of the letter came to me eventually; it was a rambling, stumbling explanation of how Liu had come to die in a routine training accident, utterly forgettable in every way. But, somehow, that first line simple wouldn't leave me alone. So the *last* thing I wanted to do was to have to explain to Mr. and Mrs. Han how their own precious son had felt so guilty over the incident that he'd regressed into a drooling vegetable. Father Murton told me that in cases like Li's they most often put the brain back into its body, and that usually did the trick.

Usually. My soul rebelled from the very concept of writing *that* letter; the only good news was that we'd be long gone from Esteppe before such a diagnosis would be in order. Maybe I'd be lucky and get killed myself before I had to write Li's parents. Then, Admiral Vlasilov would have to compose a letter to Father; he was *much* better at such things, I suspected. Certainly, he'd had more practice.

It took Ted until almost three in the afternoon to get in touch with Vlasilov; the admiral had been with the Deputy Prime Minister, the only place where Commander Knight wasn't privileged with immediate access. By then it was too late to fly anyway, and we were all sick of being cooped up in the ready room together.

"No way!" I declared when one of the counselors suggested a group-study session. "We rendezvous in orbit with *June* tomorrow at oh-nine-hundred hours; everyone needs to pack and such anyway." Then I looked into each of the sad, sober faces one by one. "I suspect a lot of us have other things to do as well, before we leave." I looked the counselor who'd suggested study directly in the eye. "Everyone present is dismissed from duty until oh-six hundred hours tomorrow. That's an order, one that you can take to the bank. I don't want to hear so much as a false rumor about a counselor showing one of my pilots a single textbook page tonight. If you don't like it go talk to the admiral; he'll either back me up or he can find someone else to wear his fancy new commander's stripes." Then I looked my squadron over again; somehow instead of faces all I could see was a bunch of unwritten death-letters. "Go relax," I told them. "Visit Li, if the docs will let you. Play if you can, either together or separately." I sighed and looked down at the ground. "It may be your very last chance. Ever."

Chapter Forty-Seven

I'd have liked to have spent my last night before shipping out playing as well. However, I had other duties and obligations. One of them was dining with the Deputy Prime Minister, as arranged many weeks previously. Originally Father and Sven had been included in the invitation, but a last-minute production emergency at the factory kept them away. I would've been disappointed, except by now I well understood that my family wasn't free to do as it pleased. We'd all become greater or lesser cogs in the United Systems war machine, such important cogs that our chances of victory really *could* be materially affected by whether or not Father and Sven took a night off. According to family legend, Mother gave birth to me less than two hundred yards from where Father stood wired to a computer, trying to force a recalcitrant milling machine to complete a Stormcrow access hatch in time for a planned morning delivery. Though Mother's delivery was a rather important one as well, Father's concentration on the task at hand was supposedly so severe that he hadn't even nodded when told I was a boy. "Ja," he muttered. "That's good. We'll name him Thomas. Now, can someone please help me with this verdammt feedstock?"

So, I smiled and nodded as Father and Sven wished me a victorious cruise direct from the factory floor, using a broad-band video-link. Father looked like he was being ripped apart inside, not being able to see me off in person, but what could he do when so much was at stake? He was needed where he was. And my smiles became real when the workers gave me three cheers, most of them still at their benches and thus off-camera. I was pretty lucky after all, I decided as Sven, tears running down his face, closed the connection. Of all the Bananas, I was the only one able to have even this much contact with my family.

And dinner alone with Alicia was pretty nice as well. "Oh, my dearest!" she exclaimed upon meeting me in the little office that was converted to a dining room for the evening; her visit was secret, so that she wouldn't have to waste hours on official ceremonies that she'd be repeating anyway tomorrow afternoon when she bade the whole squadron farewell. "I'm so terribly sorry that your father and brother couldn't be here. And where's Father Murton?"

I pressed my lips together and looked down. "At Ensign Li's bedside," I explained. "They're rotating, you see, and with him needing to help me pack…"

"Of course," Alicia replied, placing her hand on my shoulder and guiding me towards the table. "That poor boy! I'm glad that he's in such good hands. Father Murton obviously has important duties, as well." She bade me sit down, then pushed my chair in for me. It was awkward for me to do that for myself in my mannequin-body, and back at the cave she'd taken care of it at every mealtime. "We all have *so* many duties these days, Thomas."

As usual when not in the spotlight, Alicia dined very simply on a bowl of tossed greens. She caught me looking down at them and smiled. "Spencer loves human-norm cooking," she explained. "Or, at least he loves vegetarian human-cooking. He even likes a little meat in it sometimes, for flavoring. But I can't stand what most normal people call food. It's hard to believe sometimes that he and I were designed by the same gengineer."

That was one good thing about being a brain core, I decided as I watched Alicia down her greens. While I might miss eating, at least I wasn't constantly being fed stuff I actively disliked. "How did you come to be designed?" I asked eventually. "I mean, why rabbits?"

Alicia cocked an ear and blushed. "It does seem kind of silly at first, doesn't it? I think it's easier for me than Spence; he's always doing things to prove his manhood, even as old as he is. You'd think he'd outgrow such macho childishness, but he never does."

My eyebrows rose. Was it actually possible, I wondered, that Spencer Wiston did things like wreck trains and lead guerilla movements and mutilate dead Dracans because he was a little bit ashamed of being an anthro-rabbit? Because others had once made fun of him for it, a century or more ago?

Alicia's eyes glittered; she'd been studying my face and was pleased that I'd made the connection. "It wasn't easy to be rabbit-kids," she explained. "But that was the only way gengineering was legal. We started with plants and animals, you know. No one objected much to monkeying around with *their* DNA. Then, we started adding human genetic material to the animals so that we could use their hormones in human medicine, and to make their tissues more useful for various tasks." She smiled again. "Eventually, the line sort of blurred. It remained illegal to gengineer pure humans, but if you wanted to have a child designed to achieve more than Mother Nature ever intended…" She shrugged. "Rabbits were quite popular; Spence and I are hardly the only survivors. There's over a dozen bunnies alive on Earth today, or at least they were still alive before the siege began. And twenty or thirty more scattered among the colony worlds." She smiled again. "There may even be one or two fighting for the Dracans. Though I can't imagine they'd be doing so of their own free will."

I toyed with my fork. "What other species were there?"

"Oh, my! Foxes, elephants, dogs, all the various kinds of cats…" She smiled. "We were braver, then. More willing to explore, and push the limits."

"Like the Esteppan Elitemen?" I asked.

"Pretty much," she answered, not even blinking at the comparison. Clearly, she'd been expecting my comment. "You probably don't know it, but the Esteppan war is pretty much what drove Spence and I the rest of the way out of politics. We'd already been pulling back, you see." She sighed. "We were against that war, Thomas, as unlikely as that probably seems to you after seeing how bloodthirsty we can be." She pressed her lips together for a moment before speaking. "We believe in fighting to win; never doubt that for an instant. But we also believe in not fighting at all when our cause isn't just."

My mouth dropped open slightly. Alicia was right; it *was* hard to imagine the Wistons as being against *any* war, based on what I knew of them.

"Heh!" Alicia chuckled. "Spence *loved* what the Elitemen were doing, at least in terms of pushing the limits of humanity." She looked down at the tabletop. "He didn't, of course, believe in either the Autarchy or the Autarch himself; we're democracy-lovers, through and through. And what the Autarch did towards the end, to your brother Dean among others…" She shook her head in disapproval. "Someday, I'd very much like to ask your father exactly what pushed the Autarch over the edge. Was it the usual human failings? Surely they've been enough to trip up uncounted others before him. Or perhaps he spent so much time wired up to machines that in the end he became one? A heartless, soulless machine…" She frowned. "They say he didn't even flinch as he shot himself, that by then he was so far gone it was just like flipping a switch. Power on, power off."

I frowned too. "The other day I was talking to a petty officer about history and war. He said that we're all the victims of forces much bigger than we are. He even named you as an example." Alicia smiled at that. "Maybe the Autarch was a victim too, in his way."

Alicia blinked, then her eyes narrowed. "I've never compared myself to the Autarch. But I'll admit that in some ways I probably should." She sighed. "Thomas, I'm the real leader of the United Systems now that Earth's cut off. You know that."

"Queen, more or less," I agreed. "Just as the Autarch was king of a much smaller domain."

"Indeed," Alicia agreed, looking down into her plate. "I rule by absolute decree every single day, just as the Dracan Emperor does. And yet I find my hands tied at every turn. It's maddening, how little I can do and what few real differences I can actually make. I'm a queen, maybe. But in addition to the crown I wear quite an impressive set of chains." Suddenly she smiled. "I don't believe it, Thomas. You've managed to make me feel sympathy for the Autarch."

I grinned, then let the expression fade before speaking. "You *did* allow my father to jack in," I pointed out. "The Butcher Birds, too. One might make the case that you *already* felt a certain degree of sympathy. And, some might further insinuate, those long non-human ears of yours just might have something to do with it."

Suddenly Alicia's back was ramrod-straight, and her eyes hard as stones. "And what if they do?"

Very carefully, I looked down at the tabletop. "This war is a huge crisis for humanity," I explained. "And somehow, a brain-enhanced scientist, his cyborg son, various other brain-expanded and 'borged individuals, and two of the last handful of gengineered super-humans have found their way to the very center of things. Think about it; what are the odds? I mean… Each of us is the product of research that's not just frowned upon but is *hated* by the general public. Yet now that the crisis is in full bloom, here we stand front and center, trying to pull everyone else's chestnuts out of the fire." I shook my head. "Alicia… I've been trying for weeks now to figure out why people fight wars, what good if any can come of them, and what constitutes moral and ethical behavior in such a screaming madhouse. The only justification for war I've been able to come up so far with is that sometimes we can't settle our differences any other way, and the only ethical guide is that if you don't win you can't shape the peace and set the future upon its proper course. So fighting and losing is even less ethical than fighting dirty to win. Because if you lose, it's all been nothing but a horrid waste." I frowned again. "I've killed a lot of people, Alicia, and if I'm lucky I'll kill many, many more. Eventually, though, my luck will break. The odds are heavy that I won't survive the war. We both know that, don't we?"

A single tear flowed down Alicia's cheekfur. "Yes, Thomas. I've always known."

"Well, then…" I said past the lump in the throat that my brain was convinced actually existed. "Alicia, please promise me something. You gave Colonel Rotte and his men something to fight for when you promised them the right to jack in. Please, Madame Deputy, give *me* something to fight for as well. Give me a reason for all this blood and waste and slaughter, and for the death of so many children. Don't tell me lies about democracy; I've watched Parliament operate at close range, thank you very much, and not on its best day."

Despite herself, Alicia smiled. "*Hardly* it's best day, Thomas. I'll give you that one."

"What I want," I continued as if she hadn't spoken, "is something far more important. Half the people I've seen running things since the Dracans invaded Churilla have been blithering idiots. Admiral Lutjens, Sara Fowler, Parliamentarian Nagano… Today my squadron wasted an entire afternoon when we should've been flying on useless safety videos, merely because some navy idiot in the upper echelons is so wedded to regulations that he's forgotten how to think for himself. We can do *better* than this, Alicia! You're proof, Spencer's proof, Father's proof, even Colonel Rotte is proof, in his way! We can be better! Humanity can *grow*! This war didn't have to ever happen at all, and it wouldn't have if we weren't a bunch of gibbering monkeys incapable of making even the simplest of decisions." I looked up and met Alicia's eyes again. "I don't care what the majority says, Alicia, and I don't care what they're so terribly frightened of. If war teaches warriors anything, it teaches us to overcome our fears. They're *wrong* about gengineering and 'borging. Absolutely and totally wrong, or else they wouldn't be looking to us to bail them out."

Alicia nodded slowly. "I think I see. You don't seek just a political victory. You want to see us move on to another plane."

"Yes!" I declared, pounding the table for emphasis. "If I'm going to die, if all of my best friends are going to die, then let it be for something worthwhile instead of a bunch of second-rate backroom political deals."

The rabbit-woman closed her eyes and sighed. "Thomas, you don't know… I mean…"

"Yes, I *do* know," I answered her, not giving an inch. "And deep down so do you. This war should never have been fought, Madame Deputy. It *would* not have been fought, had those in power today been in charge five years ago. No battle fought is worth a damn, unless victory brings us closer to the day when no battles ever need be fought again. We should've grown past this stage in our development long since."

"You want to fight a war to end all wars," Alicia sighed, shaking her head. "Spence would be terribly amused."

"At what?" I asked.

The rabbit-woman shook her head again. "Never mind. It's really not a laughing matter, I suppose." She sighed. "You're *so* young, Thomas; on days like today it shows. It's always the young who dream. And I'm so very old." Then she smiled and looked up at me again. "But you know what? Maybe we oldsters dream too, sometimes. I can't make you promises, Thomas; as I just said, my hands are tied and to a large degree I truly am controlled by forces much larger than myself. But, I promise you this. If I can find an opportunity to help make our dream come true, I'll take advantage of it regardless of the cost to my own future. All right?"

"All right," I replied, suddenly feeling about five years old again. My god, what had I just done?

Alicia smiled, then got up and helped me pull my chair away from the table. As I was climbing to my feet, she nipped in and kissed my neck from behind. "I'm as proud of you as if you were my own," she whispered into my ear. "As proud of you as I could possibly be."

"I love you too," I whispered back. "Like the mother I never had."

"She'd be proud as well," Alicia assured me. Then we hugged, and Alicia whispered in my ear one last time. "Tonight I'm more pleased with you than ever before. Your father never really gave up hope for mind-jacking. You can see that now, can't you? And, that he's had at least the broad outline of a plan in mind since the day he quite properly sold the Autarch out?"

"Yes," I admitted.

"Then you can also see that I haven't put up much of a fight against him, now have I?" She grinned. "Thomas, your father is a brilliant man; in fact, he's one of the most brilliant human-norms it's ever been my pleasure to meet. But, knowing what you now do about him, how could you ever imagine for a moment that Spence and I are any less determined? Or, for that matter, capable?"

My mouth dropped open. "Uhh…"

She raised a single finger to my lips. "Shh, Thomas. Not a word to a soul. But Spence and I have been sitting around the fire for years, foreseeing almost everything that's come to pass and making our plans accordingly." She smiled again, wider than ever. "Don't you worry about a thing back here at home. The fix has been in since before you were born. Sometimes people need to be represented, but at others they must be *led*. I'm so pleased that you figured it out all by yourself! I don't care about your calculus grades; you're every *bit* as bright as Herr Doktor-Professor!"

Chapter Forty-Eight

Alicia's "Good Hunting" speech to the Squadron didn't include a word about brain-jacking or 'borging or gengineering. Instead she spoke of the need for sacrifice and victory against a vicious, unyielding and so far victorious foe. And yet, as she finished up her speech on the hanger deck of *The Glorious First of June* her eyes sought me out. "You're the guardians of the future," she assured us. "The men and women who will, by your courage and skill, ensure that our ethics, our sense of right and wrong and our ideas about how people ought to work and live together, shall triumph over the very different values of our enemies. As the guardians of the future, you fight to define mankind's ultimate destiny. And I salute you!"

The speech was a big hit, judging by the way everyone from Admiral Vlasilov to the lowliest mess-rating leapt to their feet and roared out their approval for the Deputy Prime-Minister as she stood and saluted us again and again and again. Vlasilov had been worried about low morale among the sailors, after so many defeats. But anyone who heard that first bloodthirsty growl arise from the throats of the assembled sailors would know that their fighting spirit was just fine, thank you very much.

"She was looking right at you!" Jimmy exclaimed as soon as we were dismissed from the assembly. He'd been sitting right next to me, so he ought to know. "Wow! I can't believe you were lucky enough to live with her and her husband for so long!"

"Aye!" Delana agreed. She'd been sitting on my other side. "Our Thomas, he flies higher *without* his Skybolt!"

There wasn't much I could do besides ignore them. It was either that or admit I'd dined with Alicia the night before, and I'd never hear the end of *that* if it leaked to my fellow pilots. Vlasilov knew, Ted knew, and of course Father Murton knew. That was already three people too many, right there.

Fortunately the squadron was scheduled to space immediately after Alicia's big speech. Since the squadron was going to carrier-qualify by landing aboard we got to watch from shore. As the big ships lifted they kicked up huge fountains of spray, and their drives lit up the winter-dark sky. Then we took a quick shuttle-'hopper ride back to the airbase and flew our 'bolts up to meet *The Glorious First of June* in orbit. There really wasn't much to carrier landings; everyone was successful on their first attempt. "Congratulations!" the deck-landing-officer greeted each novice as their landing gear mated up with the receptacles on the carrier's deck. "You're now a qualified carrier aviator, and as of today a hundred credits a month richer."

It took a lot longer than usual to get us back into our mannequin bodies; this was both because it was the first time the navy had ever tried switching all four of us over at once and also due to the fact that our bodies had to come up behind us via courier-'hopper. Eventually the job was done, however, and we Bananas were free to head for the gunroom. The counselors had arranged for a nice little get-together there to celebrate our departure, complete with a video-game tournament. But, just as we were settling down for some hardcore joysticking, the tannoy cut in. "D'ye hear there?" the ship's executive officer declared, as he always did when a ship-wide announcement was being made. "D'ye hear there?"

I reached out to freeze the game in progress, but Delana beat me to it.

"Your fleet commander wishes to address you," the executive officer continued. Then there was a clicking sound, and the admiral himself took over.

"Men and women of task force seven," Vlasilov began. "We have now departed on what will most likely prove to be the single most important cruise of the war. Indeed, perhaps the single most important cruise in modern human history."

I looked around the room; everyone was giving the admiral their full attention.

"For many weeks," Vlasilov continued, "there has been much speculation among the fleet as to what our mission will be, and how it's to be executed. We've lost many battles to the Dracans, as you well know, with the result that their fleet is at this time enormously superior to our own. All of you are aware of this; there's no point in trying to pretend that the obvious is a secret. Even with our new Skybolts and Stormcrows, we're no match for our enemies in a standup fight. So long as the Dracan fleet remains concentrated in one place, we must accept that we cannot reasonably hope to defeat it at this time.

"Of course the Dracans *are* in fact so concentrated, at New Nippon. They'd be fools if they did anything else, for New Nippon is the sole gateway to Earth. If they can starve or bomb Earth into submission, they'll win the war. Indeed, by their reckoning they probably already *have* all but won the war.

"But there's more to naval warfare than direct fleet-versus-fleet confrontation, and more to naval strategy than mere concentration of force. New Nippon is a terrible place to base a fleet; there are no convenient oceans in which to float warships while they're not actively on patrol. The Dracan fleet, therefore, must remain in space at all times. Which in turn implies a huge consumption of molecular batteries."

Suddenly a little light went on in my head. The Dracan supply lines must be stretched as taut as could be! After all, they were a long way from home. And what did it take to move batteries from system to system? More ships, which in turn burned up *even more* batteries!

Vulnerable, unarmed merchant ships!

"It's our plan," Vlasilov continued, "to relieve the pressure on Earth indirectly by striking at Dracan supply lines. Almost immediately, we believe, our enemy will be forced to divide his forces in order to protect these vital lines of communications. At that point, these non-concentrated enemy forces will themselves become vulnerable to attack."

There was a long pause. "Our task is a difficult one on many levels. It'll require us to do hard things, in many cases things which we'd very much prefer not to do. However the fate of Earth, and therefore the future of Man, hangs in the balance. We therefore move forward with resolute hearts, certain in the ultimate justice of our cause."

There was a long pause, as if Vlasilov wished to say more, but couldn't find the right words. "That is all," he finally declared, and then with another click the tannoy resumed its silence.

Chapter Forty-Nine

The counselors had good reason for letting us play video games while we could; around ship's midnight the whole squadron went to three gees of acceleration, building up a vector. Our plan was to hit Esteppe's number two Nikita Point and Roarke's Cluster beyond at quite a respectable velocity. There was a substantial chance that Dracan vessels might be lying in wait there for us, the Cluster being a significant traffic-center despite the fact that there were no habitable planets in the system. According to Ted, who briefed us Bananas while losing horribly at "Rocket Sledder", Vlasilov's staff had planned out a whole series of raids for us, all based on careful timing and our original vector. Even in the unlikely event that we ran into a superior Dracan force the squadron would hit the ground running, so to speak, giving us a good chance of getting away regardless. "Of course," Ted explained as he guided his sled-icon across the virtual snow, "that also means that we can't afford to deviate an inch from our schedule or else things won't line up for us later. That could very well bite us in the butt before all is said and done."

After some very dull hours spent at three gees, during which we weren't permitted to leave our bunks, the squadron finally dropped down to one gee for the last hour as we approached our Jump-point. This was to allow everyone to prepare for battle. We Bananas made the Jump in our fighters, guns fully charged and four war-shot torps hanging from our stub-wings.

"Now!" my ground-chief's voice whispered in my ear as, for just a tiny moment, the universe seemed to stretch and flow. Then we were through and on the other side, speeding through potentially hostile space.

"Come on," I urged my pipper, though of course there wasn't any rushing things. The speed of light was the speed of light, and that was that except around Nikita Points. First the blue "friendly" pips of the task force reconstituted themselves, shifting slowly from line-ahead Jump configuration into the enlongated-sphere of standard cruising formation.

Then the blue-giant star and its two white-dwarf companion appeared as well; at least we'd have no trouble finding mass for our motors to push against in *this* system! Minute after minute passed, until I was sure nothing was going to happen, that we'd Jumped into empty space. Then…

…there they were! One, two, three… Seven! Seven red pips, accelerating slowly between Roarke's One and Roarke's Three, just where Ted had told us to expect them. Six merchantmen and a single enemy destroyer, clearly on their way down the main supply route from Drakkus to New Nippon.

"Do you see them?" Jimmy whispered in my ear via our private link. "Do you?"

I clicked my mike twice at him, hoping the casual reply would help my friend remain calm. Jimmy got a little fidgety sometimes. Besides, my mind was on something else. Why on Earth would the Dracans escort their convoy with just a single destroyer? They had to have a good idea of what our navy still had available to it; we'd paraded right past them at New Nippon while making our escape, after all. It only stood to reason that they'd send enough to counter our known force, if they were going to provide any escort for their convoys at all. Or at least enough to cripple us, so that we couldn't go raiding again anytime soon. What sense did it make to send a lone ship?

Then the main channel came alive. "Ahoy, Dracan convoy!" an unknown voice announced. "This is the United Systems Ship *Glorious First of June*. Heave to and prepare to be boarded."

"Thank god!" another voice replied, after a short lightspeed delay. "*June,* this is *Sacramento Conveyer*. We've been forced—"

Just then, the Dracan destroyer's icon flickered, indicating it was firing. One of the other pips flared, then turned dull dead-ship blue. Suddenly, I understood why the Dracans had provided only a single destroyer as escort.

Or guard, rather. As in, prison-guard.

"Jesus!" *Sacramento Conveyor* screamed. "For god's sake, *June*! Help us!"

"Scramble!" Ted's voice rang out, overriding the comm circuit. "Scramble! Scramble! Scramble! Your target is the destroyer!"

Jimmy and I were ranged first for launch; the electromagnetic catapult threw me forward at just over twenty gees, but all I felt was a twinge in my landing gear. Then we were in space side by side, ready for our first battle together. "Full military, power," I snapped, swinging my nose towards where the Dracan had just killed another merchantman to prevent us from retaking her. *Sacramento Conveyer* was raising merry hell all over the airwaves now; angrily I shut him off so that I could concentrate on the business at hand. "We won't mess around. Full spread."

"Full spread," Jimmy acknowledged, activating all four of his torps. I'd already donethe same.

The Dracan destroyer was coming up fast now, growing in size by the second. "We're up, Thomas," a new voice whispered in my ear. It was Delana. "Orders?"

"Stay clear unless we miss." This was unlikely as hell; eight nuclear torps was massive overkill on such a small target. But, better to cover all possibilities. "In that case, engage at will."

"Roger," my second flight leader replied.

The Dracan killed a third ship as we closed, *Sacramento Conveyer* herself. Then, she finally turned her guns on us. In all the comic books and such they always talk about how the hero bores straight in, contemptuously ignoring enemy fire. Even though the Dracan, alone and unsupported, stood very little chance of hitting either Jimmy or I, my non-stomach turned into a block of ice as I weaved and dodged. Each individual laser-bolt was perfectly capable of killing me, as dead as all the other men and women I'd watched die. And the sky seemed *full* of laser-bolts! I was frankly scared shitless all through my approach. Jimmy was probably equally terrified as he twisted and jinked. For that matter, neither of us were probably as frightened as the Dracans; after all, until a few minutes ago they'd been at relative peace. Now, out of nowhere they were facing a pair of deadly super-weapons they'd probably been warned about but had never imagined they'd actually encounter on such dull, routine duty.

They died game, the Dracans did; in their last few seconds of life they fired three spreads of torpedoes at the remaining merchantmen. Jimmy and I fired our own salvos almost as one, so that it was impossible for anyone to say whose torpedo it was that first struck the destroyer. The warship blew up in an instant; there couldn't possibly have been a single survivor.

But no one made it from the merchantmen crews either, though one group managed to climb into a rescue bubble and send out Maydays for a time. Vlasilov had us search and search for all the time remaining to us, but it was clear almost from the beginning that our cause was hopeless. Then it was time to land, re-arm, and snatch a few hours rest before we hit the Roarke Nikita Number One and points beyond, deeper still behind enemy lines.

"You may think that we failed," Ted explained to us at our debriefing. "But we didn't. The poor merchies never had a chance. What happened to them was *not* your fault." He looked around the ready room, meeting all of our eyes. "What's important in the big picture is that the Emperor is now shy six shiploads of urgently-required molecular batteries, six badly-needed merchant hulls, and an old *Sun-Tzu*-class destroyer." He smiled slightly. "And, of course, there's also the fact that now you're veterans. From what I hear, the Butcher Birds are quite jealous."

I nodded and smiled and looked over at Jimmy, who was smiling too. We were the heroes of the hour, Jimmy and I. But I couldn't help wondering if, behind his smile, he was trying as hard as I was to think about the "big picture" instead of a small group of terrified, dying merchant spacers drifting about in an overcrowded survival balloon until the air finally ran out and everything went black, black, black forever and ever.

Chapter Fifty

The Roarke Cluster's Nikita points, like those at New Nippon, were especially close together. This was part of what made it such a busy place. Therefore, we only had a day to rest before *June* went back to Action Stations and we went through it all again.

This time we were raiding Dracan space, for the first time during the entire war. Shangri-La had originally been founded as a Utopian world, blessed with a mild climate and a thriving human-friendly native ecology. But the planet was only two Jumps away from Drakkus herself, and it hadn't taken long for the growing Empire to absorb such a prize. What'd once been a vacation and retirement world was now a complex of factories, largely devoted to molecular battery production.

"This system will *not* be undefended," Ted explained to us four pilots just before it was time to Jump. "So, don't expect things to be as easy as they were last time. Because there's only two Nikitas, and we're coming in with such a huge vector, there's not a lot of room for flexibility in our plans. All we can do is run from one Nikita to the other, breaking as many things as we can along the way."

Jimmy raised his hand, and Ted nodded. "Yes?"

"Are we going to raid the primary itself?" he asked.

"No," Ted answered. "We're not strong enough. Our plan is to remain a good distance out, where our fighters are effective and theirs aren't. There ought to be plenty of targets in orbit, as well as transiting to and from the Nikitas. Some of our staff officers are worried that there might be a major concentration of enemy aerospace fighters at Shangri-La." He frowned. "Personally, I disagree with that analysis. If I were the Emperor, I'd have every carrier and every 'hopper in the fleet pummeling Earth every minute of every day." He paused, then continued the briefing. "Anyway. We're giving the Butcher Birds the lead on this one, since it looks to be a fight and they *are* the longtime veterans. You

Bananas will be held in reserve until we know more." He frowned. "Watch yourselves closely. We're operating a long way out from any sizeable masses, and if you wander too far out we won't be able to come and get you."

I nodded, then pointed at the planned track of the squadron. "We are an *awful* long way out," I complained. "There won't be time for more than a single strike by each squadron. Our 'birds won't be fully responsive, because we're so far from an anchoring mass." I frowned. "Which means we're more vulnerable to enemy fire. That'll be even truer for the Stormcrows than it is for us." I shook my head. "I don't know if this is a good raid, Ted."

My co-commander frowned. "I'm worried too," he admitted. "But this is the raid that's been handed to us, Thomas. And, it's the one we have to fly."

There wasn't much argument with *that*, I decided as the ground-crew hooked me up to my Skybolt. One of them had added half a destroyer emblem to my "kill" tally; I would've objected if Jimmy hadn't been so pleased and excited to find the other half painted on his own machine. Who knew? Maybe his 'bolt's nose might also end up painted red before all was said and done. Prewar regs didn't seem to matter much anymore.

My non-heart was racing as we burst through into Dracan space, unannounced and hopefully with no warning whatsoever. This time it didn't take the pipper nearly so long to register, or else perhaps I was just growing more used to waiting. First a Dracan cruiser accompanied by four destroyers appeared just off our squadron's port bow. Clearly these were the guardians of the node. Instantly *Wright* and *Zeppelin*, with two *Chief*-class destroyers in tow, began thrusting towards the enemy. I was surprised at first that the Butcher Birds hadn't been assigned the target, then realized that they were being held back for more profitable work.

Finally, the pipper blinked and painted a new picture. This one included Shangri-La itself, along with thirty, maybe even forty, big red pips floating in orbit. A *huge* convoy!

"Launch us!" Colonel Rotte begged on the general frequency. "What are you waiting for, you idiots? We only have so much time!"

"We're prioritizing the targets, Colonel," the Operations Officer replied, his voice as soothing as he could make it.

"Bugger that!" Rotte replied. "There's a whole *skyful* of targets! You think that we're going to pick and choose one over another while they're maneuvering and firing back?"

There was a short pause, then Vlasilov's voice came on-line. "The colonel is correct," he decided. "Launch the Birds. Their mission is free chase. Seek and destroy."

"Ja!" the colonel agreed, more energetic than I'd ever heard him before. "*There's* an admiral that knows how to fight a verdammt war!"

Suddenly a new series of pips formed around *Skagerrak*, in the form of three neat pairs of Stormcrows. I wasn't on Rotte's intrasquadron channel, so I could only guess what his orders were as the Butcher Birds stooped down towards Shangri-La together.

Just then the cruiser battle began, the Dracan heavy salvoing his big guns at *Wilbur Wright*. But *Wright* was twisting and turning like a mad thing, as were *Zeppelin* and the destroyer beside them. If the cruiser got lucky and scored a couple hits before the many small guns of the United Systems ships could bear, we Skybolts might have to go bail our friends out. Therefore, I decided to focus on them and not the colonel's activities for the time being. *June* was offering me a live video feed from the hull; I dropped the pipper and accepted it.

The Dracan cruiser's gunnery was well up to snuff, I had to give them that. Her fourth salvo scored a clean hit on *Wilbur Wright*, right on the face of her number-two turret. Against all odds, *Wright*'s thin armor held. The fifth salvo missed...

...and there was no sixth. Both *Zeppelin* and *Wright* seemed to explode, but by then I knew that they were only firing their main guns. Hit after hit and hit rained down on the Dracan; most failed to penetrate but enough got through to render her a lifeless wreck. It took only seconds. Then our escorts methodically exterminated the destroyers, one by one. The last managed to get off a salvo of torpedoes; as she fired them my intercom came alive. "Thomas," Ted's voice said. "I see that you're watching the cruiser action. That's probably been the right thing for you to do up until now. But please, switch over to the raid itself. Vlasilov thinks our friends in the escorts have things under control. You won't be needed there after all."

"Right," I agreed, vaguely annoyed that I couldn't watch to make sure the Dracan torpedoes missed. My vision blurred...

...and then I was looking at the pipper again. The Birds were in among the enemy, who'd been reduced to a twisting, turning mass of ships. "Horrido!" Gustav's voice rang out on the main channel as a red pip flared and went dead-ship pink. "Horrido!"

"Jesus Christ!" a new voice interjected. "For the love of god! Cease fire! There are United Systems ships here, forced to sail by the Dracans!

We surrender! Cease fire!"

"Horrido!" Rotte cried out, as yet another ship flared and died.

Suddenly I was terribly angry, though I wasn't quite sure why. After all, anyone who hadn't foreseen this very situation was a blind fool. We had just exactly enough time to make one firing pass as we raced through this system. There was no possible way for us to accept surrenders. The ships that the Butcher Birds were destroying had sailed under Dracan orders and under Dracan escort. They were carrying Dracan cargoes critical to the Dracans in defeating Earth. It was all legal enough. And yet… And yet…

"For the love of god!" the voice rang out again. "My wife and daughter are aboard this ship with me!"

"Horrido!" Gustav declared again. "Look at her blow; full of verdammt batteries for sure!"

"Ja!" Rotte agreed. "The lot of them, full to the gills with contraband!" He paused. "Take to the survival bubbles, sailor-man, if you value your life. We'll burst no bubbles on purpose-- my word of honor. But by god if you stay aboard those ships we'll kill you all! Every goddamned one of you!"

"Horrido!" another Bird cried out, emphasizing the point.

"Thomas!" Ted's voice whispered in my ear. "You're to launch now. Free chase! Scramble! Scramble! Scramble!"

Once again the catapult launch was almost as nothing; my landing gear twinged a little more than before, and I made a mental note to have it looked at. Then Jimmy and I were shooting through the sky, pointed directly at our helpless enemy.

"Tommy?" Jimmy whispered on the private circuit. "I don't know about this. I mean…"

Then Delana was whispering in the other ear. "We're up," she confirmed. "Orders?"

There wasn't time to think about Jimmy, even though I desperately needed to. "Come in from the right and fire at will," I finally heard myself say, even though I wasn't sure if I really meant it. "My flight will take the left. One torp per vessel. Don't get in too much of a hurry; we've got enough time to make every shot count."

"Roger that," Delana replied, her voice blissfully unargumentative. "Out."

"Tommy!" Jimmy complained again as we swooped down upon the convoy, much like the Butcher Birds before us. "Some of those are United Systems ships, just like last time. Maybe even all of them. Good guys!"

I sighed, then counted to three. "We don't have time for this right now," I finally said. "Those ships are full of Dracan goods, loaded at a Dracan port and meant to resupply a Dracan fleet. We can't fight this war any other way, not if we're going to have a chance in hell of actually winning it. If that's not good enough for you, you're no warrior and certainly no Top Banana. Go back to the carrier."

"Tommy, I…"

We were almost within firing range. There wasn't any more time to argue. "Go back!" I ordered, lining up on the nearest merchantman. It was child's play, really. A mere practice run. The target wasn't firing back and a merchantman's thrusters were so weak they could barely get out of their own way, much less dodge a Skybolt effectively. "Splash one!" I heard Viktor Oudh declare on the open channel. Then I triggered a torpedo of my own. "And another!" I added as the helpless ship exploded, its death-pyre all the fiercer for its high-energy cargo. Then I lined up on a second, this one desperately careening to starboard. I was just getting ready to fire when there was another flash near at hand. "Sp-p-p-p—" Jimmy's voice said, though he couldn't quite force the words out past the sobs. "Sp-p-p-p---"

We didn't quite manage to kill all the merchantmen in the sky as Rotte had promised; there weren't enough missiles and we didn't have time for a second strike. But the threat had its effect anyway, as I now understood the colonel had intended from the moment he uttered it. Even those few merchies still intact were drifting aimlessly across the sky, abandoned by their terrified crews. These men wouldn't be carrying any molecular batteries to New Nippon any time soon.

Or ever, if they could possibly help it.

Chapter Fifty-One

I was the last pilot to leave the hanger deck, and by a large margin at that. When I described the twinge I was experiencing in my landing gear, the faces of my ground crew went all serious, and I was forced to spend almost an hour describing the sensation in detail over and over again. In theory everything I felt should've been recorded in the automatic sensor-log, but in reality there was a lot more to the brain-body relationship than anyone yet understood. My 'bolt was the Earth-built one, still suspect in the eyes of many, and after an hour of fruitless searching they finally grounded the 'bird on general principles and let me go back to my room to recover. Father Murton was waiting for me there; he'd just smiled in greeting and spread his arms for a comforting hug when the comm rang. "Hello! Is Thomas there yet?" Vlasilov's voice asked. "I hear that he's been held up due to a technical glitch."

"Yes," the priest replied, looking a bit frustrated. "He's here." I'd been seeing less and less of my old friend of late, and it was rather touching to see that he genuinely missed me as much as I missed him.

"What can I do for you, Admiral?" I asked before Vlasilov could speak again.

"Thomas…" Vlasilov began. Then he hesitated. "Thomas, first let me say that I regret asking you for a favor when you've just returned from a mission. You're entitled to a little time to talk things over with your counselor. And yet, you're a serving officer as well. We're cruising through enemy space, and a Dracan squadron could appear at literally any second." He paused again. "I urgently need to speak with you, Thomas. In private. Can you make time to come see me in my cabin?"

If there was anyone in the task force busier than Colonel Rotte and I, it was Admiral Vlasilov. "Yes, sir!" I answered. "Right away!"

"Good," the admiral answered. "And, don't worry, Father Murton. It'll only take a few minutes, and then you can have Thomas back." He paused, and you could almost hear a too-rare smile in his voice.

"Hopefully undamaged."

The admiral's batman let me into the admiral's cabin on the first knock; he must've been waiting with his hand on the hatch. "Good evening, Commander," the grizzled old petty officer greeted me. His left hand had been replaced by a simple hook; apparently he was one of those rare individuals whose personal body chemistry or religious beliefs or whatever prevented them from having a replacement grown. "The admiral is waiting for you, sir." His smile widened. "Good shooting today."

"Thank you," I answered reflexively; practically everyone I'd met in the corridors had smiled and said the same thing. It wasn't easy to be the one the cameras always focused on, I'd learned long since. "Thank you very much."

The admiral's personal office was located at *June*'s extreme stern; behind his desk the plain steel of the hull had been replaced by a huge gallery window. Shangri-La was still a discernable orb, but it wouldn't be long now before it faded away first to just another point of light and then nothing at all to the naked eye. Vlasilov's desk was made of an exotic-looking but light-colored wood; it looked vaguely extra-terrestrial to me, though I couldn't be sure. Most unusually it had a hot-plate built into it, so that off to the admiral's right a samovar of tea bubbled and boiled. It would've smelled wonderful, I imagined, if I had a working nose.

"Thomas!" the admiral greeted me, a flash of genuine pleasure passing across his face as he stood and pumped my hand. He gestured at a pair of chairs that faced the big window. "Please," he urged me, pouring himself some tea. "Sit, and let us talk for a while."

I nodded and complied, even though I was equally comfortable standing. It was the electric-motor thing again.

"You're probably wondering what this is all about," Vlasilov continued as he fussed with sugar and a sliced lemon. "And, if I remember being seventeen as well as I think I do, you're probably also wondering if you're in trouble." He smiled again. "Don't worry, Thomas. You did well today, as expected. I'm sure your father will be very proud when he hears."

Something relaxed deep down inside of me; despite everything, I *had* been a little worried.

Vlasilov grinned again, reading my expression correctly. "You did *very* well, Thomas," he repeated. "Both in completing your mission and leading your men."

And just that quickly, I knew what this little meeting was *really* about. "He'll be all right," I assured Vlasilov. "I *know* that he will." I looked away. "Admiral, he's a member of *my* squadron, not yours. If you want me to be the actual commander of the Top Bananas and not just a figurehead, then leave him to me. I'll take care of this."

The admiral's brow furrowed. "You make a powerful argument," he allowed. "There are many longstanding traditions and regulations that do indeed make this your affair, not mine." He sighed and sipped at his tea. "And yet, there are other factors that apply here as well. Jimmy, for example, is a fifteen year-old boy, not a hardened young hot-shot pilot. I bear a responsibility for him that transcends even your own in some regards; after all, you're still a boy as well. Not only that, but there are larger issues to consider. Jimmy is one of only four fighter pilots aboard this entire ship, and therefore disposes of a quarter of our effective offensive firepower." He shook his head and sighed. "I have a right to be concerned here, Thomas. A duty, even. Despite tradition."

Now it was my turn to frown. "I can see that," I allowed eventually.

"Good." The admiral put down his cup and turned to face me. "The counselors wanted you to choose someone else," he said bluntly.

"They said he was too immature," I agreed, though my fists had turned themselves into little balls at my side. "And, he *is* a bit immature; I knew that even before today. But... I still believe in him, Admiral. And, we're a near-ideal team. You've seen our scores. Delana is the best alone. Jimmy and I, however, make far and away the best pairing."

"Da," Vlasilov agreed, turning back to his window and looking out at the stars. "This is true as well." He sighed. "Though Delana is not so much better than you that I see much of a difference. And the colonel rates you higher. His opinion matters most of all." Then the admiral shook his head. "Thomas, I shall lay my cards on the table. The counselors want me to take Jimmy off combat duty, permanently and immediately. They fear for his mental health."

I pressed my lips together. "What about mine?" I asked.

"Huh?" the admiral asked, clearly caught off guard.

"What would the counselors have said about *my* mental health, had they been around when I was just getting started?" I asked. "Say, about ten minutes after Lieutenant Eaglish drifted away, dead? Or right after I got nuked and everyone all around me was killing themselves rather than die of radiation poisoning?" I smiled sarcastically. "Obviously, sir, I'm a raving lunatic and totally unfit for combat. Maladjusted, traumatized, emotionally barren..." I paused a moment, for effect. "Either that, or I'm a seventeen year-old combat veteran."

Vlasilov met my eyes again. "You *are* growing up quickly, Thomas. Perhaps *too* quckly."

"Certainly too quickly," I agreed. "All veterans do. And that's exactly what's happening to Jimmy as well. He's transforming from being a happy, well-adjusted and much-loved kid into a veteran. A killer, sir. Without even the benefit of anything like basic training or boot camp to make it easier on him; there just wasn't time. At some point Delana and Viktor will have to go through this as well; I'd guess that so far they're still in some sort of denial and it's all just a game to them, like it was to me at first. From a counselor's point of view, I'd imagine that combat-hardening looks an awful lot like mental illness. That's probably why they want to pull the plug on my wingman." I looked out at the stars and sighed. "He'll be all right," I repeated, as much for my own sake as Jimmy's. "Who else knows about this, besides us and the counselors?"

"The officers in the combat control center," Vlasilov replied. "Though they can—and will!—be ordered to keep their mouths shut."

"Good," I answered. "Let me talk to him. And to the counselors as well, of course, though you'll need to inform them up front that there's no way you're pulling Jimmy out of combat." I paused. "If you don't take a firm stand, they'll try to talk him into giving up flying instead of offering him the kind of fighting support he needs. If Jimmy listens to *that* kind of counseling, then it really *is* all over." I paused. "Do *any* of them think he's up to the challenge?

"Da," Vlasilov agreed quietly. "Petty Officer Brooks, of course. His own personal counselor. A man I greatly respect. Plus, your own Father Murton refused to offer an opinion until he'd spoken to you about the matter first."

I blinked. *That* was certainly a surprise! "Well... In that case, I'd suggest that Jimmy talk to those two and only those two, at least unless he asks for someone else."

"Very good," Vlasilov agreed, still eyeing me intently. "And his brother?"

I winced. "Does Ted know?"

"Yes," Vlasilov replied. "How could he *not* know, Thomas? Our friend's face turned scarlet with shame; I saw this with my own eyes."

I pressed my lips together again. "We've already established that this is a highly irregular situation," I ventured. "One in which you're justified in interfering in the affairs of my squadron. Right?"

"That is correct," Vlasilov agreed.

"Then, perhaps…" I sighed, then shook my head and forced the reluctant words out. "Perhaps these same extraordinary circumstances might justify my making a suggestion to you, as well?"

The admiral's bushy eyebrows shot to the top of his forehead. "Of course!" he said, waving his arm extravagantly. "Suggest away, Thomas! That's why you're here!"

Now the words came harder than ever. "You might consider," I said eventually, "having Ted visit you here for a little talk much like this one. And, you might suggest to him that he should be far prouder of his brother for being willing to fight at all than he should be disappointed by his making one little mistake. You could even go so far as telling him that it might be best for his brother, whom he truly does love very much, if he pretended only to know that Jimmy shot down four transports and willingly obeyed every order he was given, fulfilling his duty and his oath to the tee. Which is, of course, exactly what happened in the end."

"Da," Vlasilov agreed. "In the end, that *is* what happened. But…" He turned to face me again. "Thomas, this war isn't half over yet, and the most desperate times lie still before us. You Bananas, along with the Butcher Birds, are my keenest weapon. The day may come when you and your squadron-mates receive orders to do far worse things to your fellow men than what you did a few hours ago. Today's action was legal, strictly speaking. But I'd be a liar if I claimed that I'd never under any circumstances give an illegal order in defense of the United Systems. Or, even that I haven't been specifically authorized to do so at need, by Madame Deputy herself." His eyes went hard and narrow. "Thomas, in this war and under today's circumstances I expect my orders to be obeyed without question, no matter what. It's very likely that I'll know things that you do not. You understand this, I hope? Not just you, but Jimmy and Delana and Viktor as well? We *shall* win, no matter what it takes. This is my sacred duty."

"We *must* win," I agreed, looking down at the deck. "Anything's better than a future in which everyone bows to the Emperor every thirty seconds or so. Anything at all."

Chapter Fifty-Two

I spent the rest of that evening talking to Father Murton about this and that; we only rarely addressed difficult issues directly these days. I'd learned long since what he thought about most things. What I needed most from him was his actual presence, to see him smile and know that he cared about me and approved of who I was and what I was becoming. If the day ever came when he *didn't* approve of my actions, well… I didn't even want to think about it.

Apparently Vlasilov accepted my suggestion and spoke privately to Ted; the next time I saw my co-commander he was visiting Jimmy in his room, grinning from ear to ear as if there wasn't a thing in the world bothering him. Jimmy seemed pretty happy too. After everyone else had left, while I was plugging in my joystick, he placed his hand on my shoulder. "Commander Longo?"

My eyebrows rose; "Commander Longo" was what adults called me, not my pilots. "Yes?"

"Sir," he said slowly, staring at the floor. "I want to let you know how sorry I am for what happened. I was your wingman, and you were counting on me. I shouldn't… I mean…"

"Heh!" I snorted, grinning as wide as I could manage. I'd heard all I needed to hear; the awkward, half-rehearsed deep conversation I'd planned to initiate while we played *Rocket Sledder* wouldn't have to happen after all. What a relief! "Forget about it, okay? Tomorrow's a new day, and that's what matters. I understand why you did what you did; the fact that you don't like hurting people is *good*, not bad. So let's just forget that it ever happened. Okay?"

"Okay," Jimmy replied, the relief evident in every feature on his face. Suddenly, he sprang up and wrapped his arms around me. "Oh god, Tommy!" he whispered. "You're the best friend anyone ever had. I owe you *everything*! It's no wonder Dad and Ted are so stuck on you; I only wish you weren't so hard to live up to!"

I thought that'd be the end of the matter, at least from my perspective. But it wasn't, quite. Commander Bard, the nice lady who'd taught us about Alexander the Great way back when, had shipped out with us aboard the *Glorious First of June*. Though her real job was on the admiral's personal staff, Michele had decided that now might be a good time for us Bananas to learn more about military history. Once class began and I discovered what the subject matter was, I realized that it almost certainly hadn't been her idea after all.

"...is called the *guerre la main*," Bard was explaining as I walked in a few minutes late; the ground crew had unexpectedly needed me for an hour or so to check out their repairs on my 'bolt's landing gear. "That's how most naval battles and wars have been fought over the centuries. The fleets of the competing nations joust with each other for advantage until one or more major battles takes place. The winner controls the seas to a greater or lesser degree, and that's that." She smiled, then wrote again on the chalkboard. "Sometimes, however, naval wars take the form of *guerre la course*. Does anyone know what that means?"

"Attacking merchantmen," Delana answered without raising her hand.

"Exactly!" Michele said with a big smile. "And why do you suppose navies attack merchantmen?"

I fielded this one, as much to cover my awkward entrance as anything else. "Because merchantmen are the essence of sea power," I answered. "They're *why* the fleets try to control the seas, or in our case space. Trade and goods always move in merchant bottoms. So even if you can't control the shipping lanes yourself, you can still deny the enemy the advantage of his superior fleet if you can prevent his cargo ships from coming and going."

"That's mostly right, Thomas," she answered, smiling again. Some university somewhere, I decided, had lost one hell of a professor when Michele Bard chose to become a professional strategist instead. "A superior fleet can still raid when and where it chooses, even if it's losing the *guerre la course*. And, it can still mount a perfectly effective invasion. But… You've hit on a great truth, Thomas." She turned back to the board and wrote again, speaking each word as she spelled them out. "*Guerre… la… course…* is almost invariably the strategy of the weaker navy." Then she turned back to face us. "The French were the first to formally accept *guerre la course* as a valid strategic option; this was a direct response to the fact that, no matter how they tried, they were unable to overcome the superiority of the English. Later, it was taken up by the Americans, who were the strategy's most successful practitioners. A successful *guerre la course* allowed the still-weak United States to hold its own during the War of 1812, when it was seriously defeated in most other theaters of battle. Later, the United States waged the most effective *guerre la course* in history against Imperial Japan."

Viktor blinked, then raised his hand. He was always shyer then the rest of us. "Yes, Viktor?" Mrs. Bard acknowledged him.

"Well..." he said slowly, looking down at his desktop. Then he raised his eyes. "Wasn't the United States Navy far superior to the Japanese in World War Two? I thought you said *guerre la course* is for inferior fleets."

"Usually but not always," she gently corrected him. "It's hard to remember now, but back then the Pacific was a far larger place than it is today. During most of the war, Japan had absolute, unchallenged control over hundreds of thousands of square miles of ocean despite overall Allied naval superiority. It was in this area that the United States fought her greatest *guerre la course*, one of terrifying effectiveness." She turned and erased the board, giving us a moment to think. Then she drew a pantomime submarine. "Do any of you know what this is?" she asked.

"A U-boat," I answered.

"Very good!" Bard replied. "Though most people connect that specific term with the German Navy. The Germans also attempted to fight a *guerre la course*. Twice, in fact."

"They got beat," Delana commented. "Thank god. Miserable buggers, they were. Especially the second time."

"Most people feel that way," Commander Bard agreed, looking nervously at me for a moment to make sure I didn't take offense. Which of course I did not; the excesses of twentieth-century Germany could and should never be forgotten. In fact, there were monuments to the slaughtered innocents all over Esteppe. Then she sighed. "Up until the turn of the twentieth century," she explained, "there was little to choose from, ethically-speaking, between the *guerre la main* and the *guerre la course*. Given the technology of the times, neither mode of warfare was particularly lethal to those involved. In fact, far more sailors died of accidents and disease on active service than of battle-wounds. Even during the fiercest wars, a large percentage of navy men never once heard a gun fired in anger."

She sighed. "It was a time for 'clean' wars. Ships moved slowly and deliberately, and couldn't hide from each other. There were opportunities to take prisoners, plenty of space to offer them decent accommodations, even time for ritualized courtesies. Things were therefore very much aboveboard. About the dirtiest trick a captain could play was to sail under false colors, and even that didn't happen very often because there weren't all that many times when it conferred an advantage." She nodded at her little drawing. "The submarine, and later the airplane, changed all of that. Warfare hasn't been the same since."

"Because planes moved so much faster?" Jimmy asked.

"That's part of it," Michele answered. "But... Think about it. A submarine was fragile. Delicate, even. Its only real defense was its invisibility. Making war in a submarine was very different than making war from a surface ship, so much so that it changed the entire dynamic of human conflict." She pointed at her drawing. "Look at how tiny the gun is. For that matter, see how tiny the entire vessel is?" She quickly sketched in a destroyer for reference; it made the sub seem insignificant. "Yet, submarines were *effective*. So long as they didn't expose themselves to danger, they could kill any ship afloat." She looked down. "You'll also note that they couldn't possibly surface and pick up survivors. If there were any other enemy ships in the area, they might come racing up and kill the sub. And even if they tried to save people..." She paused and met each of our eyes, one by one. "...where would they *put* them?"

There was a long silence as we pondered that.

"People tried to outlaw submarine warfare, because it was so inhumane," Bard explained. "But once the Germans showed how effective subs could be in the First World War, it was pretty much futile. Because they were so potent, and because a submarine fleet was technologically complex and couldn't be improvised in a hurry, everyone had to maintain fleets of submarines in service. During the Second World War the Germans attempted a *guerre la course* strategy once again; this was probably inevitable, given how badly outnumbered they otherwise were at sea, and how much the so-called 'hunger blockade' had hurt them just a few years before during the last big war. Hundreds of thousands of German civilians starved, you see, perhaps even millions, because Great Britain chose to unilaterally reinterpret maritime law in a manner that benefited her at the expense of her enemies." She shook her head. "Germany wanted revenge, and didn't feel particularly sorry for the lost crewmen after losing so many of their own women and children. Those were not good times. And as always in war, the side with the lower ethical standard set the rules of engagement."

"But," Jimmy interjected. "You still haven't explained how the

United States fought Japan with submarines."

Bard smiled. "I'm getting there," she reassured him. "Give me time." She turned back to her board and drew a simple airplane. "As you can see," she explained. "An airplane is inherently even less humane a weapon than a submarine. It's even less able to take prisoners, and has more trouble verifying that it's shooting at a legal target." She frowned. "As Colonel Rotte pointed out recently, it's not easy for a pilot to carefully pick and choose his targets in the middle of a melee. Yet like the submarine, the airplane is such a useful weapon despite its inherent cruelty that we still us their descendants today." She smiled again. "As you four may have heard."

We laughed dutifully.

"Anyway," Bard continued, her features softening. "Through the submarine and the airplane, cruelty and callousness returned to the war at sea at a level of intensity not seen since the days of the Viking longships. The same thing happened on land, though that's another story for another day, I fear." She smiled. "Japan's war with the United States was unusually brutal from the very beginning. It started with an illegal and to Western eyes immoral surprise attack, and both sides comported themselves with the utmost savagery. Even in the day of the submarine, the war at sea elsewhere around the globe was fought with at **least a small element** of chivalry and mercy. But not so the fight between Japan and the USA!"

"This war began with a surprise attack," I said slowly. "The one we're fighting now, I mean. And, well…"

Bard smiled softly. "It's especially cruel, as well. We all know this, though we don't speak of it often. And it's growing crueler every day." She looked up at the others. "It's arguable that the United States had more reason to despise submarine warfare than any other nation on the globe; it was submarine warfare, after all, that had drawn her into a terrible war just twenty or so years before. And America had been angrily crusading against the second coming of the U-boat, as well. Yet, the Pentagon had a serious problem on their hands. Japan was *winning*, you see; we often forget today how close the Axis came to defeating the Allies in both World Wars. Japan was *winning*, and here the USA was with all these submarines just lying around…"

Suddenly the room was silent. "America chose victory over ethics," she explained softly. "Rightly, because had she chosen defeat her ethics would've been rendered irrelevant for all time. Though she had some justification in that Japan's ally Germany was doing the same thing, unrestricted submarine warfare stood directly against everything the USA ever believed in. Yet once America embraced the strategy, she did so with abandon. By the end of the war roughly nine-tenths of the Japanese merchant marine was at the bottom of the Pacific, mostly torpedoed without warning by American submarines. Hundreds of thousands of Japanese civilians were killed in the process; burned, drowned, left to die slowly in life rafts. And, there was worse.'"

There was a long pause, until Delana filled it. "What could be worse than people left to drift?" she asked.

Commander Bard closed her eyes, as if seeking strength. Then, bravely, she faced us again. "War is hard," she explained. "Its forms and circumstances are driven by technology, politics and cultural imperatives, not by how we would wish things to be. Sometimes warfare spins completely out of control. That pretty much happened in World War Two, and seems to be happening again in the current conflict."

She closed her eyes again, and this time didn't reopen them. "Here's something you all need to think very, very hard about. During the Second World War, there were four submarine commanders who indisputably and without doubt deliberately massacred the survivors of ships they or others had sunk. Such massacres were far beyond the pale; they were totally illegal and, even just a few years before the war began, would've been listed by all the peoples of the world as among the most morally reprehensible actions that it was possible for a naval officer to take. It was considered murder, pure and simple." She paused to let that sink in. "One of these commanders was killed at sea before official notice was taken of his actions. A second was tried and hung as a war criminal." Bard's face hardened. "The third commander carefully noted his actions in an official report, where his superiors read about what he'd done and acted accordingly. Shortly thereafter, he was awarded the Victoria Cross. The fourth, who similarly logged his actions and brought them to the attention of his superiors, received the Congressional Medal of Honor from the hand of the President himself."

There was a long, stunned, silence. "But..." Jimmy asked finally. "I mean, *heroes* are supposed to get those medals. Right?"

"They were the highest awards their nations could bestow," Bard confirmed. "Very few men ever received them."

"But..." Jimmy stammered. "I mean... These were survivors floating in the water, right? Helpless, in other words."

"Yep," our instructor agreed, tossing her marker into the air and snatching it again.

"What our Jimmy want to know," Delana interrupted, "is, how can a hero slaughter the helpless?"

Michele sighed, then looked each of us in the eye, one after another. "In every truly hard-fought war," she explained, "where the outcome is very much in doubt and the stakes are incalculable, there come times and places when one side slaughters the other with impunity. When thousands or maybe even millions are dying on one side, and hardly anyone is dying on the other. A time when the aerospacecraft of one side are bombing and strafing the enemy at will, and when the poor, helpless bastards on the receiving end are bleeding and screaming and cursing their gods for the miserable fate which has befallen them. A time when one side is down, and the other is repeatedly kicking them in the groin, over and over and over without reprieve, until the victim vomits blood. Then he's kicked some more." She shook her head slightly. "My children, when that time comes, and when you're inflicting that kind of slaughter and suffering on your enemy, well... there's a word for when that happens." She looked directly at Jimmy.

"And that word, Jimmy, is 'victory'."

Chapter Fifty-Three

Commander Bard asked that we pilots think hard about her lesson; I certainly did. Her image of victory as one soldier kicking the other in the genitals over and over again struck deep; it reminded me exactly of how I'd felt back on Churilla, when the Dracans had ruined all of our plans, killed us at will, nuked us, and then murdered our POW's. That'd certainly been a defeat, and Commander Bard had described it to a tee. Being defeated had been hard, the hardest thing I'd ever known. And yet…

Was it any better being the kicker than the kickee? How awful *was* war, anyway, that winning felt almost as bad as losing? It almost made me glad that I'd won all my medals as part of a defeat. It felt more honorable, somehow, even though it didn't do much for the society I was supposed to be defending.

Shangri-La's Nikita Points were a long way apart, so far that even though a Dracan task force eventually emerged behind us we had such a lead that they didn't even attempt to chase us down. Instead they just radioed obscenities at us, which *June*'s communications officer played over the tannoy to amuse the crewmen until someone reminded him that there were children aboard. It was all right, though. None of us heard any new words, though some of them were arranged in new ways we hadn't thought of on our own.

It took us almost a week to cross all the way to Shangri-La's Point One and make our next Jump; we pilots were ordered to the ready room because where we were going, there wouldn't be any gravitational anchors for our Skybolt drives to push against. "We're Jumping into empty space," Ted explained to us at our briefing. "Intergalactic space, in fact. The Black Cluster is hardly ever used by anyone except warships, because except for Shangri-La it's about seven Jumps from anywhere."

"I thought we were only two jumps from Drakkus?" Jimmy asked.

"We are," Ted answered, smiling at his younger brother. "Shangri-

La's Number Two Nikita is asymmetrical; if we wanted to go to Drakkus, we'd have to turn around and go back the way we came. Which would be kind of difficult, given our current vector."

"Right," Jimmy agreed, sounding a little saddened. I had to sympathize; it seemed a shame to come so close and not leave a calling card or two.

When the Jump finally came, I felt calm and collected. After all, this was my third combat Jump; by now it was old hat. Besides, nothing was going to happen anyway. I even silent-hummed a happy little tune to myself as I sat in my assigned seat and watched everyone else worry for a change.

Then the pipper performed its magic…

…and revealed a sky filled with a dozen dead-pink Dracan ship-corpses, along with eight blue United Systems vessels. It was a small task force built on the modern, up-to-date heavy cruiser *Nanking,* which must've been on detached duty at the time of the slaughter at New Nippon. Five of the United Systems ships glowed pale, dead-ship blue. "Whoa!" I said. "There's been a battle here!"

"A recent one, too," Ted agreed as *June* thrusted hard to starboard, just in case. It took time for a pipper to register, after all, and who knew if there might be live Dracans still lurking about?

"What ships?" a voice demanded on the tannoy; we combat pilots were linked to everything the bridge crew could hear, since in theory we were ready to launch at a moment's notice and needed to remain informed. We *couldn't* launch here, of course. But no one had bothered to modify procedures.

"This is task force seven," the admiral's voice replied. "Making rendezvous as ordered."

"Excellent, Petrov!" a new voice replied. "This is Tsu, with task force twelve. How's your back these days?"

"It still aches, of course," our own admiral replied. "From when you pinned me, you bastard!"

"You won two out of three falls," Tsu countered. "And therefore have no reason to complain." There was a long pause. "You're right on schedule, Petrov. That's good. And you've taken no losses, which is better still. How are your air groups?"

"Undamaged," Vlasilov answered. "Not only performing well, but improving with each mission." There was a long pause. "So, the Dracans showed up?"

"Either they inferred your destination and were trying to head you off out here where your fighters can't operate, Petrov, or else there's another leak at headquarters. My money is on the latter. They couldn't predict that you'd come here, where your best weapons can't operate."

"Bah! Everything back home is made of Swiss cheese; doesn't anyone know how to keep their mouths shut anymore?" Then Vlasilov spoke more gently. "I see that you've not been so fortunate."

You could almost hear Tsu shrug. "We won," he explained. "That's what matters most. Our esteemed enemy sent destroyers to a cruiser fight. My flagship shot particularly well. The rest is history."

"Indeed," Vlasilov answered. "We're on very different vectors, my friend. Is there anything we can do for you in passing?"

"No, I don't think so. We're pretty much finished cleaning up. And the butcher's bill was relatively low, thank heavens. We picked up many survivors." There was a long pause. "Petrov?"

"Yes, Tsu?"

"Our worst fears have been realized. I'm authorized to inform you that the condition is orange-five. I repeat, the condition is orange-five. The rest is left to your discretion as the ranking officer on the scene." There was a long pause. "Petrov, it's terrible to see. They used massive weapons, larger than any in our inventory and detonated in such a way as to produce huge amounts of fallout. England, the east coast of the United States, the Yangtze Valley, and the big army bases in Zaire… all were targeted. Casualties are in the billions. There's still an effective air-defense; the Dracans took heavy losses delivering those bombs. But it can only be a few weeks now. The planetary economy is shattered."

There was a long, long pause, during which the only sound was that of one of the counselors weeping. "Your family, Tsu?"

"In the billions," the other admiral replied, the deadness of his voice answering far more eloquently than the words themselves. "Our mission here is now complete. We're headed back to Esteppe for repairs and refitting. Godspeed, my friend. I look forward to sharing your excellent tea once again. Good tea may be hard to come by, from here on in."

"Good-bye, my friend," Vlasilov replied, his voice now as subdued as Tsu's had been. "**Tell** Madame Deputy that I will do all that can be done. All that *must* be done."

Then the connection was broken, and the two United Systems task forces, equally far from home, slid silently past each other in the eternal darkness of the intergalactic night.

Chapter Fifty-Four

We began thrusting again as soon as the last of the other task force vanished through the Black Nexus's Number Four Nikita. Because the Nikitas were so far apart our here, I was surprised that the admiral ordered over two gees of impulse. It would've been far easier on everyone, I reckoned, to accelerate more slowly for a longer time. It didn't make any sense. Especially since no one had much doubt as to our next destination; we all knew what was coming next. Even we kid pilots.

"I bet we're headed for Number Five," Viktor guessed. We were all clustered around the holovision, but for once weren't playing games. "Right back the way we came. Then we can beat the Dracan squadron we left back at Shangri La, and Jump right to Drakkus."

"I don't think so," Delana replied. "Our admiral, he not be looking for a fight he can avoid. Drakkus be gifted with Three Nikitas; we'll kick in one of the other doors, instead of one where we *know* there's a squadron waiting for us."

"But any other way in will take *weeks!*" Viktor answered. "We don't *have* weeks. And, we're going the wrong way to do *either* of those things." He turned to me. "What do you think, Thomas?"

I pressed my lips together and studied the map. Our vector didn't seem to make any sense at all. Yet, we just *had* to be headed for Drakkus, after what the Dracans had done to Earth. "There's a secret Nkita out here," I ventured after a time. "A Nikita that's not on the charts; perhaps an intermittent one, even. We're going through that."

"Oh, come *on!*" Jimmy countered, rolling his eyes. "Who's ever heard of an uncharted Nikita? Those things are *so* valuable!"

"Yeah!" Viktor agreed, shaking his head. I almost explained that I'd once seen a squadron much larger than this one disappear through an uncharted, top-secret Nikita, then held my tongue at the last second. Was the extra uncharted Nikita back at Churilla, in the Orion Nexus, still not publicly known? Sure, the Dracans knew about it; they'd watched the fleet's disappearing act just like I had. But…

Was it still secret? If so, why?

Perhaps because there *were* others, and the navy didn't want anyone speculating on the subject?

"I don't know," I finally answered, shrugging my shoulders and looking down at the carpet. "You're right. It's a dumb idea."

Jimmy grinned, then mock-punched my arm. "Next you'll be telling us that we're going to be attacking with top-secret antimatter missiles!" He made a silly face. "It's all right, Tommy. We still love you, even if you *are* half-nuts!"

We brain-cored people weren't terribly handicapped by two gees of acceleration; so long as we were careful not to drop anything we could get around almost as well as in a normal field. Besides, we didn't bruise or break bones when we fell, so that if something *did* go wrong it wasn't a terrible tragedy. Unfortunately, the same didn't hold true for the normal humans who made up the majority of the crew. Almost everyone else aboard *June* was pretty much chained to their bunks. It was a miserable existence, near as I could judge, with only five minutes of one-gee at the top of every hour and half an hour twice a day to handle the necessities of everyday life. Father Murton was particularly prone to high-acceleration headaches when things went on so interminably; they were why he'd asked to be transferred to shore duty, he told me once.

"Unhhh!" the priest complained as he climbed back into his bunk near the end of one of the five-minute rest-periods. "The drugs don't help so much as they used to. Either that, or I'm just getting old."

"Try lying on your other side," I suggested.

"It won't help any," he replied. "I've tried it before." He shook his head and sighed as the thirty-second alarm sounded. "How much more of this is there going to be, I wonder?"

"Not more than a few hours," I judged, even though the nearest Nikita which actually appeared on the charts was still three days away. "We're nearing maximum transit speed."

"Mph," Murton agreed. Then the five second warning rang, and my counselor laid his long-suffering head down on the pillow. "I hope you're right, Thomas."

I still hadn't worked out the best way to handle myself during acceleration changes; the best technique I'd found so far was simply to lock all of my joints in place until things restabilized. So that's what I did as our ship's main thrusters throttled up again, creating a sort of dull vibration in the hull that was almost but not quite sound. It was most irritating.

"Oh!" Father Murton moaned. "I shouldn't have tried to eat."

I shook my head and sighed; human-normal crewmen were issued special high-gee rations for long periods of acceleration. Most likely the headache was causing my friend's nausea, not the food. There wasn't much I could do to help except try and distract him from his suffering. "How's Jimmy doing?" I asked.

The priest sighed. "Pretty well, considering. You interact with him more than I do. What do you think?"

"He's pretty much back to his old self. Except that he doesn't laugh so much anymore." I shrugged. "I guess that's the best we can expect."

"Probably," the priest agreed. "After all, you don't laugh so much anymore either. I miss that more than anything else, I think. More than I would've ever guessed." He closed his eyes. "We haven't talked about you much lately, Thomas. And that's wrong. I'm sorry about that. Sometimes we counselors see you only as the brave, highly-decorated squadron commander, not a kid like all the others. We think you're Superman; the ideal outcome, under the circumstances."

I blinked. "You're kidding."

"Honest injun," he answered, trying and failing to raise his right hand like he usually did when employing the phrase. "You're the pattern, Thomas. People like Vlasilov take one look at you, and say 'Make me a thousand more just like him!'." He sighed. "They forget you're human, a boy even, because you're such a success. It's my job to never, ever forget. But I still do, what with all my other duties. I'm very sorry."

"You're busy, is all."

"Too busy, I've just decided as of this very minute. When we get back, I'm going to suggest that the chief counselor of a squadron not be assigned to any specific pilot. It's too big a workload." He smiled weakly. "You may be Superman, Thomas. But I most certainly am not." Then his face grew serious again. "We haven't talked in much too long, son. Is there anything on your mind?"

I closed my eyes. "We're going to nuke Drakkus," I answered eventually. "I think we might even kill the entire planet in revenge. No one's actually told us that, but we pilots all know it."

"Yes," the priest replied, meeting my gaze. "How do you feel about that?"

"How *should* I feel?" I asked, shrugging my shoulders. "I mean... Look, they nuked Earth. They've even nuked me personally, on Churilla.

But…" I shook my head. "I don't know. I mean, we're going to kill so *many* people. And I've seen how they die. It isn't… Humane."

Murton nodded sadly. "We counselors suspect a Drakkus raid too. And we don't really know what to do about it either. My Church, I'm quite certain, would condemn such a thing. Yet… I can't say that they'd exactly approve of the Emperor establishing an absolute hegemony over all of Mankind, either. Which I'm realist enough to understand is exactly what'll happen if we don't pull the Dracan Navy back from New Nippon, and damned soon at that." He closed his eyes. "As a historian, I'm not entirely sure that I like the idea that one planet can kill billions of people on another world without there being some kind of retaliation. In the long run, that might prove to be the worst precedent of all."

I turned away. "That's kinda what I think too," I said slowly. "But I don't like it. Not at all!"

"Good," Murton agreed. He looked up at the ceiling. "There *is* one thing I'm sure of, Thomas, in the middle of all this insanity."

"What's that?" I asked.

"That God in His mercy won't hold a seventeen year-old obeying orders, one who's sincerely sought spiritual counsel and prayed for guidance, accountable for what we both know is about to happen." He turned to face me, a single tear running down his cheek. "Neither you nor I ever wanted to come to this place, Thomas. Nor Admiral Vlasilov, I'm certain, or even Madame Deputy. But here we are, with nothing left to us but the most miserable of choices." A second tear joined the first. "Thomas, it's been weeks since we prayed together. Will you say a rosary with me? For the sake of *both* of our souls?"

Chapter Fifty-Five

It turned out that I was right about the secret Nikita; we Jumped just a few hours after my tutor and I finished our prayers. Our destination star was some kind of red giant; it was a beautiful thing, nearly filling the sky. "I sure hope we get out of here before the damn thing goes supernova," Ted groused the next morning as he and I prepared for our squadron briefing. Every porthole on the sunward side of *June* was open, allowing the eerie red light to stream in. "The physicists say it'll go any year now. That's why this route was never officially mapped."

"That and the fact that we're two quick hops from Drakkus," I opined.

"Yeah," Ted agreed, nodding slowly. "That's probably a factor as well." He sighed and turned off his computer-screen. "The admiral will be here any minute, and everything that can be done is done. Let's stretch our legs a little. I've got a feeling that this is going to be a long one."

I didn't eat or drink anymore, nor did my legs require stretching or any other sort of exercise. So instead of running off to the head or to grab a sandwich, I sat and stared out the porthole. The red star was a beautiful thing, yet dangerous beyond compare. Ted was right; the thing was going to go up in God's own fireworks display any time now; the ship's science officer had said so in our ship's newspaper. You could actually watch the needles on the dials flutter, he'd explained, as the monster-star flirted with internal collapse. She'd blow soon all right; almost certainly within my natural life-span. There'd be a titanic explosion, one of the most violent events in all of nature, and megaton after megaton of mass would be ejected at incredible velocities. Then the star-stuff would cool, precipitate out into lesser second-generation stars and planets, and maybe even spawn life as our own sun had. Supernovas, the newspaper article explained, were essential to the development of life; without them the more complex elements such as carbon and oxygen would all be locked up in star-cores.

Were wars, I wondered, essential steps in the development of mankind? Explosions of violence vital to the growth of something good and beautiful? Or were they just pointless tragedies, repeated endlessly over and over and over again? I wished Spencer were around to ask. He probably wouldn't know either. But at least he'd make me feel better about asking.

The admiral arrived right on time and took his place at the front of the room. "How are my pilots today?" he asked.

"Just fine," I answered for us all. "As ready as we'll ever be."

"Good," he answered, nodding in satisfaction. "Very good indeed." Then he frowned and began in earnest. "Our squadron is bound for Drakkus. I'm told this won't come as a surprise to any of you." He looked about the room, but no one said anything. "Then I'm equally confident that you won't be surprised with our mission. Which is, quite simply, retribution."

Again, there was only silence.

"The Dracans," Vlasilov explained, "have used thermonuclear weapons on Earth. Billions, perhaps tens of billions, are either dead or will soon die as a result of the economic upset. We don't have details, but the production and distribution of food and other essentials must've been impacted. The Yangtze valley was the rice bowl of the most populous parts of Earth; it was almost certainly targeted specifically in order to produce widespread famine. There was already a general food shortage, you may recall, due to the blockade. Dracans have traditionally used hunger as a weapon."

Vlasilov scowled and looked out at the red giant; its ruddy light transformed his hawkish features into something demonic. "It's been centuries," he continued, "since men have visited such atrocities upon each other. And never upon such a scale. The Mongol Horde's depredations and even those of more modern dictators pale in comparison." He sighed and turned back to us. "Our choice is simple. We can either bow to the Emperor and abandon our concepts of freedom and individuality in exchange for a promise of mercy, or we can strike back." He scowled, his features suddenly rock-hard. "There was never a second's doubt that we'd resist. Even the Dracans must've known this. They've miscalculated, however, in that they don't believe that we *can* strike back. We're able, however, and we shall. We owe it to all the future generations of humanity that such a crime be punished. Those who would employ such methods cannot have their efforts crowned with success. For if this is allowed, the bombs will drop over and over again forevermore."

Slowly, the admiral met each of our eyes. "Too much has already been asked of you; I lie in my bunk at night agonizing over the terrible thing that history has done to your young souls. And now, even more must be asked. For you are the only effective instrument through which we can strike back." He pressed a button on our viewscreen, and two images of the planet Drakkus appeared, one of each hemisphere. Then he picked up a pointer. "The Dracan fleet is based *here*," he said, stabbing at a shrunken ocean. Drakkus was a desert world. "Their army trains *here*. *This* is the capitol, where the Divine Emperor resides. *Here* is the place where *their* rice is grown. And *here*," he said, stabbing one last time, "is their financial center." He turned to face us, features impassive. "These are your five targets," he explained. "Earth has been hit five times now, counting the sneak-attack bombs with which this war was begun. These targets are exactly analogous to the ones the Dracans chose to attack." He closed his eyes. "It is within the power of this squadron, with the aid of the element of surprise, to sterilize Drakkus. To kill every living thing on the planet. Under Condition Orange-Five, I'm authorized to do exactly that." He frowned and opened his eyes. "I, however, am not a Dracan."

There was a long, long silence as the admiral met everyone's eyes again. "You will deliver five high-yield, fallout-enhanced thermonuclear weapons, one on each of these targets," he repeated. "I accept full legal, ethical and moral responsibility. Indeed, you will each receive written, legally-binding orders which you will disobey upon your peril."

"Thank you," Father Murton whispered.

"It *must* be so," Vlasilov agreed. "For the sake of the children." He turned back to us. "In all honesty, I'd much rather assign this mission to the Butcher Birds. Their fighters' hardpoints, however, are incompatible with our highest-yield weapons. Besides, there will be heavy air defenses. Their air-to-air experience will be invaluable in helping you fight through to your targets." He met our eyes once again. "I'm truly sorry that I must order you to do this thing. And yet, I *must* so order you."

There was another long silence. Then, I spoke up for everyone. "Aye-aye, sir!" I said, saluting as snappily as my servos allowed. Vlasilov nodded, his face as unyielding as ever. Then, after a little longer, he turned and left. "Thank you," he said from the doorway, his back still to us. "In the name of humanity."

"You're welcome, sir," Viktor answered.

Then he was gone, and we were alone with our map of Drakkus and its five blinking-red target zones.

Chapter Fifty-Six

Delana had referred to Drakkus as being "blessed" with three Nikitas, but I suspected that the Dracan Admiralty didn't see it quite that way. The more Nikitas there were, the harder it was to defend against a hit-and-run raid. Earth, for example, having only one Nikita was almost immune from such a thing; any enemy raiding force would have to loop around and leave by the same route it entered. On the other hand, Earth was a lot easier to blockade than Drakkus would ever be. So I guess it all came out even in the long run.

Drakkus's three Nikitas were far from ordinary. One was actually within the upper atmosphere, where Drakkus's air was thick enough to prevent heavy naval ordnance from functioning. The second was assymetrcal, like the Nikita back at Shangri-La. It connected to two entirely different transfer-points in systems a hundred light-years apart. And the third, while occurring at a normal distance from the planet and fully symmetrical, was periodic. Fortunately for our purposes it operated on a very long time-frame. Its current "open" phase wouldn't end for over a decade.

"What a mess!" Ted sighed as he and I contemplated the astrogational charts for the Drakkus system. He rubbed his temples. "I wish to god we had a standard war plan to work with."

We *did* have such a war-plan, of course; it was navy policy to develop war-plans in advance for use against any likely enemy. This was done to get a handle on how many and what kind of ships were needed in the fleet as much as anything else. But the plans were useless. They called for battleships and Polecats, not light carriers and Skybolts. "Look at it this way," I encouraged my friend. "All your life, you've wanted a chance to do things *your* way instead of the navy way. Now youve got your chance!"

"Heh!" Ted countered, still rubbing his temple. But at least now he was smiling. "Our routes set. That's one variable that we can't alter. We're going to come in at Number Three, balls to the wall, and brake like hell all the way to Number One."

I nodded. Number One was the Nikita located in Drakkus's upper atmosphere. If the big ships didn't slow, they'd burn up. "And I still think that's the right way to do it," I commented, not that what I thought mattered in how the big ships were handled. "That's where our teeth are sharpest. The lower, the better."

"Maybe," Ted sighed.

Finally we hammered things out in detail. Only we Skybolts could deliver the thermonukes Admiral Vlasilov wanted delivered, so all of our planning had be built around this unyielding fact. Even worse, our targets were scattered all over the planet's southern hemisphere. Ted and I gamed it out a hundred different ways, trying everything from breaking up into four single-fighter elements to keeping all of us together, under the largest Stormcrow escort we could manage. Two elements of two worked out the best, with one group being assigned three targets that were relatively close together and the other picking up the rest. With this arrangement we were able to take out all five targets about eighty percent of the time. Even better, most of the time at least one Skybolt survived.

"We don't really know what our odds are," I finally said in my final official briefing. We'd decided to hold it early, a full two days before we planned to go into combat, so that everyone would have plenty of time to study their role. "It depends entirely on how many fighters the Dracans have held back for local defense, and how many resources they've sunk into missile batteries."

Delana raised her hand. "What if they're *very* strong?" she asked. "I mean… Even we Skybolts can only shoot down so many all once, like. Are there alternate targets?"

I pressed my lips together and remained silent; Ted and I had agreed in advance that he'd field this one. "You're to break through to your planned targets if at all possible," he explained, meeting each pilot's eyes. "As you know, they've been chosen carefully, for political as well as strategic reasons. However…" He licked his lips. "Admiral Vlasilov's orders state that the number-one priority is detonating five weapons on whatever targets we can. Therefore you're empowered, if you believe you're in danger of being otherwise unable to complete your mission, to target any city within range."

There was a long, long silence. Out of the corner of my eye I saw Father Murton shift position uncomfortably in his seat. "We understand,"

Viktor said at last, nodding.

"Good," Ted answered. "Thomas will lead the first element and Delana the second, as usual. Each fighter will be equipped with two fusion weapons, so that in the event of losses we'll still be able to complete the attack successfully."

Jimmy's hand went up. "Why not four apeice?" he asked. "They're not very heavy."

Ted smiled. "Because we have something special in mind for your other hardpoints. For the Stormcrows, as well." He hit a button on the main briefing screen, and a picture of a missile appeared. "This is something that the navy's been saving for a special occasion," he explained. "It's a decoy. If the engineers are to be believed, it'll show up on the Dracan's pippers as a Polecat." His smile widened. "They even fly in formation, or so I'm told. The Dracans haven't seen any of these yet; every last one in existence is aboard our two carriers."

"Cool!" Jimmy observed. "That'll help."

"It should," Ted agreed. Then his smile faded. "We don't really know what to expect at Drakkus. There's too many variables. However, there should be heavy warships present; it'd be a miracle if there weren't, considering that Drakkus is the enemy's primary repair and training center. But we have no way of knowing which types, how many, or their locations and vectors. Similarly, we expect heavy fighter opposition--everything from training-school pilots to the top aces who do the instructing. We're running a long way in; they'll have time to scramble everything that'll fly. But, as for the details…" He shrugged. "War's like that. We'll have to be flexible, prepared to improvise at the last moment."

There was another long silence. "All right then," I said, closing the briefing. "We Jump tomorrow, then Jump again eight hours after that. From that point on we'll be continually at Action Stations until we Jump out of the Dracan home system, and maybe even beyond that. Get some rest while you can. Dismissed."

Chapter Fifty-Seven

Everyone took my advice about resting, in-between studying our targets and mission profiles. Jimmy and I spent the time in the main Gunroom lounge, with a chart of Drakkus on one side of the room and a game of *Rocket Sledder* set up on the other. We'd study together for a time, then go play. We pretty much sucked, though; neither of us could keep our mind on the game. "I won't let you down," Jimmy promised me just as we knocked off and headed for bed. "I just *won't*, no matter what I have to do."

"I know," I answered, reaching out and touching my friend's shoulder. "And I won't let you down, either. No matter what."

My wingman blinked. "But... I mean... You never let *anyone* down."

"Maybe not yet," I answered. "But that doesn't mean I haven't been sorely tempted." We stood staring at each other like that for a long time, then Jimmy laughed and turned away.

"You're the best friend I ever had," he repeated for about the thousandth time. "I wish you were my brother." And then he was gone.

Vlasilov had informed the squadron that he didn't expect opposition until we hit Drakkus itself, and when we Jumped the next afternoon I could see why. Once again, the navy had taken advantage of the concentration of the Dracan fleet at New Nippon to perform mischief elsewhere. There were United Systems ships waiting for us as we burst through, along with a dozen corpses in dead-ship pink and blue. This time it was task force eleven, consisting of a gaggle of older but very fast light cruisers and destroyers. They'd clearly been briefed on our mission, as their vector was nearly identical to our own. In a couple of hours, the new ships were fully incorporated into our formation. I was glad to see them; we'd be needing every gun and torpedo.

We pilots went to bed and at least tried to sleep, though we were terribly excited. I asked Dr. Hagen, who was the ship's doctor qualified to work with brain-cores, for something to help me rest. I don't know if any of the others did or not, but at least I got a little shuteye. In fact, I didn't wake up until they were actually hooking me up to my 'bolt.

"It's all right, Thomas," Father Murton assured me when I regained consciousness. I was a little disoriented, as I'd been having a bad dream in which Colonel Rotte was on my tail screaming "Horrido!" over and over again, and nothing I tried would shake him. "I asked them to keep you under just as long as possible, so that you'd get a little extra rest."

I tried to nod, but failed since I didn't have a head. "Thank you," I answered, once I blearily figured out which connection was live. "I think you did the right thing. This way, I have less time to worry. How're Jimmy and the rest?"

"Good," my tutor replied, sounding a bit relieved. "Everything's going perfectly, and we're twenty minutes out from the last Jump. Vlasilov's on the other line waiting to talk to you, but I'm pulling rank." There was a brief silence. "Thomas, is there anything I can do for you? Would you like to pray?"

I thought about it a moment; as I did so my flight crew plugged in another connection, bringing my stub-wings to life. And there they were, part of me. The two big, filthy nukes I was to deliver, the enders of I hadn't a clue how many millions of lives. "No, Father," I said slowly. "Praying doesn't seem right just now. Maybe you'll take care of that for me?"

"Of course, son," he assured me.

"Good," I answered, feeling my 'bolt-body come to life as connection after connection was closed. Soon, it'd be time for my pre-flight checklist. "Then... You know what I want. If things go badly, I mean. Tell Father and Sven and Dean how much I love them. Alicia too, and Spencer. Be good to Admiral Vlasilov; he'll need your support, I think, no matter *what* happens. And if you have to write letters for me, if any of the others get killed... Well, I'd rather not think about that right now. I hope it's not selfish of me."

"Not at all, Thomas. Don't worry about *that* for a moment," the priest urged. "I'll take care of it all."

"Thank you." I thought for a long minute, then decided I had only one thing left to say. "I love you too, Father Murton. You've been so good to me, cleaned up after me, were so patient..."

"Hush," the priest answered, though his voice was thick with tears. "It was my duty. My joy, Thomas. Always my joy."

It was just as well that I didn't have any tear ducts, I decided. Otherwise, I'd have had to fly the mission all blurry-eyed and that wouldn't have done at all. "I guess that's it, then. One of the good things about being seventeen is that I don't have a lot of loose ends to tie up." I sighed. "You'd better switch me over to the admiral now, Father. I imagine he's fit to be tied."

"Of course, Thomas." There was a long pause. "We don't deserve you, son. Not by half. And I love you, too."

Then there was a distinct click in the circuit, and Vlasilov came on-line. "Thomas?" he asked.

"Yes, sir!" I answered.

I could almost hear the old man's tired smile. "I fear that I've abused my authority, son. I've put my personal privacy-seal on this conversation, which is supposed to be a last-minute briefing. But it's not."

"Sir?" I asked.

"Thomas…" Vlasilov's voice was trembling heavily. "Thomas, we're asking too much of you. We've done so all along. But *this*…" There was a long pause. "Son," he said at last. "You're the finest young officer it's ever been my privilege to space with. What you've accomplished, so young and on such an impossible time scale, against such heavy odds… " There was another long pause. "Thomas, what I'm trying to say is that I feel as if I'm sending my own son, my own flesh and blood, off to battle in a few minutes. To die, or worse. I… I mean…"

'It's all right, sir," I answered gently. "Really, it's all right. It's my war too, even if I'm only seventeen. My war, my future, my freedom."

''Da," Vlasilov agreed. "So it has always been, and, Bog help us, so it may always be. What miserable creatures we men are, that we must struggle and die in such darkness?"

I didn't know what to say, even though I understood that the darkness he referred to had nothing to do with the coal-black sky of space. "Good-bye, Admiral," I said eventually. "We'll give them hell. I promise you that. Absolute hell!"

"Five times," Vlasilov agreed. "No less, Thomas! The future of humanity demands it, Bog help us again." He sighed. "And now it is time for you to do your preflight check, and for me to take my place on the bridge of my flagship. Fight well, Thomas! And come back to us!"

Chapter Fifty-Eight

A few minutes later I was sitting on the port launch rail, waiting. There were only seconds to go, but each individual one of them took an hour to pass. Why was that, I wondered to myself? I'd flown combat three times now, but it'd never been like *this*.

Maybe I was only now learning how to be truly frightened?

"Three," Otto chanted, counting down the time until we Jumped. Then, an eternity later, "Two". I mentally looked up and down my board; everything was green. "One"…

…and then *The Glorious First of June* Jumped, spanning I'd never bothered to find out how many light years in an infinitesimal fraction of a second.

"Launch!" the deck officer ordered. Time was of the essence on this mission; the carriers would be in Dracan space just long enough for us to deliver our little love gifts, plus do a little dogfighting on the way in and out. It didn't matter what other targets might be present; we were going to nuke Drakkus no matter what. So even though we were so far out that our anti-gravs would be spongy and our pippers hadn't updated yet, we were launching.

"Launch!" I agreed, mentally gritting my teeth against the pain to come. No one had been able to find whatever was hurting me in the landing gear. Then the catapult fired, there was a terrible ripping sensation…

…and I sat and helplessly watched my nosegear fly out into space at an acceleration of twenty gees.

Without the rest of me.

"Abort!" the deck officer screamed into his microphone, foremost in my ears among a sudden cacophony of voices. "Abort the launch!"

"Son of a *bitch*!" I heard Ted cry out into his microphone. "Of all the miserable, no-good…"

"Launch the other two, now!" Vlasilov cried out. Jimmy was in line behind me; until my 'hopper was hauled out of the way he wasn't going anywhere.

"No, goddamnit!" I roared. "Everything else is still in the green. Get me outside the hull and I can fight!"

"Tommy," Jimmy's voice interrupted. "It's all right. It wasn't your fault. You can't go into battle with a broken bird. No one—"

"Launching Three," the deck officer reported, his voice now calm and collected. During launch and landing procedures, his voice-channel had priority over everyone's, even Vlasilov's. "Stand by, Four."

"Goddamnit!" I roared again. "This isn't right! My bird can still fight!"

"Thomas," a new voice interrupted. It was Father Murton, trying to calm me. "Your Skybolt is seriously damaged, son. The landing gear attaches to major structural elements; even *I* know that. And... Your sitting on your nose, son. With your tail way up in the air. Your 'hopper doesn't *look* like it'll fight. Not from here. Besides, how are we going to get you out of the launch cradle any time soon without using your antigravs?"

"Goddamnit!" I roared again; for the first time in my life I understood the true appeal of profanity. If I used my antirgavs to maneuver, they'd wipe out every comuter and major electronic component aboard *June*. This was especially true since I was still inside the vessel, where there was no shielding; it was why we had launch-catapults to begin with. "Stop thrusting!" I suggested. "That'll create free-fall conditions. Get some able-bodied spacers down here in vacuum suits. *Push* me out!"

"Launching Four," the deck officer interrupted.

"....do it!" Vlasilov was ordering when his circuit came through. "He's right; his boards are still green except for the landing gear. Do exactly that! Hold Two, hold the escort. Do it now!"

"Aye-aye sir!" the deck officer replied. There was a second or two's pause, as the harried man worked out what orders to give. "Damage control party to the hanger deck!" he finally decided, and I nodded to myself in approval at his choice. The damage control parties were already suited up and were used to thinking quickly. They wouldn't freeze when faced with a novel problem.

"Tommy!" my wingman protested. "Let me go alone! You're *damaged*!"

"No!" I answered on our private circuit. "Not a chance!" Then I switched over to Vlasilov. "Switch our missions," I suggested, using as few words as possible to save time. The admiral already knew that Jimmy and I had been assigned to hit three targets, and Delana's team the other two. "We're minus on minutes here."

"Da," the admiral agreed. "I agree. You two are now to hit the navy base and the capitol." There was a long pause. "I'm switching your escorts, as well."

"Roger that," I agreed as two frantic-looking ground crewman jacked up the front of my 'hopper and stuck flashlights into the gaping hole where my nosegear had once been. Whenever I turned the landing-gear sensation- circuit on, I felt considerable pain. However, the pain was in my starboard *main*gear, which wasn't damaged at all. No wonder no one had been able to find the problem! Someone had crossed a wire back when my 'bolt was first built! I sighed to myself and pictured Father shaking his head in disappointment. "This is why you don't fly prototypes in combat," I could almost hear my brother Sven add.

Then the big red beacons began to flash, meaning that the hanger deck was being depressurized. There was a right way and a wrong way to evacuate the air from a large area like a hanger deck, and this time the navy was deliberately doing it the wrong way. There was no attempt made to salvage the valuable gasses; instead it poured out down the catapult, giving me a huge tailwind. We should have used *that* to push me out, I realized too late. It would've worked perfectly. But there hadn't been enough time to think things through. So instead of allowing me to ride the breeze, the damage control party waited until the vortex had died away a little, though not enough for safety, and then took position behind my stub-wings.

"Three!" the deck officer counted in what was clearly a pre-arranged signal that I'd missed somewhere while checking status boards and replanning the mission and arguing with Jimmy. "Two! One! Now!"

Then *June* ceased thrusting, and we were in free-fall. My Skybolt remained quite massive despite its sudden lack of weight; it was practically solid metal inside, after all. "Heave!" the damage control officer roared. "Heave!"

I shifted, then eased forward a little.

"Heave!" he ordered again, and then I was moving a little faster. The process was repeated I don't know how many times, until I was moving at a slow walk. All in all, I had to admit, I preferred the more-rapid twenty-gee method, even though this way I was able for the first time to read and appreciate all the colorful little warning-signs that lined the catapult tunnel. Apparently, it was a far more dangerous place than I'd ever realized.

"Heave!" the officer called out again, and I almost tried to stop him. I was moving plenty quick enough now, considering how tightly-confining the tunnel was. I'd just activated my voice-circuit to speak, in fact…

…when one of the suited ratings got tangled up in my portside H-weapon. "Shit!" he screamed, more in frustration than fear. "Hold up! Hold up!"

Unfortunately, you *can't* hold up when moving heavy masses around in free-fall; everything moves very slowly, yes. But it also moves quite inevitably as well. Even as I watched with an inward-turned wingtip camera, the rating's right foot caught itself in the catapult track. "No!" I cried out, there not being time for a more specific warning.

"Shit!" the rating cursed. He also knew what was coming next. "Oh Jesus God almighty!"

It was like being in the train wreck again; everything seemed to happen in slow motion. Suddenly the rating was drawn taut, his body twisting in ways it wasn't supposed to as the upper part of his person was driven forward by my 'bolt's relentless intertia. Then there was no more slack, and I felt myself slew left and crash into the tunnel wall as, somewhere in the distance, the rating screamed and screamed until someone cut him out of the radio net.

"Corpsman!" the deck officer ordered, using his super-override once again. "Corpsman to the hanger deck!"

I wanted to help the poor hurt sailor, but what could I do? So instead of sitting and watching his life bubble out in crimson streaks from a thousand unpatchable overstrained pressure-suit seams, I concentrated very hard on making sure that my status board was all still green, green, green. And it was; even the portside thermonuke that'd caused all the problems to begin with. The thing was all spattered with blood now, sure enough. But re-entry would take care of that.

"Heave!" the damage control officer ordered again, his voice now grim and hard. "Heave, goddamn you!"

There wasn't much tunnel left, thankfully. It didn't take long at all to push me the rest of the way down it; the injured rating wasn't even quite dead yet when my nosecone finally poked its way out through the hull and into the Great Blackness beyond.

And so instead of busting into action at twenty gees, ready to shoot down everything the Dracans could throw at me, I found myself drifting about aimlessly in a broken Skybolt, smeared with blood from a stupid accident and frantically working my way through the Emergency Antigrav Start checklist.

Chapter Fifty-Nine

Jimmy's launch was delayed by the fatality on the catapult; if it hadn't been for the fact that the body might've done serious damage to Jimmy's fighter, I suspect theyd've launched right over it. Time was growing very, very short.

"Hello, Thomas!" a new voice declared as I finally got my antigravs powered up. "Isn't this a fine way to begin a mission?"

"Hello, Colonel," I replied coolly. Originally, Rotte and his wingman Gustav had been assigned to cover Delana's team, while two of the lesser Butcher Birds escorted Jimmy and I. We'd intended to use careful timing and false headings to trap the Dracan fighters between two arms of a dilemma. The way things had been planned, the colonel and Gustav would've been served up dozens of confused Dracan fighters to kill, a mission they could better accomplish from Delana's attack-track. But now everything had gone to hell. If I'd had time to think things through, I'd not have switched the escorts after all. But here we were, and we'd just have to make the most of it.

"Launching Two!" the deck officer finally said, the relief clearly evident in his voice. His part in the battle was now over, and his mistakes all made. Now it was up to us.

"Form up on me," I ordered Jimmy; I'd been accelerating as hard as I could towards Drakkus ever since my antigravs had come on-line, but we were so far out from the planet that my motors had little to bite on. I'd not yet been able to make up for the twenty-gee impetus that I'd missed by not being catapulted.

"We'll conform," Rotte agreed; he was my equal in rank, and far and away my superior in combat experience. I'd learned long since that it was undiplomatic for me to make suggestions. Besides, if he wanted to do something differently than I did, you could damn well be certain that he was right and I was wrong. "Time is very short, young gentlemen," he added. "Thomas, you've been distracted by your unfortunate technical difficulties. Check your mission clock."

I'd already done so, and hadn't liked at all what I'd found there. If everything went absolutely perfectly from this point forward, if we didn't have to divert an inch from our optimum attack paths, we'd lay our eggs and arrive at the rendezvous roughly ten seconds before the squadron vanished into hyperspace. Realistically that left us no chance at all. We both knew it. "It's all right," I answered. "If we're late enough, I won't have to worry about figuring how to land this damn thing with no nosegear."

"Ha!" Rotte replied; it was easy to picture the synthetic skin on his falseface splitting in a huge grin. The hairier things became, I was beginning to understand, the more the colonel was in his true element. "That's the spirit, Thomas. We'll kill them *all*, by god!"

"We'll kill them all," I agreed without thinking. "Every last one of them." Good god! Was I in *my* true element, as well? Then I switched circuits. Jimmy was just now sliding into place on my right wing. "How are you doing?" I asked him privately. There wouldn't be much time for small-talk later. "Is everything all right?"

"We're not going to make it," he replied. "We don't have a chance." There was a long pause. "Not that it matters, mind you. We've *got* to do this. I understand that now."

"Yeah," I answered, wishing I could reach out and tousle his hair, like I had when he'd still been just an ordinary kid who smiled a lot. "We've got to, all right. And who knows? Maybe we'll get lucky."

"*Rocket Sledder* is always funnest when you know you're going to wipe out no matter what," he observed after another long pause. "You can do the craziest stuff then, stuff you never thought you could possibly pull off. Sometimes you even end up living anyway, though it's not very likely." He sighed. "Tommy, let's just have fun this last time. More fun than we've ever had before. 'kay?"

"Okay," I agreed. "We'll kill them all!" Then the pipper beeped, and suddenly the sky was full of angry Dracans.

Chapter Sixty

I couldn't honestly claim that I'd never seen a more hostile display; New Nippon had been far worse overall. And the Orion Nexus had been pretty bad too. But I'd been a mere spectator at New Nippon, and too inexperienced to know any better back when I'd flown my first mission. Besides, that first time I'd only had myself to look out for. This time, however, I was responsible for Jimmy, and indirectly for Delana and Viktor as well. That made it all different.

Ted had long ago taught us pilots that the standard method of defending a multi-Nikita system against hit-and-run raids was to station powerful squadrons at key points from which they could intercept raiders. That had worked well fairly back in the days before the war began, when ships could only transit a Nikita at a relatively low velocity. The initial high-vector Dracan raid on Churilla had ended all that, however; now both sides were hitting Nikitas at speeds undreamt-of back when all the planning had been done. Making new plans, however, took time and effort. Even worse, said time and effort had to come from a limited pool of manpower, the same group of capable, skilled individuals that did all the rest of the strategic thinking. These officers, Ted explained confidently, would all be out at New Nippon leading the Dracan offensive. That was where all the promotions and professional recognition were to be found. And sure enough, the Dracan defensive layout was nothing if not traditional and predictable.

Ted could do geometry as well as the Dracans, it seemed; he'd predicted that our opposition would consist of three squadrons of fast-moving light ships, heavy in torpedo armament and deployed in such a way that we'd find at least one of them astride our course. Additionally, he'd predicted that there might be one or two old dreadnoughts in floating reserve on Drakkus itself, though we wouldn't know about them for a while as the big navy base was on the far side of the planet, where our pippers couldn't reach. Altogether it made for a quite formidable opposition; our little squadron could never hope to survive against such overwhelming force, at least by prewar reckoning.

But pre-war plans were of little use now, as we were about to demonstrate. Times had changed. It was just too damned bad for our enemies that they hadn't yet changed with them.

The three Dracan squadrons were all of about equal strength, each centered on a pair of torpedo-heavy cruisers designed for this very job from the keel up, and a light carrier. Only one group of ships was in a position to trouble us, sitting smack-dab in our path. Delana and Viktor were almost within range of them already, with their long head start; even as I realized this I watched one of the red pips flicker, indicating that it was shooting. My comrades dodged effortlessly, at such long range. I pressed my virtual lips together angrily; we were all supposed to run the gauntlet together, not separately. Now the Dracans would get two chances to shoot us down instead of just one.

Though the Nikita we'd Jumped into the system through was a long way out, our squadron's vector was pretty high. We were diving towards Drakkus like meteors, and with every second that passed my antigravs were biting better and better. So were everyone else's; two destroyers tried to box Delana in with their main batteries, but she gracefully twirled away. "It won't be so easy, my darlings!" she laughed on the main frequency. "Thomas! Jimmy! Come and join us, loves! It's a wonderful morning to dance!"

"We're coming," I reassured her. "Fast as we can."

"Hurry!" she urged. "Or you'll miss out on all the fun-time!"

I still had several seconds left before my element was in gun-range; I used them to look back at our squadron. They were changing formation, the cruisers forming a line and moving forward so as to interpose themselves between the Dracans and the vulnerable carriers. *Ho Chi Minh City* was leading this line; she was an older vessel, though flagship of the squadron that we'd just picked up. I couldn't help but believe that *Doolittle* or *Graf Zeppelin* ought to be out in front. That was someone else's problem, however, and I had plenty enough difficulties of my own. Oddly, *Roman Nose* and *Crazy Horse* were braking harder than the rest, moving to the rear of the formation. I could understand that, in a way; *Nose* was still missing half her main armament. But why was *Horse* hanging back there with her?

"They're launching," Jimmy observed on our private channel, and I returned my pipper to forward view mode. Sure enough, the enemy carrier was pumping out fighters just as fast as she could; glumly, I watched for an unaccompanied nosegear to come flying out into space. Only whole, undamaged 'hoppers emerged, however. Apparently the Dracans weren't flying prototypes. "Thruster fighters." Gustav observed. "They'll launch a dozen, a full load. Easy meat! We haven't seen the likes of *them* in many a long year, eh Emil?"

"Ja," the colonel agreed. "We kill them all, no problem. Right, Thomas?"

"Ja," I agreed, the Esteppan syllable feeling oddly natural in my throat. "Watch Delana. She's positioned perfectly. This should be beautiful."

And so it was. Theoretically, killing enemy aerospacecraft was the job of the Stormcrows. In practice, we were flexible. This time the Bananas led while the Butcher Birds fell back and covered their tails. Delana barely had to alter course; her icon flickered rapidly, and poof, poof, poof! There were three less enemies in the sky. Viktor picked off another two, and one of the 'crows splashed a singleton who seemed lost more than anything else. It was murder to order good men to go into battle in thruster fighters against first-rate opposition, sheer murder. They should've been held back for torpedo attacks against the squadron's heavy vessels, not thrown away so uselessly. But then, what *else* did the Dracan commander have that might stop the likes of Skybolts and Stormcrows? Nothing, I knew. Nothing at all. Which explained a lot.

I was still thinking about what a miserable, short life a thruster-fighter pilot must lead when suddenly the enemy squadron ceased firing on Delana's element and switched over to us. It was easy to twist and turn through the enemy fire; the volume was relatively light compared to what I'd seen at the Orion Nexus. My jinks and dodges were smooth and professional. They also stood in sharp contrast to those of Jimmy, who was grossly over-reacting. This was his first time flying against serious opposition and it showed. Meanwhile, the six surviving Dracan thruster-fighters were ponderously forming up for an attack run on our mother-ships. I switched to Rotte's private channel. "Look at my wingman," I said. "He's nervous. Let's blood him."

"Ja," Rotte agreed. "Good plan. Let him lead."

I switched to Jimmy's frequency. "You see those fighters?" I asked. "Uh-huh."

"Kill them," I ordered. "As many as you can. You're in the best position. Lead away."

There was a long moment of silence. In point of fact Rotte was in the best position to attack, as one could always count on him to be. But the difference was trivial enough not to matter, given the caliber of our opposition. "Yes, *sir!*" Jimmy replied.

To his credit Jimmy made a near-perfect attack, probably as good a one as any of the rest of us could've managed. Making only a minimal course-alteration, he swung the four of us around behind the feeble Dracans as neatly as anyone could ask. He fired first, making a solid kill with his first shot, then the rest of us were blazing away as well.

"Horrido!" Rotte cried out, celebrating his first fighter-kill in over a decade. And I managed to nail one myself. Gustav scored twice, and there were only two Dracan thrusters left as we blazed through the remains of the formation. "Leave them," Rotte suggested. "It's not worth making a second pass."

I clicked my mike circuit twice in confirmation. We'd left two Stormcrows back with the carriers as combat air patrol. They hadn't wanted the job, by all accounts. Perhaps a couple of easy kills might make staying behind a little easier to take.

It was always easier to pass through the center of an enemy formation than to try and run by on one side, because then the enemy ships had to be careful not to shoot each other. We'd already deviated slightly from our attack-path in order to slaughter the thruster-fighters, now we did so again so as to avoid the worst of the enemy fire. It was too bad we weren't on a ship-killing mission; we could've scored with every torpedo. Even as things were, we passed so close to the enemy carrier that Jimmy and I strafed her as we went by. Our cannon weren't big enough to do significant damage in a single pass, but it was still rewarding to watch her unarmored skin ripple and tear under the punishment.

"Save your ammunition," Rotte admonished me.

"I still have more than you did when you took off," I countered. "My magazine is bigger."

He didn't reply, as just then the Dracan squadron's main batteries went into action against the oncoming United Systems ships that were following us in. The sky seemed almost to explode, we were so close to the huge discharges. Our own ships couldn't reply for fear of hitting us; yet another in the ever-growing cascade of screw-ups stemming from my failed nosegear. We'd planned better than this, but had failed to execute. Then we emerged from the enemy formation and became targets again in our own right. Dodging became pretty much a full-time job, one that didn't allow for much in the way of conversation.

Now the disc of Drakkus itself was looming up in the sky, dark and foreboding. Our approach was from the night side, though we'd have preferred daylight. There was little cloud-cover; the Dracan home-world was an arid place, geographically the exact opposite of Churilla, which was well over ninety-percent ocean. The lighted cities stood out clearly, much smaller in both number and extent than those of Earth but still quite large by colony-world standards. Most of the settlements were in the southern hemisphere, where the bulk of the oceans were. Or oversized salt lakes, rather, by Terran standards.

My pipper beeped again as The City of Imperial Peace, Drakkus's capitol, rose above the planet's horizon. In seconds, I was able to confirm it visually. "Target in sight," I reported.

"Ja," Rotte agreed. "And look! See the airfield just west of there? They're scrambling everything they've got!"

I clicked twice, saying nothing. Two, four, eight, a dozen; the Dracan fighters were rising in earnest now. Forty. Fifty… And there were other bases, too!

"Jesus," Jimmy whispered. "I mean, we never…"

"Ha!" Rotte countered. "It's just like Esteppe all over again! When we were outnumbered a mere twenty to one, why, that was a *good* day!"

"That's true," I agreed through the lump that was rapidly forming in my non-throat; I sure hoped Jimmy couldn't hear it.

"It took a hundred to one before they finally broke through," Rotte reminded me. "A hundred to one! And don't forget the most important thing of all!"

"What's that?" I asked.

"Attacking is a far simpler task than defending. If we'd been able to control our Nikita Points and attack other systems, the United Systems would've *never* beaten the Butcher Birds"

"Ja!" Gustav agreed. "Never!"

"Look at all those verdammt targets!" the colonel declared. "Just *look* at them, sitting there waiting for us! What a wonderful time we're about to have!" He waggled his wings for emphasis. "You kill the cities, boys. Gustav and I will take care of the rest. Don't worry for a second!"

Chapter Sixty-One

Rotte was posturing for me, I realized, just as I was posturing for Jimmy. Yet... He had a point. It *had* taken almost a hundred-to-one superiority to defeat the colonel's Stormcrows with Polecats; the navy finally resorted to continually maintaining so many Polecats over the Bird's bases that the colonel and his cohorts couldn't take off. *That* had finally done the trick, as a taxiing Stormcrow was just as helpless and vulnerable as a taxiing Polecat. But it'd taken a long, bloody struggle to get to that point; Emil and his friends fought viciously against every backwards step, including fun little tricks like shipping their 'hoppers to secret bases via rail and rolling out mock Stormcrows here and there all over the planet. Mostly, right next to hidden missile batteries...

As I watched, more and more Dracans took to the air until it was impossible to count them. The pipper beeped again, alerting me that it was switching to "formation" mode, representing entire groups of Dracans with single icons. That was a new experience for me; maybe this *was* the worst pipper screen I'd ever looked at after all.

"They're intercepting the others," Rotte pointed out. "Almost all of them. Because they're in the lead. Their fighter control system is breaking down. They never figured on having to make so many decisions so fast."

I clicked twice; sure enough, it looked like the majority of our enemies were forming up on Delana's group. Instinctively, they were mobbing the nearest threat. Exactly the thing we'd tried hardest to avoid, during all those now-wasted hours of attack planning.

"Look!" Jimmy added. "They've launched some decoys!" New purple icons appeared on our screens; two of them broke off to starboard, threatening Drakkus's second-largest metropolis, The City of Imperial Harmony. Thank god, three Dracan squadrons broke off to intercept. I shook my virtual head; Yes, things looked damned bad from our point of view; there was no way we were getting out of this without serious losses. But, I forced myself to remember, the Dracans had it even worse. Their 'hoppers were so much slower than ours that they could only intercept from ahead; once we were past, they could never catch up. That did a lot to equalize things right there. Plus, of course, there were the cities for the fighter-directors to worry about. And mushroom clouds.

For a moment I found myself thinking about Commander Bard's image of victory as kicking a helpless enemy in the groin over and over and over again, remorselessly and without mercy. And despite the sea of red on my pipper, I understood that by this standard we were about to win a great victory indeed, even if we were all killed along the way.

My pipper beeped again; the main Dracan naval base, our second target, was now over the horizon as well. The screen blanked, then renewed itself, displaying dozens of new icons, each representing a warship. Most were dead-ship pink, representing in this case incomplete warship hulls. But…

…right in the front row, fully powered up and undamaged, floated an *Imperial Throne* class dreadnought. All by itself, it was more than a match for every United Systems ship in the sky.

"Altering target," I ordered without hesitation; if that monstrosity ever saw space we were all dead. Period. I didn't know how long it'd take the Dracans to up-ship the thing; certainly it'd be best if we never found out. "I'm taking out the base first. Our plans are totally screwed up anyway, right?"

"Ja," Rotte agreed, his voice now cold and dead.

"I'm with you," Jimmy acknowledged.

"We're expending two missiles," I added. "Just to be sure. One from you, Jimmy, and one from me."

"Roger," he acknowledged.

"Full military power," I ordered. That'd leave the Strormcrows well behind us, but such was life. "We're going in."

Chapter Sixty-Two

It didn't take long to close enormous distances with so much vector behind us; indeed, despite the fact that Skybolts were tough 'hoppers indeed we had to brake hard as we entered the atmosphere for fear of burning up. This was unfortunate timing, since just as we did so every air-defense missile battery on Drakkus opened up on us. I switched to camera-view for a moment; sure enough, hundreds of delicate little fireflies were rising to greet Jimmy and I. My timing was lucky, because I also by pure chance got a good look at Viktor and Delana's first warhead going off. It made a pure-white, actinic flash directly over where my pipper mistakenly insisted the City of Imperial Prosperity still stood. Then the light faded rapidly as a mushroom formed to cover the planet's gaping wound.

One down, four to go.

Anti-air missiles were one of the few things that could move faster than a Skybolt, but because they used the same kind of antigrav propulsion units as a 'hopper did their guidance systems couldn't be very sophisticated. I had Jimmy fire his decoys, while behind us Gustav did the same. Then, while the enemy missiles wasted time arguing among themselves as to who was targeted on what, we dove for the safety of the ground. Lines-of-sight were short there, especially in the mountains. In a moment or two my wingman and I were, as Rotte would put it, "vermin-free". Even better, it was unlikely that the Dracans would get off another round of the evil things.

Sadly, however, we were *not* fighter-free.

It was inevitable, Rotte had taught us, that when the sky was full of enemies there would be some that simply couldn't be avoided. Jimmy and I were now running down a wide but steep-sided valley that led towards the sea, and beyond that towards the main Dracan naval base. In front of us, coming the opposite way, were a good three dozen Dracan fighters.

The colonel had taught us what to do about them, as well. I clicked over to the private circuit I shared with my wingman. "Easy, Jimmy," I whispered as the distance closed. "Easy… Now!"

As one, just as we closed to effective gun-range, Jimmy and I went to emergency power, so as to offer our enemies the briefest, most difficult shots possible. The world seemed almost to blur as the anti-gravs gave their all; even a Skybolt's airframe couldn't sustain such abuse for long. The air around us filled with laser-bolts, the vast majority aimed far behind us. Jimmy fired back, picking out a random Dracan and vaporizing him. This was extraordinarily good shooting at such a closing speed and range. I took it as a challenge and picked out one of the handful of Dracans who'd been intelligent enough to slow down and hang back, so as to have a longer period of time in which to shoot. My target exploded as well, even more ferociously than Jimmy's had. Then we were through the enemy formations and they'd never be able to catch us again. "Splash one!" I announced on the main channel.

"Me too!" Jimmy added. There was no immediate answer, however, nor time to hang around waiting for one.

There was now nothing on the pipper between us and the Dracan base, so I switched to video and took a quick look around. Dawn was just breaking in our little valley, though at ridiculously high speed as we raced towards the sunlit side of the planet. Suddenly a bright light flared above us, like a giant flashbulb in the sky. What could *that* be, I wondered? Then, suddenly, I knew. I switched back to my pipper and looked out towards space. The fleet action was underway, and with a vengeance. Half of our ships were dead, while the big Dracan system-defense cruiser was still fully in action. The flash, I realized sickly, had come from *Skagerrak*, which was now out of control and fading fast to dead-ship blue. We'd lost a carrier already! Half our landing fields! And judging by the way things were going, *June* wasn't long for this world either.

I tried not to let it bother me too much as I turned my attention resolutely towards our first target. Our entire element, all four of us, had been effectively dead men since the moment we'd decided to try and catch the big Dracan battleship helpless on the water; there hadn't been enough mission-time for such a change in targeting, and we'd all known it.

But I'd so hoped that at least Delana would make it…

"Horrido!" Gustav cried out in my ears as our relatively slow-moving escort caught up with the Dracan fighters we'd just left behind.

"Horrido!" Emil agreed. Then, "Horrido! Horrido!" He'd scored a triple! What were the Esteppans doing, anyway? Hanging around to dogfight? That'd be suicide! Then I thought things through; we were dead anyway, right? And what better distraction for the Dracans than the kind of stand-up air-to-air dogfight that we'd so far refused to offer? What fighter pilot worthy of the name could pass up a good old-fashioned furball? Even if a couple of cheats who wouldn't stand up and fight like men were nuking their fleet's home base, just a few hundred miles away? The Dracans must've been swarming on the stormcrows by the hundred!

"Horrido!" Rotte cried out again, his voice cheerful and full of joy; it must've been a slaughterhouse back there.

Then Gustav's equally-cheery voice rang out. "Hor-"

And no more.

Emil and Gustav had a private channel, just like Jimmy and I did. So, I didn't worry at first. Or, at least, not until I heard Emil on the main channel again. "I'll kill you all, you verdammt bastards!" he screamed out in genuine, heartfelt rage. "Kill you all! Horrido!"

But there was no time to mourn quiet Gustav, the best wingman there'd ever been, who'd given up so many kills in support of his good friend the colonel. Not just then. For the Dracan fleet base was just beyond the horizon, and it was time for us to make our final approach.

Chapter Sixty-Three

We were racing across the sea now, Jimmy and I, or at least we were racing across the stagnant, shallow salt-marshy kind of thing that passed for a sea on arid Drakkus. We were so close to the enemy now that the pipper was useless; I turned mine off and concentrated on the large bump on the horizon that, I knew, represented an *Imperial Throne*-class battlewagon. There was a rapid series of flashes off to our left; a last-ditch anti-air missile launch, probably. "Prepare to fire," I ordered Jimmy; he acknowledged with two mike clicks. I placed my target designator square on the bow of the *Throne*. "Beep, beep, beep," my threat-warning went; presumably, it was the missiles. "Fire!" I ordered.

My port missile leapt eagerly from my stub-wing, and so did Jimmy's. Then, and only then, I looked off to my left...

...to see a Dracan missile zooming in, already perilously close! "Break left!' I ordered without thinking, hoping to place us behind the enemy weapon. But it was not to be. Just as we reached closest approach, the damned thing decided that we were within range and exploded.

We *would've* been in range, if we'd been flying Polecats; a conventional navy fighter could never have survived such close proximity to a nuclear detonation. There was a terrible flash, then a burning sensation all over my skin. Then everything was a blur; I was tumbling through the sky, out of control! It was the work of an instant to level everything out again; a normal human pilot would've been knocked silly or more likely killed by such an impact, but I was just a brain floating in liquid, nearly immune to physical shock. "Jimmy!" I cried out desperately on our private link. "Jimmy?"

"Here," he answered, voice calmer than mine. "Everything's still in the green. How about you?"

I rapidly scanned my instruments. "Hah!" I laughed. "It seems that I've lost a main landing gear. To go with the nose gear."

My wingman giggled. "Now *that's* funny."

I giggled too; *anything* can make you giggle just after you've almost died.

Then there was a *huge* flash...

...and just a few tens of mile away a hydrogen bomb of many tens of megatons yield exploded against the nose of an *Imperial Throne*-class dreadnought. I imagined the shattered hulk being slapped viciously down into the salt-marshes, and smiled to myself. I *hated Imperial Throne*-class battleships! "Turn away!" I ordered. "Full military power! Then form up on me when you can."

"Roger," Jimmy acknowledged; the first detonation had ruined our formation. But we made that right again within seconds. Jimmy and I then outran the fusion weapon's shockwave together; for us it was a pretty light show, nothing more.

A little belatedly, I switched back to the general frequency; it was a lapse, having been away for so long. But then, I'd had good reason to be distracted. "—rido!" Rotte was crying out, "Burn, you bastard! Burn slow! Horrido!"

"First objective hit," I reported. "No losses. Moving on to number two."

Number one had originally been number two, and number two had originally been number one. But I didn't think the confusion was why it took Rotte so long to reply. He must've been fighting the tooth-and-nail battle of his life. And yet when the colonel did finally speak he found time to be polite to me. "Hooray for you two! I saw the flash even from here. And, I'm glad you both made it!"

"I'm sorry for Gustav," I answered, without thinking.

There was another long silence. "Horrido," the colonel finally replied; this time there was no joy in his war-cry. "That makes twenty-seven, Thomas. Twenty-seven! My finest day ever! And Gustav, he got five. Remember for us, won't you? Twenty-seven and five, to be added to our final tally."

"Twenty-seven and five," I repeated sadly. Clearly, the colonel was distracted by combat, or else he'd have realized that he was entrusting his legacy to pilots just as dead as he was. "We'll remember."

"Excellent!" Rotte replied; now there was a little life in his voice once more. "If I can fight my way clear of this mess, I'll try and support you on your approach. Half of these idiots are trainees or else I'd be dead by now. I'm trying to pick off the instructors. If I can do that, the rest will fall apart. If not, well..." There was another long pause. "Restart the

Butcher Birds for me, Thomas. Like the Bananas. You're both, you know. The beginning of something better and stronger than either."

"Ja," I promised. "I'll see to it, Emil."

"I should've deserted," Rotte continued. "I should've stopped the fighting sooner, as your father did. We were criminals, at the end."

"You were patriots," Jimmy offered, even though it was a breach of radio discipline for him to speak on Rotte's frequency while I was still alive.

"We were *warriors*, young James," Emil corrected him gently. Then there was another pause. "Horrido!" he cried out again, his voice filled with the old joy. "Horrido! A maneuver kill, by god! I chased him into the ground!"

"Twenty-eight," I confirmed, swinging my nose around towards the Dracan capitol and its teeming millions. "Twenty-eight and five. We'll remember, Emil!"

"Good hunting!" he wished us. "Good hunting, now and always and forevermore! Kill them all!"

Chapter Sixty-Four

Jimmy and I were now zooming northwards along a little navigation channel the Dracans had dug out in the salt marsh in order to make their fleet logistics easier. Originally Viktor and Delana had planned to follow this channel in the other direction, after striking the City of Imperial Peace. But there was plenty of room for two-way traffic, as testified to by the busy flow of barges below. Jimmy and I were already flying low in order to avoid missiles. So we shot up as many of these vessels as we could, sort of on general principles. Most of them exploded in the vicious manner that revealed a cargo of molecular batteries, but a few didn't blow up at all. Perhaps these weren't carrying contraband? If not, then maybe we shouldn't be shooting them up. But how could we tell which was which? We were moving at hundreds of miles an hour, and our targets didn't exactly have big signs on top revealing their cargos. Not that we would've believed them even if they did.

The City of Imperial Peace was located well inland from the salt marshes. While our canal would've led us all the way there, if we followed it much longer we'd have to pass far too close to a missile battery. So we swung to the right and zoomed over the open desert about fifty feet above the sand, so low that we kicked up dust trails. Nothing seemed to be particularly interested in killing us for the moment, so I decided to take advantage of the lull to update myself on the situation as a whole. "You lead for a minute," I ordered Jimmy. "I've been out of touch for too long."

"Click-click," he acknowledged, edging his fighter forward. I formed up on him, then got busy on the radio.

"Element Two," I called out. "Element Two, this is Strike Leader, over."

There was a long, long silence.

"Element Two," I tried again. "This is Strike Leader, over."

Again, there was nothing but silence.

Perhaps Delana was busy elsewhere, I reasoned. After all, I'd been unavailable for many long minutes myself. I'd try again in a little bit. In the meantime, I switched over to my pipper and looked up towards the main fleet action.

At first glance, I thought we'd lost. *Ho Chi Minh City* was dead, *Wilbur Wright* was dead, many of the destroyers were dead. Yet somehow *The Glorious First of June* had survived and was past the Dracan defensive squadron. So had *Graf Zeppelin* and *Jimmy Doolittle*, as well as most of the *Chief*-class destroyers. We'd taken terrible losses, yes. But, as was becoming more and more the pattern, it was the older ships that were doing the dying. The more modern core of the squadron, minus of course *Skaggerak* and *Orville*, had fought their way through. Since Jimmy and I had managed to shut off all chances of interception from Drakkus proper with our strike at the main fleet base, our surviving shipmates were clearly going to make it. All except *Crazy Horse* and *Roman Nose*, who were now trailing the main body further than ever. This made no sense to me whatsoever; the *Chief*s were the fastest fighting ships in the navy. Only a few unarmed messenger-sloops were rated for higher boost. *Nose*, in fact, was probably the fastest fighting ship *anywhere*, what with half of her armament missing so that she wasn't so massive as she was designed to be. Yet these two ships had fallen so far behind that they were in danger of being picked off by the other Dracan defensive squadron, the one that'd been watching the third Nikita and therefore out of position to interfere so long as we moved quickly enough. Where was the sense in this? I was just getting ready to try and reach Admiral Vlasilov to make a status report when Jimmy interrupted my thoughts. "Enemy fighters ahead, Tommy," he said over our private channel.

"Thanks," I acknowledged, turning my attention back to my own, smaller picture. Everyone who'd ever had anything to do with my training had emphasized over and over again how impossible it was going to be for someone in my position to maintain situational awareness of everything all at once. The main thing I should do, Rotte in particular had explained, was to stay focused on what was right in front of me and let those in higher command worry about the bigger picture.

"You *will* make mistakes, Thomas," he'd warned me over and over. "And, even more, you'll miss opportunities. For a formation leader, this comes with the territory. Things happen so quickly in modern combat, and at so many levels, that it's inevitable. The key is to understand going in that you're limited to doing one thing at once; no human being can possibly keep up with it all. Your job is to pick the *right* thing that needs doing, and do it well. The rest is up to Lady Luck."

Dealing with deadly threats was just about number one on my priority list; I switched my pipper over to forward-scan and eased my 'bolt forward again, retaking the lead position. Sure enough, there were two Dracan fighters dead ahead, making speed directly towards us.

"It's only two," Jimmy pointed out. "We can blow right by."

I almost agreed with him, then a little warning light went off in my brain. What had I said to myself a little earlier about Rotte? That, somehow, he was *always* in the best attack position? And now, here were two lonely Dracans, against all odds in just the right place at just the right time...

Were they the Dracan equivalents of Emil and Gustav?

"Break left," I ordered; Jimmy didn't argue. I swung our noses around until we were pointed perhaps twenty degrees to port of the City of Imperial Peace.

And even though it should've been impossible, the pair of Dracans swung right with us.

"That can't be!" Jimmy protested. "Dracans can't go that fast!"

"These just did," I countered. "They're flying Skybolts, Jimmy. Or something very close to them. Brain-cores, like us."

"Stormcrows, more likely," Jimmy speculated. "After all, this is their first generation. Probably the prototypes, even. If so, we can take them."

I thought about things for a long, slow moment as we closed with our enemies. Our mission was to kill cities, not fighters. Even if the fighters in question were valuable, high-performance prototypes. And yet...

I made a snap decision. Delana still hadn't called me back, so I had to assume that she and her entire formation was dead. And Vlasilov had called for five targets, above all else. How many had Delana managed to take out? At least one; beyond that, I couldn't possibly know. But somehow I suspected that the admiral would be happier with six than four. "Jimmy, we're going to break further left until we're closing on the City of Imperial Learning. You'll nuke it. That one will be a sure thing; no one can intercept. Then we'll take out the fighters and hit the capitol."

"Roger," he replied, voice flat and professional.

"All right," I answered, hoping that I sounded equally good. "Break... Now!"

Chapter Sixty-Five

Jimmy's second missile flew straight and true; there was a huge flash and then the whole eastern horizon went dark as a huge mushroom cloud rose over the primary Dracan educational center. Our enemies had just lost an entire generation of future scientists, doctors, and civil servants; their society would suffer for a century or more as the direct result of my snap-decision. War was insane, utterly insane! And yet insane or no, here Jimmy and I were up to our necks in the filth of it, giving our all to deliver one last nuke.

"Come back to starboard," I ordered, swinging my nose gently to the right. Jimmy's H-bomb had triggered some sort of unexpected interference on the pipper; it was clearing slowly, but for the moment I'd lost track of the two enemy superfighters. "Full military power. Stay nice and close, Jimmy. This is going to be nasty."

"Click-click," he acknowledged.

Then they were on us; my first warning was when a burst of laser-bolts zipped past my nose. "Break right!" I screamed, yanking my elevons just as hard as I could.

The world spun by as if I were on some sort of mad carnival ride; we were still practically at zero feet, to avoid the missiles. Our enemies, caught unawares by our sudden target shift, had come in from the right and attempted a high-deflection shot. They'd missed, but because of the large angle Jimmy and I weren't able to get off anything in return.

"Keep turning!" I exhorted Jimmy; if we didn't, we'd come out of the maneuver with the Dracans on our tail. "All the way 'round! Let's try to blow by!"

"Roger," he answered, again sounding calmer than me.

We emerged from our twisting headed due east, not at all the direction we needed to go, but that didn't matter just then. The Dracans were right there waiting for us, ready to take a head-on shot.

I *hated* head-on shots; Rotte had taught me that there was altogether too high a degree of luck involved. But,sometimes they were unavoidable. So for the second time that day I laid my target indicator on a rapidly-closing Dracan and hosed him down for all I was worth. Then he was firing back, our laser-bolts were crossing in the air…

…and by god my target exploded! "Horrido!" I cried out in sudden exultation. I'd never felt like that before, killing another human being. Perhaps it was because this was the first time I'd done so in a "fair" fight? "Horrido! I killed him, Jimmy! Killed him dead!"

But then there was another flash from beside me. "I'm hit!" my wingman wailed. "Tommy! I'm hit *bad*!"

Chapter Sixty-Six

And so he was; a second or two later Jimmy's fighter began tumbling, then his escape-pod fired, flinging him high into the sky. Fortunately, the parachute deployed perfectly. The last I saw of him as I roared over the horizon was the bright-orange canopy swaying in the breeze as my best friend drifted down towards the almost-equally orange desert sand.

Then there wasn't any more time to worry about Jimmy, as much as I wanted to. The verdammt Dracan that'd shot him down was arcing around behind me, hoping to try again. I wanted to give him his chance more than anything else in the world, after what he'd done to my best friend. But I was supposed to be killing cities, not fighters. So I gritted my teeth and went to full emergency power; if Jimmy was right, and the Dracan superfighters were more akin to Stormcrows than Skybolts perhaps I could leave him in my dust and worry about him later.

And so it proved; the Dracan fell steadily behind, despite his best efforts. I knew that he must be screaming on every available frequency, giving my location and vector. So I fired my decoys and changed course slightly, there being no reason I could see to make the situation any simpler than necessary for my enemies. That left only one weapon, my last remaining fusion bomb. The reduced drag made me faster than ever.

There were two air-defense missile batteries between me and the City of Imperial Peace; or, rather, there were two that we *knew* of. I didn't want them to shoot down my missile any more than I wanted them to shoot down my Skybolt. Truth be told, I much preferred gravity bombs like the simulated ones I'd dropped on my demonstration tour to missiles when attacking ground targets for this very reason. They were *much* harder to intercept. But the only large fusion warheads aboard the carriers had been permanently mated to missile bodies, and that was that. So I decided to treat my missile just as if it were a gravity bomb, by coming in close and delivering from point-blank range. I was dead, Jimmy was dead, the colonel was dead, everyone was dead. So why shouldn't I make very certain that the City of Imperial Peace, home to the Emperor himself, died as well?

I'd never actually flown into a city at such high power and low altitude before; it was an insanely difficult thing to do and I crashed as often as not when I tried it in simulation. But I never felt so capable and sure-handed in simulation as I did in combat, so I armed my warhead to ensure that it'd detonate if I crashed and blew into town like a supersonic ill wind. My motors must have done millions of credits worth of damage in their own right; at such a high power setting they'd fry every piece of halfway-sophisticated electronic gear for miles around. The physical shock wave was even worse; where during simulations I'd broken windows, now I was leveling small buildings. But all of this was nothing, nothing at all to what I was about to do.

At those kinds of speeds, even crossing a huge, spread-out metropolis like the City of Imperial Peace took only seconds; suddenly the gilded Imperial Palace reared up before me and I fired before there was really time to think about it. "Break right!" I called out reflexively, even though Jimmy wasn't there any more. Then, once again I was turning just as hard as I could…

…right back into the face of the triple-cursed Dracan superfighter I'd almost forgotten about!

"Damnit!" I cried out again; I couldn't turn back towards the city, not now that it was about to grow a jumbo-deluxe-sized mushroom cloud. Even a Skybolt couldn't survive *that*, and I'd cut my escape short already.

Which meant, I suddenly realized…

I didn't even *try* to fire as I made my third head-on pass of the day; instead I concentrated solely on dodging. It was just as well; this Dracan was a fine marksman indeed, and it took everything I had plus a little luck to weave my way between his laser-bolts. Then he flashed past me…

…and was practically on top of the hydrogen bomb when it detonated, placing him well inside the fireball and out of my circle of concerns forevermore. I sighed a virtual sigh; another task complete, another Dracan killed. My mind raced— what was the next task? What should I be worrying about now?

There wasn't anything else, I suddenly realized. It was all over. My responsibilities were now fully discharged. I checked my mission clock;

there were only seconds left before *June* was scheduled to Jump. I could never hope to make it back; it wouldn't even be close. But, maybe, there was time to make a final report? "Strike Leader to base," I said on the main frequency. "Strike Leader to base. Do you read me?"

"Thomas!" Vlasilov's voice exploded onto the channel. "Thank god! I thought you'd *never* report in!"

"I've been kinda busy, I guess. Sir."

"Busy, he calls it!" the admiral replied, his voice thick with relief. "Thomas, rendezvous with *Roman Nose*. Do you hear me? Crash land aboard *Roman Nose*. You and the other survivors in your element."

"Roger that," I replied. Crash-land? How in the world was *that* going to work?

"*Roman Nose*," Vlasilov confirmed. "You did well, Thomas! All of you did. Tha—"

And that was all; just as the admiral's voice was cut off, *The Glorious First of June* vanished from my pipper.

I recalibrated my mission clock, explaining to it that *Roman Nose* was really an aircraft carrier; suddenly, it read a positive two minutes and forty seconds, where it'd been in the red for ages now. I had a chance! Could make it easily, even!

Then I thought of Jimmy drifting slowly down onto the surface of a planet he'd just nuked, with especially fallout-heavy warheads at that, and rephrased my previous thought. No, *I* didn't have a chance. By god, *we* had a chance! All I had to do was figure out how to mount some sort of rescue. It was something I ought to be able to pull off, if I were truly worthy of my status as commander of the Top Bananas. After all, I had a good ten or eleven seconds to plan things out before I arrived back at the place where he'd been shot down.

What luxury! So much time to think was practically unheard-of, for a squadron commander! It was going to be a piece of cake!

Chapter Sixty-Seven

Picking Jimmy up wasn't my big problem. A Skybolt could hover just fine, and so long as Jimmy's survival-body wasn't damaged he could climb aboard with equal ease. Thank god that everyone had backed me when I'd insisted on adding arms despite the extra weight! The issue was, where could I put him? There weren't any good gripping-points on my outside; even if I had him lock his hands on the leading edge of my stub-wing, if I made any kind of speed the airstream would blow him off. The sky was still plenty full of conventional Dracan 'hoppers, and there was even a chance I might run into more super-fighters. I had to get him inside. But how, when a Skybolt's interior was practically solid?

Then Jimmy's wrecked Skybolt came into view, not far away from his discarded 'chute. Without hesitating a second, I closed to within gun range of the dozen or so Dracans loitering over the crash-site. "Jimmy?" I called out on the search-and-rescue frequency, while at the same time lining up on a Dracan and firing. He exploded. Instinctively I swung my fire onto his wingman, who obligingly blew up as well. "Jimmy? Can you hear me?"

"Tommy?" he answered. "Is that you?"

"Who else?" I asked, swinging my nose around into the tightest turn possible. It was growing dark, which was odd indeed for the early morning on a planet where it hardly ever rained. I couldn't figure it out, until I remembered that we were within a few miles of two nice, fresh thermonuclear strikes. Soon, it'd be black as night here. "I've come back for you, Jimmy."

"But…" he protested as two Dracans came surging in from my right, attempting a high-deflection shot. I ducked beneath their fire, practically scraping the ground, and wrenched around behind them. Then they were dead, too. *Kill them all!* I heard the colonel exhort me, deep in my heart. *Kill every verdammt one of them! Don't hesitate a second.* Then

Commander Knight spoke up. *Sheer aggression*, Jimmy's father reminded me. *Sheer bloodyminded aggression. That's the secret to winning.* "But... I mean... How..."

"How is my problem," I snapped, even though I hadn't quite figured it out yet. Surely there *had* to be an empty space big enough for Jimmy's braincase somewhere inside of my Skybolt. "Where are you?" I demanded, my voice harsher than I'd have liked. Another pair of Dracans had taken advantage of my distraction to swing in behind me. I hit the throttles hard and spun away. "I won't have long to make the pickup."

"I'm under the parachute," he explained. "It's not like there's anyplace else to hide out here. But... Tommy! You'll get yourself killed! I was just about to... I mean... I'm dead anyway, Tommy!"

"Shut up," I ordered angrily; the sky was still full of Dracans, though not quite so full as it'd been just a few seconds before. I didn't have time to shoot them all down, Rotte's normally excellent advice notwithstanding. So, how?

There was only one thing I could think of to do. "Duck, Jimmy!" I ordered. "Duck and cover! Shock wave coming!" Then, I advanced my throttle to full emergency power and flew straight up just as hard as I could, firing my cannon at nothing and, hopefully, displaying my red-painted nose bright and clear in what was left of the sunlight. "Horrido!" I cried out on the interplanetary common frequency, emphasizing my normally very slight Esteppan accent. "Horrido! I kill you all! Every last one of you beggars, ja!"

And by god, it worked! When I throttled down and yanked my nose back and over, there wasn't a Dracan left in the neighborhood. I rolled three times in triumph, it felt so good! "Horrido!" I called out one last time, to encourage my enemies on their way. Then it was time to go get Jimmy.

Chapter Sixty-Eight

Despite the luxury of having had so much time to think things through, I hadn't been able to come up with a single idea as to how to get Jimmy home. That didn't slow me down at all; in a single fluid movement I made a simple approach, then flared out and hovered not ten feet from my wingman's hiding-place. "Climb aboard and grab my wing," I was about to say, when suddenly I was distracted by a sea of red lights. Out of sheer habit, I'd lowered my landing gear during the approach. Now, my Skybolt was reminding me that much of said gear was broken, and that what wasn't broken was largely missing.

Missing!

"Climb into my nosewheel bay, Jimmy!" I ordered. "Just as fast as you can! Then hold on for dear life!"

"Right," he agreed, clambering across the sand. He was very slow. Jimmy hadn't had much time to practice with his social body, much less his survival capsule. It wasn't his fault, but the mission clock didn't care.

"Hurry!" I urged him, edging a little closer.

Then, just as Jimmy was climbing aboard, my pipper came back to life. Two Dracan fighters had finally worked up the nerve to come back. "There's not much time!" I said.

"It's *tight* in here!" Jimmy complained. "I…"

And that was that. The wingtip camera showed Jimmy as being most of the way in; I triggered my gear-doors and slammed him the rest of the way home. They met a little resistance, but closed fully. "Ow! That *hurt*, Tommy!"

I didn't have time to answer; the Dracans were closing fast. Too fast, I realized sickly. These weren't any of the gaggle I'd scared away; instead, they were another pair of super-fighters. And, not only were they on my tail, but they'd caught me with no vector and no wingman! I was a sitting duck!

There wasn't anything to do but to fight things all of the way out; I pulled sharply upwards at full emergency power, then began an unsteady, hard-to-predict turn to the left. My enemies knew they had me cold, so instead of eagerly racing in for the kill they throttled back and took their time aiming. I hunched my non-shoulders, bracing for the fatal impact...

...but it never came. Instead a familiar black shape with a red nose just like my own came streaking in from the east, easily picking off the now slow-moving Dracan wingman.

"Horrido!" the colonel declared, rolling once in celebration. "A superfghter, by god! I never thought I'd live to see the day. Horrido! That's thirty-two, Thomas! Thirty-two!"

I opened my mike, but didn't know what to say. "I... I mean..."

"Hah!" Rotte replied. "You think I'm that easy to kill, after so many combats? I'm hurt that you didn't have faith in me, Thomas! Wounded to the core!" There was a short pause while the colonel rinsed the irony out of his mouth. "There were about two hundred of them towards the end. Some of them ran into each other. I didn't count those. Finally they left me an opening, and I took it."

The Dracan leader had instinctively turned towards Rotte; normally this would've been exactly the correct thing to do. But by then I was building up some velocity too, and in just the right direction. Now *I* was on *his* tail. It was *much* better that way, I decided. It didn't take me long, from such a favorable position. "Good shooting," Rotte added as the Dracan augured in, aflame. "Burn, you bastard!"

"We're to crash-land on *Roman Nose*," I explained to Rotte. "We have twenty seconds of margin."

"Hah!" he answered, swinging his nose skywards and opening his throttles wide. "You may have twenty seconds to spare in that wonderful newfangled Skybolt of yours, but in my poor old 'crow I have only three. See you aboard!"

Chapter Sixty-Nine

Rendezvousing with *Roman Nose* sounded a lot easier to do than it really was; we were almost under the Nikita Point that she was racing towards hell-for-leather, which meant that we had to fly a long, complicated interception curve that'd end with us vectored back towards almost where we were right now, at high speed in just the opposite direction. Though both Rotte and I expected trouble, nothing rose after us in pursuit. "…biggest verdammt party Esteppe has ever seen!" Rotte was chortling. "I don't care what it costs. You and me and Jimmy. We'll open up the Aerie for an entire day and invite every VIP on the planet; none will dare turn us down after what we've done here today! Not even Madame Deputy!"

"Ja," I agreed absently. Earlier, Jimmy and I had shared a giggling fit after nearly getting ourselves killed. This was Rotte's equivalent of giggling, so I didn't shush him no matter *how* annoying his chatter became. Indeed, I felt honored that he considered me fit to share it with; this, I knew, was the nearest he'd ever come to admitting just how frightened he'd been during his long, epic stand against so many enemies. Or how terribly he mourned Gustav. I'd have cautioned anyone else trying to make such a difficult rendezvous with only a few seconds to spare to pay more attention to their flying. But Rotte was Rotte; who was I to chastise a legend?

"We'll have a band!" he chortled. "The finest band on Esteppe! Won't it be wonderful, Thomas?"

"And food," I suggested. We were well past the Nikita now, and swinging back around to match vectors with *Nose*. The Dracan squadron that'd been guarding the other Nikita was closing in fast, now. It was a coin toss as to whether they'd be able to engage or not. "The best food. We can't eat it ourselves, but we can watch the others."

"Ja!" Rotte agreed. "Watching is nearly as good!" I'd never heard the Esteppan colonel so full of good cheer before. It was false cheer, I knew. But even so, it threw a whole new light on his character. About who he might've been, if the war hadn't turned him into such a hardened, remorseless killer. I'd have liked him a lot better, I decided, if he'd never become a fighter pilot. For that matter, he'd probably have liked himself a lot better. What did that say about my own future, I wondered? And Jimmy's? I was becoming more like Rotte every day; sometimes I even *spoke* like him. Would the rapidly-accumulating scars someday render Jimmy and I equally insufferable and obnoxious?

Rotte lost a second and a half of mission-time on the approach, a performance so nearly perfect that, from anyone else, it would've been astounding. *Nose* was the very last ship in the United Systems line; because it was the fastest, it'd braked most effectively. "Steady!" Captain Ling ordered Rotte as the relatively huge destroyer closed in on the Stormcrow. The same big hatch that I'd come in through during my Churillian escape with *Tecumseh* was gaping wide open again, like a huge fish's mouth. The captain and I had already exchanged the mandatory nonsense about how, while I was always welcome to visit his ship, I really needed to learn to use the main airlock like everyone else. "Steady!"

"Ja," Rotte agreed. "It looks good from here. Steady as she goes!"

There was going to be a lot more crash than landing involved in our recovery, no matter how steady Rotte was. His Stormcrow would almost certainly be damaged beyond repair, as would be my Skybolt. But, at least this way all three of us would be alive.

"Don't move an inch!" Ling warned Rotte, "I'm making my final approach."

Just then, the Dracan cruiser opened up with its main batteries at extreme range. It was unlikely that our enemies would hit anything from so far away. Still, I was ready to dodge.

"Steady!" Ling urged the colonel again, his and Rotte's attentions both fully focused on the difficult landing. "Steady!"

"Ja," Rotte acknowledged cheerfully…

…just as the long-range salvo arrived.

It happened too quickly for me to shout a warning; a million-to-one slop shot, something that no self-respecting gunner would ever take credit for. The rest of the salvo was a clean miss. But one single heavy laser-bolt managed to find Rotte's Stormcrow while his attention was elsewhere. He flared and died instantly, without speaking another word.

"Oh, no!" Ling whispered.

"Emil!" I cried out. "Emil! Do you read me?"

But he didn't, of course. And never would again.

"What's wrong?" Jimmy demanded. I'd been relaying most of the chatter to him. "Did he... Did he..."

"Ja," I answered sadly, swinging my 'bolt in closer so that Ling could line up on us next. Another heavy salvo came screaming by, but I was too numb to notice it very much. I'd lost Rotte twice in one day, or at least it felt that way. And now I was beyond feelings. "The Ace of Aces is dead. His luck finally ran out."

Chapter Seventy

It was easier for me than it'd been for Rotte. By the time that everything was all lined up nice and pretty, the faintest ghosts of atmosphere were once more whispering around my stub-wings. That negated the enemy's big guns, and we were well out of torpedo range. The Dracan's second salvo sputtered and died when it struck the air, so that all Ling and I had to concern ourselves about was the crash-landing proper.

I could understand why Rotte had been so totally focused on the task at hand; under the circumstances, it couldn't have been any other way. It took everything I had not to flinch from the rapidly-growing destroyer when the collision-alarms began screaming in my ears and the hatch looked to be barely larger than my fighter. There was a reason for that, of course; the hatch *was* barely larger than my fighter. I'd seen this sort of thing done before, or else I'd have been even more terrified than I was.

"Steady," *Nose*'s captain whispered reassuringly in my ears. "Steady…"

And then my 'bolt was flying through the hatch, its lip ripping off my starboard stub-wing in the process. *Nose*'s crew, I'd already been assured, had improvised a nice soft place for 'hoppers to crash into, and I suppose that, relatively speaking, a nest of empty fifty-five gallon drums was indeed rather cushy. But we still hit so hard that my fuselage was bent like a banana and I lost consciousness for a second or two. "Jimmy?" I asked blearily after everything quit being so black. "Are you all right?"

"Open your gear doors!" he cried out. "They're about to cut me out!"

I complied, since being sliced into by welding torches sounded like about the most painful thing I could imagine. The doors popped open, and my wingman stuck his head out and looked around. "Wow!" he whispered. "We made it!"

Just then *Nose* Jumped; I'd never had such a good view of the process before, and the way reality seemed to slip and curve as the hyperdrive engaged. In this case, the dark stains spreading rapidly across Drakkus's southern hemisphere seemed to grow and grow and grow. I took the opportunity to count the bomb hits; there was one at the City of Imperial Prosperity, another oversized one which represented the closely-spaced strikes at the Cities of Imperial Peace and Knowledge, another over the salt marshes that represented where the Imperial Fleet had once been based…

…and, finally, a dark area was spreading over Delana's second target, Drakkus's chief food-production area. Her third target remained untouched…

…and it was only then that I knew in my heart that both she and Viktor were gone. They'd never have willingly left a target undestroyed. Never! I'd been late to take off, and the enemy fighters had concentrated against the other section, and… and…

"Come on, Thomas," a new voice was whispering in my ear. It was a pressure-suited damage control rating, come to dismount me from my 'hopper. "Let's get you out of there. Don't worry about a thing, sir; space is clear all around us. There was a support squadron waiting. You're safe now. We're *all* safe."

"Father Murton's on his way," another voice added, this one female. "Though it'll take him an hour or so to arrive on board. He's got your social body with him; for now you can wear your survival tripod." There was a short pause. I'm Keiko, *Roman Nose*'s chaplain." She paused for a moment. "Jimmy's Counselor is on his way as well, though I didn't catch his name."

I switched over to my friend's frequency again. He'd been looking out at Drakkus as we Jumped too, and apparently had reached precisely the same conclusions I had. He was crying his eyes out over the radio, though you couldn't see a thing on his survival-pod face.

"Is there anything we can do for you, Thomas?" Captain Ling asked. "Anything at all, son?"

Give me back my pilots, I wanted to scream. *Let me watch Delana dance to the sunrise one last time and look upon the special smile that she saved only for me! Let me play video games with Viktor, let me hear him laugh and make grim, Slavic jokes! Or, let me sit like a boy and listen with wide eyes to Rotte and his friends as they brag about their kills.* My eyes didn't blur up anymore, but I still cried. Just like Jimmy did, inside where no one could see. *Let me take back my missiles*, I screamed internally. *Let me not be the slayer of millions of faceless, harmless Dracan peasants, and don't make me go from audience to audience anymore where strangers smile at me and pay to shake my hand and tell me what a fine young killer I am!*

"Thomas?" Ling's voice asked again. "Is there anything at all?"

I tried to answer in a manner becoming of an officer and a gentleman; honestly I did. But all that would come out was wail after anguished wail, just like Jimmy. We'd won a *great* victory, he and I; no battle fought had ever ended in a bigger, more one-sided win. We'd kicked the Dracans hard all right, where it counted and without mercy. And even if we lived a thousand-million years, neither my best friend nor I could ever be cleansed of the stain that such a victory left on our souls.

"Good lord," Ling whispered, not quite sure what to do with us two bawling child murderer-heroes. "I don't... I mean..."

"Leave them in peace," Keiko advised. "They need to be alone. Put them in quiet staterooms, with a sentry at the door to keep everyone out. Their counselors will be here soon. They'll know what to do."

But they didn't, of course. "Would you like to pray, Thomas?" Father Murton asked, once he arrived.

I raised my head; apparently he'd been in the room with me for some time, though I hadn't noticed. His eyes were wide and his skin pale; he seemed almost to be in a state of mild shock himself. "No," I answered. Somehow, I didn't think I'd ever be able to pray again. "I just... I mean..."

Then we were standing in the middle of the stateroom floor, hugging and crying our eyes out together. "We won," I finally whispered into his waiting ear. "But..."

"Yes, Thomas," he whispered back. "I know. I feel the same way. We fought hard, and we won. Even worse, there's more battles ahead of us that also must be won, before there can be a final victory. Many of them, probably."

He shook his head and sighed. "May God have mercy upon our souls."

www.ingramcontent.com/pod-product-compliance
Lightning Source LLC
Chambersburg PA
CBHW020738250626
47155CB00003B/814